Charm City Rocks

"*Charm City Rocks* is Matthew Norman's most charming and engaging novel yet. It is impossible not to fall in love with everyone here: the happy music teacher, his teenaged son, his ex-wife and her husband, and the rock star he's loved from afar and near. This book is an absolute joy—the pinnacle of a long line of fabulous and funny Matthew Norman novels."

—JESSICA ANYA BLAU, author of *Mary Jane*

"Endearing, smart, romantic, delightful! . . . Matthew Norman has a particular talent for writing characters we can root for like dear old friends."

—ALLISON LARKIN, author of *The People We Keep*

"*Charm* is the operative word here and this book is chock-full of it. It's the perfect balance of a story that feels like a fairy tale grounded by utterly believable, lovable, everyman characters. The best love stories are the ones that sneak up on you, that end up being about love in all its forms. *Charm City Rocks* earns its place in that pantheon."

—JULIA WHELAN, author of *Thank You for Listening*

Praise for *All Together Now*

Named a Best Book of the Summer by the *New York Post*

"*All Together Now*—a delightful novel about the meaning of friendship and how we dream of being remembered by those closest to us—won me from the first page. Matthew Norman's latest made me wish I were reading it alongside its warm, wonderful characters on a sunny beach: eating too much, telling secrets, and maybe even getting a matching tattoo. . . . A fabulous vacation of a book!"

—AMANDA EYRE WARD, *New York Times* bestselling author of
The Jetsetters

"Fast, fun, and wise—the perfect summer read."

—NANCY THAYER, *New York Times* bestselling author of
Family Reunion

"Like a modern, updated *The Big Chill*, *All Together Now* features a gathering of pals who spill the truth, rehash the past, air grievances, and then let their enormous love for one another wash it all clean. I fell hard for each of the charming, oddball characters and laughed, cried, and gasped along with them as I raced from the opening pages to the final chapter in this delightful, funny, and heartwarming book."

—JESSICA ANYA BLAU, author of *Mary Jane*

"A terrific story of love and friendship and lies and secrets and how these things affect these well-rounded, very real characters. Readers will be completely entranced by Cat, Blair, Wade, and Robbie and their stories. The dialogue was rich and completely believable with each character having a distinct voice. The writing is simply beautiful. Don't miss this incredible book."

—*Seattle Book Review*

Praise for *Last Couple Standing*

The *New York Post*'s Best Books to Read in Our Age of Social Isolation

"Norman's funny and feeling writing makes for an irresistible read."

—*Esquire* (Best Books of 2020 So Far)

"Nothing is left off the table in Matthew Norman's *Last Couple Standing*, an equal-parts funny and heart-pinging novel that will be achingly relatable to both the married and the divorced—or to anyone who's ever contemplated being either. Norman's trademark humor and wit make this a page-turner you'll want to read with your funniest friend, then discuss over a couple of stiff martinis."

—SARAH JIO, *New York Times* bestselling author of
All the Flowers in Paris

"The funniest book I've read in a long time … In *Last Couple Standing*, Matthew Norman has written a heartfelt, perceptive, and thoroughly entertaining novel."

—RICHARD ROPER, author of *How Not to Die Alone*

"This warm and witty tale of a devoted couple willing to throw out that pesky 'forsaking all others' rule in order to stay together crackles with fierce energy and emotional truth."

—JUDY BLUNDELL, *New York Times* bestselling author of *The High Season*

"Only Matthew Norman can make divorce fun and funny. I smiled straight through this book, enjoying every fumbling sexual encounter, every tormented marriage, every strange neighbor. In the end, as with all of Norman's books, there's loads of heart and tenderness peeking out from behind the great comic writing."

—JESSICA ANYA BLAU, author of *The Trouble with Lexie*

"In Norman's funny and heartwarming novel ... a Baltimore couple tries to head off the demise of their marriage with an unusual arrangement.... Norman skillfully uses his gift for gentle humor to prod at the foibles and joys of marriage, parenthood, and love in this endearing charmer."

—*Publishers Weekly*

"Although Jessica and Mitch's plan may be a bit out of the box, their relationship and feelings are believable. Norman also creates a plethora of rounded, quirky side characters.... When all of those characters come together in the story's climax, the result is a scene worthy of a Shakespearean comedy.... A quick-witted and ultimately hopeful look at what it takes to make a marriage last."

—*Kirkus Reviews*

"Norman writes characters that are so relatable, you feel like they are people you know. His dialogue seems like he has eavesdropped on people at the table next to him in a restaurant. He had me laughing out loud at some of his lines, and then in the next paragraph you feel sorry for the characters. *Last Couple Standing* is a cautionary tale for married adults, where you find that the grass isn't always greener. I recommend it."

—*The Citizen* (Auburn, NY)

Praise for *We're All Damaged*

"Matthew Norman's whip-smart, hilarious dialogue will dazzle you, even as his characters crack your heart with their humanity and their in-spite-of-everything love for one another. I laughed, I cried (sometimes simultaneously), and, with every page, I wished like mad I'd written this book."

—Marisa de los Santos, *New York Times* bestselling author of *The Precious One* and *Belong to Me*

"In *We're All Damaged*, Matthew Norman has crafted a fast-paced, funny, and touching story. Comparisons to Tropper and Hornby will be made, and deservedly so, but Norman's voice and characters are fresh and all his own. . . . A winning novel that is sure to make you laugh, cry, and nod in recognition as all the best books do."

—Catherine McKenzie, bestselling author of *Hidden* and *Smoke*

"A smart, funny, and surprisingly emotional tale about letting go and moving on."

—*Kirkus Reviews*

Praise for *Domestic Violets*

"Charmingly drawn . . . All this misery makes for good comedy."
—*The Washington Post*

"Norman's debut novel is funny and incisive, and hard on sacred cows."
—*Shelf Awareness*

"Norman controls his complicated story and handles its chaos and plot twists with a steady, funny hand. . . . This is a thoroughly entertaining, light but thoughtful read."
—*Publishers Weekly*

"Norman's refreshingly witty style is perfectly suited to articulating the trials of a middle-aged cynic. Wonderfully fast-paced, hilariously genuine, difficult to put down, *Domestic Violets* is an ideal first novel."
—*Booklist*

CHARM CITY ROCKS

CHARM CITY ROCKS

A Love Story

Matthew Norman

DELL

NEW YORK

A Dell Trade Paperback Original

Copyright © 2023 by Matthew Norman
Book club guide copyright © 2023 by Penguin Random House LLC

Published in the United States by Dell,
an imprint of Random House,
a division of Penguin Random House LLC, New York.

Dell is a registered trademark and the colophon is a trademark of
Penguin Random House LLC.
Random House Book Club and colophon are trademarks of
Penguin Random House LLC.

Library of Congress Cataloging-in-Publication Data
Names: Norman, Matthew, author.
Title: Charm city rocks: a love story / Matthew Norman.
Description: New York: Dell, [2023]
Identifiers: LCCN 2022046462 (print) | LCCN 2022046463 (ebook) | ISBN
9780593499832 (trade paperback) | ISBN 9780593499849 (ebook)
Classification: LCC PS3614.O7626 C53 2023 (print) | LCC PS3614.O7626 (ebook) |
DDC 813/.6—dc23
LC record available at https://lccn.loc.gov/2022046462
LC ebook record available at https://lccn.loc.gov/2022046463

Printed in the United States of America on acid-free paper

randomhousebooks.com
randomhousebookclub.com

2 4 6 8 9 7 5 3 1

Book design by Diane Hobbing

For Kate, one heck of a piano player

Part 1

THE
MARGOT HAMMER
INCIDENT

CHAPTER 1

Here's an interesting fact about Billy Perkins: he's happy. No, for real, legitimately. It's kind of his thing, actually. If a person can have a thesis statement, that's Billy's: I'm happy. And, well, why wouldn't he be?

For starters, he has the most fantastic apartment. It's the perfect size—just big enough—and it's directly above a record shop called Charm City Rocks, so the place vibrates gently with music, as if the walls are living things that hum along. He loves his neighborhood, Fells Point in Baltimore, with its cobblestone streets and loud bars and the gourmet pretzel stand that makes his block smell like baking bread. He even loves Baltimore, because there's something thrilling about living in a city that the rest of the country assumes is on the verge of collapse. There's a bumper sticker he sees around town, BALTIMORE: ACTUALLY, I LIKE IT, and Billy couldn't agree more.

He's an independent music teacher—the founder of Beats by Billy LLC—and he loves that, too, as far as jobs go, because he gets to set his own hours and spend his days teaching people the sheer joy of rocking out, and he can wear whatever he wants. He goes with jeans and sneakers, mostly, along with an array of band

T-shirts that his students have given him over the years. He's been really into cardigans lately, too, because cardigans are the perfect garment, like, the convertible of sweaters.

He teaches kids and teenagers mostly, which is rewarding work, because he gets to shape young minds and pass on an appreciation for the arts. But there are some adults mixed in there, too, which is also gratifying, because it's never too late to learn something new, right? His oldest student is a seventy-year-old widow named Alice who always wanted to play the guitar. She meets with Billy twice a week instead of the standard once because she's determined to play a rock-and-roll medley at her daughter's wedding reception this summer. Plus, as she told Billy during their first lesson, "Once you hit seventy, it's best to get on with things."

Many of Billy's students came to him after flaming out with more traditional music teachers. Consequently, they often arrive to their first lesson shy and sullen, convinced that learning to play an instrument is lame or boring or just too much work. Billy always manages to break through, though. He's not sure why; he's just got a knack for it, he supposes. Or maybe it's the cardigans. Along with being the perfect garment, cardigans are very disarming. We can probably thank Mister Rogers for that.

Back to Billy's apartment, though.

The place is neat and clean and full of books and music and local art, and there's a wildly complicated espresso machine that Billy inherited from his grandma that looks like something built by NASA in the sixties. As great as all those things are, the true star of the place is Billy's Steinway & Sons grand piano. It's the most expensive thing Billy owns, and it's a straight-up showstopper. Even if you know nothing about pianos, and most people don't, you know that the Steinway is something special. Plumbers or electricians will be over to fix something, and they'll stop and say, "Jeez, look at that thing."

Most mornings, particularly when it's sunny, Billy opens his windows wide and loudly plays the most epic piano parts of classic rock songs, like "November Rain" or "Bohemian Rhapsody," and people wave up at him while they walk their dogs or shuffle off to work. The beer delivery guys are some of Billy's biggest fans. They sometimes shout requests, and he obliges as best he can, because playing music is such an easy way to make people happy. For example, just try listening to the intro to "Don't Stop Believin'" by Journey without feeling at least a small rush of joy.

The thing Billy loves most, though—more than his apartment or his confusing espresso machine or even the Steinway—is his son, Caleb.

Caleb is goofy and sweet, and he pokes fun at the things his dad likes, but never unkindly. And on this particular Saturday night in early spring, Caleb is stretched out on Billy's couch like a young giraffe in repose. Billy is sitting across from him in his rocking chair, which Billy refers to as "The Rocker," and they're watching a documentary series on Netflix called *The Definitive History of Rock and Roll.*

At this exact moment, 9:25 P.M. eastern standard time, there's nowhere Billy would rather be, and there's no one he'd rather be with. Billy hasn't always been this blatantly sentimental, but Caleb is a senior in high school, so lately Billy has been thinking about the finite nature of . . . well, everything. But especially childhood.

If it were possible, Billy would go ahead and pause time right here. His apartment would hum on, the streetlights outside would hit the Steinway through the window just right, and his son would be here every other week forever, stretched out and lanky, being young and silly.

But that's not how life works, is it?

———

"Did you get enough to eat?" Billy asks.

Caleb makes a noise—like a grunt of general affirmation.

"Come on," Billy says. "Use your words."

Caleb laughs, one of those fed-up teenager laughs. "Dad, stop it. I told you, I'm fine."

"I bet Gustavo still has some pretzels left." Billy goes to the window and opens it. Street sounds, like a ragtag orchestra, flood the apartment. "Hey, Gustavo!" he shouts. "You still have some warm ones?"

Down at Hot Twist, which is a pretzel stand along the brick sidewalk across the street, Billy's friend Gustavo reaches below the counter like he's checking, but when he pulls his hand back up, he gives Billy the finger. This has been Gustavo's favorite running joke for more than a month now.

"That's really funny!" Billy calls. "You should be proud!"

"Yeah, man, I have warm pretzels!" Gustavo shouts. "Having warm pretzels is literally my job! You guys should come down. We can eat, and you can watch soccer with me."

From the window, he can see the TV mounted on the back wall over Gustavo's shoulder. Elite athletes on a vast green field run and run. Billy gives his friend a thumbs-up and returns to The Rocker.

"He flipped you off again, didn't he?" asks Caleb.

"He did."

Caleb laughs. "Classic Gustavo."

"Anyway," says Billy, "if you want a pretzel, I'm buying."

"Nah," says Caleb. "I crushed three quarters of that pizza. I could probably barf."

Billy looks at the picked-over remains of the Johnny Rad's pizza on the coffee table. "You did, didn't you? Where do you put it all, anyway?"

Caleb shrugs. "Maybe I'm still growing."

What a thought that is. Caleb doesn't do anything useful with his six-foot-six-inch body, like fight crime or play in the NBA. Still, his height is a source of constant pride for Billy, just another weird thing he loves about the kid.

Billy was barely in his twenties when Caleb was born. Being that young and a single dad had its challenges—like something in a think piece about woefully unprepared fathers. The upside, though, is that they've essentially grown up together, and now their relationship is like a parent-friend hybrid.

The documentary, which moves along chronologically, is currently analyzing the nineties, so Eddie Vedder is on the TV in a giant flannel, mumble-yelling the song "Jeremy."

"I don't get the whole grunge thing," says Caleb. "Was it, like, in the bylaws that clothes had to be way too big? And what's he saying? You can't understand him."

Caleb has had a lot of opinions about the documentary series. His most unforgivable comment a couple of episodes ago was that maybe David Bowie should've just picked one look and gone with it.

After Pearl Jam, U2's mid-career evolution comes up. Bono is dressed like a fly in a leather suit and wraparound sunglasses. "And what even is that?" asks Caleb. "Was he *trying* to be an asshole?"

"He was being ironic," says Billy. "And don't swear."

This is something they're working on: Caleb's swearing. Billy is all for the subtle use of profanity, but too much just seems excessive, like saxophone solos in rock songs.

The documentary clips along, moving from the nineties and into the aughts. Nirvana comes and goes; the Red Hot Chili Peppers and Soundgarden cut their hair and begin looking like adults.

The announcer has a deep voice, like in a truck commercial. "As we go smashing our way into the twenty-first century, across the entire musical spectrum, from country to R & B to grunge to pop, female artists began to emerge like never before, loudly. And none were louder than New York–born garage band turned rock goddesses Burnt Flowers."

Billy tilts forward on The Rocker. "Oh, Cay, listen up. This was one of my favorite bands."

On the TV, four young women tear through one of the biggest songs of the aughts, "Power Pink." Billy taps out the drumbeat on his thighs.

"Yeah, all right," says Caleb. "They're not bad. Their clothes fit, at least."

Billy tells his son to shut up but is immediately ignored.

"It's like, I've *heard* of them," says Caleb, "but you don't really *hear about* them, you know?"

Billy isn't crazy about Caleb's tone, but he's not wrong. In the pantheon of rock music, Burnt Flowers have come and gone. They're a blip now—a couple minutes in a streaming retrospective. But when Billy was young, Burnt Flowers was one of the biggest bands in the United States. They flooded airwaves and sold out arenas. No lip-syncing. No choreographed dance moves. They were four talented women who turned up their instruments and rocked out.

Billy is about to explain all of this to Caleb, but the announcer keeps going.

"Plagued by in-fighting and a good old-fashioned Fleetwood Mac–style love triangle, Burnt Flowers flickered out as fast as their name would suggest. But before that—and before three hit records, a Best New Artist Grammy, and general superstardom—it all began at the tail end of the nineties with a note pinned to an NYU bulletin board by the band's founding member and drummer, Margot Hammer."

On the screen there's a black-and-white still of Margot Hammer, and a big swoony wave of nostalgia crashes over Billy.

"Whoa," says Caleb, "check out those boots. Those're pretty hardcore."

"Yeah," says Billy. "Boots were her thing. And I may have been a little bit in love with her." He meant this to be something he said to himself, but now that he's announced it, Billy braces himself, because he knows that he's about to get roasted.

"What?" says Caleb. "Really? *Her?*"

"Your mom used to tease me about it," says Billy.

The documentary cuts to a music video. Margot Hammer plays double time, hair flying wild.

"But she's so mad, though," Caleb says. "Why's she so . . . frowny?"

Billy tells Caleb to shut up again, and he longs for a more innocent time, when we fell in love with celebrities on big, boxy, standard-def TVs.

"Did you think about kissing her?" Caleb asks. "Like, with tongue?"

As a father, you can love your son madly but still fantasize about throwing pizza crust at his face. "Will you stop talking for ten seconds and *listen?*"

A *Rolling Stone* cover appears. The band is lined up behind the lead singer, Nikki Kixx, who's wearing a bedazzled crop top.

"Wow," says Caleb.

Margot Hammer stands behind her three bandmates, drumsticks in her hands. "Here to Burn It All Down," the headline reads. Billy has a copy of this exact magazine in a box in his closet. This is a fact he decides to keep to himself.

The announcer guy again. "After an infamous meltdown at the MTV Video Music Awards, Burnt Flowers was officially no more. Where are they now, you ask? Well, bassist Anna Gunn caught on in the bluegrass scene. Guitarist Jenny Switch has band-hopped for years. Margot Hammer, though—the *quiet* Flower, if you will?

Well, she walked away from all of it and has become something of a rock-and-roll recluse. Nowadays she's best known as the ex-wife of Oscar-nominated actor Lawson Daniels."

"She was married to Lawson Daniels?" asks Caleb.

"A lot happened before you were born," Billy says. "Wars, famines, celebrity weddings."

They see a red-carpet picture of Margot Hammer and the actor. Lawson Daniels—handsome in a tux—carries Margot Hammer over his shoulder.

"I mean, how cool is *that* dude?" says Caleb.

Lawson Daniels *was* cool. He still is. He's one of the most famous actors in the world. Billy is focused on Margot Hammer, though. She's wearing a blue dress. One of her shoes has fallen off. She virtually never smiled, but there she is, beaming, and for a few weeks some twenty years ago you couldn't leave the house without seeing this iconic photo.

Nikki Kixx reappears in a leather outfit. She's jumping up and down as she sings.

"And as we all know, Nikki Kixx went solo," says the announcer. "Although the singer has never quite achieved Burnt Flowers–level success on her own, she's still at it."

"You know, if I was picking rock chicks to be in love with," says Caleb, "I think I would've gone with her."

"Don't say *chicks*," says Billy. "You sound like a jerk. Also, you're wrong. Margot Hammer was the most talented musician in the band, by a mile."

Caleb points to the TV. It's a video clip from one of Nikki Kixx's solo songs. The singer has inexplicably been doused with water. "Yeah, but . . . look."

"Stop it," says Billy.

Caleb raises his palms, surrendering. "Don't hate the player, Dad, hate the—"

"All right, that's it, you Neanderthal." Billy grabs the remote and turns off the TV. "It's time for a lesson."

Caleb's shoulders sink. "Oh crap," he says. "Seriously?"

Billy's "Lessons in Art and Manhood" started when Caleb was just a toddler. They mostly covered the basics back then, like how you shouldn't stick forks into electrical outlets or eat things you find on the ground. Billy taught Caleb how to play the theme music to *Jaws* when the boy was seven, and at ten, Caleb learned that he should never, under any circumstances, be a bully. The lessons turned increasingly more complex around the time Caleb's voice changed, because Billy has always taken his responsibility as a Boy Dad seriously. His job, as he sees it, is to ensure that Caleb becomes one of the good ones—a decent young man. Tonight's lesson starts with a record.

"Oh gee, great," says Caleb. "Vinyl has entered the chat."

Billy sets the turntable needle down on Burnt Flowers's first album, *Short Not Sweet*. He isn't a vinyl fanatic, but he prefers the format for albums that he considers classics. There's that glorious two seconds of scratchiness, then track one starts, a slow burner called "I'm Not Your Girl."

"*Boom boom, pshhh, boom boom, pshhh,*" Billy says.

"Dad, stop, you're beatboxing."

Fifteen seconds in, Margot Hammer's drums erupt. Billy turns the volume up and pitches his voice over the noise. "Looks have always been part of the music business. Fine. But female artists are expected to be models *and* musicians. Total double standard."

"I believe this is called mansplaining," says Caleb. "Not a super-great look, Dad."

Caleb talks smack during Lessons in Art and Manhood; that's part of it. But when "I'm Not Your Girl" fades out and the next song, "Power Pink," starts, Caleb's expression turns thoughtful. "This is the one from the documentary, right?"

Billy nods.

"Okay, yeah, this is actually awesome."

"The drums, right?" says Billy. "They're incredible."

The first verse ends, and Nikki Kixx shouts the chorus.

"Hell, yeah," says Caleb.

"And guess what?" says Billy. "She wrote this, too."

"Who did, your girlfriend?"

"Yes. Well, no, but . . . yeah. Margot Hammer, the drummer, wrote 'Power Pink.'"

Caleb nods along. "I've heard it, but I guess I've never, like, *listened*."

Moments like this—a student finally mastering a tricky note, Caleb finding joy in something Billy likes—are among Billy's favorite things. Love for his son swells, which, as it nearly always does, blooms quickly into physical affection, and Billy reaches over and shoves Caleb. It's impossible to have a son as big as his and not occasionally shove him. "Today's lesson," Billy says.

Caleb pretends to start snoring.

"Today's lesson!" Billy repeats. "Women aren't just things for you to look at, you jerk."

The kid accepts this without eye roll or snicker.

"Your mom, for example," says Billy. "She's a woman."

"Ew, Dad, gross."

"When you were just a giant baby, she put herself through business school. Now look at her. She's a VP."

"Senior VP, actually," says Caleb.

"Really?"

"Yeah, she got a promotion. Maybe it's executive VP. I can't remember. There are a lot of different kinds of VPs."

"Well, see, then?" says Billy. "Sometimes women are senior-slash-executive VPs." Billy opens the record cover. There's a collage of band pictures inside, including a candid of Margot Hammer balancing a drumstick on her palm. "And sometimes women are the best drummers of their generation."

Caleb laughs and gently shoves his dad back. "Okay, fine. But you do realize you're totally stanning this lady, right?"

"Stanning?" says Billy. "Wait, that's a bad thing, right?"

The song fades out and Caleb laughs. "Guess it depends on how you look at it," he says. "Anyway, are you still cool if we get pretzels?"

CHAPTER 2

"Dad? Dude. Dad? You asleep?"

"No. And don't call me dude."

His dad's eyes are closed as he says this, though, and Caleb thinks, as he often does, about how much it must suck to be old. When Caleb was little, weekends at his dad's place were like slumber parties. They'd stay up late watching movies, eating Totino's pizza rolls, living it up. His dad can't hang at all anymore, though. After getting pretzels down at Gustavo's earlier, they listened to the rest of Burnt Flowers's albums. Halfway through the third and final one, *Incessant Noise,* his dad pretty much passed out. It's like he's an old desktop that's been set to go into sleep mode at exactly 11 P.M.

"Your back's gonna hurt if you sleep on the couch," Caleb says.

It's no use, though. His dad's mouth falls open and he starts to snore. *Incessant Noise* is open across his chest, like he's a teenage girl snuggling a diary. Margot Hammer and her glammed-up bandmates scowl up at Caleb. "So retro," he whispers.

Caleb goes to the snack cupboard next to the refrigerator and eats five handfuls of Raisin Bran Crunch, because the pretzel wasn't enough, and the pizza from before is a distant memory. When he puts the box back, his hand grazes something squishy in plastic. "Oh, dope," he says. "Gummy bears."

If Caleb took even a second to use the most basic powers of observation, it would strike him as odd that the gummy bears are in a Ziploc baggie instead of a regular candy package. They're shaped wrong, too—pudgy, like they've been left in a hot car. He notices neither of these things, though, because he's eighteen and hungry. He pops three bears into his mouth and spreads an old flannel blanket over his father.

"See you tomorrow, Dad," he says.

Caleb puts on some pajama pants and a T-shirt and watches the rest of the documentary on The Rocker while his dad sleeps. He flips around after that and checks out the end of a Lakers game on TNT. By the time he settles in at the cluttered little desk in his bedroom, his mouth has gone dry. Caleb blames this on Gustavo's salty pretzels. The dull buzz at the front of his skull barely registers, because maybe sometimes skulls just do that.

He gets a soda from the fridge and absolutely pounds it. Back in his room, he takes his laptop out of his backpack and opens to the Stanford University website. When he gets to the Campus Life page, he wishes like always that everything didn't look so perfect. Click after click reveals beautiful, diverse, smart-looking people doing exciting things in breathtaking locations. He did a campus visit last year: Caleb, his dad, his mom, and his stepdad, Aaron. Palo Alto was like traveling to Narnia, with distant mountains, bonkers sunsets, and single-speed bicycles.

Scrolling through images of students, Caleb imagines himself as a character among them. He'd wear a crimson hoodie and hold hands with a hypothetical girl from somewhere cooler than Baltimore. He'd wear his hair differently, maybe a little longer, and people would think it was cool that he's so unreasonably tall.

Stanford is his "reach school," so this is all probably a big waste of time. He does, however, allow himself quiet moments like this to fantasize.

But then Caleb looks at the wall above his screen and sees for probably the thousandth time the picture of him and his dad at the 9:30 Club down in Washington, D.C. It was taken at Caleb's first concert. The band was Wilco, and he was five years old, sitting on his dad's shoulders. His dad made little earmuffs out of duct tape and cotton balls to protect Caleb's virginal eardrums.

"Shit," he whispers now, because even if some academic miracle happens and he *does* get in, Stanford is thousands of miles away. It might as well be in Europe or on the moon.

His friends always talk about their dads like they're such distant, mysterious creatures. At no point in Caleb's life, though, has he for one moment doubted that he is the most important human being in his own dad's life, and now he's left wondering what the guy would do without him here in Baltimore.

Then a switch flips in Caleb's brain. A feeling like bobbing in water, mild vertigo, and, finally, a shocking burst of clarity. He looks up at the ceiling and nearly topples over in his desk chair. "Oh shit," he whispers, because he's pretty sure those weren't regular gummy bears. "Dad, what the fuck?"

He's never tried pot before, mostly because he knows his parents would kill him if they ever caught him on anything stronger than Vicks VapoRub. This, though, is a free pass—an accidental stoning—and Caleb giggles and then snorts.

Back in the kitchen, he eats more cereal, then he stares at his hand, which is something he's never really stared at before. It's a blurry and strange thing, the human hand, like anime. He goes to the couch and stands over his sleeping dad. Caleb has never really stared at his dad before either. Has he always looked this small? Caleb picks up the Burnt Flowers album off the couch cushion. Inside the gatefold, there's another serious-looking picture of Margot Hammer. Caleb holds it up next to his dad's face. He imagines them kissing, his dad and Margot Hammer. It's gross, but also nice. Caleb teased him before about having a thing for this drummer lady. He gets it now, though. She doesn't look like a rock star. She just looks like some girl in a T-shirt.

Back in his room, he googles Margot Hammer, and 180 million results pop up.

"Holy shit."

There are Wiki pages, fan blogs, and illegal MP3 sites. He briefly watches a Burnt Flowers tribute band on YouTube. Some lady in Arizona decorated her whole house with Burnt Flowers wallpaper. There's an essay from *Esquire* titled "Burnt Flowers and What Might Have Been." He scrolls by shots of a young Margot Hammer with a young Lawson Daniels. He sees pictures of her holding a baby named Poppy, then pictures of her next to Poppy as a very pretty teenager. "Damn," he says.

Stage Dive Records' website has a pull-down menu with a list of bands, and he goes to the page for Burnt Flowers. He finds a set of current pictures of the band members. Margot Hammer is sitting on a bench in Central Park in jeans and scuffed-up boots. Caleb leans in, squints because the screen is starting to blur. She looks even less like a rock star now. She looks like someone Caleb might see down at Charm City Rocks flipping through the new arrivals stack. She looks . . . normal.

A link catches his attention at the top of the page: Media Contact.

People always talk about how Caleb's dad is such a happy guy. Like, weirdly happy—happy in a time in which everyone is miserable. As a kid, Caleb just went with it. They'd eat popcorn together at Orioles games and go sneaker shopping downtown. He'd watch his dad sit at the Steinway and play "Tiny Dancer" with the window open for the whole neighborhood to hear, and Caleb would accept his dad's happiness as a given. Lately, though, Caleb has started to wonder if his dad is actually lonely.

It takes longer than it should to blink, he discovers, like his eyelids have been velcroed to his forehead. He looks at the picture of Margot Hammer again. She isn't frowning, but she's not smiling either, the way happy people do. She was a big deal once, apparently. In a band that people loved. Married to a famous actor. Now, though, she's just a lady on a bench in old boots.

What if she's lonely, too?

CHAPTER 3

A few days later, some 195 miles north of Baltimore, in Manhattan, Margot Hammer looks down at West Twenty-eighth Street seven stories below. Chelsea, which has been her neighborhood for her entire adult life, is soaked. People wearing raincoats walk dogs that are also wearing raincoats. Cabs idle at the curbside, waiting. Some tourists who didn't check the forecast stand beneath a red awning across the street.

Her apartment, which sits atop what was once a fur factory, has vaulted ceilings and exposed brick and far more space than she needs. Years ago, when she and Lawson first moved in, it was featured in some magazines. *Metropolis* called it a "crash pad," which Margot never liked, because it made it sound like they wouldn't be there for long.

As beautiful as the glossy pictures looked in print, the eighteen floor-to-ceiling windows turn the place hopelessly drab when it rains, and it's been raining all day. Shadows and gray scales, piled-up mail, and some droopy plants.

The rain against the windows sounds like a backbeat. Margot finds the 4/4 time signature on her hipbone with two fingers. A habit since childhood, she hardly realizes she's doing it, like self-soothing. In her other hand she holds her iPhone, which is open to FaceTime.

"Mum, did your connection freeze, or are you just standing perfectly still?" asks Poppy.

"They called me a recluse?" Margot asks her daughter. "Are you kidding?"

Goddammit, Netflix, she thinks.

"No, they called you a *rock-and-roll* recluse," says Poppy. "That actually sounds quite cool, don't you think?"

"No. I don't. It makes me sound like the Unabomber."

Poppy laughs. "What's the Unabomber?"

"Nothing. Just some weirdo."

"Well, weirdo or not," says Poppy, "you came off as badass. They also called you the *quiet* Flower. I liked that, too."

"Well, that's just ridiculous," says Margot. "I'm not *quiet*. I'm certainly not a recluse."

On the tiny phone screen, her daughter's mouth turns upward. "You're sure about that? Should I have Siri give us the definition of recluse?"

"Poppy!" says Margot.

"Mum!" says Poppy, teasing.

Mum. Margot is white and American; her ex-husband is Black and British. Poppy's childhood was spent being shuttled between London, New York, and Los Angeles, so her accent, like her skin, is a perfect blend of her parents'. The result is a young woman who sounds like an American playacting at being a Brit.

Poppy called ten minutes ago to give Margot the rundown on the documentary. The episode featuring Burnt Flowers premiered over the weekend. Margot hasn't watched it, because she never watches anything having to do with herself or the band. And now she's glad she didn't.

"I'm a perfectly normal person," she says. "I take walks to get my coffee, and I go shopping. I chat with my neighbors. I say hello to their stupid little dogs."

Her daughter doesn't seem to buy it. "When's the last time you took one of these alleged walks?"

"Poppy, it's been pouring all day, see?" Margot angles her phone to the window.

Poppy ignores the weather and instead takes in her mom's full reflection in the glass. "Nice jammies, by the way. Are you . . . are you not wearing a bra? Mum, it's nearly lunchtime there."

Margot turns her phone back around. "Yes, I'm wearing a bra. It's an old one. What else did they say?"

Poppy adjusts an earbud. She's at her office in San Francisco. Margot can see young professionals behind her looking at computer screens. "Relax, it was all very flattering," she says. "Rock goddesses and all that. They talked about how you founded the band. The flyer you posted. Et cetera."

Margot leans her back against the window. "What songs did they play?"

"'Power Pink,' mostly, which was cool. One of Nikki's solo songs, too. The one with the video that's like soft porn."

Margot pictures her former bandmate gyrating. Nikki's career as a solo artist has been a mix of hits and misses, but the releases have been steady, and she's stayed in the public eye by occasionally popping up as a guest judge on singing shows and somehow maintaining the body she had when she was in her twenties. "Did they show the MTV thing?" she asks.

"They didn't *show* it, no," says Poppy. "They alluded to it, though. Called it a high-profile meltdown, I think. Nothing specific."

That one stings, too: *meltdown*. Like *recluse*, it's a distinctly Unabombery word. "What about the picture?" she asks. "Did they use that goddamn picture?"

"What picture?"

"*The* picture, Poppy. Your dad carrying me into Radio City Music Hall."

Poppy bites her lip. "Well, yeah."

"Shit," says Margot.

"I know you hate that picture," says Poppy. "I get it, I guess. But I think you can understand why I love it."

Margot used to love it, too. A framed print once hung from the wall fifteen feet from where she's standing now. However, if Margot could push a button and somehow erase it from existence and the Internet, she would, without hesitation.

"Anyway," says Poppy, "your bum looked great in that dress, and you know it, too."

Her daughter is being supportive, so Margot makes a go at smiling.

Poppy leans closer to her phone. "How are you, Mum? You okay? For real?"

The rain intensifies just then—the timing speeds up—and Margot instinctively looks at her drum kit on the other side of the loft. "What do you mean?"

"I'm worried about you. You're stressed about the documentary. That and all this stuff with Dad. I don't want it to get in your head."

"I'm fine, Poppy."

"Dad's just having a . . . I don't know . . . a moment, that's all."

Her ex-husband is having more than a moment. Lawson was nominated for an Oscar for best supporting actor last year after scene-chewing his way through an ensemble murder mystery called *The House on Pembrooke*. He's been everywhere since: magazines, entertainment shows, a series of gigantic billboards for Tag Heuer watches. Divorce is never easy, Margot assumes, even years later. But consistently seeing forty-foot-tall images of your ex on the sides of buildings is uniquely not easy. And, of course, he's with someone new, like always. This time it's the young murderess from that mystery, actress Willa Knight.

"Mum? Are you gonna talk, or should I go back to work?"

Margot imagines a solo album, thirteen tracks of her screaming herself hoarse into a microphone. The title: *I'm Fine.* And then the buzzer above her apartment door blasts.

"Whoa," says Poppy. "What's that?"

A light flashes beside the door. "It's my doorman," she says. "I should go."

"Okay, fine," says Poppy. "We *will* talk about this, though. No hiding out. Also, you're not a solo bomber ... or uni-whatever. You're awesome. And I love you."

Margot tells Poppy that she loves her, too, and disconnects. The buzzer buzzes again, like a foghorn. The volume was set years ago to cut through blaring playback speakers and drum loops. She hits the answer button. "Hello?"

"Hi there, Miss H.," says her doorman, Jimmy. "Got a visitor down here for you."

"Really?" Margot asks. "Who?"

Jimmy lowers his voice. "It's a girl. Looks kinda young. Like, *real* young."

"I'm not that young, dude," says a voice. "Tell her I'm with Stage Dive Records."

Margot hears this in the background and stares at the dusty intercom. *What?*

"Yeah, I assume you heard that," says Jimmy. "Claims she's from your record label. Want me to send her up?"

There's no time to straighten up both herself *and* the apartment, so Margot opts for herself. She runs a brush through her hair and replaces her flannel sleeping pants with jeans. She looks at herself in the mirror. She's barefoot, wearing a tank top with David Bowie's face on it, and she clearly hasn't showered today. If she were a police sketch hanging in the post office, the sign would ask, HAVE YOU SEEN THE ROCK-AND-ROLL UNABOMBER?

Three assertive little knocks at the door. Margot slides the chain lock. A girl with a dripping umbrella dangling from her wrist holds out a cup of coffee. She's wearing Chuck Taylors and a vintage striped sweater. Jimmy was right; she looks like a child. "A gift from Stage Dive," she says. "Hi, I'm Rebecca Yang. I'm your publicist."

The cup is warm and familiar in Margot's hand.

"Axl told me what you like," the girl says, and then her eyes dart to the insides of Margot's forearms, where a faded drumstick tattoo runs from each of her wrists to the crook of the elbow. "I was hoping maybe we could talk."

Margot did a phone interview a few months ago for the documentary. Like the girl who's just walked into Margot's apartment, the interviewer, a research assistant from Netflix's production company, sounded like a kid. Margot can't remember his name.

"So, this is all just for background, really," he said. "Most of the info we go off of is a matter of historical record, but the writers like to add a little color when they can."

"All right," said Margot. "Are you planning on talking to the others? Anna, Jenny, and, um . . . Nikki?"

She was annoyed with herself for that pause before saying Nikki's name.

"Yeah, Nikki, for sure," the guy said. "I've got her scheduled for next week. With you being the founder and her being the lead singer, it makes the most sense. The segment will be super quick, though. Burnt Flowers will probably get between a minute and a half and two minutes, tops. So, we'll keep things high-level, if that's cool."

As Margot leaned on her kitchen counter, phone in hand, she discovered that you can be offended and relieved at the same time. Boiling their entire musical history down to ninety seconds seemed insulting, but then again . . . thank God it was only ninety seconds.

"Okay, so, question one. What, um, exactly have you been up to since Burnt Flowers broke up?"

How dare you, Margot nearly replied.

It was an obvious question, though. Margot fumbled through a summary of her days: the small birdfeeder she tends to on her five-foot-by-five-foot sundeck, the walks she takes through the city, her visits to see her parents, who've retired to Florida and are now alarmingly tan. Next, there was a question about her contact with Lawson, and another about her thoughts on the state of drumming in rock music. The guy asked Margot about exactly where she posted that now-famous flyer at NYU, the one asking if anyone wanted to be in her yet-to-be-named band. Margot was precise about the facts and vague about personal details, like her failed marriage and finances. Her Burnt Flowers money combined with her divorce settlement from Lawson allow her to maintain a frugal Manhattan existence.

"Great, great," the guy said. Margot could hear him losing interest as he typed notes. "One last thing. This is kinda off the record, I guess. I'm just curious. Do you, like . . . miss it?"

Margot didn't know what he meant by *it,* exactly. There is so much that she doesn't miss about her handful of years in the spotlight. There's one thing, though, that she misses nearly every day. "I miss the music," she said.

———

Rebecca Yang's eyes do more darting—to the bits of clutter, to the electric and acoustic guitars mounted on the wall, to the drums at the center of everything, where an entertainment center might go if Margot were a normal person. Rebecca touches one of the kit's cymbals. "Dope apartment," she says.

"Sorry about Jimmy," says Margot. "He's . . ."

Rebecca waves off whatever Margot was about to say like she's shooing a bug. "No worries. I'm not *that* young. I'm twenty-five. But, you know . . . the Korean thing. It throws the boomers off."

Margot settles into an overstuffed chair with her coffee. She wasn't aware that she even had a publicist.

Rebecca, who doesn't think twenty-five is "that young," sits on the couch and clears her throat. "Not sure if you've had a chance to read the emails I sent," she says. "I tried calling, but the number we have on file doesn't go anywhere."

Margot points to a phone next to the microwave, disconnected, strangled by its cord.

"Oh," says Rebecca. "Wow, is that a . . . a landline?"

Margot hates herself for suddenly being nervous. Rebecca is a zygote in sneakers, but she's from Stage Dive, the label. Unsure what she's supposed to say, she decides to go on the offensive. "So, how's Axl?"

"Axl?" Rebecca pauses. "Axl's good."

They're referring to Axl Albee, the head artist relations manager at Stage Dive, whom Margot hasn't heard from in several U.S. presidential administrations. "We used to be good friends," she says.

"Axl's working on strategic initiatives. He's been pretty office-bound lately. He definitely says hey, though."

Margot gets that it's this girl's professional duty to lie to her. Stage Dive has a hierarchy, like anywhere. Axl Albee deals with the big names. Any one of five other reps handle the tier below—

indie rockers, morose singer-songwriters. People like Rebecca see to artists like Margot: legacy artists.

"And, no," Margot says. "I didn't read your emails. I haven't checked lately."

"No worries," says Rebecca. "I'll summarize. We got a message over the weekend through the media contacts link. It was addressed to you."

Margot sips her coffee.

"The Netflix doc is getting good buzz all around," says Rebecca. "Chatter's up across social for bands who got featured—lots of engagement, right? But this one's different."

Another sip of coffee. Buzz and chatter and engagements. "Okay."

"It's from a little girl. And she's a drummer, like you." Rebecca takes an iPad out of her backpack and starts reading. "'Dear Margot. My name is Mazzy, and I'm eleven. I'm the drummer for the band Hot Twist, and me and my bandmates are basically obsessed with you because you rock so fucking hard.'"

"Shit," says Margot. "She's eleven?"

Rebecca tilts her head. "My niece is eleven. She called me a skeezed-out ho bag at Thanksgiving because I beat her at checkers."

"Oh. Well, go on then."

Rebecca continues. "'I attached a pic of us playing your dopest song, "Power Pink," which is hot AF, by the way. We played it for our music teacher, Mr. Gustavo. After he recovered from having his face melted off, he said we're awesome. I'm emailing you to invite you to come down to Baltimore to rock out with us, because holy shit that would make our dreams come true. Also, the pretzels here are incredible. Yours in rock, Mazzy.'" Rebecca looks up. "How amazing is that?"

"Wait," says Margot, "are pretzels a thing in Baltimore?"

Rebecca looks momentarily defeated. "Crab cakes, I think. But that's not really—"

"The point," says Margot. "I get it. Is the picture cute?"

"*Absurdly* cute. See?"

She hands over her iPad, and Margot looks at four tween girls in a garage. The little bass player has pigtails, and the guitarist is mid jump. A girl with an AC/DC T-shirt shouts into a microphone. The drummer holds both drumsticks in the air, presumably Mazzy. "That is cute."

Rebecca looks at Margot's drum kit, glances at a dying plant. "With artists who have, shall we say, been out of the spotlight for a minute," she says. "Who are, you know, between projects. It's sometimes helpful to think outside the box, right? You know, in terms of publicity."

Margot sits on her legs now, making herself a little taller. "Rebecca, I appreciate the coffee. But why are you here?"

Rebecca takes a deep breath. "I have an idea."

"An idea?"

"Yeah. And, Margot, Axl and I think it could be a *total* game-changer."

CHAPTER 4

It's Saturday again, and Billy and Caleb are on a sun-drenched side street in Baltimore a few blocks from Billy's apartment. Caleb showed up a few minutes ago, and now they're messing with the Champagne Supernova, which is what Billy calls his casually unreliable forty-year-old light-beige Mercedes station wagon.

The car has been slow to start lately, idling weird. Billy doesn't know why, because he has no idea how cars work. He tugs at some wires. "Maybe it's these things."

Caleb, who knows even less about cars, kicks a tire with one low-top Jordan.

Since Billy last saw Caleb, things have happened. A few days ago, after school, Caleb was in his bedroom at his mom and stepdad's house studying when he got a call from New York City. Normally Caleb ignores unknown numbers, because he's not an idiot, but no one's ever called from Manhattan before.

"Um, hello?" he said.

A girl, young sounding, like a teenager, told him she was with Stage Dive Records. "I'm hoping to speak to Mazzy," she said, and the air left Caleb's body all at once, like when you're ten and fall off playground equipment and land flat on your back.

There were so many things Caleb could've done next. He could've hung up. He could've told the truth. Apologized. Started speaking in Spanish. Burst into tears. Set his iPhone on fire and thrown it out the window. Instead, he panicked. "This is Caleb," he said, making his voice a little deeper. "I'm Mazzy's dad."

Billy doesn't know any of this, of course. What he does know, however, is that his son is clearly anxious. Also, he shouldn't be here. "Wait, why are you with me right now?" he asks.

"Um, what do you mean?"

"It's your mom's weekend," Billy says. "Don't be a jerk. You know it hurts her feelings when you're here on her days."

Caleb looks down at the mess of German mechanics. "I figured I'd help you, I don't know, stare at *this* thing."

A very large man walks by with a pit bull on a leash. The dog stops to sniff a tree root that's busted through the sidewalk, and the guy smiles. "Hey, yo, you're the piano man, right?"

"Hi," says Billy. "Yeah, that's me, I guess."

"Nice. How about a little Stevie Wonder next time?"

The dog sniffs up at Billy. He never gets tired of this—friendly requests from his neighbors—like Fells Point is the set of an up- beat urban musical. "Yeah, I can do that. Old-school Stevie, or are you more into 'Ebony and Ivory' era Stevie?"

"You're the pro," the guy says. "But maybe aim for old. My dad raised me on that shit."

Billy says he'll see what he can do, but he's already arranging "Superstition" in his head. When the man and his dog are gone, Billy watches Caleb look at his phone for the fiftieth time. "Okay, what's going on with you?" he asks. "You look like you ate bad clams or something."

Caleb exhales, squeezes his forehead, kicks the tire again. "Dad, I screwed something up. It's . . . it's not good."

For parents, the drawback to loving their children so much is the anxiety that comes with it—like love's neurotic cousin—and Billy grips the car's fender, bracing himself for something terrible. "Cay, what's wrong?"

"Shit, Dad," he says. "Just, like, promise you won't be mad, okay?"

Forty-five seconds later, they're speed walking.

"Jesus Christ, Caleb."

"Dad, you said you wouldn't get—"

"Maybe here's a good topic for our next lesson," says Billy. "Proper use of the goddamn Internet."

"But, Dad."

"What were you thinking?"

"I *wasn't* thinking, remember?" Caleb says. "I was stoned. So I pretended to be a little girl and I invited her here. I mean, you had them just sitting there by the cereal. You know I love gummy bears, Dad. I couldn't resist."

Billy nearly trips over a pigeon. "Would you keep your voice down?" he says. "How about we don't yell about your piano-teacher dad accidentally getting his teenage son stoned on weed gummies?"

"Whatever, it's Baltimore," says Caleb.

"What was your endgame, anyway?" Billy asks. "Fool a drummer into coming to Baltimore? Then what?"

"Okay, see my previous comment about being stoned. But hear me out for a second. I thought if she just got the chance to meet you . . ."

They turn onto Thames Street. Charm City Rocks is just up ahead. A line of cars negotiates around a delivery truck. "What, Caleb?"

"I think she'll like you."

Billy stops walking. "You think she'll what?"

"Yeah, you know, you'll be charming or whatever. And . . . she'll like you."

"Like me? Caleb, are you . . . are you *still* stoned?"

They start moving again; Caleb is a step behind. "You're awesome, Dad. I mean, you're kinda being a dick right now, but you're really cool usually. You know a ton about music, and so does she. You're a decent looking dude. And you're tall. Not like *me* tall, but you're definitely not short. Seriously, give me one reason why she wouldn't be into you."

Billy stops at the door to Charm City Rocks. He grips the handle and takes a deep breath. "Caleb, just please stop talking."

CHAPTER 5

Back when Burnt Flowers was together, journalists used to ask Margot what she was like when she was little. It always struck her as casually sexist—did anyone care about *male* musicians as kids? Either way, she knew what they wanted to hear: that she'd been an ill-behaved hellion who didn't give a shit and punched her classmates and drew pictures of unicorns with fangs. Rock-and-roll stuff.

She wasn't like that at all, though. Margot was a shy, studious girl who read fantasy novels and put puzzles together and named her stuffed animals after her neighbors' pets. To call her quiet would've been an understatement. She was so slow to speak conversationally that her parents feared something must be wrong with her.

"Got anything good to say, Margie Pie?"

Her dad asked her this all the time, to which Margot usually just looked up and shook her head or shrugged. "Eh," she might say.

Then, when she was ten, her parents lost track of her one Sunday afternoon at a thrift store in Queens. Margot had wandered off to the back where there were a bunch of old instruments. She sat at a drum kit and traced "Margie" in the dust on the snare with her finger. The high-hat cymbal had broken off, but she didn't know enough about drums yet to miss it.

The sound she made with those two sticks in her small fists brought her parents and everyone else in the store running. What they found wasn't the remnants of an explosion or a thrift store avalanche. What they found was little Margie Willis, laughing as she wailed away, practically screaming.

Later, as the owner of the shop helped her parents maneuver the drum kit into the back of their Volvo station wagon, he suggested that maybe they should get their daughter lessons. "Girl's got some raw talent," he told them. "Sounded like she was hitting these things with a couple of old hammers."

Margot thinks of that day in Queens now as she's driven through downtown Baltimore in a big black SUV. It's easy to remember being a little girl, because that's how she's felt all day, like a kid being led around by a hypercompetent mother.

"You're getting all this, right?" Rebecca asks Todd, the camera guy.

Todd shoots Baltimore's passing cityscape through the window. Earlier, back at Penn Station in New York, Rebecca told Margot to pretend Todd wasn't even there. "Just think of him as a fly on the wall," to which Todd smiled and went, "*Bzzzzz.*"

When the tires hit cobblestone, the SUV shakes, and Margot still can't quite believe she's doing this. On that rainy Tuesday morning back in Margot's apartment, Rebecca had delivered a surprisingly impassioned speech about Margot's place in the history of rock-and-roll music. "I've read about your band," she said. "Like, in detail. You were freaking legends, Margot."

It's odd to be so thoroughly shrouded in the past tense—so much so that this adult human who's old enough to have a real job needs to read up on them, like Burnt Flowers was Watergate or disco.

"Those albums stand up, too," said Rebecca. "We were listening to them at the office yesterday. Shit. Every song slaps. The interns were like, 'Who is this?' And you know what? I think people miss you."

The rain had turned wild against the window, nearly unmeasurable in terms of tempo. "Yeah, I guess we had our moments."

"I don't just mean Burnt Flowers, though," Rebecca said. "I mean *you*. Margot, I think people miss *you*."

"Me?" Margot wished she had more coffee. "But I'm a recluse."

Rebecca stood up from the couch and sat on the arm of Margot's puffy chair. "This little drummer chick, Mazzy? She was right. 'Power Pink' is the band's sickest song. By a mile. That's why Netflix focused on it in the documentary. It sounds like it could've come out this week. It's more relevant than ever. And you—*your* story? That's relevant, too. It's compelling. I think people wanna hear it."

Over Rebecca's shoulder, Margot caught a glimpse of her drum kit. Perhaps she regretted being vulnerable and telling the research assistant from Netflix that she missed the music. That didn't mean it wasn't true, though. She missed playing.

"Okay," she said. "So, what are you proposing?"

Rebecca smiled. "Do you know what it means to go viral?"

She did, generally. Videos of cats falling into bathtubs, children dancing.

"We go to Baltimore," Rebecca said. "And then you, legendary drummer Margot Hammer, rock out with a bunch of badass little girls. We bring a camera guy. He films the whole thing. We cut it into a shareable video, put it on social. And then *you* catch viral lightning in a bottle."

They hit a pothole like a bomb crater, and the driver calls back an apology.

This isn't going to be a show, of course; it'll just be four kids in a record shop. Still, since leaving New York, Margot's entire body has been buzzing with the kind of preshow jitters she hasn't felt in years, like electrical currents shooting back and forth through her arms. She used to pace, to play intros on her thighs, to close her eyes and hold her breath and listen to the sound of the crowd waiting for them.

"One minute away," the driver says. "Assuming we don't fall into one of these goddamn potholes."

People on the street look at the big SUV, and Margot thinks of rushed TV appearances, being whisked into buildings by production assistants. And yes, although she's not psyched to admit it to herself, she thinks of Lawson. In her mind, she replays the moment when Lawson picked her up as she climbed out of that limo outside Radio City Music Hall. She never did find her left shoe, so halfway through the Grammys she ditched the right one, too. When she, Nikki, Anna, and Jenny accepted their best new artist award, Margot stood barefoot on national television.

Those first few years after their divorce, she often imagined Lawson coming back. She told herself that if he did, she'd kick him squarely in the balls or jam a set of drumsticks down his throat. When he didn't come back, though, she took to wondering what kind of space she occupied in his mind. Beyond her being the mother of his child, did he think about her at all? And now, as the SUV weaves around a stopped delivery truck, she imagines him taking a moment from his life of fame and Willa Knight's lithe body to watch her tear shit up with four cute kids in Baltimore.

They stop beside a murky harbor. Todd aims his camera out the window at a place called Charm City Rocks. "Is that . . . it?" he asks.

"It's smaller than it looked online," says Rebecca.

"Parking's a no go," the driver says. "I'll cruise around. Text me when you're done."

Everyone turns to Margot. "You ready?" asks Rebecca.

Margot rubs her hands together, feeling the permanent calluses, like worrying stones, from her drumsticks.

They step out of the vehicle, and the street smells like beer. But then a breeze pushes the hair off Margot's face, and she smells something better: baking bread.

"You should go in first," says Rebecca. "Maximum impact. Todd, I'm thinking a sick over-the-shoulder shot. Get Mazzy in the frame as fast as you can. We want her reaction."

Todd says "*bzzzzz*" again, and everyone aside from Margot takes a big step forward.

"Margot?" says Rebecca. "We good?"

Margot has just noticed the pretzel stand across the street. "These girls," she says. "What'd you say their band's called?"

"I'm blanking," says Rebecca. "I can look if you want. Why?"

Thirty feet away, a guy with an impressive beard stands behind the cash register at a pretzel stand. He's watching a soccer game. Affixed to the small building's green roof, a neon sign reads HOT TWIST.

Rebecca takes off her sunglasses. "Hmm. That's a weird way to pick a band name."

Chapter 6

"Oh, hi, Billy. Hey, Caleb."

Grady Edwards, the co-owner of Charm City Rocks, holds a stack of used records. He's wearing a Beastie Boys sweatshirt and smiling. "Wanna take a look at some new arrivals before I stack 'em?"

"Hi, G," says Billy. "Now's not a great time."

"Okay. I'm actually glad you're here," says Grady. "We should really talk about that apartment thing. Because we—"

"Maybe not now, okay?" Billy scans the store. "Fair warning: I think something insane is about to happen."

The door swings open just then. Even-keeled by nature, Grady stays true to type by touching his chin thoughtfully and saying, "You know what, you guys? I think that's Margot Hammer."

Billy holds his breath as Margot Hammer walks right by him. She's followed by a cameraman and a young woman with a ponytail, wearing Chuck Taylor sneakers.

"Yeah," says Grady. "It definitely is."

"Dad," Caleb whispers. "Holy shit."

Billy knew she was going to be here. His idiot son just frantically told him so two blocks away. Still, it's difficult to process. "Cay, don't swear."

"Yeah, this kinda feels like a holy-shit moment, though, right?" says Caleb, which is tough to dispute. "You should go talk to her."

"Me?" says Billy. "This is your fault. *You're* gonna talk to her. And you're gonna apologize. Profusely."

Grady stands listening, understandably confused. He sets his stack of records on a shelf and walks over to Margot Hammer. "Hello there. This is a quite a thrill. Would you like to sign our Wall of Fame?"

Margot Hammer is rubbing her hands together, and Billy is surprised to see that she looks nervous. The young woman beside her steps up. "Hi, I'm Rebecca Yang with Stage Dive Records. You work here, right? In the store?"

"My wife and I own it," Grady says.

"We're looking for a band. Four girls. Hot Twist. We're meeting them here."

Grady looks out the window toward Gustavo's pretzel stand. "Maybe you could sign between David Simon and Laura Lippman. It's a good spot. She's a writer, and he created the show *The Wire* on HBO."

Billy tries not to stare at her. He's not doing a good job of it, though. Rebecca looks at her phone. "We're right on time. Mazzy's dad said they'd be ready. I'll text him."

Caleb was a flurry of words a moment ago as they hustled over from the Champagne Supernova. Now, though, as Rebecca thumb-taps at her phone, his son has fallen into stiff silence. When the phone in Caleb's pocket makes a noise like a cartoon robot, he whispers, "Shit."

"Um," says Rebecca.

Everyone assembled at Charm City Rocks is now looking at

Caleb. Consequently, Caleb looks like he might throw up. Or run away. Or throw up while running away. He needs Billy's help.

"Margot," says Billy. "Or . . . Miss Hammer? Hi. I think there's been a misunderstanding."

"And you are?" It's Rebecca. She's smaller than all of them but suddenly very much in charge.

"I'm Billy. This is my son, Caleb."

Margot Hammer's attention falls then on Billy, and his breath catches in his throat. She's in jeans and scuffed boots, a loose button-up with the sleeves rolled just past her elbows. Her eyes. Her drumstick tattoos. Her hair—part up, part falling across her face. She's Margot Hammer.

"Caleb? Do you have something you'd like to say?"

His son slouches, like he's trying desperately to be smaller than he is. "I'm Mazzy," Caleb says. "And I'm Mazzy's dad, too. I'm also Caleb. I'm so sorry."

Rebecca's fists move to her hips. "You're . . . who?"

"I ate three gummy bears," Caleb says.

"You ate what?"

"They had pot in them. It may've been four, actually. Dad, a couple were smooshed together. I didn't tell you that part."

"You could sign the wall later, maybe," Grady says.

"Should I cut?" asks the camera guy. "Is this, like . . . part of it?"

"I thought maybe you'd like my dad," Caleb says. "He's really nice. And he had a huge crush on you. I think he still does."

"Oh my God, Caleb," says Billy.

"Wait a minute." Rebecca takes a step toward Caleb and Caleb takes a step back, like they're waltzing. "Explain to me what's going on. Immediately."

"There's also a nice spot open next to Cal Ripken, Jr.," says Grady. "See, right here."

"Dude, enough with the wall," says Rebecca.

"There is no Mazzy," says Margot. "Right? No little girls?"

She isn't asking *everyone*—she's asking Billy. Until this moment, this has felt slapstick, like some ridiculous celebrity-encounter story he'll tell at parties for years. Margot's face changes that, though. Billy can see that she isn't just pissed off. She looks hurt. "I'm afraid not," he says.

"But you sent a picture," says Rebecca.

"I found it online," says Caleb. "Google. I added a filter."

"Did you catfish us, you asshole?" asks Rebecca.

"He didn't *mean* to be an asshole," says Billy. "He made a mistake. He's sorry."

"Yeah, this is good," the camera guy says. "I'm gonna keep filming."

"No you're not," says Margot. "Turn it off. This was stupid. I'm out of here."

Margot walks out of the store and turns left on Thames Street. Everyone who remains looks at everyone else. The sound system plays "Brandy" by Looking Glass, because sometimes soundtracks are random as shit. Then Billy does the only thing he can think to do. He goes after her.

CHAPTER 7

It takes Margot all of ten seconds to figure out that she's being chased. Which is just perfect. Even better, Billy or whatever he said his name is keeps shouting her name. His voice echoes off buildings, like he's using a megaphone.

"Margot!"

"Goddammit," she whispers.

"Miss Hammer! Margot, wait! Please!"

People turn and look, and Margot wishes desperately to be home, back in her apartment, because being a rock-and-roll recluse is better than this bullshit.

"Did he say Margot Hammer?" someone asks. Another woman says, "She was married to Lawson Daniels," because apparently people think Margot is deaf.

She passes bars and restaurants. A tattoo parlor. Some weird-looking trash wheel spins in the harbor, churning up junk. A kid up ahead is playing a set of strung-together Home Depot buckets for spare change. Billy is catching up to her fast. Years ago, she and the band were flanked by security every time they so much as left their tour bus. Now Margot is alone in a city she doesn't know at all.

"Margot! Please don't be upset!"

She stops. She has no idea where she's going anyway. Billy stops, too, and stands ten feet away and waves. "Hi," he says.

Margot relaxes a little, because at least this man, who is wearing a Neil Diamond T-shirt under his cardigan, probably isn't a murderer. A block away, the front door of the record shop opens. Rebecca points at her. Todd is still filming, the bastard. The owner is waving a Sharpie.

"Miss Hammer," says Billy, "I want to—"

"Will you *please* stop saying my name?" She takes a few steps, closing the gap between them. "People don't always recognize me. I'm not Rihanna. But if you keep yelling my name . . ."

"Oh, right. Sorry." He looks around. "Do people really not recognize you? I recognized you right away. You . . . you look like you."

The drummer kid up ahead keeps playing. A few seconds pass, and the lookie-loos move along, leaving them alone. A pigeon stands at the curb watching, cars roll by with their windows down, and there's a sign for Domino Sugar across the water.

"Where even am I?" she asks.

This could be a literal question, because Margot doesn't know. It could also be a figurative question, because Margot doesn't know that either.

"You're in Fells Point." Billy points across the water. "That's Federal Hill over there. And that's Harbor East. It's nice. Kinda touristy, with the Inner Harbor and all, but . . ." To his credit, he seems to suddenly get that maybe she wasn't looking for a rundown of the surrounding neighborhoods. "Sorry. I'm babbling. Do people get nervous when they meet you?"

Margot looks down the long cobblestone street, which fades into urban blur, and she wonders what she's going to do with the rest of her life, because there seems to be finality to this moment.

She hasn't recorded music or performed in front of anyone in years. Somehow, though, she's never stated, even to herself, that her career as a musician might be over, and it's a suddenly devastating thought. Because if she isn't a musician, what is she?

"Well, *I'm* nervous," says Billy. "I'm a . . . a big fan. But that's beside the point. Obviously. Again, hi, I'm Billy. Billy Perkins. My son lied about who he was. I know that's bad. Also, creepy, in context. I'll talk to him—ground him, maybe? Can you ground people who are half a foot taller than you? I don't know. But it's kind of my fault, too. I had these edibles behind the cereal. I'm not a big drug guy. My friend Gustavo gave them to me. He thought it'd be funny. Caleb thought they were candy. He's smart. He's *really* smart, actually. His SAT scores are nuts, especially the math part. He created this app for a school project that aggregates basketball statistics. It's pretty amazing. But you know how sometimes really smart people can be complete idiots? That's him. And I may've told him . . . we were watching this thing on Netflix about you. I let it slip that I may have had a crush on you back in the day, and . . ."

Margot realizes that if she doesn't say something to stop him, Billy will just keep talking until he passes out, like those goats that faint when they're startled. He looks nice, actually. Maybe it's the cardigan. "Just stop, okay?" she says. "I get it, I guess. Not really, but, what're you gonna do?"

"Margot, you okay?" It's Rebecca, shouting from outside Charm City Rocks. She has her phone to her head.

"Are you gonna sign the wall?" the shop owner asks.

"Jesus, he really wants me to sign that wall."

"Yeah, he's pretty proud of it," Billy says. "I'd consider that spot next to Cal Ripken. That's prime real estate in this city."

Margot watches the drummer kid. Some ladies in jogging shorts drop change in his bucket. "He's not bad," says Margot.

"I know. The tempo, right?" Billy cups his hands to his mouth. "Hey, Daquan, do you know 'Power Pink' by Burnt Flowers?"

Daquan stops playing, thinks, then shrugs. "Nah, man. Never heard of it."

"Oh," says Billy. "Well, shit."

"Nice," says Margot.

"Yeah, I imagined that going differently," he says.

Daquan starts playing something new. In seconds, his hands are a blur, and Margot remembers playing "Enter Sandman" by Metallica at her junior high talent show five hundred years ago. Her stunned classmates stood and cheered for her for two full minutes. Her principal had to finally shout at them to stop.

"He reminds me of you," says Billy.

"Who, him?"

"Yeah. That intensity. Like he's got a personal vendetta against each drum. It doesn't matter that he's playing buckets. That sound, you know? Pure percussion."

The big black SUV pulls up to the curb. Rebecca is in the front seat, hanging out the window like a terrier. Todd, whom Margot would like to throat-punch, is still filming.

"Let's get out of here, Margot. And *you*." Rebecca points at Billy. "Don't be surprised if you and that lanky creep hear from our lawyers."

"I appreciate the warning," says Billy. "Also, I don't think you'd think he's a creep under different circumstances. He's actually a good kid."

Margot is that little girl again. Mom is telling her it's time to go, and there's nothing left to do but obey.

"Wait," says Billy.

Margot stops, her hand on the car door.

"You came all this way," he says.

Rock-star Margot would've grabbed Todd's stupid camera and

chucked it into the harbor. Present-day Margot does her best to ignore him as she watches Billy put his hands in his pockets and look at his sneakers.

"Can I maybe buy you a beer?" he asks.

"Are you fucking serious, dude?" says Rebecca. "You're lucky we're not calling the cops right now."

"I know, and *again,* I'm sorry. I'll buy you and Mr. Camera Guy a beer, too, to make up for it. What do you say? I just feel like if you drive off without me asking, I'll regret it."

"Damn," whispers Todd. "That's a decent line."

"Todd, it's time to cut, seriously," says Rebecca. "Margot, are you ready? You shouldn't have to deal with this."

Margot looks over at a bar across the street: the Horse You Came In On. A neon Orioles sign blinks. A few twenty-somethings with beards smoke outside. It's just some bar, like any one of a million in any city anywhere. Since the band broke up, she's avoided places like it, instead opting mostly for her apartment. There's a whole generation of people who have no idea who she is. People her age, though, remember what a mess everything was at the end. It'd be nice, she thinks, if she could just step out of being Margot Hammer, like a kid stepping out of a Halloween costume. No one would give a shit who she once was or who she used to be married to or how she had a high-profile meltdown at the MTV Video Music Awards.

Margot looks at Billy's vintage T-shirt and wonders what his favorite Neil Diamond song is. Hopefully not "Sweet Caroline," but probably, because people usually don't surprise you.

"Margot?" says Rebecca. "You ready?"

Margot opens the car door. "Maybe next time," she says.

CHAPTER 8

It's a surprisingly small city, Baltimore—another thing Billy loves about it—and there's nothing special going on, like a festival or an Orioles home game. So, in the few minutes it takes Billy, Caleb, and Grady to order pretzels at Hot Twist and tell Gustavo about the craziest thing that's just happened, the black SUV carrying Margot Hammer and her crew makes it across town to the Ivy Hotel in Mt. Vernon.

Gustavo doesn't believe them at first, obviously. Now, though, he points up the street with a pretzel stick, devastated that he missed it. "This all happened right . . . *there?*"

"Yeah," says Grady. "At Charm City, then up by where Daquan's playing."

Gustavo looks up the street at the busking drummer. "You ate *how* many gummies, Cay? Three?"

"Might've been four," says Caleb.

Gustavo shakes his head. Out of respect for the situation, he's muted the volume on his soccer game. "I'm impressed you could even type."

"That's what I said," says Grady. "Remember, you gave me two last year at the store's anniversary party? I almost fell into the harbor. I would've had to get a tetanus shot."

"Didn't realize you guys had a legit cartel going on down here," says Caleb. "I'll be more careful next time I'm looking for snacks."

"Stop it," says Billy. "No more drugs. Or at least, not until you're . . . I don't know, older." Billy grew up on "Just Say No" and "This Is Your Brain on Drugs," so he's torn here between his liberal stance on drug laws and feeling like a horrible father. He hands Caleb the second half of his pretzel to eat. "Maybe we don't mention this to your mom, though," he says. "Or to anyone else, ever."

Gustavo serves pretzels to an older couple. When they're gone, he smacks the countertop. "So, what was she like? Was she nice? Did she look good? I need details."

Billy doesn't know where to start. Margot's outfit was so effortlessly cool. And those eyes. He'd seen them in pictures and on TV hundreds of times, but in real life they were so startlingly blue beneath her wild brown hair that he'd only been able to maintain eye contact for small allotments of seconds. "She was beautiful," he says.

Gustavo touches his chest. "Really?"

"Her boots were cool," says Grady. "Very rock and roll. She's shorter than you'd think, though."

"When I was a kid, I was in love with Alyssa Milano," says Gustavo. "I wanted to build a fort for her in the basement and have her live in it with me."

Caleb chews his pretzel. "Yeah, Gustavo, that sounds like kidnapping."

Gustavo sneaks a glance at his soccer game. "Fair. I won't mention it to her if she ever swings by for pretzels."

"Paula Abdul," says Grady. "She was my crush. I wanted to be the cartoon cat from that 'Opposites Attract' video and synchronize dance with her."

"Oh, right," says Gustavo. "I would've built a fort for Paula, too."

"Are these, like, *celebrities* you're talking about?" asks Caleb, but they ignore the question.

"And then what?" says Gustavo. "You just asked her out for a beer? Like it was nothing? Like you're Richard Gere or something?"

"That *was* pretty money, Dad," says Caleb. "But who's Richard Gere?"

They ignore this one, too.

"It was inspiring, Billy," says Grady. "You know, you shot your shot."

Gustavo hums an *mm-hmm* with his deep voice. "Billy Perkins," he says. "Nice guy. Piano teacher. Local hero."

As his friends and son eat pretzels and tease him, Billy looks back at Charm City Rocks. He hasn't recovered yet from what just happened, so maybe he's being overly romantic, but that cluttered little shop beneath his apartment will now forever be the place where he briefly met Margot Hammer. He replays the big moment in his head: going after her down Thames Street. To Caleb and Grady, it must've looked spontaneous. It wasn't, though.

Nineteen years ago, less than a mile from here, Billy proposed to Caleb's mom, Robyn. They were at La Scala in Little Italy, her favorite restaurant. Billy's Caesar salad had just arrived. Robyn was eating crackers and drinking club soda, because morning sickness for her had been more like evening sickness. Billy took a deep breath and got down on one knee beside their table. His napkin fell on the floor. It's funny the things you remember: a fallen napkin, a young waiter who was trying to grow a mustache.

The place went as quiet as a funeral home. Billy hadn't planned on the fact that everyone in the restaurant would instantly know what he was up to and turn to stare. He also hadn't planned on how small the diamond would look. He moved the box in his hand, hoping to catch the light and give it some sparkle.

Robyn stared silently at the ring. For exactly how long he's not sure, because the passage of time is tricky when you're on one knee. Then she said, "Oh Jesus, Billy," and ran out of the restaurant.

He stayed there, the floor cold and hard through his jeans. Eventually, he sat back down at the table. He could practically feel the strangers around him urging him with their minds to get up—to *do* something. He was hurt, though. Embarrassed, too. So much so that all he could bring himself to do was sit quietly and eat his salad.

That night, Billy *didn't* go after Robyn. For years, he regretted it. Then, he accepted it, the way we grudgingly move on from the dumb things we do and don't do. Either way, few days have gone by since in which he hasn't thought about it. So, thirty minutes ago, when Margot bolted from Charm City Rocks, Billy knew what he had to do. He's been waiting to do it for nearly two decades.

CHAPTER 9

She's supposed to just be grabbing her stuff.

Rebecca was clear about the plan. "Let's meet in the lobby in fifteen. We'll head to the train station and G-T-F-O."

It took Margot a moment to parse out "G-T-F-O," like she was decoding Poppy's text messages. *Oh, right, yeah. Get the fuck out.*

Five minutes after stepping into the cool, clean suite, though, Margot is stretched out on the bed, boots off. Her socks, she realizes, don't match. It's been forever since she's been in a hotel room, particularly a plush one, and it makes her think of the days when *all* the hotel rooms were plush. When they were on the road, each of the four members of Burnt Flowers had their own rooms, but they'd inevitably pile into one until late to listen to music or to work on songs or to gently trash the place.

Nikki and Margot were the night owls. Anna and Jenny would slink back to their own rooms at some reasonable hour and Nikki would pour a last drink. Her real name isn't Nikki Kixx, and Anna's and Jenny's last names aren't Gunn and Switch either, but Burnt Flowers made a pact before their national television debut on *Late Night with Conan O'Brien* that it was glam names only henceforth.

"Just you and me, rock star," Nikki would always say, and they'd clink glasses of whatever it was they were drinking, even though Nikki was the *real* rock star. She was the one Margot, Anna, and Jenny stood behind in publicity photos. She was talented and electrifying and gorgeous. She was also the one who ruined everything.

According to the clock on the nightstand, Margot has five minutes to get downstairs. That said, what're they going to do, leave without her?

The day has been a thorough clusterfuck and she's tired and the bed is nice and the sun currently lowering itself over Baltimore through the window looks all right. If she had one of her notebooks, she'd write down something about that window or this hotel room, or about how it feels to be here alone. It wouldn't matter, though, because she writes down things like that all the time and nothing ever comes of it. Her notebooks sit in their little pile, their insides slowly fading.

She feels dumb for being tricked, but she feels even dumber for how excited she was. She conjures up the image of those four little girls from Rebecca's iPad. She'd have counted off for them—five, six, seven, eight!—and there would've been that divine instant just before her sticks hit the drums.

She climbs off the bed and goes to the mini bar, where she finds a bottle of white wine with a French-sounding name. It's a twist-off, so it seems silly not to have some. She pours a glass and says, "What's up, Baltimore?" in her best Nikki Kixx voice. She taps the thin remote, and the flatscreen across the room comes to life. It's a smart TV, like her one at home, so the Netflix logo sits in the middle of a grid of other logos. Margot is surprised to find that she knows her login and password by heart.

The documentary appears immediately. *The Definitive History of Rock and Roll.* The description reads: "From the bands you know to the bands you should know: a comprehensive deep dive into the most influential rock-and-roll musicians of all time."

"Oh, fuck off," she says.

Margot was content to have the past remain firmly in the past, but then Netflix fucked everything up. Some faceless kid on the phone asked, "Do you, like, miss it?" and now she's in a hotel room in Baltimore pining for the music she used to make.

And then she hears her name. Two muffled voices. One is Rebecca's. It takes her a moment to recognize the other one, but when she does it's unmistakable. Axl Albee.

The door next to the minibar is one of those pass-throughs that divide conjoined hotel rooms. It's probably supposed to be locked, but when Margot gently turns the handle, it gives. She risks a glance and sees Rebecca's laptop open to a video call. Axl's hair is more salt than pepper now, but it's still long and pulled back. "You said you got this all on film?" he asks.

"Yeah," says Rebecca. "Todd was persistent."

Axl laughs, dismissive. "Keep it. We'll play it at the holiday party. The troops'll love it. Now get back to New York. Return Margot to her depressing loft and put her out of your mind forever."

Margot grips the doorjamb.

"That's it?" Rebecca asks.

"For Margot it is. For *you,* you pitch me another idea Monday. And then another one Tuesday. That's how this works. Next time maybe focus on one of our artists who people care about, though. Might improve your chances."

It feels like something being torn open, but Margot wills her eyes not to fill.

"Do you know if she's still making music?" Rebecca asks.

"Is she what?" Axl sounds annoyed.

"She had instruments. Her place, it was like a little studio."

"It doesn't matter, Rebecca," says Axl. "*Margot* doesn't matter. She hasn't for years. The most interesting thing about her is that she managed to get knocked up by a movie star. End of story."

Margot holds the cheap hotel wineglass, unable to get a full breath.

Axl brought her flowers when the band officially broke up. He showed up at her apartment door with a big bouquet and a bottle of wine. Lawson had moved out and the apartment felt big and empty. He told her how talented she was. He told her that he still believed in her, even if she didn't believe in herself. But no, Margot isn't going to cry. Not for this fucker.

"Whoa there, you okay, miss?"

The bellhop is a tall, slightly stooped man with gray tufts of hair above his ears.

"I'm looking for a bar," she says.

He laughs, like, *Aren't we all?* "Well, you're in luck, miss. There's a whole city full of them out there."

"No, a specific one." She stands in her unlaced boots trying to remember details of the bar she saw earlier. She looks back at the hotel entrance. She's never run away before, and she imagines Rebecca coming after her, fists clenched. "I don't know," she says. "It had *horse* in the name, I think."

"Okay. Could be a couple different ones. You know which neighborhood?"

She remembers Billy rattling things off. "Fells something," she says. "Fells Point?"

The bellhop smiles and whistles at an approaching cab. "Look at us, coupla masters of communication, you and me." A yellow car squeaks to a stop at the curb. He opens the door and gives Margot a little wink. "Take this young lady to the Horse You Came In On," he says. "And make it quick. Looks like she could use a drink."

CHAPTER 10

Billy is at the Steinway back in his apartment trying to figure out how to play "Power Pink" on the piano. It isn't an obvious song for keys, what with all the power chords and rage-drumming, but in his experience you can play anything on the piano if you sit with it long enough, because the piano is the greatest instrument ever made.

Lately, his go-to song to teach his beginners has been "She's a Rainbow" by the Rolling Stones, because Billy always gets a kick out of hearing kids slowly work through those perfect opening notes. Maybe it's time to change it up, though, switch to something more raucous.

Saturdays are the only days Billy doesn't have lessons. His weekdays are full, Sundays half full. No one has been more surprised by the success of Beats by Billy than Billy himself. It started on a whim after he and Robyn broke up—a way of filling the time—and it took off from there. His accidental career.

Billy's grandma taught him to play. She was a long-fingered natural, but a classicist, so she insisted Billy learn by playing the oldest, deadest, malest artists in the history of music. When he started Beats by Billy, he hung signs downstairs at Charm City

Rocks and in coffee shops and bus shelters around the neighborhood. He included his tagline and general philosophy: "Because Music Should Be Fun." He let his students play what they wanted to play—*whatever* they wanted to play—and it somehow worked. People liked it. They liked him.

When his grandma passed away ten years ago, she left him a modest sum of money. She labeled it "Billy's Steinway Fund" in her will. It wasn't quite enough, so Billy made up the rest by selling his old Yamaha piano and digging into his savings. The first song he played on the Steinway was "Prelude and Fugue No. 1 in C Major" by Bach, in his grandma's honor. The delivery guys hadn't left yet, so they stood and listened, still sweating from hauling the gorgeous monster up the narrow metal staircase that ran around the side of Charm City Rocks to his door.

"Wow, man, you're really good."

"Thanks."

He stares down now at the bass staff on his sheet music while his left hand struggles to produce something that sounds like rock and roll. Like most Burnt Flowers songs, "Power Pink" starts with drums. He's been at it for nearly two hours, and his head is starting to hurt. This is work, technically, but what Billy's really doing is thinking about Margot Hammer.

Is it possible to miss someone you only knew for five minutes? He figures yes, especially if you've also known that person for twenty years.

"Hey, Billy! Billy! Wherefore art thou, Billy?"

He goes to the window and finds Gustavo standing on the sidewalk.

"Hey, sexy," his friend says. "What're you playing? I don't recognize it."

"Oh, nothing," Billy says. "Just working on some lesson plans."

The lights are dim at Hot Twist. Gustavo has hung up his Back

IN 15 MINS sign. "Come get a beer with me, then," he says. "I wanna be at least a little buzzed for the nighttime rush."

Billy looks at his notes sprawled across the lid of the Steinway.

"I think that cover band is playing at the Horse," says Gustavo.

"Um."

"Please?" says Gustavo. "It's your day off, right? Saturday night. Your pretty piano can wait 'til tomorrow."

CHAPTER 11

The beer that Margot is drinking isn't good. It's called National Bohemian, but the bartender called it "Natty Boh," and she told Margot it's the official beer of Baltimore. The logo is weird: a cartoon man with one eye and a big mustache.

When she sat down alone at the bar over an hour ago, the bartender gave her that look that people give her when they know who she is but aren't sure they should say anything. The closest she's come since to acknowledging Margot's identity was when she asked, "So, what's someone like you doing in a place like this, hon?" as she dropped off Margot's second Natty Boh.

Good question. Margot wasn't sure. Two Natty Bohs later, she still isn't.

The Horse You Came In On is exactly as she'd imagined it'd be: stuffy, ordinary, a little sticky. She takes a sip of her beer and spies a sticker on the mirror above the bar: I GOT CRABS IN BALTIMORE. The nearby TVs are playing several different baseball games. The Baltimore team, the Orioles, are playing in Chicago, and they're losing badly.

The fact that Natty Boh is kind of shitty doesn't mean Margot doesn't like it. All beer is kind of shitty, after all, like something you try on a dare—sushi or hot yoga. The reason people drink it in the first place, she's convinced, is because of the associations they make when they taste it, and Margot thinks of going to rock shows with Nikki in tiny clubs before they were famous. She thinks of the early days of Burnt Flowers, huddling in back rooms next to hot water pipes with her bandmates while they waited to go on-stage.

She left her hotel fighting back tears, but now she's edging toward anger. This is often Margot's emotional journey—an initial shock of sadness followed by a quick trip to rage—and she re-members how it felt when her drumstick cracked in her right hand all those years ago, just before she kicked her drum kit across the stage, live on MTV.

"Another Boh, hon?" asks the bartender. She's a big lady, late middle age. Her name is Beth, and if Margot isn't mistaken, she has a full-on perm.

"Yeah, okay," says Margot.

Beth sets the bottle down. "You aren't paying for any of these, by the way. My treat, hon. It's an honor having you."

"Thanks," says Margot.

"I wasn't gonna say anything before, because I was trying to be cool," says Beth. "But I figure I'll just go ahead and tell you. I think my first son was conceived to 'Power Pink.'"

People have said a lot of things to Margot over the years, but no one's said that. "Well, now *I'm* honored," she says. "Short song, though. Like two minutes, thirty seconds."

"Yeah, that sounds about right," says Beth. "Enjoy the Bohs, hon. I'll keep 'em coming."

Margot looks up at the TV just as Baltimore's baseball team loses. Someone on the other end of the bar shouts, "You bums!" A band is setting up on a small stage at the other end of the bar. Two guys and two girls, young looking, and Margot tries to guess who's in love with whom, because someone's always in love with someone.

She's starting to like Natty Boh, as opposed to just tolerating it—the way it burns the back of her throat.

By the time the band finishes setting up, the bar is more crowded. A few people have noticed her, but they're being chill about it, which Margot appreciates. The band's drummer—one of the two girls, it turns out—keeps glancing over but pretending not to. When someone young recognizes her, it's either because they're a musician or obsessed with Lawson.

Beth slaps the bar and shouts, "Gustavo!" Then she says, "And Billy Perkins, is that you?"

Billy Perkins? The name registers, and by the time Margot turns, she remembers. The guy from the record shop is standing wide-eyed next to a man she also recognizes, the guy at the pretzel stand across the street, Hot Twist. Margot wonders if she's in an episode of *The Twilight Zone.*

"You," says Billy. "You're . . . *here.*"

"What the hell?" says Margot. "Did you foll—"

"No," he says. "I live here."

"You live in a bar?"

"No, I . . ."

"He lives above Charm City Rocks," says Beth. "Billy, do you know Margot Ha . . ."

Moments like these lead to so many half sentences and trail-offs. "Hi, Beth," Billy says. "We met earlier. And I wasn't following you. This . . . this is my neighborhood. We came for a drink."

Margot thinks about this. It checks out. She left, and now she's back, and apparently Baltimore is the smallest goddamn city in America.

"I'm Gustavo." The guy with the beard holds out his hand, which is warm, and he smells like butter and salt.

"What are you doing here?" asks Billy.

"She's drinking some Bohs, that's what she's doing," says Beth.

"Oh . . . *really?*" says Billy. "Bohs, like, plural? That's . . . do you like them?"

"Oh, stop being such a snob," says Beth. "Should I get you one of your fancy IPAs, Your Majesty?"

Billy says yes, and Beth gets him and Gustavo beers. She doesn't ask specifics, she just knows what they want, and for some reason, maybe because she's mildly intoxicated, Margot finds this funny. They're regulars here; she's wandered into these people's lives. "You live above that record shop?" she asks. "The one from today?"

"His place is really cool," says Gustavo.

Billy seems embarrassed. Margot can tell the two are friends, he and Gustavo, the way they talk to each other with their eyes, and Gustavo turns to the band, which is about to start. "These guys are pretty good. You should check them out."

"Looks like you wanted a beer after all," Billy says.

"Several, apparently," says Margot. "It's been a . . . a day."

"Can I buy you another one?" he asks. "Maybe one that doesn't taste like barbed wire and clinical depression?"

"Wow, you really *are* a snob," says Margot. And then she sees Neil Diamond's smoldering eyes on his chest. She points, fully prepared to have her suspicions confirmed. "By the way, what's your favorite song by him? Just answer, don't think."

"Oh," he says, clearly thinking. "Probably 'Solitary Man.'"

Margot was about to take a sip of her beer, but she stops. "'Solitary Man'?"

"I think Neil's best when he's a little dark, you know."

So does Margot. She resumes that sip, surprised to be surprised.

Beth leans on the bar between them. "What are you talking about, you idiot? It's 'Sweet Caroline' all the way. My sister threw her bra at Neil once while he was singing it at the Verizon Center down in D.C. Almost got us kicked out. Apparently, you're not supposed to do that. Which is bullshit. I mean, how could you not toss your underwear at that man?"

Then, without comment or introduction, the band opens with a loud, uneven cover of a Killers song. Margot and her odd new group of pals watch. The drummer girl and the bass-player guy are messy, lagging on the downbeat, and the dude singing sounds like he needs to clear his throat. The lead guitarist knows her shit, though.

"Can I tell you again that I'm sorry?" Billy shouts.

"Whatever!" Margot says. "It's done!"

"My son is—"

"It's done, man!"

Billy recoils, like she's shoved him.

Shit, Margot thinks. He's a nice guy, and she can see in his eyes that he likes her—that "crush from back in the day" thing. Of the four members of Burnt Flowers, Margot elicited the fewest crushes, she supposes, but she had her fair share, and they always looked at her like Billy's looking at her now, like he's hoping she doesn't ruin everything by being different than he imagined.

Beth sets a new beer in front of Margot—a colorful label, not Natty Boh. "His royal highness, the Lord King of Baltimore, thinks this beer is more befitting of your station, Ms. Hammer!"

The second song is better, "We Got the Beat" by the Go-Go's. The lead guitarist has taken over the mic, and she's very good. Gustavo is bobbing his head, enjoying the show. Billy is pretending to watch the band, but Margot can see that he's glancing at her out of the corner of his eye, and she wonders if it's so bad to be liked.

Poppy was back in New York for Christmas last year. They

walked together through the holiday market at Columbus Circle and talked about men—specifically, the lack of men in Margot's life.

"But I don't like very many of them," Margot told her daughter.

"Well, why would you?" her daughter asked. "Most are dreadful. I wanna push them into traffic, generally speaking. But, well, surely not all of them, though, right? And the occasional shag is okay, now and again."

She looks at Billy's cardigan. His jeans, sneakers. During all that ridiculous shit before at the record shop, he was nice to Margot—concerned for her, in a dopey way—and he was protective of his weirdly tall kid. She pokes his arm now. "Hey!"

Billy turns, and Margot tries to think of something nice to say. Maybe she'll compliment his choice of Neil Diamond song or tell him that it's cool that he didn't turn out to be a murderer or sexual predator. But then the band abruptly finishes the Go-Go's, and the girl who's just been singing says something into the mic. It's garbled, because acoustics in bars are shit, but she gets the gist, because now everyone is looking at Margot.

"At first I thought I was hallucinating up here," the singer says. "But nope. Ladies and gentlemen, we've got an honest-to-God rock music goddess in the house right now!"

Margot doesn't move. "Oh shit," she whispers.

Beth claps while Gustavo yells, "Woot woot!" Beside Margot, Billy smiles. "You don't think she's talking about me, do you?"

The Horse You Came In On is smaller than it was a moment ago. Hotter, too.

The singer is looking at Margot, her hand over her chest. "I mean, it just seems like any other gig. You put on your sexy outfit, and you start playing, and then you look out there and you see Margot *fucking* Hammer."

People cheer, and Margot knows what's coming, like a musical inevitability. She looks quickly at the drummer. Her kit is basic but nice, cared for. Margot imagines the weight of the sticks in her hands, smooth against her palms. When she was a teenager, Margot used to bite her sticks. She'd sink her teeth into them hard, but not quite hard enough to make them splinter in her mouth.

"Can we get you to come up here and join us? Pretty please? Just one song . . . or maybe, like, ten songs? We can negotiate the details."

"'Power Pink'!" shouts Beth. "Mama feels like getting pregnant again!"

A big, joyous collective groan and more cheers. People start chanting Margot's name, breaking it in two: *Mar-got, Mar-got, Mar-got.* Billy tips his fancy beer to the stage. "No, she's definitely not talking about me."

She's off her barstool and walking before she even realizes it. As she weaves through people, she understands how much she wants this. Maybe she doesn't matter anymore. Maybe she barely ever did. Fuck it. Right now, Margot really, really needs to hit something.

The drummer hands over her sticks. She's so young up close— a kid in too much makeup pretending to be a rocker.

"Sorry about this," Margot says.

"Sorry?" she says. "Ha! You're saving me. I have no idea what I'm doing up here."

When Margot sits, the rest of the band gathers at the front of the kit. The bass player is older, maybe late twenties. "If we don't play 'Power Pink,' I think that bartender's gonna burn the place down," he says.

"Do you know it?" the female singer asks him.

"Close enough," says the bassist.

"My dad used to play it," says the dude who choked through the Killers song. "I can figure it out. Hi, Margot. I'm Tim, by the way."

"Hey, Tim," says Margot.

"Emma," says the singer. "You're awesome, by the way."

"Dave," says the bassist. "Ditto on the awesome thing. Welcome to Baltimore."

No glam names yet—a bad sign, she thinks. "So, 'Power Pink,' huh? We giving 'em what they want?"

"Fuckin' A we are," Emma says, and she tells Tim that she's taking lead, "obviously." She goes to the mic, and Tim and Dave assume their positions to her right and left. Margot slides her boot into the kick drum. The light over her head makes the cymbals glow perfect and gold.

The bar has gone quiet, and Emma is looking at her, waiting. This is exactly what Nikki used to do. *Ready, rock star?* she'd mouthed before every Burnt Flowers performance ever, from those little clubs to cramped TV studios in skyscrapers to windy open-air festivals to jam-packed auditoriums across the country. Because everything started with Margot and her drums.

A strand of hair falls across her face, but she leaves it. Cellphones—dozens—rise up, the dots of their tiny lenses homed in on her. Margot relegates everything that isn't the drum kit to a peripheral fog, and then she slams her sticks together four times.

"Five, six, seven, eight!"

CHAPTER 12

"Goddamn. I mean, god*damn*. Seriously. That was . . . that was . . . shit. I'm sorry. I don't usually swear this much. But, Margot, holy shit. Could you hear yourself up there?"

Billy isn't articulating himself very well.

He saw Burnt Flowers years ago, from the cheap seats in Philly. Robyn surprised him with tickets, and they drove up from Baltimore. It was a solid show, but nothing like what he just witnessed.

"Power Pink" blew the roof off the Horse You Came In On. For the first thirty seconds, people stood watching, mouths open. But then there was a collective realization in which everyone remembered all at once that it's an absolutely perfect rock song. By the time Beth climbed onto the bar to shout along with the chorus, people were dancing and jumping. Passersby gathered at the front window to look in, like, *What the hell's going on in here?*

Outside now, Billy and Margot sit on a bench looking out at the Inner Harbor and eating cinnamon pretzels. Billy breathes in, tells himself to at least *try* to be cool and maybe speak in coherent sentences.

"That singer, Emma," Margot says. "She was pretty good. The guys, though . . ."

The two men had trouble keeping up. It hardly mattered, though, because they quickly became superfluous.

Margot takes a bite of her pretzel.

"Try to get as much of the sauce as you can," Billy says. "It's the best part. You have to go full dunkage to really appreciate it."

Gustavo threw in an extra cup of caramelized sugar for Margot—a reward, he said, for shaking the whole neighborhood. She sinks her pretzel as far into the little cup as it'll go and takes another bite. "Okay, yeah," she says. "That *is* pretty good."

Some guy yells into his phone across the street. "This rocker chick lit it up at the Horse earlier! . . . I don't know! . . . Yeah, I can't remember her name—something weird! But she was fucking awesome!"

Margot rolls her eyes and laughs as she wipes a glob of sugar off her bottom lip.

Billy likes the way she laughs—like a kind-of laugh, like she's trying not to. "Your name's not *that* weird," he says.

"We sounded okay, you think?" she asks.

She licks the glob of sugar, and Billy marvels at the understatement.

She sat in for five songs—four Burnt Flowers tracks and a cover of "Let's Go Crazy" by Prince. You'd never guess Margot and Emma had just met; they sounded like they'd been rehearsing for weeks. As good as the performance was, though, Billy keeps thinking about the moment it was over. As everyone applauded, Margot set her sticks down gently on the snare drum, stood up, and did a little bow. Then, probably because he was the only person there that she knew, Margot returned to her spot at the bar next to Billy.

"You're the best drummer I've ever seen," he shouted into her ear over what had quickly become a standing ovation. Beth rushed over and told Margot that she could have free Natty Boh at the bar for life. "I'll write you an IOU and everything!" Then—with no idea what else to do—Billy held up his hand and offered his rock-and-roll crush a high five. Before slapping his palm with hers, Margot smiled at him. Like, *really* smiled.

A breeze blows in off the water now. "When was the last time you played in front of a crowd?"

She takes another bite. "The MTV thing."

"Oh," he says. "Wow. *The* MTV thing."

"Mm-hm. The one and only."

Billy hasn't seen the clip from the MTV Video Music Awards that she's referring to in years. He was watching it live that night, though. At first, when Margot kicked her drum kit off its stand and pushed her cymbals over, he thought it was all part of the show. Everyone did. Confusion set in quickly, though. Before cutting back to a stunned-looking Chris Rock, who was the host that year, the camera moved into a close-up of Margot's face as she stood over the wreckage. Her eyeliner had just started to run down her cheeks.

The *New York Post* put the angriest picture of her they could find on its cover the next morning. "Margot Hammers Away." *Rolling Stone* chronicled the event later that month, detailing the band's immediate split and Margot's separation from Lawson Daniels. Billy and Robyn had recently broken up. The apartment they'd shared above Charm City Rocks—*their* apartment—had become *his* apartment. He remembers feeling sad for Margot— this famous drummer on whom he'd had such a silly crush— because he knew what it was like to have something important be so suddenly over.

He takes a bite of his pretzel. "Well, welcome back," he says. "We've missed you."

A police boat zips along the inky black surface of the harbor, and Fells Point buzzes behind them. He'd stop time here, too, if he could, because it's a perfect moment. But then Margot says, "Well, thanks for the pretzel."

"Oh, of course."

He implores himself to say something else. *Use your words!* he thinks. Finally, he manages, "We could get another beer if you want. Beth didn't make me pay for that IPA I ordered for you, so I still technically owe you one." He tries to laugh, to make it sound casual, because it's embarrassing how badly he wants her to stay.

She stands, and he stands, too. "Thanks. But I should go. I think I'm gonna grab that cab over there."

Billy has sometimes wondered over the years if there's anything he could've said to make Robyn stay—some insight, a bit of hapless charm, some promise he could've made that would've saved them. He wonders the same thing now, too. Unfortunately, like then, he doesn't have much. "Well, if you're ever in Baltimore again . . ."

Margot Hammer is already walking away. She steps off the curb, jogs toward the dented yellow car outside 7-Eleven. Billy watches her climb into the backseat. He waves as the cab passes, but she's not looking at him. One headlight burns brighter than the other. Then she's gone.

Fells Point is its typical Saturday-night obstacle course of humanity. Billy dodges an Uber, waits for drunk people to pass, smiles politely at someone's dog. Police officers stroll by, keeping tabs. Couples hold hands. Someone is clearly smoking weed nearby. Teenagers speed across cobblestone on rented scooters that they will almost certainly crash.

The lights at Charm City Rocks are dim, because the place is closed, so he doesn't notice Grady and his wife, Patty, standing in the doorway until he's practically on top of them. "Hey, Billy," says Grady from the shadows.

Startled, Billy nearly trips over a crack in the pavement.

Patty is wearing her jean jacket over her favorite Dolly Parton for President T-shirt. "Got a sec, Billy?" Her voice is somber, and Billy gets that this isn't happenstance.

Grady looks at his wife and then at the ground. "Patty, can't we do this some other time? Tomorrow, maybe?"

"Grady, no. We went over this." She's taller than Grady, even more so than usual tonight, thanks to her wedge heels and the softball-size bun at the top of her head. "Billy, we've been trying to get on the same page with you about this apartment thing. You've been avoiding us."

She's right. He feels bad for ducking them, but he chalks it up to denial.

Down the block, people are gathered outside the Horse You Came In On, as if at any moment Margot Hammer might return and blow the place up again.

"I can't tell you how sorry I am about all this," says Grady.

"Will you stop apologizing?" says Patty. "It's *our* building, Grady, and this is *our* business."

"It's okay, G," says Billy. "Patty's right. I'm here. Let's talk."

People walk around them on their way to and from bars, and Patty sighs. "You're a good friend, Billy. You always have been."

"A *great* friend," says Grady.

"But this is a good opportunity for us. And your lease expired like ten years ago."

In truth, Billy never had a lease. He and Robyn signed a napkin once, but that was mostly a joke and probably not legally binding. "I get it," he says. "But does the neighborhood really need *another* coffee shop?"

"It's a new revenue stream for us," Patty says. "Music downstairs, coffee and pastries upstairs. Little sandwiches, too. We're still working out the details."

"Charm City Grinds," Grady says. "Get it? Synergy. You can come by whenever for a coffee or a fancy latte. On us."

Patty puts her hand on Grady's shoulder. "We'll discuss that."

Through the front window, Charm City Rocks looks ramshackle in the low light. "Aren't record stores dying?" Billy says. "How can you be expanding?"

Grady smiles at Patty. "Well, funny thing is, we're doing really good. Records are cooler than they've been in years. *We're* cooler. What's old is new again, right?"

"Maybe it's just a trend," says Patty. "But we're gonna capitalize on it."

"There are other apartments," says Grady. "Maybe you can find a new place around here. Somewhere even better."

It's a nice thought, but heartbreakingly naïve. All three of them know that Fells Point is mostly luxury condos now, or tiny row houses tucked quietly away from everything that Billy loves about living here. His apartment is one of a kind.

"I'm sorry, Billy," says Grady, and this time Patty doesn't scold him for it.

Gustavo catches Billy's eye from Hot Twist. Oblivious to what's happening, Gustavo smiles, then gives Billy the finger. Daquan drums down the street, and people shout and laugh and sing. "Yeah, G," Billy says. "I'm sorry, too."

Part 2

CARDI PARTY

CHAPTER 13

Billy is late. Which is why he's running, kind of, across the shadowy Ruxton Academy parking lot in northern Baltimore. He isn't built for speed, and he smoked in his twenties, so his shoes sound like anvils on the pavement, and he's gasping more than is reasonable for a forty-five-second jog. He weaves between BMWs, of which there are many, and a few Land Rovers. He hip-checks a silver Jaguar as he rounds a corner heading for the entrance. The alarm chirps out a shrill little warning.

His lessons ran until six, then he decided he should probably change, because he was wearing a Sex Pistols T-shirt, and you shouldn't have "sex" written across your chest at parent-teacher night. Then, of course, the Champagne Supernova chose tonight to be difficult. Traffic was snarled in its usual places, too. These are reasonable excuses across the board, but Billy is preparing himself for the look that Robyn will give him.

Oh, Billy, come on.

He pushes through the front doors and comes to a sliding stop atop the Ruxton Academy crest, which is inlaid into the floor. Billy can either go left or right. He chooses left, which works out. Robyn texted that the room, 118, is in the English department, and Billy sees stenciled drawings of Shakespeare, Dickens, and Poe on the walls. He passes Mr. Butler's office, Ms. Stringer's office, and then Mrs. Duncan's office. 118 is next to Maya Angelou and a small caged bird.

Three faces turn, six eyes, two of which narrow.

Oh, Billy, come on.

"Hey, everyone. Sorry. My car . . ." He leaves the rest to their imaginations, hoping they'll come up with something harrowing—a multivehicle pileup, escaped animals on the highway.

Caleb's academic advisor, Ms. Modell, stands and shakes Billy's hand. She's a serious-looking young woman in a navy-blue blouse and checkered skirt. Robyn and her husband, Aaron, have come from work, so they're dressed like they're initiating a corporate takeover. Robyn looks terrific, and Billy wishes he had a wardrobe do-over. Something with a collar would've been nice, and khakis, perhaps. Realizations like this, unfortunately, always come in retrospect.

Aaron shakes his hand, squeezes his elbow. "Billy," he says. "Good to see you."

Billy kisses Robyn's cheek. "Sorry," he whispers.

"You didn't miss a thing, Mr. Perkins," says Ms. Modell. "We were just chatting about Caleb. I should apologize myself. I didn't realize until this evening that Caleb is from a nontraditional household situation."

Billy assesses the furniture as he sits. An extra chair has been dragged over to accommodate the odd shape of their parental unit. "Well, that's us," he says. "I'm dad, she's mom, and he's the stepdad."

"Some might say co-dad," says Aaron.

"We're still workshopping that term," says Billy.

"Billy and I were never married," says Robyn. "So Caleb has

only known us as two separate homes. Aaron and Billy are both very involved. They're good dads."

"I can see that," says Ms. Modell. "Well, whatever the arrangement, it works. You should all be very proud. Your son is a fantastic student. Top ten percent—officially now."

Caleb's three parents smile. Billy knows how hard Caleb worked this year to break the top ten, and a lump of pride forms in his throat.

"As you know," says Ms. Modell, "Caleb has applied to some very competitive schools. U. of Maryland is a definite yes. He's in-state, and his grades are stellar. I'm confident about Hopkins, too. We have a wonderful relationship with the admissions department over there. Stanford, though . . . well, Stanford is our reach. Your influence as an alum, Mr. Frazier, could definitely help, but you never know. Stanford is unpredictable."

Everyone nods; Billy unbuttons his cardigan, hoping not to start actively sweating from all that accidental cardio.

"In years past," says Ms. Modell, "they've focused heavily on extracurriculars over there—athletics, student government, that sort of thing. Lately, though, with quants and computer programmers doing so well out in the world, they've made room for more academic-minded kids like Caleb. The app he built for his analytics class is a perfect example of that."

Another lump forms, and Billy insists to himself that he won't turn weepy in front of these beautifully dressed professional people. He clears his throat. "One heck of a piano player, too."

Ms. Modell smiles. "Certainly is. Caleb said you helped film his video essay, Mr. Perkins."

Seven minutes of Cay at the Steinway wearing a dress shirt and tie they tied with the help of a YouTube video. He played a medley of his favorite songs. "Nailed it in three takes," says Billy.

"So, for the sake of discussion," Ms. Modell says, "if Hopkins and Stanford were to both come through, we'd want to—"

"Clearly Stanford," says Robyn.

The HVAC ticks on, and Ms. Modell is briefly flustered by being interrupted.

"Sorry," says Robyn. "Hopkins is fabulous, obviously. But the chance to go out west—a new experience—it seems like an easy decision. No?"

"A reasonable point of view, Mrs. Frazier. Four years at Stanford would be an incredible opportunity. I should tell you, though, after speaking with Caleb, he's not ruling out staying in town. In fact, as of yesterday morning, I'd say he's leaning toward it."

"Wait, what?" says Robyn.

"He wants to go to *Hopkins*?" says Aaron.

"*Not* necessarily," says Ms. Modell. "There's a pull to stay local. It's perfectly natural. We see it all the time."

Billy leans forward in his chair just as Robyn and Aaron lean back in theirs. Sneakily, he feels a hit of joy shot directly into his veins. Hopkins. In Baltimore.

"In other words, folks," says Ms. Modell, "Caleb's got some thinking to do."

Robyn crosses her arms and then her legs. "I guess he does." She's speaking to Ms. Modell, of course, but she's looking right at Billy.

"Will someone please tell me why this is such a bad thing?" he asks.

They're walking through the parking lot—three of them among a gentle stream of couples. He knows why Robyn and Aaron are pissed, but there's power in good-natured obliviousness. "Is this really the *worst* problem we could have? He's just keeping his options open."

Billy and Aaron walk side by side. Robyn is a step ahead, her shoes tapping out an agitated beat. Sometimes in moments of tri-parental tension, Billy and Aaron form careful alliances. Not tonight, though.

"It's more complicated than that, Billy," says Aaron. "And, all due respect, I think you understand that."

"You went to Stanford, Aaron," says Billy, "and you loved it. I get it. But Hopkins is one of the best schools in the country. And it's right here." Billy points. "It's literally down *that* street."

Aaron shakes his head as the three of them stop at a red Audi. He looks at his wife and then at Billy. "This is me," he says.

Billy eyes the roadster—two-door, sleek, and fast looking. "Damn. Is this new?"

"Couple of months," says Aaron. He unlocks the car with a key fob and the headlights flash.

Billy touches a smooth fender. "It's nice."

They easily could've been adversaries, Billy and Aaron—toxic masculinity and such. Ten years ago, though, when Aaron and Robyn got engaged, Billy invited Aaron out for crabs, and they decided that it'd be easier for everyone involved if they simply liked each other. Now they're friends, in the broadest sense of the term.

"I'm parked up that way," says Robyn. "I'll see you at home."

Aaron tells Robyn that he'll start heating up the lasagna, and then he gives Billy a look that says, *Glad I'm not you, you dumb bastard.*

Alone now for the first time in a few months, Billy and Robyn walk up a slight incline. She asks where he's parked and he waves up ahead, trying not to be specific. There aren't as many streetlights in this section of the parking lot, so it's darker the farther they get from the school. "I'll walk you to your car," Billy says. "You never know who's lurking in these private-school parking lots."

Robyn slows and makes a clicking sound with her mouth. "Billy? Is that the Charm City Rocks van over there?"

He'd hoped she wouldn't notice, which was a silly thing to hope, because it's a big baby-blue conversion van with CHARM CITY ROCKS stenciled on the side. A helicopter would've stuck out less. "Grady let me borrow it," he says. "The Champagne Supernova is having some trouble with its . . . whatever makes cars start."

"He evicts you from your apartment, but you're perfectly fine borrowing his van?"

Billy flushes. He hoped she wouldn't notice that either: Billy's pending homelessness.

"Caleb told me," she says.

"Right. Well, it's not Grady's fault. It's just business. I'm being gentrified."

Robyn is the sort of person who's perpetually in motion. She paces. When she sits, her right leg bounces, electrified by caffeine and anxiety. She dashes from one appointment to the next, cell-phone in hand. She's often in the middle of a call, and it usually seems like things on that call aren't going great. Tonight, though, she doesn't appear to be in any hurry to get home, so she and Billy stand for a while beside the Charm City Rocks van. She's wearing heels, which puts her almost exactly at Billy's height. Leaning against the driver's side door, she pulls her hair out of its tight bun.

"Oh, hey," he says. "Your hair's shorter, right? I like it."

She looks at her reflection in the van's window. "Stop being nice. I'm mad at you."

"Well, in that case, your blouse is hideous."

Robyn laughs, which comes with a head shake, and it reminds him of when they were young. He half expects her to pull out a cigarette, even though she quit nineteen years ago when she was pregnant with Caleb.

"You aren't talking shit to Cay about Stanford, are you?" she asks.

"What?"

"I don't know, poisoning the well? Calling it fascist or whatever?"

"No. Stop it. First of all, I'm just being supportive. It's *his* decision, right? Secondly, I don't think Aaron is a fascist. He has fascist hair. We've discussed that. But he's a nice guy."

Yes, Billy and Aaron are friends, but Billy takes every opportunity to poke fun at the man's hair, which is sandy blond and wavy and oddly perfect.

"I would've killed to go to Stanford," Robyn says. "You know how many doors that would've opened for me?"

"Rob." Billy lifts his palms. "Come on, you got through some doors."

"*Fought* through," she says. "I wouldn't have had to fight if I'd gone to Stanford."

Billy has no idea if that's true; this is her department, not his. "Maybe he's afraid he'll be homesick."

Robyn gives him an expression that reminds him of portraits of bank presidents. "Do you honestly believe that, Billy?"

"It's thousands of miles away," he says.

"It's you," she says.

"What's me?"

"If he leaves, he's afraid that *you* will be homesick for *him*, you moron."

"What? That's crazy. I'm . . . I'm fine." But now it's his turn to lean against Grady's van. "Goddammit," he says. "Did *he* tell you that? That he's worried about me?"

Robyn shrugs. "You want me to snitch on my own kid?"

Billy and Robyn agreed years ago to keep their son's secrets when it's appropriate. This seems like a gray area.

"Maybe just this once," he says.

Robyn straightens Billy's cardigan with a quick tug. "He told me everyone leaves you. That's what he said. 'Everyone leaves him, Mom. I don't know if I want to be one of those people who leaves him, too.'"

This feels like a punch to the midsection. Kids do that to you. When Caleb was in third grade, he wrote a composition for school stating that his mommy makes money at an office and his daddy plays the piano all day.

"Not *that* many people have left me," he says. "*You*, most notably, but that was before he was born, so I don't think it counts."

"What about that kindergarten teacher you were seeing?" she asks.

"She moved to Milwaukee," says Billy.

"What the hell's in Milwaukee?"

Billy wasn't sure. A job? A guy, maybe—someone who wasn't Billy.

"And the dogwalker?" Robyn asks. "I liked her. She was sweet."

"She went to Pittsburgh."

The dogwalker's name was Amanda. The kindergarten teacher was Tricia. Both women flutter briefly through Billy's mind now. Amanda with her cargo shorts full of biodegradable dog-poop bags and Tricia with her soft, patient voice. Yes, they'd left him, but does it count as leaving if he didn't ask either of them to stay?

There's a police siren somewhere nearby.

"I just don't want him to get stuck here, Billy," she says. "If he goes away and decides to come back on his own, like Aaron did, fine. This city, though. It . . . it absorbs people."

This has been a humbling conversation, because it's clear what Robyn is saying: Billy is among the absorbed.

"Anyway," she says. "I haven't seen you in a while. How are you?"

The real answer is that Billy has been down. The Margot Hammer Incident, which is what he now calls it, was ten days ago, and he's having trouble forgetting about it. He wonders if this is what people who survive semiserious accidents experience: a mild sort of trauma. Because that's what meeting Margot Hammer was: mild trauma. "Yeah, you know," he says. "I'm good."

"So, what are you gonna do?"

He isn't sure exactly what she's referring to.

"Billy, where are you gonna live?"

"Oh, that? No big deal. I'll figure it out. It's a renter's market, or . . . something."

Robyn looks out at the parking lot, which has almost entirely emptied. The van and her SUV a few rows away are among the only vehicles left. A school security guard watches them from a golf cart a hundred yards away. "Hear me out on something, okay?" she says. "I have a proposition for you."

Billy waits, nervous suddenly.

"What would you think about staying with us for a while?"

"With you and Aaron?" He laughs. "Are you kidding?"

"Not *with* us," she says. "You know the little apartment above our garage? It's perfectly nice. We're not using it. And there's plenty of space for the Steinway."

"I get that we don't chat about money a lot, Rob, but I'm not destitute. I have a job. I can affo—"

"I know," she says. "It's not that. It's . . ."

"What?"

"It's Caleb's idea."

"Caleb wants me to move in above your garage?"

"Just until he starts college—*wherever* that ends up being. He didn't say this, but I don't know, maybe he wants us to be something like a normal family for once. For a little while. He never had that. And, well, this is the end of his childhood, right?"

"Goddammit," says Billy to no one in particular, and he and Robyn lean on the van some more.

"When he was little," she says, "when I'd drop him off at your place, he'd be like, 'Why can't you just stay *here*, Mommy?'"

"He told me once if I just moved the piano there'd be plenty of room for you," says Billy. "Like us not living together was about square footage."

They look at the ground, and Billy thinks of the Twizzlers Robyn used to cut into cigarette-size pieces after she quit smoking, just before they broke up. He'd snap his fingers sometimes, pretending to light them for her.

"You don't think we fucked up our kid, do you?" she asks.

"I wonder sometimes," he says. "I think that's just part of being a parent, though. In our defense, the money we've spent on his sneakers alone should be worth something."

Robyn doesn't laugh this time; she just shakes her head.

"Oh, shit, I almost forgot," says Billy. "I brought you something." He opens the van door and grabs a paper bag from the passenger seat that contains one jumbo Hot Twist pretzel.

"Oh my God, you didn't," says Robyn.

"I did. Sorry, it's not warm anymore, but—"

"Who cares," says Robyn. "I haven't eaten since lunch."

"Yeah, I figured."

Robyn digs in, rolls her eyes with pleasure. She tears off a piece for him, and for a moment they eat in silence as the security guard frowns from a distance.

"He's gonna drive over here and shoot us, isn't he?" she asks.

"Nah," says Billy. "We'll be fine. The worst he'd probably do is tase us."

When Robyn is gone, the security guard sighs loudly enough to be heard from across the parking lot and drives off. Billy hops into the van and enjoys the smell of vinyl mixed with pretzel. He takes his iPhone out of his pocket and turns it back on before dropping it into one of the cupholders. As he twists the key in the ignition, his phone lights up and chirps. Then it chirps again . . . and again and again.

"Shut up," Billy says.

His phone doesn't shut up, though, not for at least ten seconds, because Billy has nineteen missed calls and thirty new text messages. He sees one from Caleb that includes a link. It reads: Dad? Have you seen this? Holy Sh*t!

Chapter 14

It wasn't exactly lightning in a bottle. Margot's performance at the Horse You Came In On went viral slowly, over about a week and a half, fueled by YouTube, TikTokers, and social media algorithms.

Who knows how many original videos exist? Margot would guess she saw fifty phones go up the moment before she counted off. Four videos broke through the clutter. One is eighteen minutes long and includes all five songs. The sound is surprisingly clear. The three others are shorter, taken from different angles, their quality fine enough, because even the cheapest smartphones are like tiny movie studios these days.

Likes, red hearts, retweets by the thousands. The link was copied from YouTube and dropped into text chains and emails over and over. Instagram, Instagram Stories, Instagram Reels, TikTok, Twitter, Twitch, Facebook. The videos were sent by twenty-somethings to older brothers, sisters, cousins, and parents with questions like *didnt u like this chicks band???* and *do you kno who burnt flowers is?* and *remember her?*

For a few days, like a communicable disease, the videos quietly spread, mutated. The long-form YouTube video was cut down to one broadcast-worthy clip of "Power Pink" that people thought was awesome. Like Caleb, they knew the song but had never really listened—or hadn't listened in years. Kids who weren't even alive when the song came out played it loudly through Bluetooth mobile speakers and thought, *Do I like this?* And then a TikToker named MusicBae99 posted herself dancing in a pink sports bra to "Power Pink." Her mind-boggling number of followers watched, influenced.

The algorithms took over, relentless in their mathematics. Anyone who'd ever watched and/or liked any music video or any video of an attractive dancing girl was fed the clip. The other platforms followed, serving videos up to people who had liked MusicBae99 or followed female musicians, alternative-rock bands, Burnt Flowers, Lawson Daniels, any of Lawson Daniels's movies, and so on.

Automated robots at Spotify, Apple, Amazon, and the other streaming music services logged the uptick in "Power Pink" streams and moved the song higher on their lists. Apple featured it on a playlist called "Girl Power Summer."

The online news site *HypeReport* jumped on it before *BuzzFeed* and posted a story with the caption "Remember Margot Hammer? Well, she's back and we're here for it."

Likes, loves, thousands of comments, forwards, retweets, quote tweets, and Margot Hammer knows absolutely nothing about any of it, because she's stayed as far away from social media as humanly possible. To Margot, social media is just *Us Weekly* for computers, and she wants no part of it.

Rebecca Yang keeps calling, but Margot has let those calls go straight to voicemail. Rebecca is a direct link—guilty by association—to Axl, and Axl can fuck all the way off.

As Billy circles his neighborhood looking for a place to park Grady and Patty's Charm City Rocks van in Baltimore, Margot sits on her couch in New York with her acoustic guitar. She's messing with some lyrics she started thinking about in the hotel room back in Baltimore. It's the first time she's tried putting actual music to one of her would-be songs in years, but performing ten nights ago in front of actual people has made her more acutely aware of how much she's missed being a musician. Her notebook is held open beside her by a plastic clip designed to keep potato chip bags closed.

When her phone rings, Margot knows it's her daughter, because FaceTime has a particular ringtone, and Poppy is the only person who FaceTimes her.

"Hey."

Poppy's face comes into focus. "Mum, for fuck's sake," she says, which isn't a surprise, because Poppy swears like a British football hooligan. What *is* a surprise is that she's crying.

"Pop?" Margot sits up. "What's wrong?"

Poppy wipes her nose with a balled-up tissue. "I saw you play."

"What?"

"I've only seen the old you play. Never the *you* you. When were you in Baltimore? *Why* were you in Baltimore?"

Margot has no idea what Poppy is talking about. "What?"

"There are videos all over the Internet."

She thinks of Todd, the goddamn camera guy—of Axl laughing at her. "There was this thing. It didn't work out. But how did you see it? It wasn't supposed to—"

"It's a little concert," Poppy says. "At a bar. You played 'Power Pink.' Other songs. You—" The girl's lower lip wobbles. She's a grown woman, an adult, but she's just a girl to Margot when she's crying. "Mum, you were amazing."

They talk it through. Margot tells Poppy about being ambushed in the record shop, about how Baltimore smells like bread and beer, and about overhearing Axl.

"Twat" is Poppy's response, which is Margot's favorite of her Britishisms.

Before calling, Poppy watched the videos. *All* the videos, including new content created in response to the originals. She watched with her two roommates, who agreed with Poppy that Margot looked and sounded fantastic.

"It was just a few songs. It wasn't—"

"Bloody hell it was. You should see the comments. My God, you're basically Beyoncé."

"The comments?"

"Yeah, Mum, there's this thing on the Internet called comments. Usually, they're a godforsaken shitshow of racism and misogyny, but people love you." She looks off camera at her laptop and starts quoting. "'This is the most badass thing I've ever seen.' 'I think I just fell in love with Margot Hammer.' 'I like how she looks mad but also sexy.' 'Am I crazy or is MH a legit snack?'"

"Snack?"

Poppy laughs. "That's a good thing. Oh, and here's an interesting one."

"Please, don't read them all," says Margot. "I'm begging you."

Poppy wrestles her hair into a bun, and it makes Margot miss her. She's a marvel to look at, this girl, even on a tiny screen. There's so much of Lawson in her face—an infuriating amount of him, the bastard. Her eyes, though, are all Margot, undeniable proof that the girl is hers.

"'Dude in the cardigan looks sweet,'" Poppy quotes. She scans more comments; the screen reflects off her eyes. "'Who's the dweeb in the Neil Diamond T-shirt?' 'Lots of big dad energy from dat cutie in the cardi.' Oh, here's another good one. 'Cool move with the high five, brah. Well played.'"

Margot is surprised to find that her face has just gone hot. "Dweeb is a little mean."

"No shit it's mean. It's the comments, remember? The trolls raise a good point, though." Poppy rests her chin on one fist. "Who's dat cutie in the cardi, Mum?"

It's not just her face now; her whole body heats up. "He's a guy I met in Baltimore," she says. "He's . . . he's no one."

Margot has no idea why she's just told one truth and then a lie. When she got back to New York, late on the night of her impromptu performance, Margot spent the next two days buzzing from playing again. It was all she could think about. As that began to fade, like adrenaline, she found herself thinking about Billy. And she *kept* thinking about him.

You're the best drummer I've ever seen.

He'd said that so earnestly—he really meant it. And now Margot finds that she can't remember why she was in such a hurry to leave him there holding his pretzel. In Burnt Flowers's old club days, just before their first album hit, they did blisteringly quick thirty-minute sets—nine songs, two for an encore, and then out the door. Leave 'em wanting more was the idea. Maybe that was good for a band who only had eleven songs to play, but it's a questionable strategy in terms of human interaction, because it might've been nice to have one more beer with the nice man in the cardigan who thought Margot was the best at something.

Either way, Poppy clearly doesn't believe her. "Hmm," she says, "right. Well, that nobody from Baltimore did something pretty freaking outstanding if you ask me. He made Margot Hammer smile."

"What? I didn't . . . I . . . I *smile,* Poppy."

"Do you, though? I've been talking to you for half an hour. I just told you you're Beyoncé on the Internet and that thousands of strangers think you're a rock-star snack. And you know what? Your facial expression hasn't changed. Not once. No smiles. Nothing."

"That's ridiculous."

"There, that was like *half* a smile, at best. Mum, I'm texting you a video. Right now."

"You know I don't watch—"

"Yourself. Yeah, yeah, I know. I'm sending it anyway. Skip the part where you're drumming, I guess, if you wanna be neurotic about it. It's worth it. Trust me."

The phone vibrates just then in Margot's hand as Poppy's text arrives.

"I'll think about it," says Margot.

When Poppy hangs up, Margot's phone screen turns black, so she can see her own reflection. She looks like she's always looked, she thinks, not pissed off or sexy or like a snack. She opens her camera and tries smiling at herself. It doesn't go particularly well, like the muscles in her face don't work properly. She tilts her head, tries again. "Whatever," she says.

Because we can't all be smilers.

CHAPTER 15

"Dad, what? No. Seriously?"

When Billy got home, Caleb was standing in the middle of the apartment, waiting for him, holding his laptop in one hand and his iPad in the other, like tall Moses. Billy tried to ask him about the college thing—and about why Caleb thought Billy should live above his mom's garage—but the kid only wanted to discuss one thing. Now they're arguing about whether Billy should casually call a rock star.

"Just hit her up," says Caleb. "Say hey. Like, 'Sup, girl?'"

"Cay, I don't talk like that. I don't think *anyone* does. Also, that's not a good idea."

"Orrrrr . . ." says Caleb, "it's the greatest idea in the history of human thought." He holds out his iPad as evidence. "The hardest thing about calling girls is that you never know what to say, right? Well, you've *got* things to say. You're both all over the Internet."

"When have you . . . Caleb, have you called a girl before?"

Caleb's eyes shift from side to side. "I don't tell you everything."

"Really? That's grea—"

"Well, people don't really call each other," says Caleb. "It's more like texting now, or maybe DMs. Oh, you should text her! Texting is casual. Less pressure. Like, 'Hey, so I guess we're both Internet famous now, el-oh-el.' I'll hit up Rebecca. She can give me Margot's number."

"Cay, that's *really* not a good idea. Rebecca thinks you're at best an Internet pervert. She's not just gonna hand you a famous musician's phone number."

Caleb jams a handful of Goldfish crackers into his mouth. "Dammit," he says.

"It was just a fluke thing," says Billy. "That's it. We need to move on."

"We have to try *something*, though, right?"

Billy just now notices that Caleb is playing Burnt Flowers's second album—track four, a song called "Slash Waitress." Margot's drum bed is subtle, just under the surface of the guitar, like something approaching. He nods up at the sound. "Good choice."

"I can see why you liked them so much," Caleb says.

"They were a helluva band. But, Cay, the thing is: I *did* try."

"I know, you went after her after my cluster-eff at Charm City. And that was a baller move. But—"

"No, after that. After she played at the Horse. We were down by the Harbor, having pretzels."

"Cinnamon?" asks Caleb.

"Yeah."

"Nice."

"I told her how great she played," says Billy. "It felt like, I don't know, we had a moment. So I asked if she wanted to get a drink."

"What'd she say?" Caleb asks.

"She said no. Then she left."

"Left?"

"In a cab."

Caleb collapses onto the couch, digs in for more Goldfish.

"Just because you like a girl—a woman," says Billy, "it doesn't mean she owes you something. It's not her job to like you back."

"But she *does* like you," says Caleb.

Billy hangs his cardigan on a hook by the door and sits next to his son. Burnt Flowers plays on the turntable next to the Steinway. Caleb offers Billy some Goldfish crackers. *What if Robyn is wrong?* Billy wonders. Would it be so bad if Caleb stayed in Baltimore? If after graduating from Hopkins he got a job downtown and lived a few miles from Billy? He thinks of hitting concerts with his son—of taking him out for a beer when he turns twenty-one, of having him . . . well, here.

"I get that you don't wanna be, like, *that guy*," says Caleb. "You know, pushy. But, before you give up, I don't think you're respecting the full enormity of this situation, Dad."

Billy laughs. "Enormity? Isn't that a little dramatic? A couple of YouTube videos?"

Caleb shakes his head. "Give me my iPad. You need to see something."

CHAPTER 16

A few days later, Margot is thinking about fifteen minutes of fame: the Andy Warhol thing from the sixties. The members of Burnt Flowers used to talk about it all the time. Anna and Jenny were convinced that their clocks were rapidly ticking, and after some symbolic quarter of an hour everything would go poof, and they'd be four nobodies again. Anna joked that she'd open a restaurant called the Gunn Show, and Jenny figured her dad could get her a job selling life insurance in Trenton if she somehow managed to hide her tattoos, particularly the one on her collarbone. Nikki thought that was all bullshit, though.

According to the lead singer, they were on their way to becoming icons, the first all-female rock band to go nuclear and, more importantly, *stay* nuclear. U2 with uteruses, an edgier R.E.M. in short skirts, Zeppelin with curves and on less coke. She went on about their staying power—about becoming multigenerational entertainment powerhouses. "That's how goddamn good we are," she told *Spin* magazine. "I'm personally here to give fifty years of rock-and-roll misogyny the middle finger. Better get used to it, too. If fucking Jagger can prance around stages in tiny T-shirts at *his* age, you think I won't be able to? Just wait."

Margot didn't talk to the music media as much as Nikki did, because her attitude was that nobody wanted to hear from the drummer—*any* drummer. When she did talk, though, she preferred to talk about the music, because that was what she loved. "My dream was never to be famous," she told *Mojo* once. "The day my dad set my first drum kit up for me, my dream was to be in a band. To make music. Being famous just makes me anxious."

When the issue of *Mojo* came out, Anna read that quote aloud to the band. The four of them were eating sushi together in the deep, dark depths of Madison Square Garden before a rehearsal. "Interesting point of view from the only one of us currently married to a movie star," Anna said. Jenny laughed and said, "Busted," while Nikki looked down at her little block of raw tuna—suddenly, it seemed, unable to meet Margot's eyes.

As Margot walks now through her neighborhood, she wonders what Andy Warhol would say about social media. He'd probably talk about reality stars and influencers and artificial fame and about how made-up it all is. Well, artificial or not, Margot is aware of the extremely real fact that people are looking at her more than usual.

Poppy texted earlier that Jimmy Fallon talked about her last night in his monologue, and that *Good Morning America* played "Power Pink" as they went to commercial. Poppy called it the "next stage of viraldom."

And these are just the things Poppy told her about. Margot doesn't know that the episode of the Netflix documentary that features Burnt Flowers is the streamer's third most watched unscripted program. She doesn't know about the vlogger who's figured out who Billy Perkins is and is currently telling the world. She hasn't found out about how Urban Outfitters is selling "Team Margot" T-shirts for $34.99.

Did you watch the video I sent you or what?

Poppy asked her that over text an hour ago.

No, Margot hadn't. Watching videos of yourself is a slippery slope. Because there are always more of them, like bugs camped out under stones.

"You rock, Margot!" a woman shouts from across the street. She gives Margot devil horns with her fingers. Two guys recognize Margot while she stands waiting for a light to change. They're holding hands. One of them openly stares, the other apologizes. "Sorry, he loses his shit around famous people. Love that jacket, by the way."

"Thanks, guys," she tells them.

Lawson was better at being famous. Mostly because he loved it so much. He made friends with the handful of photographers who lurked outside their apartment. He brought them donuts. Margot would squeeze his hand in a vise of anxious energy as their flashbulbs flashed. "This is part of it, love," he told her.

Her phone buzzes. Rebecca Yang again. She considers answering but doesn't. When Rebecca's name disappears, her daughter's pops up again with a new text.

Are you ignoring me?

Margot sees the video file again, attached to Poppy's previous text. She holds her thumb over the image from YouTube. The last video she watched of herself—her MTV meltdown—is still burned onto her brain.

A guy wearing a sweater passes. It's not a cardigan, but she thinks of Billy anyway. Cardigans don't work for everyone, but they work for Billy, and she imagines him letting her wear one of his. It'd be too big for her, of course, but it'd be so warm.

"Jesus," she says to no one. "What's wrong with you?"

The light turns red again. She's been standing there spaced out like a drunk tourist through the walk signal, so now she's stuck for another cycle. There are people to her left and right. Someone whispers to someone behind her. Four blocks up, one of Lawson's billboards looms over the street. She knows that it's there, because she's been avoiding it for weeks.

The light turns green again, finally. "You know what?" she whispers. "Fuck it."

In New York, a few blocks in any direction can mean a wholesale change of climate. Going this way, it's windy and cool, so Margot buttons her jean jacket. She looks at her phone and nearly crashes into a sign about street cleaning. Finally, holding her breath, she taps the video.

Her reaction to seeing herself is visceral, like rain down the back of her shirt. She barely hears the audio, but she can see by her drumming that it's the last few seconds of the Prince cover. Only Emma and Margot are visible. Emma is facing Margot, singing and playing, while Margot drums. Emma jumps, strums one last time, and Margot lets the cymbals crash and reverberate to silence while people cheer.

Whoever took the video follows Margot with their phone, zooms in on her as she walks offstage. There's Billy in his cardigan.

It's funny how dumb our memories are. She's been thinking about him a lot, but she'd forgotten exactly what he looks like. She remembered his sweater being black, but it's more of a gray. He's taller than she thought. His face is nice—friendly. She watches him as he waits for her to talk to the bartender. It was the moment when Beth offered her free Natty Boh for life. Then, when Billy holds his right palm up for a high five, Margot sees what Poppy was talking about.

"Shit," she says.

Yes, Margot Hammer is capable of smiling. But the smile she sees on her phone now is so big and bright that it causes her to stop walking. She looks up to get her bearings, which is when she sees the giant billboard of Lawson. Along with not smiling much, Margot doesn't laugh often either. She has to now, though, because there are currently two men on scaffolding removing her ex-husband. They sway in the breeze, fearless in their helmets and straps, chiseling away at his face.

"Hello, you bastard," Margot whispers, then she opens Face-Time.

Poppy answers. "Did you watch it? Tell me you watched it."

"Okay, yeah," she says. "I get it."

Poppy emits a delighted squeal. "See? I don't mean to sound like an old man here, but you really are pretty when you smile."

"Shut up."

"*You* shut up." Poppy is at her workstation. She looks around, draws her face closer to her phone. "Also, there's this. I'm sending you an image. *Us Weekly* just posted it."

"Oh Jesus," she says.

Her phone vibrates. Margot clicks on Poppy's text and immediately sees herself twice: two images side by side. On the left is the picture she's been avoiding for years: Lawson carrying her. On the right is a still frame from the video taken seconds after high-fiving Billy. Margot as a young rock star in a dress, as happy as she'd ever been. Middle-aged Margot in a dive bar beside Billy. Her smiles are identical—two moments of joy divided by decades. *Us Weekly*'s caption reads: "Good for You, Margot Hammer."

"This guy, Mum," says Poppy. "You should go see him. In Baltimore. Surprise him."

Margot walks a few steps, stops again. "You mean just go there? Like, show up? I shouldn't call him first?"

"Nobody calls anyone anymore. Just go. He'll be thrilled."

Margot doesn't have his number anyway, and there's something exciting about the thought of the look on his face when he sees her, exciting in a way that makes her feel a little sick to her stomach.

"Oh, by the way," says Poppy. "You're trending on Twitter."

"I don't even know what that means. I just—"

"What did he say the last time you saw him?"

Margot thinks. "He said if I'm ever in Baltimore again . . ."

"Wait," says Poppy. Her mouth becomes a straight line. "Mum? Is that . . . Dad?"

"Where?"

Poppy points. "There. Behind you."

Margot looks over her shoulder at the men scraping Lawson's cheekbones from plaster, turning him into flakes of dust. "Yeah," she says. "They're taking him down."

CHAPTER 17

Caleb stops at the mailbox on his way up the driveway. The previous owners built it to resemble the look and feel of his mom and Aaron's house, complete with white shutters and a little matching roof. It's cheesy and suburban, but actually kinda cool, too.

A few years ago, when his mom and Aaron decided to change the color of the house from beige to greenish, Caleb helped Aaron paint the mailbox to match. It was a Saturday afternoon. They drank sodas and chatted as they worked; an Orioles game played on the old-school radio Aaron found in the basement. Chatting always feels more forced with his stepdad than his *dad* dad, but Caleb has grown to appreciate the effort Aaron always makes.

Birds sometimes try to build nests between the mailbox door and roof in the spring, which can scare the living shit out of you if you're not prepared. A UPS guy knocked the whole thing over a few years ago while backing up. He pinned a note to the tipped-over wreckage afterward: "My bad!—Travis."

Caleb opens the mailbox door slowly, in case any sparrows have tried to set up shop, but it's all clear. Generally, the mail is just catalogs and glossy ads for window cleaners and landscapers. Beginning earlier this year, though, things started arriving addressed to him.

He can't imagine how stressful trips to the mailbox must've been back in the day, before universities started sending their acceptances and rejections via email. Every trip out to the curb must've felt like life or death.

The cadences from the University of Maryland and Johns Hopkins were identical: an acceptance email followed a few days later by a packet of pertinent information delivered by snail mail. Maryland's packet had a cartoon terrapin on it. Johns Hopkins's info was more formal-looking—serious blues and grays. Mr. Butler, one of the English teachers at school, had already told him he got into Hopkins, though, so the email and follow-up packets were just for show. Mr. Butler called Caleb into his office last week.

"Congrats," he said. "If you accept, I have a blue jay stuffed animal for you. It's cute."

"Thanks."

"You applied to Stanford, too, right?" asked Mr. Butler.

"Yeah."

The English teacher rubbed his chin. He wears a corduroy blazer all year, even when it gets hot. "You don't wanna go there," he said. "California? You can't study when it's seventy-two and sunny every day. You'll fail out in a month. Baltimore is perfect for academia. The weather is just bad enough."

Caleb does a quick peek into the mailbox and finds that there's nothing interesting: catalogs, a letter from AAA for Aaron. He hasn't gotten his email from Stanford yet, so he wasn't *technically* expecting a packet. But who knows? Maybe they do it differently.

His neighbors the Gundersons drive by and wave. Their chocolate Lab, Tessa, wags her tail from the backseat. Caleb waves back and tucks the junk mail under his arm.

He takes his phone out of the back of his uniform khakis as he walks toward the house. He hardly realizes he's doing it, because checking his phone comes as naturally as blinking or breathing. TikTok, then Insta. When he opens his email and sees the message at the top of his inbox he stops walking. The letters he's carrying fall to the pavement.

Stanford University Office of Undergraduate Admissions.

"Oh jeez," he says.

His backpack feels heavy. His knees go weak, like he's run here. But then he closes his email app and puts his phone back in his pocket, because he's not ready to know. Not yet.

CHAPTER 18

Margot packs in her head as she walks. Underwear, socks, toothbrush.

What if it's hot? What if it's cold? What if it rains? It hardly matters, because all her clothes are basically the same: jeans, gray button downs, black T-shirts, the boots she's wearing now. The best outfit she has is the one she wore to Charm City Rocks. Will Billy notice if she wears it again?

The idea is to keep moving, because if she stops, she'll realize this is crazy. She's an adult. Adults don't just get on trains and show up at strange men's doorsteps. Margot said these exact words to Poppy ten minutes ago.

"Says who?" Poppy asked.

"I don't know, civilized society?"

"Whatever. And he's not strange. You know him. Just keep walking."

When she pushes through the glass door to her apartment building, her doorman Jimmy is standing behind the desk, the knot of his tie loose. "Oh, hey, Miss H. Good timing."

Margot doesn't break stride. "Hey, Jimmy. I think I'll need a cab in a bit."

"No problem. But, uh, first things first. The kid's back."

Margot finally stops. "The kid?"

"Dude, seriously, enough with that. I'm twenty-six years old."

"Sorry," says Jimmy. "Miss H., I believe you know Miss Yang."

Rebecca stands in the lobby wearing her Chuck Taylors, a different vintage sweater this time. "Hey, Margot."

"You said you were twenty-five."

"Monday was my birthday," says Rebecca.

This is annoying, because a little clearing of sympathy forms now in Margot's anger.

Jimmy clears his throat. "This okay? I could ask her to leave if you want."

Jimmy has been her doorman since she and Lawson bought the place. He was like this back then: protective of her. He'd shoo away photographers, close the door quickly behind her when she entered, shake her packages. Seeing him take that posture again is sweet, but weird, especially now that he's become an old man. "It's okay, Jimmy."

"In that case, happy belated, Miss Yang," says Jimmy. "Got a few lollipops back here if you want one."

If Rebecca is trying not to look young, taking a sucker and immediately jamming it into her mouth probably isn't a good idea, but that's exactly what she does. "Can we talk?" she asks. "Can I come up or something?"

Margot looks at the elevator. "No, not up. But, here . . . sit."

They settle onto the old leather lobby couch under a painting of Central Park. "I'm in a hurry. I don't have time to—"

"I'm sorry," says Rebecca.

On the other side of the lobby, Jimmy pretends not to be listening.

"I didn't get why you bolted, back in Baltimore. Then I saw that door between our rooms. You heard him, didn't you? Axl."

"I heard *both* of you."

"Margot, he's my boss. I'm sorry I didn't defend you. That was shitty. I was afraid he was mad at me for getting you catfished. I thought I was about to get fired. But he was being a total dick—that stuff he said. And I'm sorry if he hurt your feelings. If *I* hurt your feelings."

Axl is a weird-looking little man with a dumb-ass ponytail. But Margot knows how important he is—she was scared of him when she was young, too. "His real name is Stuart, by the way," she says.

"What? Axl?"

"Yeah. Next time he makes you feel bad, just think of him as little Stuart Albee."

Rebecca smiles. "I will. Anyway, the *official* reason I'm here. Requests are coming in."

"Requests?"

"Yeah," she says. "Appearances. Google wants to use 'Power Pink' in a commercial. A new phone or something. I guess it's pink. Also, are you familiar with that show where famous people perform in elaborate costumes and people try to guess who they are? They want you as a guest."

None of that sounds interesting. Worse, stopping, as she feared, has made her re-rethink her nonplan of a plan. Maybe Rebecca has Billy's number—or at least his son's. But no, Poppy was right. Margot doesn't want to talk to him on the phone. Margot hates the phone. She wants to see him. Oddly, she wants to see Baltimore, too. She was only there for half a day, but it was nice.

"Rebecca, I have to go."

"Really? Don't you want to talk about—"

"Call me, okay? Later. I'll answer . . . probably." Margot stands. She'll throw some things in a bag, have Jimmy get her that cab. She'll get a drink on the train if she gets nervous, then maybe another one.

"Wait," says Rebecca. "One other thing."

Margot waits.

Rebecca stands now, too, beside the old couch. "I was right, you know."

"About what?"

"You. People missed you, Margot. And now you're awesome again."

When Rebecca is gone, Margot steps into the elevator. Jimmy calls her name, so she hits the hold button.

"Um, just so you know, Miss H.," he says. "Maybe it's not my place to say. And I'm sorry for eavesdropping. I've got the YouTube here on my PC. I saw you play, and you were real good. Thing is, though, you never *stopped* being awesome." Jimmy puts his hands in his pockets. "You've been awesome this whole time."

CHAPTER 19

"Okay, kiddo, one more time, with feeling."

His student, Sophia, draws a big, weary sigh, as if Billy has just asked her to pick up the Steinway and walk around the apartment with it. "Didn't I do it right, though?"

"Yeah, you're doing great. But you gotta do it over and over, until your muscles remember it without you even having to think about it."

Sophia's only a few months into her lessons, so she's not sold yet on "over and over." She's nine and very small. Her hair frizzes at the ends, and her feet sway a few inches off the floor. "Fine," she says.

"You warm enough?" asks Billy. "That sweater's not *too* too big, is it?"

She pushes the sleeves up on the cardigan. Billy let her borrow it because she was cold. "No, it's okay. I like it."

"Don't think I'm just gonna let you walk out of here with it, though, okay?"

"I won't," she says. Then, with the grim determination of a Depression-era gravedigger, Sophia plays the intro to "Levitating" by Dua Lipa. Billy always asks students to bring in a few of their favorite songs so they can learn to play them. It helps Billy convince them that the vast instrument before them is something to be enjoyed.

"Keep going. Little louder. Hit those keys now, show Dua some love."

The girl fumbles over notes, but she does so with impressive force. When she gets to the end of the first verse, which is as far as they've practiced, Billy finally gets her to smile by suggesting that maybe he briefly lost consciousness and the *real* Dua Lipa climbed in through the window and started rocking out.

"No, it was just me," Sophia says.

"If you say so."

There's a knock at the door. Billy checks the clock. "Probably your mom. Moms love sneaking back early to see the action."

"She says you're famous," says Sophia. "My dad said so, too."

"Who, me? Nah, I'm *Internet* famous. Barely counts."

She's just a kid, but Sophia seems to get the distinction. "Is that why you're moving out? Are you gonna live in a mansion, like The Rock?"

There are packed boxes stacked in orderly rows all around them. The walls are bare, and his TV and stereo are unplugged. His old acoustic guitar sits on a crate of *Rolling Stone* magazines. There's a second knock at the door. "I've been to The Rock's place a bunch of times. Not super impressed. You ready to show your mom how well you're doing?"

Billy hops off his teaching stool and heads to the door. As he opens it, he says, "Hope you're ready to be impressed." The first thing that crosses his stupid mind is that Sophia's mom looks different. His second thought is a happier one. So happy that it's difficult to fully trust what he's seeing.

Margot Hammer pushes the hair out of her face. "Hi."

A few seconds pass. Could be three, could be twenty. Probably somewhere in between. "You," he says. "Again."

"I forgot to sign your friend's wall," she says. "Kind of a bitchy move, right?"

Billy is thrown. Maybe this is the sort of thing famous people do. They return to cities far away from their own to sign their names next to local authors and retired baseball players. But then Margot pushes the same bit of hair out of her face again.

"I'm joking. Can I come in? It's windy out here."

CHAPTER 20

"What are you . . . what are you doing here?"

Margot has had some time to think through the answer to this inevitable question. Two and a half hours on the train, plus fifteen minutes with a cabdriver who seemed to care very little whether they lived or died.

They're tearing my ex-husband's face down. I only went to college very briefly, but a metaphor like that can't be an accident, right? Also, my daughter thought I should come find you, and she's often right about things. I'm trying to prove to her—probably to myself, too—that I'm not a recluse. And I saw on the Internet how you made me smile, and the last time I smiled like that I was very, very happy. Oh, and I know this is weird, but I wanted to see the look on your face when you saw me. And now that I have, I'm pleased to report that you looked thrilled. And it's nice when someone is thrilled to see you. Right?

She decides to distill all that, though, because it'd probably be too much. "I wanted to see you."

"You did?"

Just then, Margot realizes two things. Billy's apartment is packed up and barren, and there's a little girl in a giant cardigan staring at them with her hands over the keys of the most gorgeous piano she's ever seen.

"Should I start?" the girl asks.

"Oh," says Billy. "No, actually, why don't you chill for a sec, Soph? Margot, this is Sophia, my student. Sophia, Margot."

"Hi," says Sophia. "I like your boots."

Margot looks down at her feet. She's interrupted. Billy is working, and she's just shown up to his weirdly empty apartment, assuming he'd be sitting here waiting for her. The bag over her shoulder seems horrendously presumptuous now. All that time for thinking, and she's forgotten to work through the logistics of where exactly she's going to sleep tonight. "Thanks," she says. "I like your sweater."

Sophia points at Billy. "It's his."

"Yeah, the Soph-meister was chilly, so I hooked her up."

"We're having a cardi party," says Sophia.

Billy is wearing a cardigan, too, and Margot wonders how many of them he has. "I could come back. Maybe we could meet up or some—"

"No," says Billy. "Are you kidding? Stay."

Margot rubs her hands together. As lovely as it was to see the look on his face when he opened the door, this—the fact that he so adamantly doesn't want her to leave—is even better. Maybe we're all overthinking it, and everybody just needs someone who wants them to be there.

"Soph, how about we show Margot what we've been working on?" says Billy.

Sophia reaches for the keys. "'Levitating'?"

"Nah. You're killing that one, but let's do the one I showed you last week, remember? The rockier one?" He shuffles through some papers and finds handwritten sheet music. "Okay, let 'er rip."

Sophia shakes out her hands and starts playing. Margot doesn't recognize it at first. The notes are too slow and careful. But then the girl relaxes, and her fingers start to flow across the keyboard.

"That's it," says Billy. "Keep going, Soph. Sounds great."

He's right. She's never heard "Power Pink" played on a piano by a child, but it sounds fantastic, and Margot is very happy that she came.

CHAPTER 21

If there's anyone in Baltimore who's as happy as Billy, that person is Grady Edwards. He's trying to play it cool, but his face is like Christmas morning as he hands Margot his Sharpie. "Right here, next to Ripken. It'll be perfect."

"Okay, if that's what you want," says Margot.

"Don't worry if you mess up. We can paint over it with Wite-Out, and you can do it again."

Margot puts the cap back on the marker. "Well, now you're just making me nervous."

"Okay, yeah, sorry. I'll shut up. Go ahead. I can't tell you how much I appreciate this."

And now Billy is nervous, too, as if Margot has never written her name before.

Fortunately, though, she has, and she does it perfectly: a big scribbly *M* followed by "Hammer." It's a rock-and-roll signature if ever there was one.

"Awesome," says Grady. "Kid Rock stopped by a few summers ago. He said he was too fucked up to sign, which I totally get. He bought two Lynyrd Skynyrd records and a T-shirt, though."

Margot looks around. "I really like your store," she says.

Grady beams. "Yeah? Well, thank you. Are you back to . . ." He moves his Sharpie from one hand to the other. "Wait, why are you back? Is it . . . is it because of the Internet stuff? You and Billy?"

Margot looks at Billy, clearly embarrassed, and so is Billy, and now Grady is smiling at them like a dad before prom. "Are you two, like, on a date?"

"G, stop it, we're just . . ." Billy doesn't know what comes after the word *just*.

Margot twists the toe of her right boot into the smooth cement floor. "I was in a hurry last time I was here," she says. "I feel like maybe I should've stayed for one more drink."

"Yeah, totally," says Grady. "So, what're you guys gonna do?"

Grady was right before, back at Hot Twist a week and a half ago. Margot really is shorter than you'd think. Billy read somewhere once that her real name is Margie Willis, which is far less intimidating than Margot Hammer. Margie Willis is just a pretty woman, smart- and shy-looking, who showed up at his door earlier with a little bag slung over her shoulder, like a time traveler. And now she's standing in a record shop, waiting to hear how Billy answers Grady's question.

His mind goes blank, as minds do, as if he hasn't lived here his entire life. He and Caleb sometimes play a game called Wrong Answers Only, so a few seconds pass during which he can think only of terrible options. A couple of foot-longs at Subway. A quick swim in the disease-infested Inner Harbor. A dogfight followed by the Dunkin' Donuts drive-thru.

He looks out the front window. It's breezy out there and late-day sunny—just the right amount of warm. Behind Margot, scrawled next to her newly added signature, he sees Cal Ripken, Jr.'s distinct autograph, and the night starts to take shape in his mind. Food, drinks, a sunset, a nice view of the stars. "Do you like baseball?" he asks.

"Baseball?" says Margot.

"Oh, right," says Grady. "Good idea. The goddamn Red Sox are in town."

"I like baseball," she says.

"Oh, and look at this." Grady jogs to the other end of the store and returns with a new Orioles cap, fresh off a rack of hats. It's black and white with the old-school cartoon bird logo and an orange bill. Margot slides it onto her head and looks up at them.

"Perfect," says Grady. "On the house. Don't tell Patty, though. She hates when I give stuff away."

"Does it make my ears look weird?" Margot asks.

Billy assesses Margot's ears. They're sticking out a little, because that's what happens when women put on baseball caps, like a weird quirk of their anatomy. "Nah," he says. "They look great."

She touches a lobe, obviously doubting this. "They have drinks there, right?"

Grady waves at them on their way out and tells them to have a good time—still dad-like. He even stands at the door smiling when they leave.

"Hey, is that . . ." someone asks someone else as they pass. Margot ignores them, so Billy does, too. Some other people look, which is weird but exciting. No one's ever really looked at him before.

Tonight is Billy's last night in Fells Point. As they stand on Thames Street, he imagines the neighborhood from Margot's perspective. Daquan is one block over, pounding away. The sun is moving toward the horizon. The twinkly lights strung around the outdoor eating area at the Greek restaurant next door come on, and people are out with their tattoos and interesting outfits and cool beards. Like always, there's music everywhere.

"It's not like how everyone says," says Margot.

"What isn't?"

"Baltimore," she says. "I thought it'd be, I don't know, more murdery."

Billy might never see this woman again after tonight. That's a very real possibility—maybe even a likelihood. At any moment, she could hop into another janky cab and simply vanish, like before. As long as she's here now, though, he figures he might as well enjoy it.

"Be patient," he says. "The night is young."

CHAPTER 22

Burnt Flowers performed the national anthem at Yankee Stadium before a game once. It was the postseason. Margot doesn't remember the round or level or whatever. It was cold, though, and the game didn't start until nearly 9 P.M. Derek Jeter looked like a skinny teenager back then. He gave the band a thumbs-up on their way off the field to a respectable level of applause. Nikki had gone on a few dates with him the summer before.

"Good kisser, that one," she shouted into Margot's ear. Nikki had managed to display her entire midriff, despite the October chill. "Whatever, though. I think he still has a thing for Mariah Carey."

Margot was always at her best during proper concerts—full-on, exhaustive performances. The one-off things like national anthems and late-night talk shows always felt rushed. The Yankees gig was over in ninety seconds, give or take. Jenny did her best Hendrix impersonation with her guitar while Nikki sang. Anna's bass got drowned out by Jenny's amp, and the little kit the grounds crew dragged out for Margot hardly seemed worth the trouble. The field was nice, though. She remembers that—bright green grass with damp dirt the color of clay.

That odd minute years ago represents the sum total of Margot's experience with baseball. She knows only the most basic things, like the bats and balls and throwing and spitting. She didn't mention this to Billy, though, because it didn't really matter where they decided to go. She just wants to be with him and to see if he's as nice as he seems.

She was nervous earlier, as they stood outside the record shop. She had no idea which way the stadium was, so she was helpless, and she could feel her ears jutting out from the sides of her new cap. Plus, she hasn't been on a date in three years.

Time is the worst: the way it stacks up so fast. One day you decide that maybe you'll take a break from relationships to focus on yourself, then suddenly, thirty-six months have passed, and you wonder if you've forgotten how conversations work.

Margot briefly dated an actor after she and Lawson divorced. He worked mostly in the theater, so he wasn't nearly as successful as her ex-husband. Lawson hung over their short relationship like a ghost, fueling impossible comparisons and inferiority complexes. There was a hedge-fund guy nearly as old as her father, who collected music memorabilia. The symbolism wasn't lost on Margot. She may as well have sat in his enormous study behind protective glass. There was an aging chef with tattoos who drank and an acerbic stand-up comedian who also drank.

These men told her how smart she was—how cool—but Margot understood that that was their way of telling her that she wasn't as pretty as they wished she was.

Margot is famous, and famous women are so very often famous for being beautiful, but Margot is famous for hitting things. If she wasn't pretty enough for them, fine, because they weren't worth her time anyway. They didn't make her happy. None of them were good people. None of them were nice.

The walk from Charm City Rocks to wherever this baseball stadium is is lovely.

They've been walking for twenty minutes, and Billy knows something about every block, like an easygoing tour guide. "Federal Hill used to be a nice little neighborhood," he says. "Now it's mostly drunk kids right outta college."

"Hey, dude, check it out!" shouts a drunk kid who looks to be just out of college. "It's the drummer and that guy from the Internet!"

They aren't in Federal Hill long, because the neighborhoods clip by quickly, like breezing past small towns on a train. They pass a playground of shrieking children, a small church that looks very old, and a convenience store. Baltimore is like if someone carved out a slice of Manhattan and made it into a whole city.

Margot stops to look at her own reflection in the window of a liquor store. She never wears hats, but she's surprised to see that this one looks nice on her.

"See, told ya," Billy says. "You're *wearing* that thing."

Billy isn't particularly tall, but there's a ranginess there that she likes. He's taken his cardigan off and tossed it over one shoulder. Historically speaking, Margot isn't a big hand holder. Holding hands is overrated. It throws off your balance and makes you look needy. She can imagine holding *his* hand though, maybe, someday.

They walk on, and a woman smoking a cigarette says, "Go O's!" when she sees Margot's cap. It's the third time someone has shouted this since they started walking.

"Why do people say it like that here?" Margot asks.

"You mean the accent?" Billy asks.

"Yeah. They draw it out, like, 'goaow aows.'"

He laughs. "That's pretty good. Yeah, OG Baltimoreans add completely unnecessary letters to some words. But then they *take away* letters from other words. Right now, you're not in *Baltimore*, you're in *Balmer*. Water is *wooter*. No idea why. If it were Tuesday right now, it'd be *Toosdee*. And your name isn't *Margot*, it's *Marghaow*. Like with an *h* and an *a*, maybe even a *w* thrown in there for no good reason."

"That's how Beth at the bar said it. And she kept calling me *hon*."

"Of course she did," says Billy. "*Hon*'s big here, and Beth's about as OG Baltimore as it gets."

"Why don't *you* have an accent?"

"My grandma," he says. "She said Baltimore accents hurt her ears, like wrong notes on the piano. It stuck."

Up ahead, a big brick building stands against a darkening blue sky: Oriole Park at Camden Yards. Yankee Stadium has always looked cold and corporate to Margot. This, though, looks like someone's elaborate home.

Margot drank two little bottles of wine earlier on the train, but she only ate a fun-size bag of potato chips, so she's hungry to the point of shakiness. They stop at a food tent outside the stadium with a hand-painted sign that reads DOLLA DOLLA DOGZ. A traffic cop blows a whistle and dances as he directs a stream of cars into the parking lot. Billy orders them two hot dogs, and when he hands Margot hers, he seems unsure of himself. "Wait, is this okay?"

"Is what okay?"

He looks at the hot dog wrapped in foil. "We can find something nicer, if you want," he says. "Something better than this."

His concern is sweet, but it's silly, because this is perfect. "Shut up," she tells him. "And give me that ketchup."

CHAPTER 23

This feels like a first date, while also not feeling at all like a first date. The nerves are there—that jumpy feeling, like you've had too much caffeine, like you're sweating in places that you don't normally sweat, like your voice sounds weird in your own ears.

Is that really how I talk? I've never said "all righty" before in my life. Why am I saying it now?

What's different, Billy realizes as the sun drops below the first-base side of Camden Yards, is the lack of mystery here. Because, he really *has* known Margot for twenty years. He was a fan of the band because they were incredible. They played the sort of music he'd want to play if he were in a band: brash and loud, but smart and political, too, like the Clash but with better voices. His crush on Margot wasn't weird or obsessive. It was as harmless as the celebrity crushes everyone has, like daydreaming about a different life, like building a fort for Alyssa Milano. He liked Margot for her talent, which was celebrated and well documented. He liked her, too, because of how pretty he thought she was behind her drums. He loved the intensity in her eyes when she played, and how she peeked out through her hair to look at Anna Gunn, the bassist, during transitions.

As a fan of Burnt Flowers, he paid attention when they were profiled, featured, and interviewed, which they were often back then. And as someone with a crush on the drummer, he paid particular attention to the Margot parts of those profiles, features, and interviews. So, while he gets that he doesn't *know her* know her, he knows more about her than anyone he's ever gone on a first date with. He knows what she looked like when she was young and how she got her first drum kit. He knows that she dropped out of NYU, and that Nikki Kixx was the only person to answer Margot's flyer, and that they became fast friends at CBGB when they were eighteen. He knows who Margot married and what her daughter's name is. He's seen the famous photo of Lawson carrying Margot a million times. My lord, that smile! He knows exactly how, when, and why her marriage ended. And he knows what the worst day of her life probably was: the MTV Music Video Awards where she broke down in front of the whole planet. So, even though Billy doesn't *know her* know her, he knows a lot, which is why, nervous jitters aside, he's surprisingly relaxed. Relaxed enough, even, to be himself.

"See the warehouse out there?" He points at the long brick building beyond the right-field fence. "It used to be a railroad station. It looked so perfect there that the Orioles decided to keep it when they built this stadium. Now it's one of the most famous backdrops in baseball."

"I like it," she says. "It's pretty."

They're on the aisle, first-base side, fifteen rows up, because if ever there was a time to get good seats, Billy figured this was it. It's the fourth inning. Neither team has scored, and the beers he bought on the way to their seats are nearly empty. "We should get more of these," he says.

Margot makes a face that suggests *Um, yeah.*

From a distance, he sees his favorite beer vendor, Clancy. Billy waves, catches Clancy's eye, and gives him a nod. He resists the urge to shout, "Fancy Clancy!" like he normally does, because, relaxed or not, no one is *totally* themselves on a first date.

"So, scale of one to ten," Billy says.

Margot is watching the players on the field. She looks up at him now. The bill of her new cap runs low and straight across her forehead. She looks wonderful.

"How glad are you that you came back?"

She swirls what's left of the beer in her plastic Orioles cup. "You said it yourself, right? The night is young."

He's about to tell her that he's at a ten—maybe a nine-point-five so as not to seem overeager—but then Clancy sets his iced box of beers down on the metal stairs with a clank. "What's up, Billy?"

"Hey, Clance. Nice night, huh?"

"Baseball and beers, my man," says Clancy.

"We'll take two."

Clancy gives Margot a sly wink. "Hope you don't mind me saying, miss," he says. "But I like you more than that giant kid he usually shows up here with. You fit better in the seat."

Margot says that she doesn't mind at all, and Billy swipes his credit card. "I'll tell Caleb you said hey."

"Good deal. I'll be back. You two look thirsty. Like your cap, miss. Suits you."

Someone yells, "Fancy Clancy, beer me!" and Clancy is gone in a rush.

"You know a lot of people, huh?" says Margot.

"Nah. Everyone knows Clancy. He's a local celebrity. NPR did a feature on him a couple years ago. Sorry I didn't introduce you. You got mad at me when I yelled your name during the Margot Hammer Incident. I didn't want to draw unnecessary attention."

Margot sips her new beer—a big stadium can. "The Margot Hammer Incident?"

"Yeah," he says. "That's what I call it."

Margot looks around. "Well, knock yourself out," she says. "I don't think it matters anymore."

She's right. Since they started their walk across town, Billy has been absorbed in the space immediately around him and Margot, like they're in a protective bubble. A quick 180 scan, though, is all it takes to see how many people are aware of them.

"It's *totally* them," someone somewhere says. A guy in an Orioles jersey gives Billy a nod on his way up the stairs. "Respect, dude." A woman a few rows over is definitely taking their picture. Someone else nearby, a guy, says that Margot is surprisingly short.

"Who knew so many people have the Internet?" Billy says.

The Orioles third baseman pops out, and a woman somewhere behind them says that she thinks Margot deserves something good to happen.

"How does this work, exactly?" Billy asks. "Do we pretend people aren't looking at us? Do we act like we can't hear them?"

"You guys are adorable!" a young woman at the other end of their row shouts. She's in her twenties, wearing a sideways Orioles cap. "It helps when they say *nice* things," Margot says as she tips her beer at the woman.

"Isn't it exhausting?" he asks.

Margot looks up. The first handful of stars are doing their best against the stadium lights. "You'll get used to it," she says, and it might be the most thrilling thing anyone's ever said to him, because it sounds like a promise.

The Red Sox score a bunch of runs. Between innings, the stadium crew entertains the crowd. A guy in a bird costume dances on top of the dugout. Pretty girls in orange tank tops throw T-shirts into the stands.

When the Red Sox are finally out in the sixth inning, the "kiss cam" appears on the large scoreboard screen, and the whole stadium watches. An elderly man and woman, a young husband and wife, two shy teens in matching hoodies. Each is shocked, then embarrassed, before kissing to polite applause. The whole thing is sponsored by a local florist. Then Billy sees someone who looks very much like himself: a man in a cardigan beside a woman in an Orioles cap. It isn't until he hears "Power Pink" being blasted over the stadium's PA that he realizes the man is him and the woman is Margot.

"Oh," he says.

People around them cheer; some sing along with the chorus. Not everyone was looking at them before, but now *everyone* is, and Billy feels his stomach drop. An old man in front of them turns in his seat. "You see that up there?" he says. "That's you two. Means you gotta kiss. Those are the rules."

"I guess we should," says Billy.

"Yeah, probably," says Margot.

He's seen hundreds of kiss-cam kisses. Sometimes they're chaste little things, followed by smiles and giggles. Sometimes either the guy or the girl hams it up for the crowd. One time, Billy saw a guy turn away from the mortified girl beside him and pretend to kiss his beer. When Billy's mouth touches Margot's, though, despite the rising volume all around them, he somehow forgets that they're in the middle of a stadium.

He takes her chin. The bill of her cap bumps his forehead, but she adjusts and then sighs into his mouth as they sink into each other. Four seconds, maybe five. But who knows, because it feels like slow motion.

"Okay, that's enough," the old guy says. "Come on, there's kids here."

CHAPTER 24

Justin: *Just open it ffs!!*

　Shin-Soo: *Yeah . . . DO IT.*

　Caleb: *I will. Shut up!*

Caleb is messaging with his friends Justin and Shin-Soo from his laptop. Among the academic top 10 percent in Ruxton Academy's senior class, Justin, Shin-Soo, and Caleb are the only males. Junior year, Justin tried coining the nickname "the Bro-Brain Triumvirate," but it didn't stick. Among their classmates, the three friends are mostly just known as the nerdy dudes who sit together at lunch. Caleb is the tall one. Justin has glasses. Shin-Soo breakdances at pep rallies to uproarious applause. He's inexplicably good at breakdancing and has more than fifteen thousand followers on TikTok.

Justin sends a GIF of a robot twiddling its fingers: *We're waiting!* Shin-Soo highlights the GIF with an exclamation mark.

Caleb looks at his phone on his desk, which is open to his email inbox. If it were a letter—sent on actual paper like in the days of yore—he imagines the corners would be as sharp as throwing stars, weaponized.

He doesn't want it to say yes, but he totally wants it to say yes.

Caleb has decided that he's staying in Baltimore. He's never actually said those words aloud, but he's committed to them in his mind. Either way, it'd be nice to be wanted. To know that he'd been invited in.

Shin-Soo: *It's totally gonna say yes. It's time a straight white guy finally catches a break in this country.*

Justin: *Hahahhahaa*

Plus, there's the element of competition. The other two bro-brains both got into Ivies last week. Shin-Soo is heading to Yale and Justin to Penn, the bastards. Fine, Stanford isn't *technically* an Ivy, but pretty damn close.

Caleb shifts the chat box on his laptop and goes to his browser, where he opens the Stanford site. He looks at the same students/models he's been cyberstalking for months. He knows all about impostor syndrome. Everybody does. Still, despite his Hoops Compendium app and his GPA being legit great, everyone on the screen looks smarter than him—better looking, too. Does Stanford give extra points to prospective students for hotness?

He hasn't been rejected from a university yet, so he's not sure how the email would start. *Dear Caleb, we regret to inform you . . . Dear Caleb, we're sorry to report that . . . Dear Caleb, go fuck yourself.*

Regardless, it'd be nice to have the decision made for him—to have the Stanford door slammed shut. Yeah, it'd be a body blow, but he'd recover. He'd claim his blue jay stuffed animal from Mr. Butler. He'd buy a cool Hopkins hoodie and start the next part of his life: the college part. He and his dad could watch rock documentaries together and poke around under the Champagne Supernova's hood for years to come. A couple of weeks ago, before accidentally getting stoned to bejesus and emailing a rock star, Caleb thought about how sad his dad would be if Caleb left. Caleb is smart enough, though, to know that he'd be just as sad.

He tentatively explained this to Justin and Shin-Soo at lunch earlier this spring. They were respectful, because they think Caleb's dad is cool and all, but: "Come on, dude," said Shin-Soo, "Cali is insane."

"Yeah," said Justin. "You could sell your app to the Golden State Warriors for like five million dollars and date Olivia Rodrigo. Pull your head out of your ass."

The little flatscreen TV on the other side of his bedroom is set to *SportsCenter* on ESPN, which Caleb isn't paying attention to.

Justin: *Working Theory: You need to go where the most nerds are. Among nerds, you're a solid 8. In gen pop tho with all the hot people, you're a 5 at best. This is just math. Don't hate.*

Shin-Soo: *TRUTH!*

Caleb picks up his phone. "Here goes," he says, tapping the email from Stanford.

Across the room, the ESPN announcer says, "And now, finally, it's that time of night. Time for Today's Best."

It's Caleb's favorite part of *SportsCenter:* when they count down the ten best moments in sports for the day. The first one is some crazy header goal from a soccer match in France. An MMA punch is next—an act of pure violence. He's too busy to deal with sports, though. This is his life, after all.

There are so many words in the email, hundreds, arranged in neat lines and stacked in paragraphs. Only one word registers, though—the only one that matters. *Congratulations!*

"Motherfucker," says Caleb.

"But enough about cricket," says the announcer. "This is America, right? Slow news day? Maybe. But for number one, we take you to beautiful Camden Yards in Baltimore, Maryland, where, along with the smell of crab cakes, romance was in the air."

Caleb looks up at the TV. The announcers riff.

"You remember the aughts, Tina?"

"Eh. I mean, I was alive."

"You have the Internet, though, right?"

"I do indeed, Bobby."

"Well then surely you've been following this story out of Charm City."

Caleb has never seen his dad on TV before, so it's the cardigan he recognizes first, as in *My dad has the same sweater as that dude on TV*. But then Margot Hammer is there. As the crowd cheers, his dad and Margot . . . start kissing.

"Wait, what?" says Caleb.

"I give you world-class-rock-drummer-turned-viral-sensation Margot Hammer, seen here on the kiss cam at an O's game with everyone's new favorite random cardigan guy."

"At least someone in an Orioles hat got to first base tonight."

"Zing! But, yeah, Tina's right, the Orioles got beat down by the Sox. But who cares? I mean, come on, look at those two. Go get 'em, Cardigan Guy!"

Caleb's laptop screen pings.

Shin-Soo: *Dude. Cay. Are you watching SportsCenter?*

CHAPTER 25

"It's a beautiful piano."

"Thanks," says Billy. "I catch myself staring at it sometimes. Is that weird?" He plays a few lazy bars of his go-to, "She's a Rainbow," and offers her an espresso.

Margot frowns at the robot octopus of a machine on the counter. "I'd be up all night," she says. "And no, it's not weird at all. I stare at my drums all the time."

They're back from the game, side by side at the Steinway, and he logs these details about her: she can't drink coffee at night, she stares at her drums. Also, she doesn't know how to match socks. "Those're different," he says.

Margot looks down at her feet, curls the toes of the right one. "I'm a little color-blind."

"Okay. Are you a little *blind* blind, too? Because that one's striped and that one's got polka dots."

"I guess it's been a while since I cared," she says.

This could mean a couple of things. Perhaps she's too much of a mad genius to care about such inconsequential things as socks, like how Einstein used to forget to put on pants. Or maybe it means she's been on her own for a while, and there's been no one around to match socks for.

On their way back from Camden Yards, he asked if she wanted to stop for a drink or maybe ice cream. "I think that'd be more of a production than you realize," she told him. After the kiss cam, their cover was totally blown. People came up to them to wave and take pictures, to shout encouragement and to tell Margot that she rocks. Billy found it impossible to follow what was going on in the game. Now that he thinks about it, he's not even sure who won.

"I have other things to drink," he says now. "Beer, soda? I have some pot gummies. That was a true story, by the way—the gummy bear thing."

"All good." She holds her palms over the keys and leans in to look at the sheet music he made for Sophia. "I like how you simplified it." She plays it perfectly.

"Damn. So, you're not . . ."

"Just a drummer?"

"Would that be an insult?" he asks. "Is being called *just* a drummer offensive, if you're one of the best drummers of your generation? Like, oh, so, LeBron, you're not *just* a basketball player, you play a little tennis, too."

"Stop it," she says, smiling. It's not a break-the-Internet, full-wattage smile, but he'll take it. She plays the beginning of "Let It Be" then "Karma Police," and it makes him dizzy to imagine the Billy of twenty years ago seeing this: Margot Hammer in mismatched socks, afraid of caffeine, wearing an O's cap, playing Radiohead beside him. He's glad she didn't want to get a beer or ice cream earlier, because what could be better than this?

"All right, move it, sister," he says. "My turn."

He plays "Goodbye Yellow Brick Road" by Elton John, then "Oh! You Pretty Things" by David Bowie.

Margot rolls her eyes. "Ugh, dudes," she says, and then plays

"Borderline" by Madonna so well that all he can do is watch with his mouth open.

"Did you prepare for this?" he asks. "I'm calling bullshit. You rehearsed."

"What, this?" She keeps with Madonna, starts "Like a Prayer," but stops because someone is yelling outside.

"Yo, Piano Man! Where's my Stevie at?"

They look at each other then go to the window. It's the guy with the pit bull. He and his dog are looking up from the sidewalk.

"Hey, man," says Billy. "How are you?"

"Good. But I don't remember requesting no Madonna."

"Hold up a sec." Billy guides Margot back to the piano bench. "You don't know any Stevie Wonder, do you?"

"Not off the top of my head. Do you know that guy? Do people just yell at you from the street?"

"Sometimes, yeah. Here, you can help me." He finds his iPad under some books. "I have to cheat on this one. I didn't practice." He searches his sheet music app and sets "Superstition" on the stand between them. "You play these," he says, pointing. "I'll play these. Ready?"

Billy starts, then Margot comes in after him. "Goddamn right!" he hears from outside. The dog barks a few times. "That's what I'm talking about, Piano Man!"

Billy returns to the window. "What do you think?"

"I think I'll take that over some old white lady any day. I'll swing by next week with some more requests. Maybe Jay-Z. Need some hip-hop in this neighborhood."

When the man and his dog are gone, Billy lets his eyes linger on his view of Fells Point. By next week he'll be gone, of course. As far as goodbyes go, however, this isn't so bad, because Margot is there at the Steinway. She pushes her sleeves up over her elbows and looks at the keys like she's trying to decide what to play.

"I know I said it before, but you really do look great in that hat."

She touches the bill. "It's kind of itchy, but I like that it's like I'm hiding."

He sits again and takes the cap off her head, sets it on the Steinway. "Why would you want to hide, though?"

She doesn't respond, but he gets it. The world hasn't seen her in a long time, and that's probably not an accident. There's a red line across her forehead from the cap rubbing against her skin, and he kisses her there. The small overnight bag she brought sits by the door next to their shoes, and he's not sure what to make of it.

"You like the Stones, huh?" she says.

"Well yeah," he says. "Who doesn't?"

"'She's a Rainbow' is pretty good," she says. "I like this one, too."

Billy sometimes does a warm-up exercise during lessons. He and a student will take turns playing for each other, and they'll see how many notes it takes to name the song. Despite having a good ear, it sometimes takes Billy a while. Songs out of context with no lyrics, even great ones, have an elusive quality, like seeing someone you know in a crowd and not quite remembering their name. That's not the case now, though. He recognizes "Let's Spend the Night Together" right away. "Yeah," he says. "A classic."

She doesn't play the whole thing, just the intro. She plays it again.

"People always want you to pick, right?" he says. "Beatles or Stones. Can't we just all agree that they both changed the world? Why do we have to—"

Margot starts the song again, louder this time, cutting him off. She's not looking at the keys now; she's looking at him.

"Oh," he says.

CHAPTER 26

Margot can't believe she did that, the Stones thing.

She can practically hear Poppy in her head. *Who, even, are you, Margot Hammer?*

She blames the kiss cam. You wouldn't think kissing someone in front of thousands of people on a jumbotron would feel intimate, but it did.

The anatomy of a kiss: two people lean in, mouths touch, eyes close, lips part just barely. All those things happened, like always. Other things happened, too, though, like a joyful feeling in Margot's chest, like that sensation right before you laugh. She reached for his hand and found it near his lap just as his other hand took her by the chin. Based on the kisses before theirs on the screen, Margot supposes it was just meant to be a peck. Their kiss, though, lasted, like neither was quite ready for it to end.

People kept cheering even after the game started again. Margot—flushed still, heart racing—thought, *I'm going to sleep with him.*

It was the second time in her life she'd felt this way with such certainty. The first time had been the night she met Lawson at a Super Bowl party on the immense penthouse terrace of an obscene luxury apartment building in Battery Park owned by a tech mogul. Three of the four Burnt Flowers were there, forty stories up. Jenny had ditched at the last second, claiming a migraine. Nikki was inside at the bar pretending to know the first thing about football, so Anna and Margot, the band's rhythm section, stood near a glowing space heater at the edge of the terrace.

"Is this caviar?" asked Anna.

They assessed the small pile of gunk on Anna's appetizer plate. A cigarette hung from Anna's lips.

"Maybe," said Margot. "Is it good?"

"I don't think that's the point with caviar," said Anna, and they gave each other little upward nods that said, *Can you believe this shit?* Their first album had come out that summer and they were the hottest new band on the planet. They were rock stars.

"Okay, don't be a total spaz and turn and look," said Anna, "but, you know who Lawson Daniels is, right?"

"The actor?"

"Yeah, dum-dum, the actor. British. Scorching hot. He's . . . well, he's staring at you."

"What? Where?"

Margot has never been good at the whole "don't turn and look" thing, so, after turning and looking, she saw Lawson Daniels smiling at her from beneath a different glowing space heater.

Like Margot, Lawson was in his early twenties then—famous, but newly so. His first movie, a little British heist called *Piccadilly Hustle,* had been an indie hit. He was a little too skinny. His teeth weren't capped yet. He was dressed a notch too casually for the party, and his leather jacket was too big for him. But he was still handsome enough to make her swear aloud the first time she laid eyes on him. "Goddamn."

"Uh-oh," said Anna. "And now he's coming over."

Lawson was en route, his eyes locked on Margot as he weaved

around people. Anna made a quick exit. "I'm gonna ditch the fish eggs and get some of those little hot dogs. Good luck, babe."

She had five seconds to prepare herself. She decided to feign obliviousness, as if she had no idea that a beautiful actor was bee-lining for her.

Lawson leaned against the railing, smiled. "Evening, love."

No one had ever called Margot "love" before. The effect was like being on an airplane that suddenly loses altitude. "Hey," she said.

"I'm Lawson."

She'd recently discovered something odd about being famous. Even when everyone in the room knows exactly who everyone else is, you're still expected to introduce yourself. So she played along and said her name, and they stood looking out over the terrace. A couple in an apartment across the street ate dinner. Lawson took a sip of his beer and smiled at the cold, blinking city. "Remember when we used to have to look up at all these fancy buildings?" he asked.

He didn't know her, but he knew enough to know that a view like that was as new to her as it was to him. They were married six months later.

Billy asks now if he should draw the shade. "I should, right? Duh. The whole neighborhood can see in here."

He gets up off the piano bench and pulls the gauzy thing down over the window, then he stands like he's not sure what to do next. His anxiety is like moths fluttering around his head. Margot gets it. Years ago, late into the night on that Super Bowl Sunday, Margot was matter-of-fact about being in a cab with Lawson as they sped through the city toward his apartment. She was impossibly young, and his hands were on her body, and they felt amazing. He whispered sexy things into her hair and kissed her earlobe as the poor driver looked at the road ahead. She slept with Lawson that night because she wanted to. That's about as much thought as she gave it. Now, though, sex is a minefield, and she finds that she, too, is nervous.

"Sorry," she says. "I don't normally do things like that."

"Like what?"

"Ask men to sleep with me via piano."

Billy looks at the closed shade. He pokes the drawstring, watches it swing.

"And now that I have, I don't know if I'm . . ."

"Yeah," says Billy. "I understand."

"Maybe we can wait?"

Billy tells her that they can definitely wait—that he isn't going anywhere.

"I got carried away," she says. "The kissing thing, at the game. That was really nice."

"Can I . . . ?" he asks.

She slides over, and he plays the intro she just played. He fumbles a few notes and plays it again. "In fairness, we don't technically know if this song is about sex."

Margot touches middle C. "No, it definitely is."

"Okay, yeah, probably. But music is interpretive, right? Maybe for us it can be about kissing again and then going to sleep. I assume you have pajamas in there, right?"

Margot looks at her bag. "You want to kiss me and then go to sleep?"

He slides closer. "Well, it sounds weird when you say it like that," he says. "Listen, I know you don't know me that well. But if someone had asked me six hours ago if I wanted to play the piano with Margot Hammer tonight, make out a little, then have a slumber party, I would've definitely been down with it."

Well, shit, Margot thinks. Because that's the hottest thing anyone's said to her in a decade.

He holds her chin again, which must be something he does when he kisses. She likes it, because it's nice sometimes to be gently guided. That joyful feeling again. Heat radiates at the center of her chest. This isn't a kiss. This is a big, soft sledgehammer. He eases her head up and kisses her jawline, then her throat, then her lips again, and she whispers that it's different without a crowd present, and he tells her that if she wants, he'll go see if that Stevie Wonder guy and his dog want to come over and watch, and she laughs. When was the last time she laughed—genuinely? Margot can't remember.

"Okay," he says. "You should probably get some sleep. You've got a big day tomorrow."

"I do?"

"Yeah, you're helping me move."

Margot assumes he didn't just say what it sounded like he said. She'll ask him a clarifying question later. It doesn't matter now, though, because she wants to kiss him again.

CHAPTER 27

The time between Margot playing the beginning of "Let's Spend the Night Together" and Margot deciding that she didn't want to actually spend the night together—at least not in the Mick Jagger sense—couldn't have been more than thirty seconds. Still, for Billy, it was quite a ride. Sudden elation, obviously, like stumbling into dumb luck. That was trumped quickly, though, by a crashing wave of anxiety. Then, ultimately, he felt relieved because he wanted to wait, too.

Sleeping with Margot would've felt too fast. Not in a puritan way. We're done saving ourselves when we're in our forties. It would've felt too fast because Billy still hadn't wrapped his head around the fact that she was here in the first place, in Baltimore, in his apartment. For that he needed a minute.

And now she's quietly breathing beside him.

A bed is such a different thing when there's someone else in it with you—like a whole other structure entirely. For starters, the topography is off. It's a fine-enough mattress, but their combined weight creates the slightest dip in the middle, giving him the sensation that he's being drawn to her physically. Secondly, her warmth is unignorable. It practically hums.

"Are you asleep?" she whispers.

Billy laughs, because he couldn't be further from asleep. If asleep is the sun, Billy is Pluto, or some other demoted celestial object, hurtling through darkness. "Well, I was," he says. "Thanks a lot."

They roll at the same time, facing each other. The lights are off, but it's not fully dark because of Fells Point outside. Margot is wearing a plain, threadbare T-shirt and lounging pants. It's not sexy but also incredibly sexy in that way that anything can be sexy in the right context. Her bare foot brushes his shin.

"I'm not scared of sex," she says.

They're close enough that her breath is warm. It smells like toothpaste—*his* toothpaste, because she packed her toothbrush but not toothpaste.

"Okay," he says. "You can be, though. Sex is kind of scary. Nobody talks about that."

"You had a crush on me when we were young, right?"

This has been established. Still, Billy is embarrassed. "I did."

"Why?"

"I . . ." he says.

She watches him while he thinks. It's a difficult question to answer.

"You liked how I played?" she asks.

"That was part of it," he says. "But it wasn't just that. I had a crush on . . . on *you*."

"You were attracted to me?"

"Of course."

Margot asks him to close his eyes. He asks her why and she tells him to just do it. It's a vulnerable feeling to be this close to someone you can't see.

"When did you start having a crush on me?" she asks.

"The first time I saw you."

"When was that?"

"That first *SNL* performance, I think. Yeah, definitely then."

"Right," she says. "I was nervous. We all were. Anna puked before the show."

Billy doesn't know if having his eyes closed means that he's not supposed to touch her—the rules aren't clear here. He chances it, though, and pushes through a tangle of comforter to find her hip. His eyes are still closed. "You didn't seem nervous."

"Yeah? Okay, well, think of what I looked like then."

They played "Power Pink," then a song called "On the Run." She wore a tight black T-shirt. Her hair was up for the first song, then down and wild for the second. His mind quickly wanders to other stored imagery. *Rolling Stone* spreads, maybe a dozen TV performances, album art, promotional materials, tabloids, Margot being carried by a movie star.

"Okay, open up." She's looking directly at him. "See. I'm not that person anymore."

"What do you mean?"

"When you had a crush on me. I'm not saying I was ever hot, like Nikki. But I was professionally lit. Makeup experts spent hours on me, tending to my appearance. And I was young. I'm not now. I'm . . . *this*."

She's mostly covered by his comforter. If she was wearing makeup before, she wiped it off before bed, and she's not lit—professionally or otherwise. "I like this, though," he says. "Very much."

She shows him the inside of her arm. "My tattoos are faded."

"They look great."

"And I'm shorter than I was," she says.

"Really?"

"I was five-three forever. I had a physical a few months ago. Five-two-and-a-half. I made them measure me three times. Has that not happened to you?"

"I haven't checked," he says. "I'm probably shorter, too, so maybe it evens out."

Margot pushes the comforter down, just below her knees. "I haven't had my clothes off in front of someone in—"

"I have my mom's legs," Billy says.

"Your mom's legs?"

"Yeah," he says. "From the waist up, I'm normal looking, right? But my mom's got these stumpy little legs. I got them from her. I've always been sensitive about them. See?"

"They are kinda short," she says. "Not bad, though."

"Thanks."

"I get it," she says. "I got my mom's ankles?"

"Really? Let's see."

Margot kicks the comforter down to the foot of the bed. She pulls the left hem of her lounging pants up and rolls her foot at the ankle. "See? Thick, right? That's why I always wear boots. They're kick-ass, obviously. But cankle camouflage, too."

"Stop it," he says. "They're lovely."

When she puts her leg back down, she rests it on his, and it's warm beneath the loungy fabric. "What else is wrong with you?" she asks.

"My hair is thinning."

She squints at his forehead. "It doesn't look like—"

"No, not there." He shows her the crown of his head, and she runs her hand over it.

"Okay, yeah, a little."

"The lady that cuts it says she can hide it for a few more years. All bets are off after that, though."

"I find grays sometimes," she says. "I just yank the fuckers."

He goes to her hip again, pulls her closer. "Don't even get me started on my stomach," he says. "My twenties, it was good. Thirties, decent. I even had one of those V things for a while. Now it's more of a U. I have a U-shaped stomach."

Margot smiles, and Billy wants to kiss her again. He will soon, he's nearly certain, but for now he's enjoying this part. This is foreplay in your forties: pointing out all the things you don't like about yourself and just going with it. She rolls onto her back and slides her T-shirt up, revealing the pale skin from the bottom of her ribs to the waistband of her pants. "Mine's held up pretty well," she says. "I actually still kind of like it."

Billy swallows and then touches her there. She sighs, a sound like *hmm,* that he could listen to all night.

"How long has it been since I said we should wait?" she asks.

Billy consults his digital alarm clock, which is among the only electrical devices in his apartment that are still plugged in. "About an hour and a half."

"Yeah," she says. "That's long enough."

CHAPTER 28

Robyn Frazier considers herself a social media voyeur. Caleb called her that once, and she liked it, despite it sounding creepy. The idea is that while she *has* social media accounts, she never actually posts anything. Instead, she uses them to keep up with her friends and relatives, liking photos of their dogs and children and birthday cakes. She's glad the people in her life post these things because it gives her something to look at while she waits for hair appointments or sits in traffic jams, but she has absolutely no interest in putting herself out there online in any way. Who cares what her salad looks like?

Consequently, the algorithms keep Robyn at a distance, showing her only the tips of icebergs—the surfaces of rabbit holes. Which is why Robyn only knows the basics about the Margot Hammer Incident. Some of her friends have texted her about it.

Is this really Billy?

That's Caleb's dad, right?

Seeing the shots of Billy all moon-faced next to the drummer made her laugh at first. She imagined him making a fool of himself trying to talk to her. But then she remembered how annoyed she used to be at his Margot Hammer crush. It wasn't like Robyn hadn't had her own music crushes. She'd been quietly in love with Jack White, for example, and Justin Timberlake *still* does things to her insides. The thing that irked her was that Billy really liked Margot Hammer—as a person and an artist. If he'd wanted to grind up against the Spice Girls like some horny idiot, that would've been one thing. Expected, even. But seeing him with his big earphones on air drumming to her music had been a sore spot. Plus . . . well, Margot Hammer wasn't even that pretty.

That's a tremendously bitchy thing to think, Robyn knows. Sure, Margot Hammer was a rock star, which came with some built-in appeal. The whole mousy, regular-girl-turned-rocker thing was annoying, though, and frankly, played out. The fact that she'd been married to Lawson Daniels of all people was and remains a complete mystery. Whatever, though . . . celebrities are weird.

She's standing at her kitchen sink now, eating a low-fat English muffin, waiting for Billy and his piano to arrive. The window overlooks the driveway and the front door to the little guest apartment over their garage. Things are starting to turn green again, flowers blooming. Springtime in Baltimore. A male cardinal sits on the backboard of Caleb's basketball hoop, shouting into the sky, looking for a girlfriend.

"Honestly, though, I just think this whole thing is weird. The entire concept of this. Weird." Aaron is at the kitchen table reading *The Wall Street Journal* on his tablet.

"Your position has been noted," says Robyn. "You're just pissed because I made you move your Peloton."

"A little, yeah, but that's not all," he says. "I get that this is what Caleb wants. I do. But Caleb's eighteen. If we did everything eighteen-year-olds want, the world would spin out of control."

She finishes as much as she's going to eat of her muffin and drops the rest into the garbage disposal. "Mm-hm," she says.

"You know I like Billy," Aaron says. "*Everybody* likes Billy. It's just . . ."

Her husband is searching for a word other than *weird*, which he's dramatically overused these past two weeks. A female cardinal lands on the rim of the hoop outside and chirps up at the male. *Oh, good for you two*, she thinks as both birds dart away.

Robyn is willing to concede, in her own head at least, that her ex-boyfriend and the father of her child moving into the room above their garage might seem odd, in theory. But . . . it's Billy. It's fine. Caleb asked for this, and when he did, she could tell by the look on his face that he really wanted her to say yes, so that's what she did.

Robyn doesn't say any of this, because marriage is exhausting enough without having to replay the same conversations on a loop.

"Speaking of eighteen-year-olds," Aaron says, "I take it we haven't heard from Stanford."

"Cay said no email yet."

Aaron sets his iPad on the table. "You hear Justin and Shin-Soo got into Yale and Penn?"

She did; their mothers told her, and Robyn wishes there were boxes you could tick on college applications next to the words "Good Kid," because Caleb is such a good kid. She wants him to get into Stanford for all the obvious reasons. She also wants him to get in because she knows that he wants to get in. She's caught him looking at the school's website a hundred times, the way she imagines other moms catch their sons sneaking onto the Victoria's Secret homepage. Parenthood was easier when he was little. She could just tell him what to do and what to want. Now she's expected to stand by and watch as he wanders toward something she knows he'll regret.

"Is he up yet?" Aaron asks.

"Yes," she says. "He said he'll help you and Billy move Billy's stuff in."

Aaron laughs and shakes his head. "Who's that you got moving in above the garage, Aaron?" he says, changing his voice to sound like someone else. "Oh, that guy? Just the wife's baby daddy. No big deal."

"We're too old to say *baby daddy*."

"We are, aren't we?" says Aaron. "When did that happen? It's a good expression." He stands now and does some halfhearted arm stretches, preparing himself for a rare bit of manual labor. "Well, at least we don't have to move that goddamn piano. That thing would kill us all."

Robyn enjoys the ridiculous image of it: Billy, Aaron, and her beanpole of a son hoisting a piano. Just then, the wood floor beneath her feet shakes, and a moving truck rumbles up the driveway. Calvert Piano Movers, Inc.

Aaron calls up the stairs. "Cay! It's go time, buddy! Rock and roll!"

Outside, three giant men hop out of the truck. A few seconds later, Billy's old Mercedes pulls up beside them towing a U-Haul trailer. Robyn goes to the fridge for the Gatorades she bought for everyone.

"Um, Rob?" says Aaron.

She chose orange Gatorade because it's Caleb's favorite. Maybe she'll order some pizza later. "Hmm?" she asks.

"You know all that stuff about Billy meeting Margot Hammer a few weeks ago?"

"Yeah. What about it?"

Aaron leans close to the glass. "She's . . . um. I'm pretty sure she's standing in our driveway."

CHAPTER 29

Turns out Billy *did* say what Margot thought he said last night. He's moving. Today. Right now, in fact. There's nothing weird about that. People move. It's *where* he's moving that she still doesn't fully understand.

They're in his car, which is towing a small U-Haul trailer. His Mercedes reminds Margot so much of her mom and dad's ancient Volvo station wagon that she feels like she's traveled back in time as Billy weaves his way across the city through narrow, potholed streets. She thinks of her first drum kit sliding around in the back on their way home from the thrift store. Her mom let her hold the sticks, which she used to smack away at the back of the driver's seat. Her dad smiled in the rearview mirror. "Don't know if you know what you're doing, Margie, but that sounds pretty good to me."

The leather interior of Billy's car—the Champagne Super-nova—is faded, cracked in spots like an old couch. The floormats are as thick as carpet, and the whole vehicle smells like Billy. She noticed it when he opened the door for her earlier—a big whiff of him—and she's annoyed with herself for letting it turn her brain to fog. Having sex this morning probably contributed to that, too.

Margot again imagines her daughter's voice in her head. *Last night* and *this morning? Shit, Mum. Get it.*

They woke in their underwear. Billy put on some music and climbed back into bed beside her. He ran his fingertip up and down the drumstick tattoo on her left arm while he went on about the tricks to making the espresso machine work. Something about holding a lever and not putting in too much milk. She hardly listened because it felt so good to be touched like that, like the nerves on the surface of her skin were connected to every other nerve in her body. Eventually she pulled him on top of her.

"Oh, yeah, okay then," he said.

They stop at a red light. Two teenage boys step into the intersection with squeegees. One sprays blue liquid on the windshield while the other wipes, smiling at Margot.

"Hey, guys," says Billy through his open window. "Careful. It's a classic."

"We gotcha, man."

He gives them a few dollars and they hustle off to the next car.

"So, *where* are we going again?" she asks. "Where does . . . *she* live?"

"A neighborhood called Roland Park. Not quite the burbs, but close. Nice place."

No amount of Billy-scented European leather, no number of morning-time orgasms, could make her dimwitted enough to not find this strange. "So, she's . . . your son's mom?"

"Mm-hm. Robyn. You'll like her. Wound a little tight, but she's great."

"And you're moving in with her . . . above the . . . garage?"

"Not moving in," he says. "Just staying awhile. It's her and her husband's place. You'll like Aaron, too. He looks a little like the murderer in *American Psycho,* but super nice guy."

"You're all . . . friends?"

Billy steers around a pothole the size of a small bathtub and smiles—finally, it seems, picking up on the long pauses between key words. "Sounds weird, right?"

"Maybe a little." *Or maybe a fucking lot.*

"I know. It's not, though. It was Caleb's idea. We've never lived together in his lifetime, Robyn and me. I think he just wants that for a little while, even if I'm on the other side of the driveway. But seriously, it's nothing. Rob and I are friends—like, partners, like in Caleb, Incorporated. That's all. It's nothing."

Margot looks through the windshield. One of the squeegee boys missed a spot—a single, anxiety-inducing line of blue liquid spreading in the breeze. He called her Rob, not Robyn, just now. She noticed that. She noticed, too, that he said "nothing" twice, and she imagines the utter back-assed absurdity of moving into one of Lawson's pool houses.

Oh, hi, Margot, Willa Knight says, looking up from a downward goddamn dog while she does yoga in a bikini. *You want a Vitaminwater? This is nothing, right? Nothing!*

They drive along a highway called 83. They catch up to the moving truck that's hauling the Steinway and follow it onto an exit. Then they move slowly through a tree-lined neighborhood with bike lanes and cozy-looking midsize homes. Billy was right when he said it wasn't quite the suburbs. The houses sit close together, and the streets are lined with cars and bus shelters. There are Black Lives Matter signs and Orioles flags and bumper stickers with crabs on them, and joggers and dogwalkers.

"Just up here a bit," he says.

Maybe Margot's being unnecessarily dire. She does that sometimes. As they pass a coffee shop and a little market called Eddie's, Poppy's voice starts up again.

What? You're worried about some boring lady in the sorta burbs? She probably wears mum jeans and crochets throw pillows with little inspirational messages on them. Stop it. You're Margot fucking Hammer!

Which is true, she is. Earlier, in bed—Margot still naked but wrapped in sheets, Billy holding a cup of espresso—he smiled, happy and warm beside her. "I'm so glad you came back," he said.

She probably has nothing to worry about. Families have their own rules. Especially broken families. Just because Margot and Lawson aren't friends—far from it; they haven't spoken in years—that doesn't mean Billy and this Robyn woman can't be on good terms.

The moving truck turns on its blinker and slows. "Okay," Billy says. "Here we go."

It's one of the nicest houses on the street—big, but not a mansion—nestled among a bunch of steadily blooming trees. It's green with bright white shutters. A ten-speed bike leans against the pole of a basketball hoop. Birds watch them from branches, then scatter when the moving guys jump out of the truck. You'd have to drive an hour to find a place like this outside of Manhattan.

Billy shifts to park. "Caleb's gonna freak when he sees you, by the way."

Margot steps out of the car and immediately spies the place above the garage. It's more of a miniature house than an apartment: two big windows and a red door. Yesterday, she packed an overnight bag and hopped on a train heading south like a girl in a country song. Now she's here. She doesn't know why, exactly, but she knows that she doesn't want to leave. Not yet.

The front door of the main house opens. That door is red, also. A man wearing sneakers and a T-shirt steps out. Billy was right. He's eighties-killer handsome—tall, perfect hair. He shakes his head, miming disbelief. "Hey, Billy," he says. "And hello there . . . Margot Hammer?"

Margot is about to say hello back, but then a woman appears holding Gatorades. Sometimes dire thinking is best, because, of course, this is Robyn—*Rob*—and she's very, very pretty.

The window above the front door opens and Caleb sticks half his long body out of it. "Dad! Holy shit!"

Margot feels Billy's hand on her lower back. "Cay, come on. No need to swear."

Part 3

ACTUALLY, I LIKE IT

CHAPTER 30

The stunt car pitches right, then left, then shimmies more than any real car ever would, like it's about to explode. Lawson Daniels jams his foot down on the gas pedal, which is connected to nothing, then he pretends to be shoved back in his seat by raw horsepower. *Acting!* he thinks. He shifts from third to fourth gear. He checks the rearview mirror, holds for two beats, then delivers the line.

"Good luck, you stupid motherfuckers."

There was a whole discussion about "stupid motherfuckers." An R rating versus PG-13 matters—there's a whole box-office calculation. Lawson did fifteen takes this morning saying, "dumb bastards," then twelve before lunch with "dumbass bitches," which made absolutely zero sense and was a complete waste of everyone's time.

"Dumbass bitches?" he asked earlier as the crew stood watching, hands on hips. "I've never heard a British person say that in my bloody life."

"Maybe just do it," replied Hugh Ward, the childlike director. "Could be good for a laugh, yeah?"

"Is this a comedy, though?"

Hugh didn't know and didn't hide that fact. This is his first feature. His reel to date is entirely made up of student films and Adidas commercials. "We'll sort all that in post, mate. But for now, let's think in terms of action-comedy, but with an edge."

Hard turn now. More acting. Jerk the wheel, grimace, grunt like it hurts. Hold the wheel, straighten. Another shimmy like he's speeding over debris. Sound will be added later—debris, too. Gas pedal again. Line: "Yep, that's what I thought. Cheers."

For fuck's sake, he thinks.

Lawson is trying to remember who's chasing his character, exactly. Is it the drug dealers or the Russian mafia blokes? He's always prided himself on a certain level of engaged professionalism, but he's found his attention drifting these last few weeks of shooting. More flubs than usual. More clarifying questions to the assistant director, Harry, who's somehow even younger looking than the director. Lawson committed to this nonsense before the Oscar nom, now he feels like the prince of bloody Wales cutting the ribbon at a new Sainsbury's in Liverpool.

"Annnnd cut!" shouts Hugh. "Fantastic, mate! That's a shot for the trailer, for sure." Hugh is very concerned about the teaser trailer, which is due next week, even though there's still a month of shooting left.

After a loud buzz, the hydraulic arm holding the silver Porsche 911 relaxes, and the stunt car settles, like something in an amusement park.

"That's it, then?" Lawson asks. "Good? We've got it? Please say yes."

Hugh sticks his head in the driver's-side window. "Yeah, yeah," he says. "But no. I'm thinking maybe we go head on. Do a few like that. You staring down the audience. The audience staring you down. Fuck the fourth wall. Effective, right? Especially for IMAX."

Lawson notes the rig of cameras—seven by his count—all set

and focused for a day of profile shots. Changing and relighting will take hours. "Bloody kettle better be on, then," he says.

"'Course, mate," says Hugh. "We brought England with us, remember?"

The car doors don't open properly, because they aren't real, so Lawson contorts himself into a pull-up and climbs out the sunroof.

"Take five," Harry shouts into his megaphone, and the set takes a collective breath.

Lawson stretches, then walks across the sound stage. It's a dull cement building in Los Angeles, like an airplane hangar, but movie magic will turn it into the leafy British countryside soon enough.

"Tanya, can we get Lawson a bit of a touch-up?" Harry shouts.

Tanya springs to action and starts rolling her makeup cart toward him. Lawson points to the tea station that the crew set up for him, Hugh, and Harry, who are the only Brits on set. "Teatime, love," he says.

Tanya redirects to the plush leather chair that's written into Lawson's contract.

"How do I look?" he asks.

Tanya tilts her head, squints her left eye, chews her gum. These are lovely affectations—among the few highlights of this preposterous project. "Little ashy," she says. "Forehead's shiny, too. Especially that last take."

"Can't have that, now, can we?"

An assistant whose name Lawson can't remember—Trig, possibly Trey—hands him a cup of tea and a small stack of Hobnob biscuits on a dish.

"Interest you in a cup, Tan?" Lawson asks.

Tanya makes a disgusted face—their little inside joke. She guzzles the battery acid that is Diet Pepsi all day but turns her nose up at tea. He sips, and she works his skin with tickly little brushes, and Lawson does his best to ignore the makeup artist's breasts, which are inches from his face behind a thin layer of cotton. Tanya is older than Willa Knight but younger than Lawson, and he briefly imagines a simpler life with a gum-chewing makeup artist from Malibu. Lawson does this: he falls carelessly in love with nonactors on set. He's not sure why, maybe because it's less complicated than falling in love with his costars, which is also something he does. Tanya stands on her toes and bites her lower lip as she smooths and pats down Lawson's hair.

Maybe just have a seat right here then, love, he thinks but doesn't say. Instead, he redirects. "Can I ask you something?"

Tanya says, "Hmm?"

"You ever been to Baltimore?"

"Maryland?" Tanya's nose crinkles. "No, why?"

"I'm having the damnedest time finding anyone who has."

"I think it's near D.C. I don't know the East Coast very well."

Then Lawson does something he's done often recently: he takes out his mobile so he can digitally spy on his ex-wife.

Quite the journey Mar has been on of late. Sweet at first—that little concert with the amateurs in the pub. The look on her face as she drummed was like some surgical deep dive into Lawson's long-term memory. Brow furrowed, jaw clenched. And, of course, that hair falling across those eyes.

"Well, look at you, Mar," he whispered the first time he watched it; then, again, the twentieth time he watched it. This was back in London. The production for *Car Chase* hadn't shifted to L.A. yet. Yes, the movie is called *Car Chase,* because they didn't even try coming up with a proper title for this floating turd.

It's not as if Margot hasn't come up from time to time over the years, what with them sharing a child and her being one of the most celebrated drummers of her era. He'll hear a Burnt Flowers song on the radio or playing in some posh shop. He watched her alongside Nikki and the other two on that Netflix documentary a fortnight ago. He sees her frowny face in his record collection back in the London flat. These new videos, though, have affected him more than that old rubbish. The reason, he supposes, is that this is the *real* Mar, not some past version. And, well, real Margot Hammer looks quite fit.

He glances over Tanya's shoulder at the messy set—green screens, a carved-out shell of a Porsche. What would Margie think of all this buffoonery?

Didn't you used to do Shakespeare?

Easy, love. A few for the studio, then a few for me. That's the game.

Sounds like a dumb game.

"Close your eyes for me a sec," says Tanya.

Lawson does, and she powders his eyelids. "As long as I'm asking questions." He holds his phone out. There's a shot from *HypeReport* of Margot and Billy at an outdoor restaurant. They're holding hands at the middle of the table, talking. "What do you think of this bloke? Honest opinion."

Tanya tilts her head, more gum chewing. "Oh yeah, I saw this one. They're cute."

"Cute?"

"They work, you know," says Tanya. "They're a good couple."

Lawson holds his phone closer to his face. Mar is smiling, and he very much doesn't like that, because Margot Hammer doesn't bloody smile. "What do you think of *him*, though? Mr. Pasty Face here?"

Tanya sets her brushes down, gives his phone a good look.

"Go on then," says Lawson. "Suspense is killing me, love."

"Well, he's not handsome. Not *handsome* handsome. But he has an appeal."

"An appeal?"

"*I* think so," she says. "Good for her, if you ask me. Honestly, I'm rooting for them."

"Like a football club?" His eyes are open again, and he sees that Tanya is blushing. "Shall I have Harry get you a Team Margot shirt?"

"Don't tease." She touches his arm. Lawson is secretly mad at her now, though, so he doesn't allow himself to enjoy it. Falling out of love with crew members is even easier than falling in love with them, he's found.

"He seems like a nice person," Tanya says. "And . . ."

"And?"

"She looks happy."

Lawson has been thinking about the Grammys lately. You see a picture of yourself a million times on telly and in magazines and it sticks with you. He can still feel the weight of Mar slung over his shoulder. He remembers the way she slapped at the back of his head while the cameras popped off like machine-gun fire. He didn't see her actual smile until later when the photograph went everywhere. He could somehow feel it, though, the warmth of her happiness radiating down from above.

"Put me down, you dickhead!" She was laughing, though, her face a burst of bloody sunshine. He couldn't believe some twat from *Us Weekly* last week had the nerve to put their photo—*the* photo—next to a new one of her with . . . him. This Billy something-or-other.

Life is a series of fuckups. When you're rich and famous, the lion's share of those fuckups simply evaporate into the ether—forgiven, forgotten, replaced by public triumphs and shrewd management. Some fuckups linger, though, like the dog's breakfast that he made of his marriage to Margie.

"Have you always categorized your divorce as a fuckup, Lawson, or is this a new realization? As in, new since your former wife's reemergence?"

His therapist, Dr. Winston, asked him this yesterday in a video telesession.

Whatever, mate, the chronology is moot as far as he's concerned. Call him old-fashioned, but Lawson is a firm believer in epiphanies, and nothing crystallizes regret like seeing someone you made so miserable look so happy.

He checks himself in the mirror mounted to Tanya's cart. "All right, enough about all that," he says. "How do I look? Sorted?"

Tanya smiles. "Perfect once again."

He winks, bored now with her and this banter. "Off you go. I need to ring my daughter."

Tanya wheels away to go eat grapes at the craft-services table, and Lawson taps Poppy's name on his mobile screen. It rings a few times.

"Hello, Dad."

"Pop Star!" he says.

"Hmm," Poppy says. "I guess I like that one better than Popcorn."

"I know you do, love. See, I listen quite well."

"Mm-hm. If you say so."

Lawson smiles. He loves the sound of her voice, how her accent exists between two places, like coordinates plotted over the Atlantic Ocean. "How are things up in San Fran, then? They're treating you well? You don't need me to bust anyone up for you? I can do that, you know. I'm famous and powerful, and I'm quite good at pretend fighting."

He can hear her typing. His daughter is in a bloody office, of all things—in something called a cube.

"So, how's the starlet?" she asks.

"Be nice, now," he says. "Willa sends her love."

"I'm sure she does," says Poppy. "So, what's up, Dad? I have a meeting in six minutes. I'm presenting something."

Often, when they talk, Poppy begins by setting parameters.

"Righto. Just wanted to ask, you keeping track of this business with your mum?"

The space between them goes silent. "What do you mean?"

"This American chap. In Balti-wherever, which I've recently learnt is somewhere near Washington, D.C. Just seeing if everything's on the up-and-up. The Internet and all. You can never tell what's what, exactly."

"She's fine," says Poppy. "More than fine. She's . . . Dad, she's good."

"So, it's real, then, this thing?"

Another silence. Lawson wishes he'd called on FaceTime so he could see her expression. "Dad, I'm gonna ask a favor, okay?"

"Anything, darling."

"Just . . . just leave her alone."

Fifty feet away, three cameramen have started disassembling the machinery attached to the fake Porsche. "Bit harsh, love," he says. "I'm just trying to make sure—"

"Come on, Dad," she says. "Don't screw this up for her. Okay?"

CHAPTER 31

Margot thinks about that research assistant from Netflix again—that kid who apparently lives rent free in her head.

"What, um, exactly have you been up to since Burnt Flowers broke up?"

When he asked her that, Margot wanted to know his address so she could go there and slap him across his stupid face. The question had pissed her off for two reasons. First, although it was a reasonable question, there were about a dozen different ways he could've asked it that would've sounded less accusatory. Second, and more importantly, it pissed her off because she had no idea how to answer it without sounding like . . . well, the Unabomber.

Margot forgives him now, though, whatever his name is, because she keeps imagining him asking her a slightly different version of the same question. *What, um, exactly have you been up to since you got to Baltimore?* Her answer, this time, would sound like a fantasy camp for wayward adults. Her answer, this time, would sound like bliss.

When Billy's not giving lessons, they go places together. They've been to a few small concerts at a place called the 8x10. At each show, Billy and Margot stood together at the back of the cramped club and were the oldest people in attendance by a long shot. They've been to two more Orioles games. Once it was just the two of them; the other time Caleb came, too. Clancy the beer vendor complimented her Orioles cap both times and officially gave her permission to call him Fancy Clancy. They've been to Charm City Rocks a few times, too, mostly to see Patty and Grady and to hang out with Gustavo across the street and eat pretzels. Gustavo is considering naming a special pretzel after her, and Grady recently upgraded the lightbulbs above the Wall of Fame to a higher wattage so people can see her signature better.

"It's more noticeable this way," Grady proudly told her. "Plus, it gives the wall some legitimacy, you know. Some real star power."

Billy took her out for crabs the other night. Margot had no idea what she was getting into. She had to use a special little mallet and wear a bib like a toddler. The whole thing had been funny and messy and gross, because crabs are really just giant sea bugs, but it was an experience.

She walks to Eddie's, the little market she saw that first day in Roland Park, nearly every day and hangs out at the coffee shop next door for hours on end. When dogs approach her, she pets them, and when people approach her, she signs things for them. A barista she sees often brought one of her dad's old concert T-shirts for her to sign. Two high school kids asked her to autograph a CD for their music teacher. The dilapidated jewel case practically crumbled in Margot's hands, like a shell washed up on the beach.

On their way out of a movie on Saturday evening, they stopped to watch Daquan, the drummer kid down the street from Charm City Rocks. Daquan smiled and invited her to take over. A small crowd gathered as he gave her a brief tutorial on which buckets made what sounds. She played for a few minutes, which, of course, ended up all over YouTube and Instagram. Margot didn't play anything specific—just a couple of drum loops she made up on the spot—but she enjoyed it very much. Drums, buckets, whatever, it feels incredible to play music again.

This morning, Margot and Billy took a ride up north in the Champagne Supernova. A few minutes outside the city, the land opens into acreages, and things turn hillier than she would've imagined. They parked and then hiked for about a half an hour until they came to a white picket fence outside an enormous horse farm.

"We're here," Billy said.

"Where?" she asked. "This isn't where you murder me, is it?"

"No, not yet," he said. "I'm saving that for later. I wanna show you something."

"What?"

"A cow," Billy said.

"You brought me here to show me a cow?" she asked.

"Not just any cow."

They stood for a few more minutes eating protein bars and sipping the water they'd brought. For a while, nothing but mosquitoes showed up, but Billy told Margot to be patient. Then, finally, a few horses trotted out from a big barn. Among them was a lone brown cow doing its best to keep up.

"There she is," said Billy.

"Oh wow," said Margot. "I don't think I've ever seen a cow run."

Billy rested one foot on the lower rung of the fence. "She's famous," he said. "Well, locally, anyway. She escaped from a slaughterhouse somewhere in the Midwest a couple years ago. Just bolted, apparently. Found a gap in the fence and made a run for it. Some hedge-fund guy found out about it and bought her. Now she lives here."

Margot watched, touched by the animal's story. She was skinny for a cow and had pretty white markings across her wide red-brown face. "Do you think she thinks she's a horse?" Margot asked.

Billy smiled. "Who cares? Look how happy she is."

When they got back to the apartment an hour ago, they had daytime sex like a couple of dumb, carefree twentysomethings. And now they're relaxing in bed. Margot is on her stomach, nearly dozing, while Billy runs his hand back and forth across her lower back. She loves that his hands are so soft—a piano player's hands. He told her that he likes how rough her hands are, calloused from her sticks. With his other hand, Billy's holding a copy of *Us Weekly*. It's not just any copy of *Us Weekly;* it's their copy.

"You're obsessed with that thing," she says.

Billy eyes her over the top of the magazine. "Well, yeah. I know you're an old pro at this, but believe it or not, I'm not. Being in gossip magazines is new for me."

For this, Margot thinks, Billy should consider himself fortunate.

"Whirlwind" is what they called Margot and Billy's relationship. It's a stupid word, *whirlwind.* Not as stupid as *recluse,* but it's one of those words those magazines use that have the power to diminish.

Margot halted her *Us Weekly* embargo last week at Poppy's request. "Seriously, Mum, you gotta see it!" the girl said.

Featured in the issue was a short article and an accompanying photo of Margot and Billy sitting at an outdoor table at a restaurant by Billy's old place. They've just ordered. Their water glasses sit between them, paper straws dissolving. Billy's arm rests at the middle of the table, and Margot has, just seconds before, laced her fingers into his without even realizing she was doing it. Billy is only visible in profile, but Margot's full, oblivious face is on display, smiling again.

Someone told her once that the tingly, gooey feelings you feel when you first meet someone eventually fade because of a trick of evolution. The reasoning is that all that lovestruck stupidity makes you vulnerable to predators. Margot rolls onto her side now and looks at the photo of herself, and that's exactly what she sees: vulnerability. The woman on the glossy page looks like she could be attacked by wolves at any second, because liking someone is dangerous.

"Recluse No More," reads the headline. "The whirlwind romance between former rock star Margot Hammer and everyone's new favorite music teacher continues in . . ." blah blah blah.

"I don't think *former* rock star is fair," says Billy. "Once you become a rock star, aren't you *always* a rock star? Like a Jedi?"

"That's a dorky way to say it," says Margot, "but I agree. They can go to hell."

"And who took this picture, do you think?" he asks. "Are there paparazzi in Baltimore?"

Margot sits up and wraps herself in sheets. "I think I'm gonna go to the coffee shop."

"Yeah?" he asks. "What do you do there all that time, anyway?"

"None of your business, that's what," she says, because she doesn't want to tell him that she's writing. She doesn't want to tell anyone. Nearly every day since getting off the Amtrak train in Baltimore, Margot has sat huddled over her notebook writing things that might be lyrics but also might be nothing. Either way, she's enjoying it.

Poppy called her out on it the other day over FaceTime. "You're writing again, aren't you, Mum?"

"What? I don't know. Why? How do you know?"

Her daughter snorted. "Why are you so weird? I can just tell. And you should keep doing it, by the way. You're less bitchy when you're writing."

"Gee, thanks."

Poppy tilted her head. "He's your manfriend, isn't he?" she asked. "You have a manfriend."

"Stop it."

"Gentleman caller?"

"Oh Jesus," said Margot. "That's worse."

Now Margot climbs out of bed. "I'm getting dressed."

"Ugh," says Billy, "clothes are stupid."

She sits cross-legged on the floor beside her open carry-on bag and looks inside. There's a wrinkled T-shirt, two balled-up pairs of underwear. "Shit," she says.

"What?" asks Billy.

"I'm out of socks."

This is the second time Margot has run out of socks since she arrived. She only brought five pairs, after all, and she's been quietly washing them and her underwear in the stacked washer-dryer combo in the closet off the kitchenette. This, however, sitting barefoot on the bedroom floor of this apartment that isn't hers, feels significant. Margot is a guest here. And the thing about guests is that they tend to leave right around the time they run out of clean socks.

They haven't talked about the logistics of all this. Margot doesn't necessarily want to, because doing so would be like shaking herself out of a very pleasant dream. She does, however, want to know if it's cool to keep dreaming for a little while longer. "I've been wearing the same three shirts for two weeks," she says. "I don't technically have pajamas. And your shampoo is making my hair flat. I didn't buy any at Eddie's, because I didn't know if—"

"Your hair looks great," he says.

Say what you will about men, but sometimes moments like these are lost on them. Socks are just socks, right? Shampoo is shampoo. Billy, though, after a brief silence, seems to understand that something is happening here. He sets their *Us Weekly* down and looks at the clock. "I don't have a lesson until this evening."

"Yeah?" she says.

"Yeah," he says. "Let's go shopping."

CHAPTER 32

The view from Robyn's office on the twenty-third floor looks like something shot by the Baltimore Department of Tourism. Boats floating, swaying trees against an urban landscape, planes drifting in and out of BWI airport. It's just after midday, so pedestrians are out down below, walking in friendly groups. Across the harbor, people exercise on the greenspace behind the Under Armour headquarters.

She remembers those days, the first decade of her career, when her schedule allowed for big breaks to go to the gym and shower, maybe grab a salad. Her current day's schedule is up on one of her four monitors now. Every half-hour block is color-coded and accounted for, stacked like Legos.

She can see her assistant, Trevor, approaching, because her office walls are glass. He smiles as he enters, sets a stack of papers on her desk. "Printed the decks for you," he says. "A few changes to the P&L, but nothing major. They'll go over everything at three."

"Great," she says. "Thanks."

"You've still got that personal thing now, right? 'Til 2:30?"

"I do," says Robyn.

Having an assistant is a godsend, but it's weird having someone else control her schedule. She had to email Trevor last week and have him block out ninety minutes, like a permission slip.

"Cool," he says. "Anyone comes looking, I'll fight 'em off. I'll text you if there are any emergencies, but only as a last resort."

"Thanks, Trevor."

This is usually when he shoots Robyn with finger guns and walks briskly back to his desk. Instead, Trevor lingers.

"Anything else?" she asks.

He touches his tie, which has little crabs on it. "Um," he says, "can I ask you something?"

She glances at the clock. No, he can't; there isn't time. "Of course," she says.

"It's kinda not work related." He looks back through all the glass, and Robyn wonders what he's going to say. She knows very little about him, aside from his collection of ties. He loves tennis. He's gay, dating a guy with a German shepherd. His name is Grant, she thinks. The guy, not the dog.

"Some of us were wondering. You know, the assistants. You were married to him, right? Billy Perkins?"

Robyn stifles a sigh. Of course that's what he wants to talk about. It's what *everyone* wants to talk about lately. "Not married," she says. "We were together when I was younger than you. In other words, a long time ago. Now we're friends. Co-parents."

"And you live in Roland Park, right?"

The news and gossip sites have been vague about exactly where Margot is staying. Baltimore is a small town, though. A middle-aged rock star shuffling up and down Roland Avenue en route to the coffee shop every morning gets some attention. Last week, the *Baltimore Sun* printed a picture of her in the style section petting a dog in front of Eddie's Market. Neighbors have started slowing when they pass Robyn and Aaron's house on their morning jogs and evening walks.

"Hey, Aaron. Hey, Robyn. What'ssss . . . uhhh . . . new with you guys?"

She tells Trevor yes, that she lives in Roland Park, hoping to leave it at that. He takes a step closer, though. "What's she like?" he whispers. "Margot Hammer. Is she, like, cool?"

Yes, she *is* cool. Margot Hammer is impossibly cool, with her roughed-up jeans and tattoos and windswept hair. She's also quiet and weirdly stone-faced. Robyn is nervous around her because she's never been around a famous person before. And she's prettier in person than Robyn gave her credit for when Robyn was young and jealous. Margot's eyes are striking, and she gives off this aura of not caring about anything, which is intimidating. She has laugh lines, but she makes them look badass. And she and Billy play music together on the other side of the driveway at all hours, and sometimes she hears them laughing.

The other day Robyn made up a reason to go to the garage, and she stood perfectly quiet looking up at the garage ceiling, wondering if Margot and Billy might be having sex up there. Because that's what new couples do: they have sex. She wondered if that applies to people in their forties, though. She also wondered what it would be like to have sex with Billy when you'd previously had sex with Lawson Daniels. Is it possible to enjoy it, or does having sex with Lawson Daniels render all other men simply *not* Lawson Daniels?

Robyn doesn't go over any of this with Trevor, because it would be wildly inappropriate, particularly the sex part. Plus, she needs to leave immediately. She stands and grabs her jacket. She considers switching to the cushy sneakers she keeps under her desk but opts to stay with the heels she's wearing. She may not be a rock star, but her legs look great in these awful things. "Weren't you like five years old when she was famous?" she asks.

Trevor laughs. "Um, not sure if you're on the socials much, Robyn, but . . . she's pretty famous again."

In the elevator, Robyn digs her phone out of her purse. Caleb taught her about the search functions on Twitter and Instagram the other day, so she's advanced from social media voyeurism to full-on cyberstalking.

She thumbs out "Margot Hammer" and sees pictures of the drummer in Roland Park and videos of her playing at the Horse. There's Margot writing in a little notepad at the coffee shop. She sees a picture posted by someone she doesn't know in which Margot is standing under Caleb's basketball hoop looking up at birds. *I saw her!* the caption reads, and there are tongue and guitar emojis. The post has 427 likes. "Jesus," says Robyn, because she is 100 percent certain that she doesn't even know 427 people.

At the crosswalk outside her building, she types "Margot and Billy," and there they are, no last names required.

Luv them.

Good for her.

Go Margot!

Team Margot 4LYFE

Is it weird that this gives me hope?

Suck it Lawson Daniels!

Find a guy who looks at you like Billy looks at Margot!!!!

That last one was posted by HellaBella93, and she has a point. In the image, Billy is looking at Margot the way an infatuated teenager would, and it's impossible not to remember when Billy used to look at Robyn like that.

Another post reads: *i luv them, but i kinda love him more!!!* *#luckymargot*

Robyn gets it. He was easy to love; he still is. Last Saturday, she was in her driveway watering flowers. Billy opened the apartment windows and played "Rhiannon" by Fleetwood Mac on the Steinway, which he knows is Robyn's all-time favorite song. "Rob!" he shouted. "These acoustics! I'm never leaving this place!"

She closes Twitter and opens Instagram, where she finds a video titled "Why I Love Margot & Billy." A girl with pink hair and thick-framed glasses wears a T-shirt with cats on it.

"Okay, so, yeah," the video girl says, "my hot take? How could we *not* love Margot and Billy? The world's the worst, right? Death, disease, the Supreme Court . . . the patriarchy! And then along comes this rainbow of happiness. We love Margot and Billy because they're something good and sweet in a pretty shitty world. I just hope I find my Billy. If you're out there, hit me up, Boo."

"Oh, get a life," says Robyn.

Now she stands at the foot of another tall building downtown. She closes Instagram, checks her email. She was due on the twelfth floor five minutes ago in office 2112A. A quick text to Aaron. *On my way up.*

Two women in business-casual dresses look down at Robyn's heels in the elevator, and she feels good about them—like a power move. When the door opens, the ladies hustle off in their lunchtime Nikes.

Inside 2112A, a young receptionist looks up. "Hi. Robyn, right?"

"Right. Here to see Mr. Sommers."

"They're expecting you. Head on back."

Industrial carpet beneath her feet, Robyn walks down a long hallway until she finds Aaron and a man with gray hair sitting at a conference table. "Hey, Robyn," the man says, standing. "Ed Sommers. Good to see you."

"Hey, Robyn," says Aaron. His voice catches her off guard—the serious tone of it—and for the first time the gravity of what's happening hits her. After offering Robyn and Aaron tea, water, or sodas, Mr. Sommers starts. "Now, my role here," he says, "is to be a guide. I'm here to help you two find the clearest path to what's next. You've opted not to use divorce attorneys. From my perspective, with as friendly and amicable as you two seem to be about all this, well, that's a good decision."

Aaron offers Robyn a sad little smile. They've talked about this at home and at restaurants and on walks for more than a year. They've grown apart. The distance between them is too great. They'll always be friends. They still love each other, in a way. Once Caleb starts college in the fall, they'll divide up their lives. Uncouple. Begin their separate journeys.

My marriage is ending, Robyn thinks.

For the purposes of easy math, she's always assumed she'll live to be a hundred. The 10 percent of her life that she's spent with Aaron will soon be over, facilitated by a jowly man named Ed Sommers. All it takes is a three-block walk in heels on a sunny day, and she wonders, *Is it supposed to be this easy?*

CHAPTER 33

Margot is on her way back from the coffee shop, thoroughly decked out now in new clothes. She's carrying her notebook and an iced coffee, and the sun is out. It feels weird to not be wearing her boots, like she could take off at a dead sprint if she needed to.

About twenty minutes after stepping into Target with Billy yesterday and finding some hair products suitable for females, Margot realized something: Billy drove her there in a car. That car was, in fact, in the parking lot right outside the store. Margot hasn't had consistent access to a car since the Jaguar Lawson kept in a garage seven blocks from their apartment when they were married. Consequently, for years now, whether it be groceries, clothes, electronics, or whatever, Margot has only been able to buy as much as she could carry. Standing in the hair-care aisle at Target, it hit her that she could buy whatever the hell she wanted.

"Are there other stores?" she asked. "Not just Target?"

Billy laughed, like she was kidding. A teenager had just taken Margot's picture with her iPhone and run away, embarrassed. "Oh, you're serious," he said. "Uh, yeah, we've got stores in Baltimore. We've got a mall and everything."

She bought socks and underwear, a couple of gray and black T-shirts that were slightly different from her other gray and black T-shirts, a new pair of jeans, some legit Target pajamas, a pink shower loofah, and the pair of squishy Vans that she's wearing now, like sleek little pillows for her feet.

Billy was delighted by the loofa. "Margot Hammer uses a pink loofah," he said when they checked out. "You don't read about stuff like that in *Rolling Stone*."

She decides to hit Eddie's for baby carrots and—*well, as long as I'm here, right?*—to flip through the newest *Us Weekly*. In the Stars—They're Just Like Us! section up front, Margot sees herself with Billy at Camden Yards. Fancy Clancy is there, too, but poor Caleb has been cropped out. "They drink brews at ball games!" reads the caption. Margot's ears are definitely sticking out the sides of her Orioles cap. Ten or so pages forward, Willa Knight is beside a pool in an article about how celebrities are prepping their beach bodies for summer, as if twenty-six-year-old genetic lottery winners have to do anything aside from exist.

Her phone vibrates in her back pocket as she steps out of Eddie's. It's a New York number. Margot answers, because maybe it's Jimmy, her doorman, telling her that her building is engulfed in flames. There's no one there, though, just dead air.

When she's about a block from the apartment, she can hear guitar riffs reverberating off the pavement. Billy's inside with Alice, his oldest student, and she's surprised none of the neighbors have called the police.

Her phone rings again. Same number. Margot stops walking. "Hello?"

Still nothing. Margot nearly disconnects, but then there's a sharp intake of breath in her ear. It's just a sound—not even a word—but it's a sound Margot knows instantly, because she's heard it a thousand times, in microphones, playback speakers . . . her own memories. "Nikki?" she says. "Nikki, is that you?"

Another breath, then the line goes dead.

Margot says, "Shit," to a tree, then taps the number on her screen, calling it back.

"Hello?"

"Nikki?"

"Margot? Sorry. I sort of freaked out when you actually answ—"

Margot hangs up. Ten seconds later, her phone rings again. She answers, aware that she in no imaginable way should. "What?"

"Margot?"

She's rehearsed things that she might someday shout at Nikki. She wishes now that she'd written those things down, because her mind is a barren, horizonless nothing. "What do you want?"

"Um, did you *literally* just call me back so you could hang up on me, you psycho?"

"Yeah," says Margot, "and I'm about to do it again."

Inside, Billy is sitting in The Rocker while Alice jams out in a full rock-and-roll pose, leg up on the coffee table. She stops when she sees Margot, turns shy.

"You're back," says Billy. "Did you hear that? 'Sweet Child O' Mine.' Alice just blew my eardrums out. I'm probably gonna have to go to the hospital after this and get them reattached."

"Sounds really good, Alice," says Margot.

"Oh," says Alice, "thanks. I'm . . . you know, figuring it out."

"You okay?" asks Billy, because Margot must look like she's not as she stands at the door with a grocery bag dangling from her wrist and a knocked-out expression on her face.

"I'm just gonna put this down. I don't wanna interrupt."

Not counting the small bathroom, the apartment consists of two rooms. The kitchenette and main sitting area make up one. Margot steps into the bedroom and closes the door as Alice starts again from the top.

The bedroom is a mess, not because they're slobs but because they're two people in transition—the way hotel rooms always look like a bomb has just gone off. Margot's overnight bag sits on her side of the bed, her new clothes stacked beside it. The floor is lined with Billy's unpacked boxes. A cardigan hangs from the bedpost. She sits on Billy's spinning desk chair and lets herself slowly rotate. An old box of Billy's *Rolling Stones* sits at her feet.

The last time Margot spoke to Nikki, Margot said she never wanted to see her again. Ever. It was a week after the MTV Video Music Awards. Axl had arranged for the two of them to meet at Stage Dive, and Nikki stood next to a stupid fax machine like some beautiful, sad-looking deer, head hung, hands shoved into her pockets, belly-button ring twinkling. "So that's . . . it? Like, it's over? For real?"

As Alice's guitar wails on the other side of the bedroom door, Margot starts sifting through the magazines, noting each cover. Stipe, Green Day, Springsteen, Britney. She stops when she sees Nikki, Anna, Jenny, and herself.

"The Flames Go Out."

Margot was more nervous than usual that night.

Big, multi-act shows were stress machines of logistics and strung-out crew members. Their third album, *Incessant Noise,* still felt new, so Margot had to think through every move. Anna would stay close so they could talk with their eyes and get through the performance together. Still, Margot was uncomfortable.

Axl wore an all-black suit. He kept calling out vaguely threatening words of encouragement backstage, like "The whole world is watching, girls!"

Lawson was there . . . somewhere. An odd concoction of famous people milled about, and models in tight dresses stood frowning in the corners of the room, looking hungry. Eminem walked by. Jenny bobbed her head to something on her headphones. Anna held a gin and tonic and a cigarette and stared down at the red bass in her lap. A young woman with a buzz cut wearing an MTV lanyard shouted, "Burnt Flowers to stage B in two minutes!" No one knew where Nikki was.

Margot did a breathing exercise to relax herself and played the intro on her thighs.

Lawson appeared first, entering from a dark hallway. Margot's eyes found him, as they always did. And then she saw Nikki beside him. The room was a shitshow—people everywhere, pressed together. Margot could see, though, that Lawson and Nikki's proximity to each other wasn't an accident. She didn't know where they'd been, but they'd been there together.

Time slowed as she observed more things. Lawson's shirt wasn't quite right, crooked. Nikki's cheeks were flushed. Then, just before separating, Lawson's and Nikki's hands touched. Just a graze—pinky to pinky—followed by nearly imperceptible smiles.

Margot might have been able to explain these things away to herself. Any threads of doubt snapped, though, when she saw that Anna was looking at her. Anna had seen what Margot saw, and she'd seen Margot see it. Margot found out later that Anna knew. And then she found out that Jenny *didn't* know—not technically—but suspected.

"Burnt Flowers, you're up!" the buzz-cut girl shouted. Then she spoke into a headset. "Burnt Flowers is en route. Repeat, Burnt Flowers is en route."

"Let's go, bitches!" shouted Nikki.

Anna and Jenny fell into line behind their lead singer. Margot, though, froze. She thought of just leaving. She could bolt through the back door where the crew took their smoke breaks, and she could wander into pedestrian traffic in her rock-and-roll outfit. She would make it home, relieve the nanny, curl up beside Poppy, chain-lock the front door. Margot wishes now, of course, that she had. Everyone would've been screwed for a few chaotic minutes, but they'd have figured it out. The host, Chris Rock, would've done some jokes about musicians being assholes and thrown the broadcast to commercial. The pull to the stage was too strong, though, like a gravitational force. Drumsticks in hand, Margot walked.

"Hit 'em hard, love," Lawson said somewhere behind her.

Anna looked back over her shoulder, her expression pleading, *Let's just get through this, okay? We can figure everything else out later.*

Aside from glow-in-the-dark strips of tape, the stage was pitch black, so people wearing headsets escorted them to their marks. Margot sat on her stool. Her kit was on a raised platform, five feet above the rest of the band. Her earpiece went in, courtesy of a young man with a goatee. "You good?" he asked.

Margot somehow nodded that she was. Twenty-five yards away, Chris Rock was bathed in studio lights, reading from a prompter. The director's voice spoke calmly in her right ear. "Greetings, Burnt Flowers. Fifteen seconds. Lights'll go up when Rock cues you, then you're on. Break a leg."

Margot looked beyond her cymbals. Anna was to her left, Jenny to her right, waiting. Between them, center stage, stood Nikki. Crop top, jet-black eyeliner. She smiled at Margot. "Ready, rock star?" she mouthed.

". . . the four baddest white chicks I've personally ever had the pleasure to meet!" shouted Chris Rock. "Give it up for Burnt mother-effing Flowers!"

"Cue band," said the voice in her ear as the lights went up. "Cue band," the voice said again more urgently. Margot didn't know what to do, so she did the only thing there was to do. "Five, six, seven, eight," she whispered.

Her delay threw everyone off, so they were immediately out of sync. Nikki looked back before doing the little opening-verse bunny hop she'd come up with during rehearsal. Anna and Jenny adjusted, angling toward Margot. Her eyes met Anna's.

Don't do this.

Nikki started singing, her back to the band, and Margot watched her friend from behind, slinking in her leather pants. Other than the first few rows, the crowd was hidden behind pulsating lights. The eyes she could see, though, were aimed, as always, at the lead singer. Nikki had everything. The *real* stardom, the attention, the literal fucking spotlight. Anger welled, like adrenaline, which caused her timing to speed up. Nikki looked back again, touched her left ear, which was her symbol for them to slow down. Margot was louder than she'd been at soundcheck, so she drowned the other three out before the engineer pulled her levels down. That same engineer pulled her down again seconds later, but it was no use, because Margot was hitting her drums harder than she ever had before. Halfway through the song, Nikki moved up from the front of the stage. She sang still, but her eyes asked, *What the fuck, Margot?*

The kickdrum came apart when Margot's right foot broke through the strap. She felt the calluses on her palms open, and her hands went slick with blood. When her left stick cracked, she kept hitting, unfazed. When her high-hat cymbal came loose, she punched the stand and sent the whole thing crashing. Voices shouted in her ear.

Anna stopped playing first. She stood, bass at her hip. Jenny played a few more chords before giving in to a splitting burst of feedback, then it was just Margot and Nikki as the singer tried to power through disaster.

Fuck her, Margot thought. *And fuck this.*

She was still hitting her drums when she stood, and then she kicked the base of the kit and it fell off the platform. If Nikki hadn't scrambled out of the way, it would've crashed down on top of her. The mic wired to the falling snare broadcast Nikki's scream.

All the eyes that had been so dutifully trained on Nikki were now, finally, on Margot, and the audience fell silent. Just offstage, Lawson stood with his mouth open amid a swarm of scrambling crew.

Fuck him, too.

"Well, goddamn, ladies!" shouted Chris Rock. "That's what I call rock and roll!"

CHAPTER 34

"So, you're the world-famous Billy Perkins, then?"

"That's me," he says. "Nice to finally meet you."

He wonders if *finally* is the right word. It's only been a few weeks with Margot, but those few weeks have felt longer, more significant. This probably has something to do with the fact that he and Margot are living together. He didn't ask her to move in, exactly, and the closest they've come to discussing their current arrangement was when Billy invited her to go shopping, but he's woken up beside her every morning since she arrived, and now he's meeting her daughter on FaceTime.

"And you must be Caleb," says Poppy. "I've been misled. You don't look all that tall."

Caleb laughs and crumples his napkin. They're at Kooper's Tavern in Fells Point, sitting outside beneath a large umbrella. His phone is propped up at the center of the table against a water glass. They used it to call Poppy, because Margot's phone was nearly dead.

"In fairness, he's sitting, Pop," says Margot.

"Right, well, hello from San Francisco, both of you. It's a pleasure."

Caleb croaks out a word that's probably meant to be "Hello." Despite being a giant, his son still gets nervous around girls. Earbuds in, head tilted, Margot's daughter is just lovely. The resemblance to her famous dad is obvious: that narrow face and impossible jawline. This would be unnerving if it weren't for the obvious traces of Margot. "You've got your mom's eyes, Poppy," says Billy.

"I do, don't I? I'm a brown girl with blue eyes, thanks to this one."

Billy sets his hand on Margot's shoulder. "Lucky you, they're beautiful."

"Oh, stop being adorable," says Poppy. "I made Mum arrange this call because I wanted to make sure you're a suitable manfriend for her."

"Poppy!"

Billy laughs. Poppy does, too, on the little screen.

"Well, I'm struggling with the terminology. You're quite grown. And Mum rejected *gentleman caller* on account of it being gross."

"Ew," says Caleb. "Yeah, good call."

"Right?" says Poppy. "Gave me shivers."

"Is that what I am?" Billy tucks some rogue hairs behind Margot's left ear. "Your manfriend?"

"Ugh, fine," she says. "At least until we come up with something better."

"Deal."

"Ah, the agreeable type," says Poppy. "I like it. You've made her happy, Billy. So that's something. And you mostly don't look like a murderer."

"That's sweet, Poppy," he says. "Thanks."

"Where'd your name come from?" Caleb blurts this, then clears his throat. "I mean, I don't think I know any other Poppys."

Billy smiles at his son, who looks disgusted with himself.

"Yeah, Mum," says Poppy. "Good question. Why don't you tell them about my namesake."

Margot sips her beer. "How did it only take us forty seconds to get to your name?"

"We're skipping the boring parts," says Poppy. "Right to the good stuff. Go on."

"Fine," says Margot. "It was Lenny Kravitz's idea."

"Lenny Kravitz?" says Billy. "Like, *the* Lenny Kravitz?"

"Is there more than one?" Poppy teases. "Lenny Kravitz the tax attorney? Lenny Kravitz the dental hygienist? Yes, *the* Lenny Kravitz. He suggested it to Mum when she was pregnant with me, so here I am, the only Poppy you two lads have ever met."

"It sounded cool when he said it," says Margot.

"I'm sure it did," says Poppy. "Anything sounds cool when you've got a twelve-pack. He was shirtless at the time, right?"

"Of course he was shirtless," says Margot. "I don't think Lenny even owns shirts."

Billy and Margot laugh, but Caleb is confused. "Who's Lenny Kravitz?"

"What?" says Margot. "Are you serious, Caleb?"

"Oh man," says Billy. "We'll hit Charm City, hook the kid up. We can't have this."

Poppy leans closer, like she's telling a secret. "You know Zoë Kravitz, right, Caleb? The hottie? Catwoman?"

"Oh my God," says Caleb. "Yeah."

"Lenny's her dad," says Poppy. "Google him. I think the best way to describe him would be very much *not* a dental hygienist. Although Lenny Kravitz rummaging around in my mouth doesn't seem all that bad."

"Poppy, are you drunk?" asks Margot.

"No. Wouldn't mind one of those wacky gummy bears, though. Caleb, you mind hooking a sister up?"

And then Caleb, red-faced and speechless, dies at the table from embarrassment.

They do hit Charm City Rocks after lunch, where Margot buys Caleb a copy of *Are You Gonna Go My Way*. Billy gets him a pretzel after that, even though they just ate. And now they're stepping out of 7-Eleven, because somehow Margot has never had a Slurpee.

"How is that even possible?" asks Caleb. "You *are* American, right?"

Margot shows Billy and Caleb her tongue, which is electric blue. A couple recognizes Margot and smiles, which has been happening all day.

"It's cool being with you," says Caleb. "You're my favorite celebrity now, by the way."

Margot tells him that she's flattered. "It's cool being with you, too. You're the tallest person I've ever met. It's charming, like you're a friendly tree."

Caleb laughs, clearly loving this. "I get that I shouldn't have pretended to be a little girl and sent you that email," he says. "Like, as a general rule, I guess, dudes shouldn't pretend to be little girls. But I'm glad I did."

"Me too," says Margot, and Billy fights the urge to tackle them both into a hug on the street.

They're walking back toward the Champagne Supernova, their pace leisurely. They pass a toy store, more bars, a cookie shop, Daquan, then Caleb clears his throat. "So, I guess I should tell you, Dad," he says. "Like, officially."

There's a tone Caleb uses when he's being serious, and Billy recognizes it. It's the tone he used his freshman year when he announced that he wasn't going to bother trying out for basketball and was going to join the Academic Decathlon Team instead. The tone he used when he showed Billy the email from Stanford.

"I'm gonna go to Hopkins, I think."

Billy stops. Margot and Caleb stop, too. "Cay?"

"I don't *think*," says Caleb. "I know. I'm going. It's a great school. And it's . . . it's *here*."

Billy doesn't know exactly what he wanted. Well, that's not true; he's just been playing it cool. Billy wanted his son to be here forever. As he looks at Caleb now, though—slouchy in his tall-kid way—Billy has to force himself not to shout with joy. "This is what you want? What you *actually* want?"

One of the great things about Baltimore is that it has impeccable comedic timing. Before Caleb can answer his dad, a drunk guy is forcibly ejected from Max's Taphouse across the street. The security guard gives him a shove, and he stumbles over an industrial-size ashtray before sprawling onto the pavement. "Yeah, well, fuck you and your stupid little bouncer shirt, you asshole!" he shouts.

Caleb smiles. "Well, obviously. Who'd ever wanna leave this place?"

They're nearly back to the car, and Billy is thinking about Robyn, wondering if she blames him for this, wondering if she *should* blame him. That's the toughest part of parenting: not knowing if the things you want for your kids are what's actually best for your kids. And then he hears a familiar voice.

"Yo, Piano Man! Hold up!"

It's the guy with the pit bull. He and his dog are with a little boy.

"Don't move, Piano Man! I've been looking for you!" The cars inching along the cobblestone stop as man, boy, and dog cross the street.

"Um, Dad, are you about to get your ass kicked?" Caleb asks.

Billy shakes the man's hand. "It's good to see you."

"Where've you been? You play me Stevie like some kinda music tease then peace out? Not cool."

"I moved," says Billy. "Sorry. They're making my old place into a coffee shop."

From here they can make out the bright-red COMING SOON sign that Grady hung above Charm City Rocks.

"Well, that's some bullshit."

"Hey, you're LaVar Barber, right?" says Caleb. "You play for the Ravens."

"Yes, sir," he says. "Just settling in."

Billy didn't recognize him before, but the name places him. He's the Baltimore Ravens' new defensive end, acquired from the New Orleans Saints in the off-season. Billy introduces himself, although LaVar says he likes Piano Man better than Billy, which is fair. Billy introduces Caleb and Margot.

"This is my son, Jackson," LaVar says, putting his hand on the boy's head.

Jackson is maybe eleven, twelve. He's a skinny kid in glasses, a stark contrast to the bulk of his father.

"Is your dog pettable?" asks Caleb.

"Who, Lincoln? Yeah. He's not one of those rip-your-throat-out pitties. Get in there."

Caleb pets Lincoln's bowling-ball-size head. The dog doesn't have much of a tail, so he wags his entire rear end. Margot joins, scratching Lincoln's smooth back, and the dog tips over onto the pavement.

"Yeah, that's my guard dog for you," says LaVar. "Anyway, Jackson's the reason I wanted to talk to you. I got another boy, too. Younger. Absolute monster. Tears the place up."

Jackson nods, agreeing that his brother is a monster.

"Jackson, though, he's real musical. A piano man, just like you."

"That's great," says Billy. "How long've you been playing, Jackson?"

"Since I was six. Well, five and a half."

"Had to say goodbye to his piano teacher when we left New Orleans," says LaVar. "I asked around. Folks tell me you're the best music teacher in the city."

Margot and Caleb smile at Billy, and he feels a rush of pride. Lincoln smiles, too. He's a friendly gargoyle sprawled out on the sidewalk.

"I'm thinking we should hook you two up," says LaVar. "You'd like teaching him. You're a good kid, right, Jackson? And he can play. No joke. Kid's legit."

Jackson pushes his glasses up. "Dad, stop it."

"Nah," says LaVar. "I wish I had five more just like you. What do you think, though, Piano Man? Got any openings on your roster?"

Internet fame has been good for Beats by Billy. For the first time in years, he has a waiting list. A universe simply doesn't exist, however, in which Billy could tell this man who's advocating for his son anything other than yes. "What's your favorite song to play?"

Jackson thinks. "Probably 'Für Elise.' You know, Beethoven."

"Who?" says Billy.

Jackson is startled at first but then gets it. "Oh. Yeah."

Billy hands LaVar one of the business cards he keeps in his wallet, and LaVar claps him on the back, which nearly sends Billy into traffic. "And maybe after you get going," he says, "you can give us some advice on pianos. Thinking we're ready for an upgrade."

Billy tells them that he'd be happy to.

"I miss having you around, Piano Man," says LaVar. "You made this place sound like the French Quarter. Felt like home."

When LaVar, Jackson, and Lincoln are gone, Margot hands Caleb her Slurpee to finish, because it's too much for her, even a size small. "By the way, I take it back," she says. "*That* is the tallest person I've ever met."

Caleb sips Margot's Slurpee, stands up straight, sighs. "Well," he says, "it was fun while it lasted."

CHAPTER 35

On Friday, Billy pokes his head into the bathroom. "The Baltimore Department of Water called. They said they're almost out."

Behind the shower curtain, Margot says, "Good one."

Yesterday he tapped the bathroom door and asked if she'd fallen. The day before that he asked if she wanted him to install a water-proof chair for her. He can tease her all he wants, but the water pressure here is amazing, like something you'd have to be sleeping with the mayor to get in New York. "I'll be out in a minute."

"Okay, but . . . technically we're late."

She looks at her new pink loofah, soapy and dripping. They're going to Robyn and Aaron's for dinner tonight. "I can't believe it's taken us so long to ask you two over," Robyn said yesterday. She and Aaron came to the apartment door to formally invite them. Aaron gave Billy and Margot a look that said, *I assure you, this wasn't my idea.*

She isn't nervous, exactly, but the list of things she'd rather do is long and includes things like dental appointments and mammograms. As the hot water works the back of her neck, Margot imagines chatting, passing salt and pepper shakers, complimenting window treatments, and for the umpteenth time in her life she wonders what it'd be like to be a normal person.

"Well, since we're late anyway," Billy says, "you want a shower beer? I got the crappy kind you like."

She tells him to go away, but then reconsiders. "Yeah, actually, I should probably be at least a little drunk for this, huh?"

"Atta girl."

Billy returns and pushes a cold Natty Boh through the curtain. "Normally I'd come in and help you drink this swill," he says, "but I just got my hair perfect."

When she takes the can, he kisses a streak of water off one of her drumstick tattoos. She calls him a pervert, and he leaves. Her iPhone plays music out on the sink. "The Ghost in You" by the Psychedelic Furs comes on, and Margot thinks about happiness. It's such an elusive thing; it can vanish for years at a time, and then suddenly a nice man wants to bring you drinks and kiss your arm while you're in the shower.

The music stops and her phone rings, and Margot frowns at the shower curtain. Nikki's call the other day has boosted her anxiety to a low, steady hum. Margot doesn't want to talk to Nikki, but she also wants to know what Nikki wanted. They used to talk so much, about life and music and sex and the future of Burnt Flowers. And then one day they never spoke again. It was like mourning a death: awful at first and then progressively less awful.

Finally, she turns off the water and wraps herself in one of Billy's towels. He's playing the piano in the other room. The din of baseball commentators and the Steinway have been pleasant constants since her arrival, like a really good soundtrack. She picks up her phone and wipes the steam off the screen. The call wasn't from Nikki this time; it was from Axl, and there's a voicemail.

"You fucker," she says.

This makes five voicemails from Axl. The first was quick. "Margot, we should talk." The second was his version of an apology. "I'm told you overheard me being unkind. I regret that. But I think we can both agree that I'm not kind." The third was just a sigh, the fourth an even longer sigh. Now this: "Do you have any idea, Margot, how rare second chances are in this awful business? Enough of this. Let's talk."

She leaves the message marooned with his others, then she hears Billy singing, mostly on key. His singing voice is an octave higher than his speaking voice, like he's in a boy band, and she smiles at her own reflection. But then she listens to the words.

"Where'm I even going? Why did I feel such fear? Will things get any better, now that I'm here?"

She pushes the bathroom door open, and Billy stops. Her notebook is propped open on the Steinway.

"I wasn't snooping," he says. "I made the bed. It was under your pillow. You have terrible handwriting. It's like cuneiform. But this is great."

Margot doesn't say anything.

"You're not mad, are you?"

She continues not saying anything as he flips pages. "It's almost full."

The residual heat from her marathon shower dissipates, and she shivers. "Those weren't meant to be seen. Definitely not sung."

"But they're . . . songs."

She tightens the towel across her chest. Margot isn't mad. She's aware, though, that this is complicated, because her notebook is a secret. Relationships are so beautifully uncomplicated at first, and then someone finds something, asks questions. "They're not songs. They're . . . I don't even know what they are."

He touches her words. "Verse, chorus, verse. That's a song. Do you wanna sing it?"

"I'm not a singer."

"So?"

"What do you mean, 'so'? I'm a drummer."

"Did you hear me just now?" he asks. "I'm not a singer either. Most singers aren't singers. You ever *really* listen to Mick Jagger? He sounds like an old British lady. But it works because it's rock and roll." He turns back to the keys. "Here, listen."

But then Caleb is yelling at them from the driveway. "Dad! Margot! You guys coming over or what?"

Margot cinches her towel again, saved by a shouting teenager. "I better get dressed," she says. "We're late for dinner with your son and the woman you used to have sex with."

CHAPTER 36

Lawson can't remember the last time he flew commercial. That probably sounds like a rich person exaggerating—like the ultimate first-world problem—and Lawson acknowledges to himself the pure assholery of even thinking it. But he literally can't, as if the part of his brain that houses pre-celebrity memories has been damaged. Too much champagne, probably, brought to him on silver trays by startlingly blond flight attendants on private jets.

And it's not just about being rich. The sheer logistics of someone like him being crammed into a flying tube full of civilians are harrowing. He was in first class, of course, which was fine enough in a pinch, but that placed him at the very front of the plane, so he was the first thing his fellow passengers saw as they shuffled aboard back in L.A.

"Oh my God."

"Holy shit."

"Whoa."

"You're . . ."

Lawson just kept smiling.

"Right. 'Ello, mate."

"Cheers, love."

"How do you do?"

"I am indeed."

He took pictures with the crew and pilots and with anyone else who asked as he waited, boarded, flew, and finally *de*boarded. He has three signature smiles, developed over a couple of decades of professional smiling. He went with the friendliest one, occasionally adding a peace sign or a thumbs-up.

"Cheers, now."

"Appreciate it."

"Well, if you say so, mate."

"Thanks for watching."

During the flight, two teenagers kept filming him with their phones on the sly and then frantically typing with their thumbs, the cheeky buggers, as if he couldn't tell. Truly relaxing is out of the question when every moment of a six-hour flight is likely being beamed to God knows who all over the sodding planet. On long hauls he usually pops an Ambien and wears a velvet sleeping mask that feels like kitten kisses against his skin. Not today, though. How would that look: Lawson Daniels half-zonked, dozing, mouth agape—snoring, God forbid? Pictures like that, even hypothetical ones, are enough to make him shudder. Consequently, he spent most of the flight rereading a Colson Whitehead novel that he's trying to get adapted. It's the kind of project he's determined to do: actual dialogue, a plot that doesn't hinge on things exploding around him.

The woman seated next to him on the flight seemed impressed. "I love that book," she told him at some point over the vast middle of America. She'd spent the better part of two hours building up the courage to speak to him, he knew.

"Brilliant, yeah?" he said.

It's exhausting to be constantly game for conversation, but that lady in her yoga pants and flip-flops will tell the story of this flight beside him for the rest of her life, so no harm in giving her a bit of a show. He held up his free bag of cheese crackers. "Care for my snack, love?"

"Really?" she said. "Are you . . . are you sure?"

He said that he was deadly sure. Then he warned her that if she fell asleep, he'd surely nick her wallet, and her sudden delighted laughter bounced through the plane like a cricket ball.

And now he's walking through this strange, bigger-than-you'd-think airport, following signs that say GROUND TRANSPORTATION.

Often in the wild, Lawson holds his iPhone to his ear. It's easier to ignore people if they think he's on a call—an old celebrity trick. Now, though, he really is on a call, and the person he's talking to, his manager, Rufus, is bloody furious.

"For the love of God, Lawson. We're screwed."

"Oh, don't be so dramatic, mate. They could prop a sodding mannequin in the driver's seat for that next bit. No one would notice."

"That's not the point," says Rufus.

"I was upfront," he says. "I told them I needed to sort some personal matters. Mental wellness check. Work-life balance. That's all the rage now, right?"

"That doesn't apply to people like you."

"Well, that's hurtful." He passes a woman dragging a bag that's big enough to transport dead bodies. "If you cut me, do I not bleed, Rufus? If you tickle me . . ."

"Right," says Rufus. "You're a real man of the people, Laws."

"Okay, well, if you're gonna be a cunt about it, I'd like to address the quality of material that's been coming my way of late."

Rufus goes quiet. A guy with a goatee is approaching Lawson from the left, holding out his mobile. "Dude, can you call my wife?" he asks. "She'll absolutely shit herself."

"Sorry, mate," says Lawson. "Cheers to your missus, though. Rufus, you there?"

"I am. Lawson, I don't want to keep having this conversation."

"Perhaps I do."

"Better scripts will come. They're on the way."

"I'm an Oscar nominee, for fuck's sake."

"*Nominee*, Laws. *Supporting.* Those are two big qualifiers in this equation. Stick with the plan. Do the movies they want you to make and cash the checks. Then we make the turn back to more serious work."

Shit. Lawson has gone off in the wrong direction—figuratively, but also quite literally. People are pointing at him, aiming their phones. A lady in a Southwest Airlines vest waves at him with both hands and simply screams.

"Cheers, love," he says.

Where in the hell is he? He prefers the private airports; they're smaller, and fewer people scream at him.

"There are pictures on Instagram of you on a commercial flight," says Rufus. "If you left the state of California, Universal is gonna send someone over here to cut my nuts off."

"No way, mate," he says. "Wasn't me. Maybe that handsome lad from the sexy Netflix show."

"All righty then. I'll go ahead and say goodbye to my nutsack. Thanks for that."

Christ, Americans—all Big Gulps and castration analogies.

"What if I'm ready to make the turn now?" says Lawson. "I've done my time with the blockbuster rubbish. I was a Shakespearean actor before all this. Enough with the fucking green screens. You ever try acting in front of a green screen? It feels ridiculous."

"Um, that *blockbuster rubbish* has put your favorability among teenage males at ninety-seven percent."

"Who the bloody hell cares?"

"*Me,* Lawson. Because teenage males are the only people who actually go to movies. And they love you."

"I'll gladly trade a few million lads for a script that doesn't make me want to gouge my eyes out, Rufus. In a heartbeat, mate."

"We'll get there," his manager says. "I promise. And not for nothing, going AWOL off the set of a seventy-five-million-dollar movie isn't gonna help your cause. A shift like you're talking takes political capital. You know that."

A sign leads Lawson to escalators. He heads down behind a family of tourists: two bickering kids wearing sneakers and headphones.

"What do you want me to tell Universal?" asks Rufus. "Quote unquote personal matters isn't gonna cut it."

Through a bank of windows, Lawson sees a bright orange sun just beginning to set. He was expecting some bombed-out urban war zone, but this doesn't look bad at all. "Well, you know how I am when it comes to maths, mate," he says. "But you've been taking ten percent of my money for an awfully long time. I trust you'll come up with something." And then he hangs up on his manager.

At the bottom of the escalator, he signs autographs, poses for two more photos.

"Loved you in *Counterstrike,* man," a police officer tells him.

"Cheers, mate." Lawson bumps the man's knuckles, noting the gun on his hip.

This whole thing came about quite quick—Lawson is going mostly on impulse—but he did think to arrange a car, and he reckons the black Escalade parked outside by the long row of taxis is it. It dawns on him now, though, that he doesn't know where he's even going. He fishes his mobile back out of his black Levi's and tells it to call Pop Star.

"Hey, baby girl," he says when she answers.

"Hi, Dad."

"Question, love. Where'd you say your mum's staying again?"

Poppy's voice turns stormy. "I didn't. Why?"

"Doing a bit of research. I shouldn't say more. It's all quite hush-hush."

"Oh shit. Dad, you promised me."

The exit doors part as he approaches, set with sensors. It's chillier outside than it was back in L.A. He nods at the Escalade, and the big truck comes to life. A sign up ahead glows pinkish. It's dirty with grime and soot, but friendly looking.

WELCOME TO BALTIMORE!

CHAPTER 37

The adults are hitting it pretty hard.

Caleb's dad usually just drinks a beer or two here and there, maybe at an O's game or when he and Caleb watch movies on Saturday nights. Caleb can tell he's buzzed now, though, because he's laughing, and his face is flushed. A moment ago, he looked into the wine bottle at the center of the table like it was a telescope and asked, "Did someone spike this thing?"

Margot has had as much to drink as Caleb's dad, but she's tougher to read. She looks cool tonight, pretty. She keeps drumming her fingers on the table to the music that's playing over the Sonos. Caleb wonders if it's a drummer thing—if she even knows she's doing it. He also wonders if his dad knows that he keeps looking at her and smiling.

Dinner started a little rough, with everyone just staring at one another. The low point was when Margot said, out of nowhere, "Your windows are really nice," then everyone looked at the window and nodded for, like, forty-five seconds.

But then Aaron swooped in with the save. "Well, here we are," he said. "Just a totally normal collection of people in a perfectly ordinary situation, right?" Everyone laughed. "Should I get more wine?" he asked, and the group agreed wholeheartedly that he should.

"Co-dad for the win!" Caleb's dad said.

"Oh, you're embracing the terminology, Billy," said Aaron. "That's fantastic."

Caleb doesn't spend a ton of time with grownups, but it seems like alcohol is a pretty big part of adulthood. He gets this, he supposes. Alcohol is like a smoothing device—it takes rough things and turns them into softer things. For example, Aaron gave Caleb a glass from one of the red wines he opened half an hour ago, and Caleb feels warm and light now, like he could do pushups or have a conversation with Poppy without humiliating himself. He wonders if she has a boyfriend, but he can't think of a casual way to ask Margot. Since meeting her on FaceTime the other day, Caleb has started following Poppy on Instagram. He's also googled her about twenty times.

"So, you two need to take me through all this," his mom says. "The Billy-Margot journey."

The adults are done eating. Caleb is finishing his mom's chicken.

She swirls her glass of wine. She looks pretty, too, and Caleb can tell that it's on purpose. Her hair is done—curled at the ends—and she's wearing new distressed jeans with small tears in the thighs. She never wears jeans like that.

"What do you mean?" asks his dad.

"I worked back through YouTube and social media," she says. "My assistant loves you two, by the way."

Caleb watches a series of events. His dad puts his hand on top of Margot's hand, his mom sees it, and then Aaron sees his mom see it. His mom shifts in her seat, takes a sip. "But the thing I haven't figured out. You live in New York, Margot, right? What were you doing in Baltimore? At the Horse You Came In On?"

Caleb and his dad look at each other. His mom sees this, too.

His mom sees everything; it's her most devastating power as a mom, like she's an X-Man. *X-Person? X-Mom?* "What was that look?" she asks. "I see you two."

"Well, it's convoluted," his dad says. "Right? She was . . ."

"I was invited," Margot says. "It was a thing for a fan, through my label. But it didn't work out. So there I was, outside the record store."

His mom leans onto her elbows. "Wow, you two would *not* be good FBI agents. You're hiding something."

"It was because of me," Caleb says, surprising himself. He swallows.

"What? You? How?"

His dad shoots him a cautious look.

"Dad, I mean, I feel like we can tell her, right?"

"Can we, though?"

"I'm eighteen. You're letting me drink wine at dinner."

His dad turns to Aaron. "Yeah, Aaron, let's maybe cut the minor off."

"Come on. Are we just *never* gonna tell her?"

"Well, now you *have* to tell me," his mom says. She fills his dad's and Margot's glasses, does a little chair shimmy. "This is exciting."

"I think Robyn can handle it," Margot says.

"*Thank* you, Margot. Caleb, proceed."

It's a thrilling feeling for Caleb, this life of crime. "Okay, but you can't get mad."

"That's not how anger works, sweetie," she says.

"Right?" his dad says. "I've been telling him that since he was five."

"I'll do my best," his mom says. "No promises, though."

"Okay, so, Gustavo," says Caleb.

"Gustavo?"

"Well, apparently, he . . . partakes," says Caleb. "Did you know that?"

"Oh jeez," his dad says, and Aaron is laughing.

"Partakes in . . . ?" His mom slowly gets it, though. "Ah, so this is why you spend so much time at your dad's. Pretzels and weed, rock stars wandering in and out. I'm glad you'll be able to continue your life here in Baltimore."

Caleb tries to redirect the conversation, noting the subtext in his mom's comment. Actually, it was more *text* text then subtext. "Mom, stop. Okay, so, anyway. Dad had these gummy bears in the cereal cabinet. *Special* gummy bears."

"Gustavo gave them to me as a joke," Caleb's dad says.

"Doooo you still have those?" Aaron asks.

His mom is very still as Caleb tells the story of how Billy met Margot. Candy that wasn't *just* candy. Finding Margot online while stoned. The made-up band of little girls. The frightening woman from the record label who yelled at him. How he wondered if pretending to be a tween girl on the Internet is illegal.

"No, but it probably should be," says Aaron. "Can we all agree?"

His mom stops swirling her glass when he's done talking. Margot stops drumming her fingers; everyone waits for his mom to react.

"Well, I'd like to have a little talk with Gustavo," she says, finally.

"You're not mad?" says Caleb.

"Oh, come on," she says. "This is fun. You think I can't be fun? I can be fun. You were afraid to tell me this, like I'm *soooooo* scary. Here comes Robyn the fun hater, everyone hide your fun. Do you all think I'm so straightedge?"

"Noooo," says Aaron. "What? You?"

"Mom, you're one of the wildest senior vice presidents I know," Caleb says.

She folds her arms. "You all think you know me. Well, did you know I got stoned once and tried to climb into the popcorn machine at the Senator Theatre?"

Aaron raps his knuckles on his placemat. "I did *not* know that."

"Mom? Really?" Caleb laughs. "That's awesome."

"See, I used to be cool."

"You're *still* cool," says Aaron. He holds up his wineglass. "Seriously, though, how big was that popcorn machine?"

"Billy," she says, "you remember that night, right?"

"I do," his dad says. "We were very politely asked to leave."

"And then we made out in the Royal Farms parking lot."

Caleb laughs, and his dad says, "Ohhhhkay."

It's impossible to imagine any of this: his mom stoned, his mom getting kicked out of . . . well, anywhere, his parents together and kissing. "The story continues, though," he says. "So, I'm standing there pretty much frozen in terror at the record shop, wondering if Rebecca Yang is gonna punch me in the balls or have me arrested. Then, boom, Margot takes off. Just runs right out the door like the place is on fire."

"I don't blame you," says Robyn.

"I was still fifty-fifty on whether they were murderers."

"And then," says Caleb, "dopest move of the *century*. Dad goes after her, leaves poor Grady and me standing there with our mouths open, chases his old-school crush down Thames Street. Epic."

It's been fun for Caleb these last few minutes, having the full attention of a room of adults. As he says this last thing, though, something changes. Aaron is still laughing. "Strong move, William," he says. Margot is enjoying it, too, having inched herself slightly closer to his dad. His parents, though, aren't laughing. His mom sets her wineglass down. She smiles, but it's a smile that makes her look hurt. "You went after her?"

"Yeah," his dad says. "Just an impulse, I guess. A reflex."

He's only seen his mother cry a few times—sad movies, mostly, and after the 2016 election. This is different, though, because she's so obviously trying to hide it. "Mom, are you okay?"

"Ha. What? Stop it." She stands, gathers some plates. "I'm fine. I'm just gonna get these out of the way. You all sit, keep talking."

CHAPTER 38

Nineteen years ago, Robyn waited outside La Scala in Little Italy.

She was pregnant, nauseous, uncomfortable with incessant heartburn, a little chilly. She stood for a bit, paced. When she got tired of standing, she leaned on a parking meter. At one point she sat at a bus stop, but buses kept trying to pick her up.

"You gettin' on or what, hon?"

That whole time, she watched the door beneath La Scala's awning, waiting for Billy to come after her.

If he's not out here in sixty seconds, I'm leaving, she'd tell herself. But then a minute would come and go, and she'd still be standing, leaning, or sitting. "Come on, Billy," she whispered. "What're you doing in there?"

What he was doing was proving that all the doubts she'd ever had about him were well founded. She was young, but Robyn had had boyfriends since she was fourteen, and she knew without question that Billy was the sweetest guy she'd ever been with. Attentive and loving. Gentle. He made her laugh, and he joked about her being better looking than him, even though Robyn knew that Billy was cuter than he gave himself credit for. But he was also aimless and immature, and he showed no signs of ever being anything other than that. No signs of fight. No drive. He'd gotten his music degree from Towson, but he was a waiter at a terrible seafood restaurant who didn't own a decent pair of shoes and had irrational crushes on rock stars and played piano in bars for crumpled bills on Thursday and Friday nights.

All of that may have been fine, because men are allowed to be children for as long as they want—they're practically celebrated for it—but Robyn was ready to be an adult. And even if she wasn't ready, she was pregnant. She didn't have the luxury of arrested development.

When Billy knelt and showed her the ring, Robyn was eating crackers, which was about the only food she could keep down. At first, she thought he'd fallen out of his chair, like he'd fainted, which was just what she needed: dealing with a sick Billy while she herself felt like warmed-up garbage. But then . . .

"Robyn, will you marry me?"

It makes sense, in retrospect, that he interpreted her running out of the restaurant as a definitive no. It hadn't been, though, not at first. In truth, with all those eyes on her in that stuffy little place, she just needed some air to deal with all that was suddenly happening. But then he never came after her.

If he's not out in thirty seconds, I'm gone.

A half minute later, her future started to become clear. She began to make what was her first adult decision. She also started to make a plan. Robyn was going to have the baby, because she knew she could. She was lucky. She had a support system, career prospects, some savings built up. She'd just gotten into grad school, but she'd defer for a year. It would be hard, especially at first, but doable. She would head immediately to her parents' house. They would help her. Billy would help her, too, because she knew he'd want to. He'd be involved. He'd be doting and sweet and all the things she knew he was capable of being. But they would *not* be together. No more artificial sixty-second deadlines. No more waiting for him to be the person she needed him to be. Robyn and Billy were done.

And now she's alone on the deck at the side of the house listening to music coming from the apartment. It's the Steinway, and if she's not mistaken, Billy is singing.

Someone used the term *doom scrolling* recently, and Robyn thought it was the most perfect thing she'd ever heard. She's doing a version of that now on her iPhone beneath the stars, flipping her thumb up and up, reading about how sweet and cute AF Billy and Margot are. Some woman posted a photo of Billy and Margot walking in Fells Point. The caption reads, *Your daily dose of adorbz from Baltimore. #amiright*

"Oh, shut the fuck up," Robyn says.

She's brought a thick flannel blanket out, but she's still cold. The firepit sits empty at her feet.

The side door opens, and Aaron appears holding the bottle of cab. He fills her empty glass without comment and then goes about the quick work of building a fire for her. He puts on a pair of gloves, arranges wood into a tepee, twists some old newspaper. She watches, taking note, aware that she's going to have to do this on her own soon. She's getting the house, so she'll be staying here. Aaron will move to an apartment downtown. He knows a few divorced guys who live in some big complex on the water. She imagines a building of lonely men, their TVs the size of sideways refrigerators.

Aaron strikes a long match and sets it into the structure he's built. Smoke appears, and then a weak flame. "There we go." He sits in the chair beside her.

Warmth touches her skin as the flame grows. "Thanks."

They listen to the muffled sound of Billy's piano.

"So, what was all that in there, Robyn?" Aaron asks.

Billy and Margot left fifteen minutes ago, and Robyn headed out here without comment, leaving the dishes and cleanup to Aaron and Caleb.

"Do you have feelings for him again? Is that what this is? Two decades later?"

"No," she says. "I mean, yeah, of course I do."

"Well, that clears it up."

"I haven't had feelings for Billy in years, Aaron. But obviously I have feelings for him. Again, before, probably always. That's how it works."

She notes the hurt on his face and then watches it dissipate like the smoke from the fire. They know each other's backstories, each other's pre-marriage loves and losses. "It's complicated," she says. "Like how you and I are no longer in love, but we love each other."

This was the realization they'd had, articulated over the last year of talking and reflecting. Maybe if they'd had kids, it would've been different—perhaps a family would've tethered them to each other in a way that felt permanent. Or maybe they've just run their course. Who knows? They tried, sort of. Last summer, Caleb stayed with Billy for twelve days while she and Aaron went to Hawaii. They stayed at the same hotel they'd stayed at during their honeymoon. They snorkeled and got day-drunk and sunburned. They had a pleasant time together, because it was Hawaii, but they both knew that nothing between them would ever go beyond simply pleasant again.

Aaron stabs at a log with a metal poker. Orange embers float up and quickly vanish. "If it makes you feel better," he says, "I would've chased after you."

"I know," she says, and smiles, because he's going to be a good friend. Her other divorced friends will be jealous of how amicably they fell out of love, like a blueprint for the end.

"Who would've thought," he says. "Apparently inviting your ex to live above the garage was a mistake."

"Oh, go to hell," she says.

He fills his own glass. "I meant what I said the other day at the arbitrator's office," Aaron says. "I'll help with Caleb's tuition. I'm happy to. The one good thing about him picking Hopkins . . . it's cheaper, right?"

The fire is at a full roar, crackling and bursting.

"That's very nice. But he's mine, Aaron." In her head, that seemed like a nice way of telling Aaron that Caleb isn't his. There's no nice way to say that, though. The hazards of nontraditional household situations.

"Are you nervous about being single again?" she asks. "About, I don't know, sex and stuff, dating?"

He holds up his glass and inspects the red wine against the flame. "Sometimes I look forward to it, like an adventure. Sometimes, though, it just seems like so much work."

"Right?"

"Dating apps," he says.

"Ugh," she says.

The music from the apartment stops, starts again. "I don't think I've ever heard Billy sing before," Aaron says.

"It's not great, is it?"

"No. I guess we know why he never became a real musician. My God, is that an electric guitar? How many people are up there?"

Robyn looks up at the stars. There are planes up there, too, dozens slowly streaking across the sky. She used to track planes like these with her eyes when she was young and watching the nighttime sky. Other people would look up and point at constellations or try to spot shooting stars. Robyn just wondered where all the planes were going. Paris, London, Hong Kong?

"If you met him now?" Aaron says. "The forty-whatever version? And if Margot wasn't part of this weirdness? If it was just you and him, and the last twenty years hadn't happened?"

"Oh God," she says, because she doesn't want to think about it—because she *has* thought about it. "I have no idea, Aaron."

Another hurt look, because he wanted her to immediately say no to the question he wasn't quite asking. She tries to imagine how to explain how she feels, but then headlights appear, and a rumbling black SUV pulls into the driveway.

"Who the hell's that?" asks Aaron.

She can hear friendly chatter down by the mailbox. A "thank you" and a muffled "goodnight, mate," British sounding and familiar, although Robyn doesn't know any Brits. A car door shuts.

"Maybe they ordered food?" Aaron says.

"We just ate," says Robyn.

A voice, footsteps. "Oy! 'Ello. Black man approaching in the nighttime. Nothing to fear. Just popping up for a chat."

"Can we help you?" Aaron asks.

A man wearing black jeans, a white V-neck T-shirt, and a leather jacket climbs the short flight of stairs to the deck. His handsomeness registers first, followed by how perfect his teeth are. They're as white as his T-shirt, like they've been color coordinated. Then Robyn realizes who she's looking at. A month ago, this would've been shocking to the point of absurdity. Now, though, it makes total sense.

"Oh," says Aaron. "Right."

"How lovely," says Lawson Daniels. "A fire. Don't mean to disturb you. A little bald bloke from a music shop sent me here. I'm looking for Margot Hammer."

CHAPTER 39

Margot wrote the lyrics to "Power Pink" on the back two pages of her Western civ notebook her freshman year at NYU. It was the first song she'd ever finished.

"You wanna see something I wrote last night?" she asked Nikki, hands shaking.

Nikki sat across from her at a bar near campus that played things fast and loose with IDs. "What, like, a song?" When Margot flushed red from her collarbones up, Nikki pushed her beer aside. "You wrote a song, you bitch? Yeah, I wanna see it."

"It's not . . ."

"Gimme, Ringo! Now."

Margot handed over her notebook.

"Ha," said Nikki. "Western civ. I can't wait 'til we drop out."

Margot watched her friend's eyes as she read, and then as she slowly started to smile. "Shit, rock star. I could make this sound fucking rad."

The song sat, though. Nikki was the band's lyricist, and by the time they were ready to record their debut album she'd written ten bangers. At the last minute, though, Axl said he wanted eleven songs because ten songs "is too predictable—too even numbered."

By then Nikki was tapped out. She hated quick-turn songwriting, and deadlines made her nervous. "Wait," she said. "Margot, you still have that pink song you wrote, right? From your notebook?"

"Power Pink" was an immediate hit, but an accidental one. More importantly, it was a one-time thing. Nikki was Burnt Flowers's songwriter, Jenny was the guitarist, Anna was the bassist, and Margot played drums. That was the arrangement that had made them all famous. Margot explains all this now to Billy, who's sitting at the Steinway.

"Yeah, but that was then," he says.

Margot slides her boots off, finds one of her beers in the fridge. "Why are we even talking about this, anyway?" she asks. "Are we seriously not gonna discuss what just happened over there?"

Dinner dispersed quickly after Robyn's miniature, weirdly composed meltdown.

Billy taps out the opening bars that he came up with earlier. "Honestly, I'd rather play your song."

"Jesus, I told you, it's not a song."

Billy closes the lid over the keys. "You know what? You're right," he says. "This is rock and roll. We should do it on the guitar." He takes the electric Fender from its wall mount, plugs it into the amp by the piano.

"What are you doing?"

"Do you know how to play guitar?"

"Of course I know how to play the guitar," she says. "I can play anything."

"Well," says Billy. "La-dee-dah. Check it out. These feel like power chords to me up front." He sets his fingers, strums twice, and starts singing Margot's words.

It's hard to stay annoyed with someone while they're singing, particularly if they're singing badly. He stops after the first verse but keeps strumming.

"It's dark, right?" he says. "It's about being lost. Maybe? But maybe it's about being found. It's as dark or *not* dark as you want it to be. That's why it's good."

She scoffs, because scoffing is easier than allowing herself, if even for just a dumb, fleeting moment, to wonder if he's right.

"A guitar solo here would be nice," Billy says. "Some haunting, drawn-out thing before the chorus. You know, played by someone who's better at it than me. Rock-and-roll bass underneath. Like a G note. Second verse'll get a little faster, a slow build." Billy nods to Margot. "Here, go, let 'er rip. Sing it."

He waits for her to sing, but she doesn't, and she won't.

"I can't hear you," he whispers. "You're gonna have to be louder."

"Stop it."

"Why?"

She takes his right hand, silencing the Fender. "Billy, we had, what, thirty-five songs on three albums? Twenty of those songs were really good. Ten were great. Nikki wrote all of those but one. And you and I both know 'Power Pink' wouldn't have been great if she hadn't sung it. Without her, it doesn't work. I'm nobody."

He sets his guitar down. "Nikki wasn't at the Horse You Came In On, was she?" he asks. "And yeah, it wasn't Madison Square Garden. But it was a room full of people who had an unforgettable night. That wasn't because of anyone else. It was because of *you*."

It's more complicated than that, but, technically, he's right.

Billy touches her notebook, traces his finger across her words. "These are good songs. That's all you need. Music isn't about big, glitzy album releases anymore, Margot. You could record these right now on Caleb's computer if you wanted to."

"But then what?" she asks.

"You release them," he says. "Right? That's how it works."

"After the band broke up, every time I left the house—every time I looked at a magazine cover or turned on the radio—I was told and I was shown how much better Nikki is than me. Hotter. More talented. More bankable. More *fuckable*. If I put out some lo-fi vanity record by myself, it's gonna be that all over again. Probably worse. I need you to understand that."

"No," he says. "You're better than her."

"Billy, shut up."

"No, I won't. You are. There, I said it. You're a better musician than Nikki Kixx. I don't care what she looks like."

Outside, a car pulls into the driveway. Its headlights paint a grid of shadows on the walls as they blast through the blinds.

"It's sweet that you think that," she tells him. "But you're an idiot."

"This is the one thing I'm not an idiot about, Margot. Can't you trust me on that?"

She touches the top of his head, runs her fingers through his hair, lingering at the thinning parts that he's sensitive about. "Robyn still has feelings for you, by the way. If you can't see that, then you really *are* an idiot."

"What?" says Billy.

"You were each other's first loves, right?" she says.

"Yeah, but—"

"First loves brand you, Billy. They burn themselves on you forever." She's thinking of Lawson, of course, because not a day has gone by since their divorce in which she hasn't, at least for a moment.

There's a knock, then Robyn is calling them from behind the door. "Billy?" she says. "Margot? Um, you guys? I think you need to come out here."

CHAPTER 40

He could easily think some generic thing, like *Holy shit, I can't be-lieve this is happening*. Billy doesn't think that, though, because he *can* believe it. He's been waiting for it, actually. Well, maybe not this specifically: Lawson Daniels sitting at Robyn's kitchen table wearing an incredibly cool leather jacket. But he's been waiting for *something* like this to happen. Something that would shake Mar-got out of whatever this is and make her realize that it's time to go, that she's better than all this. Better than him.

Because, up until now, this has all been just too good, hasn't it? Too easy?

He's standing next to Margot, but they're not touching. He imagines putting his arm around her and announcing that he's her manfriend and that he's seen the pink loofah she uses in the shower. Robyn, Aaron, and Caleb are seated across from Lawson, and they're all staring at the actor. The only person in the room who looks as if this is all perfectly normal is Lawson.

"I signed that little bloke's Wall of Fame," he says. "He was quite happy about it. Signed right next to you, Mar. Your signa-ture's still a mess. Like it was scribbled by a toddler. But it was fun to see us there, side by side."

Billy makes a note to give Grady the silent treatment next time he sees him.

"Can I get you a drink?" asks Robyn. She stands as she says this, and her chair slides across the floor and strikes the wall. "Beer or . . . or maybe some wine?"

"Appreciate it, love," Lawson says. "No booze for me, though. Truth is, I'm a bit pissed already. Went on an adventure to find our little Miss Hammer, here. Stopped at that music bar where you played, Mar, the Horse something. Rather boisterous lady there sent me to the record shop, but not before making me drink a few bottles of the most godawful beer I've ever tasted. Nappy or Natty something or other. Tasted like a mouthful of bubbly pennies."

No one present knows it yet, but pictures and videos of Lawson Daniels drinking at the Horse You Came In On are currently being shared all over social media, and, therefore, Earth. Billy will later see a shot of Beth kissing Lawson on the cheek while he demonstrates disgust at a bottle of Natty Boh.

"I'd love a cup of tea, though," says Lawson.

"Like, *tea* tea?" Robyn asks.

"Well, we Brits only say it once, but I suppose you can call it what you like."

Robyn rushes to the cupboard above the coffeemaker, stumbles over a pair of Caleb's giant sneakers on the way, then nearly drops the kettle on her head as she pulls it off the shelf.

"Careful now," says Lawson.

Billy can see that Robyn isn't just nervous, she's scared. Billy can relate. As much as he wishes Lawson weren't here, he's so starstruck by him that his heart is racing. The guy isn't just handsome; he's beautiful.

"Earl Grey okay?" Robyn asks.

"Well, you've gone and made my night, Robyn," says Lawson, and Robyn laughs, nearly dropping the kettle again.

"Lovely home you have," says Lawson, smiling. "Nice little city, too. Mar, I see why you've settled in here. You're . . . you're in that little flat, then?" He points over his shoulder with his thumb. "The one over the garage?"

He pronounces *garage* like a British person—"*gay*-raahj"—and something about the posh lilt hurts. Billy has spent the last couple of decades building a life that he's cautiously proud of. Seeing it now, though, through Lawson's eyes is embarrassing. "It's only temporary," he says. "It's just—"

"Lawson, what the hell are you doing here?"

These are the first words Margot has spoken since she and Billy came out of the apartment and saw Lawson standing in the driveway.

"Nice to see you, too, love," he says.

She folds her arms. "This isn't funny. What are you *doing* here?"

A few years ago, when Robyn and Aaron redecorated their kitchen, they sprang for something called an induction stove top. The product's claim to fame is that it uses magnets capable of boiling water in a matter of seconds. So, as Lawson leans forward and levels everyone in the room with another smile, the kettle begins to howl like an approaching locomotive.

"Well, isn't it obvious, love?" he says. "I've come to win you back."

Five minutes later, Billy is sitting outside on the deck by the firepit with Robyn, Aaron, and Caleb. As a group, they're quiet, because what is there to say? Aaron throws a log on some burning embers. Caleb says, "You guys want me to go get some marshmallows or something?"

The fact that his son is seriously asking this would normally make Billy's heart swell with love at the tone deafness of youth, but his heart is otherwise occupied.

"Nah," Caleb says. "On second thought, going back in there would be awkward."

They left Margot and Lawson alone inside . . . to *talk*. This seemed reasonable five minutes ago, but now Billy wishes he could crash back through the side of the house like the Kool-Aid Man.

"You know, he's shorter than I thought he'd be," says Aaron, apropos of nothing. "So's Margot, though. Maybe that's just how it is with famous people."

Billy wonders what they're talking about in there. Maybe they aren't even talking; maybe they're kissing. If so, he's screwed. He's *seen* Lawson Daniels kiss, on screens the size of barn doors, many times. It seems like he's pretty good at it.

"Listen, Dad," says Caleb. "I don't think this is necessarily all that bad."

Billy exchanges looks with Aaron and Robyn, looks that say, *Kids, right? They're dipshits.* "Maybe you're right, Cay," he says. "The woman I'm in love with is alone in a house with a rich and famous movie star who looks like he was sculpted from marble by Italians. That movie star has come to *win her back*. And I'm out here looking at a firepit . . . in a cardigan."

"Oh," says Caleb. "I guess I didn't think of it like that."

"You love her?" The fire reflects off Robyn's eyes, which are watering again.

He hasn't told Margot that he loves her. He hasn't told *anyone* that he loves her. But isn't it obvious? "Of course I do," he says.

"*Her* her?" says Robyn. "The real her? You love her?"

Billy nods into the fire.

"Maybe she loves you, too," says Caleb. A burned-up log crumbles. "I mean, isn't that why we're all here in the first place? Because I was right? I said if she got the chance to meet you, she'd like you?" Caleb leans forward. "You have any idea how many pictures there are on the Internet of Margot frowning? Believe me, I know. I investigated. Thousands. And now every time I see her, she's smiling. That's because of you, Dad. Looks aren't everything. Money either. I mean, yeah, his jacket is dope as ffff . . ."

Billy sighs as his son stops himself from saying the f-word. "It isn't as simple as that, Cay."

"He hurt her," says Caleb. "Remember? Like, famously. Him showing up now doesn't change that. Just because he's in movies and cheesy watch commercials doesn't make him a good person. It definitely doesn't make him better than you."

Billy's heart is capable of at least a small swell now. He reaches over, squeezes Caleb's knee. He wishes he could believe him, because it sounds like something that *should* be true, the way his Lessons in Art and Manhood *should* all be true. Billy *doesn't* believe him, though. And it's not necessarily for the obvious reasons. Maybe Margot does love Billy. Or if she doesn't love him yet, maybe she could, someday. Maybe she's happier now than she was before she met him. What worries Billy, though, are Margot's own words.

"First loves brand you, Billy. They burn themselves on you forever."

Billy thinks about Robyn all the time. He's not still in love with her, but the cumulative effect of their history together has created something very close to love. He gets nervous and tongue-tied sometimes when he sees her after a long spell of not seeing her. He thinks she's beautiful, and he admires her for her determination and success, and he roots for her from a distance. If Margot thinks about Lawson half as much as Billy thinks about Robyn . . . well, he could be in real trouble.

CHAPTER 41

"So, what's your plan, exactly?" she asks. "You wanna talk first, or should I just take these clothes off?"

Lawson's still at the kitchen table, smiling. The purple mug of tea steams between his hands. "Well, I hadn't thought it through totally. I took a bloody commercial flight, for fuck's sake. But if you're game for option B, just give me a minute to freshen up."

Margot shakes her head as she eases into the seat across from him. "I can't believe you just showed up here."

Lawson smells his tea. "This is gonna be dreadful, isn't it? She had no idea what she was doing."

Margot's phone rings. She checks the screen, then sets it between them so Lawson can see that their daughter is calling.

"Probably just wishing us well," he says.

When the ringing stops, a text arrives. *mum you there? is dad there? WTF!*

"All right, here goes," Lawson says. "Wish me luck." He takes a sip of his tea and immediately contorts his face. "What's the matter with this country? Is it really that difficult? Here, I'll make us some proper cups."

As her ex-husband goes to the cupboard and starts rummaging like he owns the place, Margot takes a moment to check him out. She's seen him a handful of times since their divorce because they share a child. He missed both Poppy's high school and college graduations, though, because he was shooting movies in far-flung places, so her visual references for nearly a decade have been limited to screens, magazine pages, and billboards. He's taken his jacket off, so he's just in jeans and a T-shirt now. There's a chain around his neck, picked by a stylist, she's sure. He's leaner, more muscular than when they were married. She was only half kidding about taking her clothes off. Regardless of how much time has gone by, she knows that there's a part of this man that assumed she would simply jump into his arms.

"Oh, well, looky here," he says. "Robyn was holding out. Saucers, sugar cubes. I'll get us sorted."

He didn't ask if she wants tea, which she doesn't, but he's making it for her anyway, because he's Lawson. He fiddles with some knobs on the stove top and then leans on the counter, checking *her* out. "You look good, Mar."

"Stop calling me that, *Danny*."

He laughs. When they were together, they rarely called each other "Margot" or "Lawson," because those aren't their real names. It seemed more intimate to be Mar, Margie, Dan, or Danny. And then he went and fucked a girl in a crop top from Long Island named Nicole Schwartz, and intimacy went straight out the window.

"Fair play," he says. "*Miss* Margot Hammer, you look lovelier than you ever have."

"You look pretend."

He clutches his chest like he's taken a bullet. "Ouch, love. But you're not wrong." A twirl, a little bow. "This is the uniform required. I do what I have to."

The kettle screams, and Lawson startles. "Is this some sort of bloody super-stove?"

He prepares their tea in silence, concentrating. She watched him perform this ritual untold times when they were together. He finds some cream in the fridge, drops a bunch of sugar cubes in hers, places the cups on saucers. In lieu of what he'd call "biscuits," he settles for a few Nilla Wafers, then returns to the table.

Margot looks down at the cup he's slid before her and makes a note not to touch it, even though taking a sip would feel like returning to a home she's long since left. Her feet in his lap while they watched *The Sopranos*. Sunrises when he had early call times on New York shoots. Steaming mugs after walks in the park in the fall. Margot never particularly liked tea, but she liked having it with him, the fucker.

"Yes, I look a bit absurd," he says, dipping a Nilla Wafer. "I still regret getting my teeth done, if I'm being honest. Like I betrayed king and country. It was Rufus's idea, though. Part of the bloody uniform."

Margot doesn't reply.

"*You*, though," he says. "I'm not just being polite. You look wonderful. When I saw you online—that little show you played. Couldn't take my eyes off you. You looked smart. Mature. Powerful. A grown, proper adult woman. You looked sexy. You *look* sexy. The years, love, they've agreed with you. Well done."

The tea smells good, and the house is chilly, so she gives in and takes a sip, and he smiles, like he's won a minor battle. "Lots of sugar cubes," he says. "A bit of cream, enough to make it not taste so much like tea."

"You remember how I used to like my dirt water," she says. "I regret every bad thing I ever said about you. Here, let me just take these pants off."

Lawson slaps the table. "See, Mar, *that*. That's what I miss. That *edge.* That *bite.* You, my dear, are the real deal. All these years, more birds than I could count, and I have met exactly no one quite like you."

"Quite a feat there," she says. "You're telling me how good I look while also referencing how many women you've slept with. Bravo. But just showing up here? This is my life. You're not part of it anymore."

Lawson's phone rings. He looks at it, laughs, shows Margot. Poppy again. "She's just like you, you know. I'm proud of her. I told her she didn't need to bother with a bloody job. I'd open whatever doors she wanted—movies, music, entertainment management. But no, she's determined to go out on her own and be a . . . what is she again?"

"She's a graphic designer at an ad agency, Lawson. And she's very talented."

"Ah, right."

When his phone stops ringing, Poppy texts him. *dammit dad!!!*

"Counterargument to the whole showing-up-was-bad thing," he says. "If I'd just called like a normal person, would you have answered?"

Margot admits that she wouldn't have.

"Plus," he says, "I wanted to get a look at this bloke. This Billy chap who you've gone and made semifamous. Snogging at baseball games, Mar? You saucy minx. What do we think, love? Do we . . . do we fancy this one?"

Margot feels herself get defensive. "Yes," she says.

"Really? All right. I'm not particularly blown away, if I'm being honest. Just an American in a jumper. And . . . *this*?" He gestures vaguely. "You like this, then? Baltimore? Flat above a bloody carport?"

She doesn't owe him an explanation. She doesn't owe him anything.

"And can you fill me in on the supporting cast? That friendly couple, their enormous child. Are you being held against your will? Mar, blink twice if you need me to save you."

"You're being an asshole," she says. "What I like and what I don't like are none of your business. You forfeited your right to an opinion a long time ago."

He sips his tea. "Did I mention I'm sorry about all that hullaba-loo from before?"

Margot laughs. She can't help it—the understatement, the nerve. "The *hullabaloo*?"

"That naughty business from . . . what year was that again?"

"You're referring to the affair you had with my best friend and creative partner that broke up my band, destroyed my livelihood, ended our marriage, and ruined my life?"

"A bit dire that, but . . . well, yeah."

"Let's table the time machine," she says. "Focus on the present. Aren't you living with . . ." As Margot trails off, she's surprised that she has trouble saying her name aloud, the actress. "You know, the skinny child with the boobs I keep seeing you with."

Lawson takes a longer sip of tea now, hugs the cup with his hands. "Willa, like these perfect teeth, was also Rufus's idea."

"What does that mean?"

"There's a certain synergy to it, you'd have to agree. Our own little Oscar campaign. And she's a darling girl. You'd like her, if you unclenched for a moment."

"Oh my God," she says. "You're serious?"

"The older I get, Mar, the younger they *have* to get. That's strat-egy. I get to look like the sort of man who goes to bed with a girl like Willa Knight, and Willa gets to jump the queue and become a household name."

This feeling is new, so it takes a beat for Margot to process it. For obvious reasons, she's repulsed by every word that has come out of Lawson's mouth in the last thirty seconds. She's relieved, though, too, and she knows it. Judging herself harshly against a beautiful twenty-six-year-old has taken more of a toll than she'd like to admit. There have been others, of course, a long, busty line of them, working backwards chronologically all the way to Nikki. But at least she can take Willa off that list.

"Does *she* know the truth about this little arrangement?" Margot asks. "Willa?"

Lawson looks into his tea. "Willa will be fine," he says. "She's talking to bloody Marvel next week. You think that would happen if she was still dating that idiotic TV actor?"

Margot doesn't even know who he's talking about, but the whiplash of now sympathizing with the wealthy model-turned-actress she used to hate by default is jarring.

"Can we take a walk or something?" he asks. "This place. It's very . . . I don't even know what the word is. Suburban? Or, no, *normal*. It's very normal, isn't it? We're not normal, Mar. You and me. Certainly not you. Frankly, this place is freaking me out."

Goddamn this son of a bitch, she thinks, because he can just come here and start digging around in her head.

Lawson grabs his jacket. "Come on, love. Let's get out of here."

When they step out the front door, Margot finds Billy, Robyn, Aaron, and Caleb sitting at the firepit at the side of the house. Billy is next to Robyn, and Caleb is next to her, like the busted-up little family that they are. When Billy sees Margot with Lawson, his eyes turn stricken. "Oh, hey," he says. "Are you . . . leaving?"

"We're going for a quick walk," she says. "To talk."

"That's bollocks!" says Lawson. "Don't believe that, mate! I've swept her off her feet again, and we're running away together. It was nice meeting you all. Cheers!"

"Um," says Billy. "Okay. I'll be here."

Margot and Lawson walk up the driveway. "Was that necessary?" she asks.

He leans into her gently. "Ah, lighten up, Margie. Bit of fun." Then he takes off his jacket and drops it over her shoulders. "You're chilly, love. I gotcha."

It's as heavy as a weighted blanket, and it smells like leather and . . . Lawson. He's been tweaked, tightened, straightened. There's more of him in some places, like his chest and arms. But in his waist and cheeks, there's less. This, though, Lawson's smell, is the same, and it enters her nose and works quickly through her nervous system like a party drug.

Shit, she thinks.

"Now that we've escaped," he says, "who the hell are those people?"

She tugs his jacket tighter. "Robyn is Billy's ex. The tall one, Caleb, is Robyn and Billy's son. The guy with the hair, Aaron, is Robyn's husband. Billy and I are staying in Robyn and Aaron's guest apartment because Caleb wants us to."

"Right-o" is all he says. One of the advantages of having a conversation with someone whose life is like make-believe is that nothing you tell him comes off as particularly strange.

A block of silent walking later, he asks if there are any bars around. "Turns out I could go for another drink after all. What do you say?"

"No. We'd be all over the Internet in five minutes."

"Little late for that," he says. "Between the airport and my little jaunt downtown, I'd say half of Baltimore has a shot of me on their iPhone."

"Fabulous," she says.

"Oh stop. Mar, you know you love it."

"Love what?"

"*This,* all of it. Mattering once more."

She laughs—again, unable to help it. "You really think any of this matters?"

"Bloody right I do. And so do you, love."

"You don't know the first thing about me."

"Don't I? Liar. Those videos? I was telling the truth. You looked amazing. But there was something else, too. Your eyes. They were ablaze. I hadn't seen that fire in a long time. I know you were never keen on the celebrity rubbish. But Margot Hammer was born to play the drums. She's a proper rock star. I loved seeing her again. And you know as well as I do that you loved *being* her again, din'cha?"

She doesn't bother telling him that he's right.

"Going off the grid like you did, though . . ."

"Why does everyone think I'm a mole woman now? I live in Chelsea, Lawson, in *our* old apartment."

"You know what I mean," he says. "You think giving it all up was a way to punish me. Nikki, too. And it worked. I can't speak for her, but I felt like shite—I *still* feel like shite. But what's that worth if you're just punishing yourself as well?"

"You playing a shrink in your next movie or something?" she asks.

"Bloody wish," he says. "I'm in talks to thwart more fucking aliens."

Billy's old neighborhood is a scene at night—bustling and noisy. This place, though, is quiet after dark. Adults pass them. Couples walk expensive dogs, talk politics. A few of them do double takes when they see Lawson, but no one says anything. Eventually, he sits on a bench. Margot sits beside him. Eddie's Market is across the street, closed for the night. The *E* in the Eddie's sign flickers. Lawson touches some words stenciled on the backrest between them. BALTIMORE: THE GREATEST CITY IN AMERICA. "Bit of a bold statement, don't you think?"

"Go fuck yourself, hon," she says, doing her best Baltimore accent.

"Beg your pardon?"

"They're proud of their city," she says. "Good for them."

"Right. Ironic, though, innit, considering there's a rat over there?"

"What? Where?"

Lawson points at shadows across the street. "See, the wee beady eyes?"

"No, that's a . . . a cat. Right?"

It isn't. The rodent stands on its haunches and assesses them before it disappears into the sewer.

"Fair warning," says Lawson, "that thing comes back, I'm using you as a human shield."

The lights at the coffee shop next to Eddie's shut off; two teenagers in green aprons walk out, lock up. Neither sees them.

"You warm enough, Mar?"

"I'm fine."

"Good, because I'm freezing my tits off, you fucking cow."

Margot lets loose her first spiteless laugh of the night, and it feels like letting go. Two things can be true at the same time: you can be epically pissed at someone and you can miss them, too, and Margot has missed this man on an atomic level.

"If you'll indulge me, love," he says. "Back to the time machine?"

"Oh God. Fine. What?"

"I really am sorry."

"You said that. Five minutes ago. You said it back then, too."

"Bears repeating."

"It would've hurt less if you'd loved her," she says. "If you'd cared about her. But it was just an affair. You ruined everything for . . . an affair."

Lawson hugs himself. "I understand. But listen, Mar, if it hadn't been Nikki, it'd've been someone else. I didn't know what the hell I was doing. Every woman I met suddenly wanted to shag me. It was bloody overwhelming."

"Got any tissues in this jacket?" she asks. "I may start weeping for you."

"All right. I know how it sounds. Absurd, right? Not wrong, though. When I was in primary school, birds ignored me. I was a . . . what do you call it here . . . a theater nerd? Suddenly, when I was eighteen, I transformed into a young version of this." Lawson points at his own face. "Then, after *Hustle* came out, nothing was ever the same again. Suddenly, temptation was everywhere. I loved you, Mar—so bloody much. And I thought that marrying you would force me to grow up, like adult boot camp. No such luck, though. Turnt out I still had the emotional intelligence of that skinny lad from nowhere. I failed you. Failed us—Poppy, too. And yeah, I said it before, I know. But . . . I'm sorry, Mar. I am."

An old man with a beard rides by on a squeaky bicycle, and Margot allows what Lawson has just said to sink in. From his perspective, it's the most sympathetic version of the story of their end. Hearing him tell it, though, it rings true. They never stood a chance. Lawson wasn't ready. They were kids, basically. They married too young, both of them in search of normalcy. Maybe it's time to stop being mad at him for that.

He's practically shivering beside her now, which he deserves, she supposes. She pokes one of his biceps, which feels like smooth skin stretched over stone. "What do you even eat, anyway, you skinny bastard?"

He scoffs. "Not much. It's all laid out for me by my nutritionist. Little packets that I heat up. Everything tastes like oatmeal."

"Poor thing."

"I'll give you a thousand quid right now if you have a buttered roll."

"Sorry, mate," she says.

They're a former husband and wife—parents—smiling on a bench in a city that, despite a few rats, is nicer than either of them would've previously guessed. Margot looks up the street. There are a few restaurants with decent bars over the hill. A drink would be nice, because a drink is always nice. Not tonight, though, because it'd be a shitshow. This bench, however, is quite pleasant, and she's in no hurry to leave it.

"I liked myself more when we were together," Lawson says.

"Shut up," she says. "You love yourself always."

"Right, true. I was less awful, though. My roles were better. I was taken seriously."

"Eh. You were always too pretty to be a serious actor."

"Fuck off. I'd be British Denzel by now if I hadn't cocked us up. You joke, but I was legitimate. I was in films I was proud of. I wasn't having a laugh before about that alien thing. In my next film, I will likely be playing Dr. Trent Hammersmith, intergalactic negotiator for the United bloody Nations."

"Shit, really?"

"I've become very much a joke, Mar. It's possible to love yourself while also loathing yourself. Trust me."

"Wait, did I watch the wrong ceremony on TV?" she asks. "Were you not nominated for an Oscar?"

"Supporting," he says. "Important distinction there, I'm told. And I didn't win. Also, I had to beg my way onto that cast. Did it for scale. And I've got nothing to show for it. The parts I want are still going to the other blokes. You legitimized me. You were part of my cachet, love. My cool. I'm ridiculous without you."

She wants to laugh—to dismiss this. But Lawson was part of what made her cool, too, and she knows it.

"Not a bad team back then, you and me, right? Tell me you weren't happier."

Margot doesn't tell him that. She says nothing.

"I'm not proposing here. I didn't show up with a ring. I'm just saying, baby steps. Have dinner with me. Maybe come back to L.A. for a bit. Or New York. Is our sushi place still there? The one you liked with the dodgy aquarium?"

"No. It's Thai fusion now."

"Well, somewhere new then."

Lawson's naïveté seems intentional, like he's constructing an alternate reality in which they're in their twenties again. He takes out his phone, taps a few times, and shows it to her. "Remember these two gorgeous idiots?" It's the photo from the Grammys. The smile seen round the world.

"I've avoided looking at that picture for years."

"Really?" he asks. "I look at it quite often. Especially when I need a wank. I mean, your bum, love. Look at that thing. Here, turn over. Lemme get a bite of it. Just one."

"Stop it, you idiot," she says, but she's laughing, because forgiving him has allowed her to admit once again that Lawson is actually quite funny.

He holds his phone between them. "Look at us. All promise. You, the badass drummer of the hottest rock band on the planet. Me, the next big thing."

"That was a long time ago," she says.

He puts his phone away, and they watch the quiet street. "I almost came back, you know."

A few weeks ago, when she heard Axl say that she didn't matter, the hurt was instantaneous. The hurt rises more slowly now, like something that's lingered inside, waiting to unfurl itself. "When?" she asks.

"Right away. Nikki and I thought we'd make a go of it, right? But that was a bloody disaster. She's quite a handful, you know. More important: I missed you. I missed seeing Pop Pop every day. I thought, what if I go back? Just show up. Jimmy would've let me up. He always liked you more than me, but I coulda slipped him a tenner."

Margot imagines what that knock at the door would've been like, his face in the peephole, an alternate two decades. "Why didn't you?"

"I was scared," he says. "Of you, mostly. You're quite small, but you're scary. And I knew I'd blown it. I also knew I didn't deserve you."

He's right, he didn't, but she knows how quickly she'd have opened that goddamn door. "Why are you here, Lawson?" she asks. "And don't say to win me back. Because we aren't those people anymore."

He takes her hand. "Fair. But imagine the *new* us. This little resurgence of yours? The return of the great Margot Hammer? Tip of the bloody iceberg." He kisses her hand. His lips are cool but soft. "This bloke, Billy? Nice chap. I get it. And I've seen how he looks at you. Poor tosser's crazy about you. But, Margie, love, we'd be unstoppable. Biggest story on the planet, us."

Margot breathes in, meaning to sigh and tell him to fuck off, but the sudden intake offers a fresh blast of Lawson's scent from his jacket.

"And you wouldn't have to worry about . . . well, any more of that dirty business. I'm ready to give that up. It's bloody exhausting anyway. A little tacky now, as well."

When her phone vibrates in her back pocket, it's a relief, because she doesn't have to think about what he's just said. She takes her iPhone out. Poppy again.

"We should answer that, yeah?" he says.

He's right again. Earlier was the first time Margot has willingly not answered one of their daughter's calls. She slides the bar at the bottom of the screen, and there's Poppy, concerned.

"Hi, honey."

"Mum?"

Lawson puts his face next to Margot's. "Pop Star! There's our girl!"

"Oh Jesus," their daughter says.

"How are you, love?" says Lawson. "Your mum and I are catching up a bit. We just saw a rat the size of a bloody Yorkshire terrier. You should've seen it. Your mum was terrified!"

CHAPTER 42

The next morning, Billy hears Caleb shooting baskets outside. Which is horrifying, because Caleb is just a little boy, and there's no hoop outside his apartment in Fells Point, just a street and cars bouncing up and down the cobblestone. Billy startles awake before he remembers that Caleb is eighteen. Billy isn't in Fells Point, and this isn't his apartment. If he inhales deeply enough, he can catch lingering whiffs of exhaust, because he's currently above a garage.

When he rolls over, the space where Margot should be is empty. He touches the sheets, which are cold, and he sees a note torn from her notebook. *Went to a farmer's market with Robyn. -M*

He stares. Her handwriting really is terrible. "A farmer's market?" he says, because he can't imagine a more improbable location: an underground rave maybe, or Mars.

More dribbling outside. From the swishing sounds every ten seconds, he wonders if Caleb has been practicing. Billy helped Aaron put the hoop up a few years ago. The two of them pouring concrete together went surprisingly well, although they had to throw their shoes away after.

Billy chose to pretend to be asleep when Margot returned to

the apartment last night after her walk with Lawson. He was trying to make a point, he supposes—his way of saying, *Well, you were certainly gone a long time. So long, in fact, that I am no longer conscious.* He listened to her in the dark as she brushed her teeth, took off her boots, slid out of her jeans. When she eased in next to him, she touched his back and took a breath, like she might say something. Billy waited. But then the warmth of her hand was gone, and she rolled over. He'd like to know what she almost said. One of the worst things about being a person is that when you don't know something, you assume the absolute worst.

Lawson and I made love in a parked car down by the dry cleaners. In case you were wondering, he's way better at sex than you are. I'll be leaving with him today and we will continue to make love in various exotic locations around the world. Come on, Billy. You assumed this would eventually happen, right? I mean, look at him. Look at you.

He gets out of bed and goes to the espresso machine, where he turns the appropriate levers and sets his little glass beneath the spout. Then he looks out the window into the driveway and discovers that the person shooting hoops isn't his son, it's Lawson Daniels. Lawson is wearing the same thing he wore last night. His leather jacket is folded neatly on the pavement. The actor pivots fifteen feet from the hoop and drains a jumper.

Swish.

"Well, 'ello there, mate."

"Hey, man," says Billy. He's standing on the stairs outside the apartment overlooking the driveway. He's not sure what compelled him to come out, but now here he is, committed to what he can only imagine will be among the strangest conversations of his life. "Did you stay here last night?"

Lawson nods up to the main house. "Extra bedroom. Not a bad

little setup. One of those feather beds. Like sleeping on a giant Muppet."

Billy tries to imagine Robyn leading him up the stairs, handing him clean pillowcases.

Lawson tosses a ball up underhanded. It rolls around the rim and falls in. "You haven't seen our girl yet today, have you?" he asks.

"She's apparently at a farmer's market with Robyn."

"Perfect day for it. Hey, is that an espresso?"

Billy looks at the little glass hooked to his index finger.

"Reckon that's quite good."

Billy can hardly believe the question he's about to ask. He has to ask it, though, right? It's just common decency. "Um, do you want one?"

"That'd be lovely. Thanks, mate."

A moment later, Billy returns to the driveway with an espresso for Lawson and a new one for himself. Lawson holds Caleb's basketball in his armpit and clinks his little glass against Billy's little glass.

A jogger passes, a woman a few years younger than Billy and Lawson. She does a double take, then a triple take, then stumbles over the curb.

"Morning, love!" Lawson calls, then he drains his espresso in a single gulp. To Billy, he says, "Fancy a shoot-about?"

"A what?"

"One-on-one? Twenty-one? Horse?"

"Do they even have basketball in England?"

"Here and there," says Lawson. "I played rugby when I was a lad. Picked basketball up stateside. I was up for a part. A Spike Lee Joint about a phenom baller from the inner city. When I started playing, it just . . . well, came natural. I'm a bit of an athlete, as you can tell." He rolls the ball to Billy, then jogs in a short circle. "Here, mate, feed me."

Billy passes Lawson the ball. The actor banks it off the glass. Not a difficult shot, but Billy is aware that he's yet to see him miss.

"Lawson, I don't wanna sound unfriendly, but . . . what are you doing here?"

Lawson seems almost offended. "I think I made my intentions quite clear last night. To you. To Mar. To the rest of the lot. That said, I understand that this puts you in a somewhat awkward position."

Billy isn't sure where he should be aiming his eyes. Looking directly at Lawson, he finds, is unsettling, and the two espressos he's had are starting to enter his bloodstream like a swirl of tiny jackhammers. "Yeah, I guess you could say that. So maybe you should, I don't know . . . go?"

"Go?" says Lawson. "Go where?"

"Away. A hotel. Or back to . . . where did you come from?"

"Last night? Oh, L.A. Flew commercial."

"L.A., then," says Billy. "Go there. Or anywhere that isn't here. Seriously, anywhere."

Lawson dribbles twice, hits a quick layup, then he and Billy both turn at the sound of the front door opening. Caleb steps into the driveway wearing joggers and sneakers, a long-sleeved T-shirt.

"Perfect," says Lawson. "We've got another player. A tall one at that."

"Dad?" Caleb says. "What're . . . what're you guys doing?"

"We're just talking, Cay," says Billy. "It's fine."

"Here, show us your moves, stretch." Lawson passes to Caleb. Caleb catches it but clearly has no idea what to do next.

"Go on, then," Lawson says. "Shoot. Pop the J. Fire the rock. I could go on with basketball phrases if you'd like. I know quite a few."

Caleb walks over to the hoop and lays one in.

"Well done. Now, Billy, back to our discussion. Just because you and I want the same thing—i.e., one Margie Willis—that doesn't mean we can't be civil about it."

"Wait," says Caleb. "You two aren't gonna, like, fight, are you?"

"What?" Lawson laughs, and then he laughs again, which Billy can't help but take personally. "Stop it, mate. Of course we aren't. Caleb, I like your dad, and I like you, too. But as far as having a row goes, well, lads, the way I see it, none of this is up to us. The options have been well presented. Me. You, Billy. New York, L.A. . . . this garage here in Baltimore. But this is Mar's decision, right? Not mine. Not yours."

"Her decision?" says Billy.

"Yeah."

"What do you mean? What did you two do last night?"

"Relax," says Lawson. "It wasn't like that, mate. We talked. I presented my case. Convincingly. I told her I want her back."

"What did she say?" Billy asks.

Lawson spins the ball on his finger. "She said she needs to think about it."

"Shit," says Caleb.

Billy looks at his son. He can't bring himself to admonish the swearing because, yeah, shit. Another one of the worst things about being a person: when we're not busy imagining the worst, too often we allow ourselves to imagine the best, and that almost never pans out.

The front door opens again, and everyone turns. Aaron steps outside in his running gear. He's oblivious to them at first, because he's wearing wireless earbuds. He grabs one foot, stretches. Eventually, when he realizes that the three of them are standing in the driveway, he removes one bud. "What the hell's going on out here?" he asks.

"Excellent," says Lawson. "Who's up for a bit of two-on-two?"

CHAPTER 43

Margot isn't exactly a farmer's market kinda girl. As she stands sipping iced chai tea, or whatever this peppery bullshit is that Robyn bought for her, she's staring down at a big basket full of some weird fruit that looks like it shouldn't be real. "Star fruit?" she asks. "Is that a thing?"

"It's good in smoothies," Robyn says.

They're a ten-minute walk from the house. Margot woke an hour ago with a text from Robyn inviting her along. Under normal circumstances Margot would've dunked her phone in the toilet and claimed never to have seen the message. *This* morning, though, milling about looking at space fruit is preferable to dealing with the awkwardness of having Billy and Lawson on the same property.

Lawson kissed her on the cheek last night before they parted ways. He'd kissed her hand earlier, and she'd felt very little, but her face was a different thing entirely—different nerves, wired to different memories.

"I suppose that doesn't change your mind, love?" he asked her after, sensing that his kiss had had an effect.

She shook her head.

"What if I try a different location?" He touched her chin, just under her lower lip. "Like, maybe *here,* for instance?"

She shook her head again, and it felt powerful, the certainty of it. "No."

"No?" he asked.

"Yeah," she said. "No."

"Care to elaborate?"

"I don't think I hate you anymore," she said. "Which is nice. It was exhausting hating you. But I don't want to be with you again. I mean, I *really* don't."

"Just like that?" he said. "You don't want to think about it? It's a big decision."

"I've been thinking about it for years."

"For fuck's sake," he said. "Because of *him?* Because of Billy bloody Perkins? Really?"

"No," she said. "I like Billy. I might like him a lot. But I don't want to be with you because of *you.*"

"Well, shit," he said. "That hurts, love. It's my teeth, then, innit?"

"Yeah, a little."

Now, with the star fruit behind her and stands of more weird fruit and produce ahead, Margot finally drops her chai tea into an overflowing recycle bin.

"Not for you, huh?" Robyn asks.

"Eh," Margot replies. "I mostly run on coffee, alcohol, and anxiety."

Robyn looks around, leans closer. "Well, that lady over there at the green bean stand sometimes has mimosas. Wanna check it out?"

Margot isn't really a mimosas kinda girl either, but sometimes in life you have to adapt.

———

"I almost got a tattoo because of you."

The chill from last night is gone—burned off by a sunny, breezeless morning—so Margot's sweater is around her waist. She looks down now at her own arms, fading ink on bare skin. "Yeah?"

"He thought you were so cool. I don't know if he's downplayed it, but Billy *really* liked you back then."

Margot sips her plastic cup of spiked orange juice, unsure what to say.

"He was my boyfriend," says Robyn. "I knew he loved me. But he had this crush on you. I'd catch him reading about you in magazines. And he'd play your albums and be like, 'Robyn, listen to this tempo change' or whatever, like I had any idea what that meant. He was crazy about you. But we were so different, you and me. That annoyed the shit out of me. Is that weird? You were, like, my nemesis. I was pissed at you, a total stranger."

Margot looks up at the woman before her—taller, skinnier, lighter hair, angled cheekbones. Robyn is right; it's like she's looking into a mirror that reflects opposites.

"Obviously, I didn't know you," Robyn says. "You weren't even *you*. You were some famous chick. It's not like he'd ever actually meet you, right? Ha! But do you know how much it messed with my head that my boyfriend was nuts about someone who looked absolutely nothing like me? Who was different from me in every way?"

Margot might know a thing or two about that. "Well, if it makes you feel better," she says, "you're very pretty."

"Oh, stop it."

"No," says Margot. "You're prettier than me. It's an objective fact. The first time I saw you, I did that thing in my head. I was like, 'She's prettier than me, goddammit.'"

"Well, thank you," says Robyn. "*You're* pretty. And you're cooler than me. Obviously. Just look at you. God, I could never pull those boots off. Anyway, why do we do that? It's not healthy."

Just then, a blond mom in yoga pants who is arguably better looking than either of them walks by holding a giant bag of carrots. She's wearing an infant on her chest in a BabyBjörn, and Margot and Robyn both look at her ass.

"Doubt we're gonna solve that one here," Margot says. "I mostly blame the Internet."

Robyn buys strawberries. Margot offers to carry them, because the cloth NPR tote bag Robyn brought is starting to look heavy.

They continue, moving at museum-stroll speed. Some twenty-something girls tell Margot that she rocks. Others notice her, too. Margot senses photos being snapped by poorly concealed iPhones, their computerized clicks just audible. When they make it to the last stand of the farmer's market—a guy in an Orioles cap selling locally sourced goat cheese—Margot and Robyn stop. It seems like Robyn has more to say. "Robyn. You're not *still* pissed at me, are you?"

Robyn laughs. "No, of course not."

But Margot watches as the woman's face changes—a slow, downward slide.

"Maybe a little," says Robyn. "I know how sweet he is. And he's very gentle, right? The way he is with Caleb—his students. And he's *nice*. Like, he's a legitimately nice person. And you think, how can someone be as nice as he is? Nobody's that nice. Not anymore."

To Margot's semi-horror, she sees tears form at the bridge of Robyn's nose, like last night at dinner, and she thinks of the kettle back in the kitchen: a harmless-looking thing that boils over in seconds. "Are you okay?"

"He *is* all those things," Robyn says. "He was back then, too. But he was also a fucking moron. Completely directionless. No motivation. He had no idea what he wanted to do with his life. I had no choice. What was I gonna do, wait around for him to spontaneously become an adult?"

"Believe me," Margot says. "I know how stupid twenty-something-year-old men are."

She means this to be funny, but it's not, and Robyn's sharp laughter takes a sad-sounding turn. "Right," she says, "but at least you got to be with Law—No, nothing. My point is, I broke his heart. And it broke *my* heart to do it. But me giving him up was the catalyst for Billy getting his shit together. It made him who he is now. Then you swoop in, with your tattoos and your hair that does that fall-across-your-face thing, and you get to have the *good* Billy. The grown-up. It's not fair."

Robyn's right, it isn't. Good or bad, life is all about timing. We're either its victims or its beneficiaries. Margot picks out a strawberry for herself and then one for Robyn.

Robyn smiles as she chews. "It's good," she says.

"Very fresh," says Margot.

"We could get some star fruit if you want," Robyn says.

Margot tells her that maybe they should take things slow, and Robyn laughs. Then Margot does something she couldn't have imagined doing earlier: she hugs Robyn. The other woman stiffens, surprised, which is understandable. She relaxes, though, and hugs Margot back. It's nice. Farmer's markets. Who knew?

"Ready to go back?" Margot asks.

"Yeah," says Robyn. "In a sec. Maybe another strawberry?"

She holds out the carton, and Robyn takes a few. "Usually I wash them first," Robyn says. "But fuck it, right?"

They walk, finally, in the direction of home.

"So, yeah," Margot says. "It didn't work with you and Billy. The timing was off, like you said. But you have a sweet son. And a great house. And Billy says your career is going well. And you have Aaron, too, right?"

Which is when Robyn bursts into tears.

CHAPTER 44

Caleb is staying positive about this "Dad vs. Lawson Daniels" stuff.

Okay, yeah, apparently Margot is going to choose between them, *Bachelorette*-season-finale style. And at least on the surface, that doesn't bode well for someone like Billy Perkins, him being not famous and just a normal guy and all. But Caleb is sticking to his original line of stoned thinking: Billy Perkins is *still* the best person Caleb knows.

That said, Lawson Daniels really is cool as fuck.

"I'll take you, mate," he told Caleb a few minutes ago. "You and me against Club Dad Bod here."

Caleb isn't used to being picked when it comes to athletic things. "Me? Really?"

"Yeah. You're Shaq, I'm Kobe."

How would he even begin to explain this to Justin and Shin-Soo? He didn't tell them about Lawson showing up last night while the three of them played *Grand Theft Auto* online, because he was afraid they'd log off immediately and race over. Now he and Lawson are playing pickup basketball in the driveway like besties.

Lawson dribbles between his legs, jukes Caleb's dad with a

crossover, and hits Caleb with a high lob. Caleb dodges Aaron and lays it in.

"That's it, mate! See? You're a foot taller than these geezers. Keep the ball high and they can't stop you. You're a bloody scoring machine."

Caleb tosses the ball back to Lawson, who checks it with Caleb's dad. "Ten two, mate. Should we get some oxygen for you? You don't have a tank up there in the flat, do you?"

Billy checks the ball back.

They play on, make-it-take-it, and Caleb and Lawson continue to dominate. Caleb knows that he's not good at this sport or any other, but Lawson's advice was solid, and he hits a few more shots. It helps that his dad and Aaron are objectively terrible.

Lawson drains one from the crack in the pavement that they've all agreed marks the three-point line. "Apparently there's ... *reign* in the forecast, lads," he says. It's a total dad joke, but it's funny when he says it.

"Are you even trying to guard him?" Aaron asks Caleb's dad.

"You can help, you know," his dad responds, and Caleb is startled by his tone. He wouldn't need one whole hand to count the number of times in his life that he's heard his dad raise his voice.

The tension has been building since they started playing. His dad grabs at Lawson's arms on defense, and Lawson keeps driving into him with his shoulder. Caleb gets it, since they're both competing for Margot, like a driveway duel. What Caleb doesn't get, though, is why Aaron seems so mad at his dad.

"Jesus, man!" Aaron throws his hands in the air after Lawson hits a reverse layup. "Are you kidding?"

"Aaron, I'm a piano teacher!"

"All right, lads," Lawson says. "Simmer down. Maybe make-it-take-it isn't working. Here, ball's yours, Billy. Caleb and I'll play a little D. Change things up a bit."

The teams switch sides. Lawson slaps Caleb's ass. "I'll work the perimeter, mate. You just stand down low and keep being tall."

His dad moves to the top of the driveway, checks the ball to Lawson.

"Don't feel bad, mate," Lawson says. "I'm sure you're a better pianist than me."

"We don't have to be dicks, though, right?" Caleb says.

When Lawson laughs, Caleb can think of at least three movies he's seen in which Lawson laughs just like that—like a big, head-tossed-back thing. The people stopping and watching at the end of the driveway add to the weirdness of all this, the way each goes through the same process of realization. *Is that? No. Wait. What? Oh my God.*

His dad dribbles, steps back, surveys the driveway. He passes to Aaron, but Aaron immediately fires the ball back. His dad catches it right at his face. He passes back to Aaron, but the same thing happens: Aaron throws it back, hard, with a grunt. This repeats itself a few times. At first his dad seems confused, but with each toss he looks more pissed. "What the hell, man?" he asks.

"Here!" says Aaron, throwing the ball back.

Caleb and Lawson ease out of their defensive crouches, and now they're watching as the piano teacher and corporate lawyer heave a basketball back and forth at each other's faces in the driveway.

"Guys?" says Caleb.

"Interesting offensive strategy," says Lawson.

"Fucking take it!" Aaron grunts.

"You take it!" says Billy.

"No!" Another throw to the face.

"Aaron, why are we doing this?"

Finally—inevitably—Caleb's dad can't handle one of Aaron's tosses. The ball comes in too hot, shoots through his hands, and hits him squarely in the left eye like an uppercut. His dad collapses in the driveway.

"Dad!"

"Oy! Ouch, mate."

Caleb kneels next to his dad. "Are you okay?"

"Aaron, Jesus Christ!"

"Yeah, mate, have to agree with Billy. That's no way to treat a teammate."

"Will you please shut the fuck up for five . . . goddamn . . . seconds?" Aaron shouts at Lawson.

"Oy," Lawson says. "Getting heated."

"Everything's working out just like you've always wanted, huh, Billy?"

Caleb's dad sits up, palm pressed to his eye. "What are you talking about? You just hit me in the face, you asshole. You think I wanted *that*?"

"You're just gonna swoop right in, aren't you?"

Caleb doesn't know what Aaron is talking about. He holds his finger in front of his dad's face. "Do you, like, see more than one?"

"Three. No, wait, four."

"Ol' nice guy Billy Perkins," says Aaron. "You've been skulking around for ten years, just waiting for us to fall apart. And now here you are—above the goddamn garage!"

"What are you talking about, Aaron? Who's falling apart?"

Maybe it's because his dad has just taken a pretty significant shot to the head. Or, well, maybe Caleb's just smarter than he is. Either way, he's a step ahead, and suddenly things make sense. The vibe between his mom and Aaron has been different lately, the changes subtle, like barely perceptible temperature drops. He looks up at his stepfather. "What?" he asks. "Aaron, you're . . . you guys are falling apart?"

Aaron tosses the ball over his shoulder. It bounces away, stopping in a hedge, scattering some birds. "Cay," he says. "It's . . ."

Then a big black Cadillac Escalade pulls into the bottom of the driveway. One of the back doors opens and an old guy with a creepy ponytail steps out. The woman who gets out next is maybe his mom's age, but Caleb is immediately certain that she's the most beautiful woman he's ever seen.

Lawson is the first to speak, and he does so smiling. "Well, this is a surprise. Hello, love. Come here; give us a hug. You look wonderful."

CHAPTER 45

Robyn is embarrassed for crying. In front of Margot Hammer. At a farmer's market.

Worse, she's mad at herself for all the times she's judged other women for going off the rails in the face of domestic bullshit. How many times has she heard about a lady from work or another mom from Caleb's school melting down at the grocery store, having an affair with a T-ball coach, or getting hammered at a charity luncheon and thought, *Jesus, lady, get your shit together?* Now, though, with her shit very much not together—frankly, her shit is all over the place—Robyn gets it.

She's walking through her neighborhood. The former drummer of a rock band that she never particularly cared for is clomping along beside her. And for the first time in her adult life, Robyn doesn't have a plan. She had one, and she executed the hell out of it. But that plan was recently torn to pieces and tossed up into the wind. Robyn tried to keep loving Aaron because that was what her plan called for. It turned out Aaron was trying, too, because he also had a plan. Their marriage had been a merger, and that merger has come undone—it's being spun off into two separate entities.

As she rattles through this analogy in her mind, Robyn is aware that she should probably stop thinking about her life in corporate euphemisms. Maybe that's part of her problem. She's treated her marriage less like a marriage and more like a meeting with HR in which a problematic lack of synergy is being discussed in detail.

The upside of not having a plan, though, is that Robyn can now do . . . anything.

She can start running if she wants to. Literally. Robyn could drop this tote bag full of expensive organic crap on the pavement right now and just take off. Margot would never catch her, with those boots and her short little legs. Robyn could chop her hair off and dye it some daring color. She could seduce that handsome nerd Mark in accounting or get a boob job. She could switch things up and let Aaron keep the house, and she could move to some edgy place in the city—a loft, something with exposed brick and cool views and the constant drone of police sirens. Seriously. Anything.

"You're a fast walker," says Margot, struggling to keep up.

Robyn does her best to slow down, but it's difficult, because Robyn walks the same way she does everything: with a purpose.

No. She's being stupid. Cool apartments? Sex with accountants? Silicone? These aren't solutions; they're just more problems. What Robyn needs is a new plan. And she needs it right now.

Margot has stopped walking. Robyn doesn't realize this for a full five strides, because she's been busy self-analyzing.

In the short time Robyn has known Margot, she's rarely seen the woman's facial expression change. When Robyn turns back now, though, she sees that Margot looks shocked. More than that: she looks upset. As Robyn follows Margot's gaze back toward the house, she understands why.

Billy is sitting in the driveway with a swollen face. Caleb is kneeling beside him. Aaron is standing in his running clothes with his hands on his hips, and Lawson Daniels, whom Robyn has somehow forgotten about, is smiling and chatting with a gorgeous woman. A man with a ponytail stands beside her. A few neighbors watch from a distance; some are taking iPhone pictures. The woman looks familiar. Then she looks more familiar. "Oh shit," Robyn says, because the woman is Nikki Kixx.

It's ridiculous that Robyn knows exactly how Margot's marriage ended. But she does, every sordid, stupid detail. Lawson's affair with Nikki Kixx. Margot losing it on MTV. The band breaking up. Margot's life and career unraveled. Robyn read about all of it in some magazine years ago, probably while she got her hair cut or waited in line at Giant to buy groceries. It's taken her until now, though, to consider how much all of that must've hurt.

"Margot?" she says. "Are you okay?"

Margot is still holding the carton of strawberries. She takes a step backward, as if she, now, is the one thinking about running. Aaron's voice carries up the block. "So, does everyone in the entertainment industry know where I live now or what?"

"We can go if you want," Robyn tells Margot. "We can just bolt. You want to?"

Billy is the first of the crew in the driveway to notice them. He looks up from the pavement and shakes his head.

"No," says Margot. "Thanks. But I need to finally deal with this."

Nikki Kixx sees Margot next. She stops talking to Lawson and takes a step toward them, waiting. "Okay," says Robyn, because she knows that for Margot there's no going back now.

CHAPTER 46

Lawson sips his pint, sighs, smiles. He smiles a lot, Billy has found. "Intense morning, innit, mate?"

Billy and Lawson are sitting in the bar section of a restaurant called Johnny's, a few blocks from Robyn and Aaron's house. When the dumbstruck bartender came over for their order a few minutes ago, Lawson asked, "What's the most proper English beer you've got?" That ended up being something called Boddingtons Pub Ale. Lawson ordered two, along with a plastic bag of ice. "For my mate here's cocked-up face."

Billy sips the ale now. It's delicious—smooth, creamy, like a lighter Guinness. "I wonder if I have a concussion," he says.

"Well, if you feel like having a puke, aim that way," says Lawson. "I only brought this one pair of jeans."

The restaurant tables are full of people eating brunch. The bar, though, is empty. Lawson chose a corner spot, which means everyone here can see him. It's the exact opposite of how Margot handles being in public. She hides, angles herself away from crowds, stays as low-key as she can, while Lawson announces himself to the world.

A girl in a Roland Park Country School hoodie approaches

with her iPhone. "Can I . . ." She's unable to finish her sentence, though, stricken by shyness.

"'Course, love," Lawson says.

A pose, a smile, a blushing teenager with braces, and they're alone again.

Along with putting Lawson on display for the entire restaurant, their seats have camped them directly across from the big mirror behind the bar, so every time Billy looks up, he's treated to a side-by-side comparison of himself and the most handsome man he's ever seen in real life.

Lawson nods at Billy's eye. "Give us a look."

Billy removes the baggie, and Lawson hisses. "Is it bad?" Billy asks.

"Seen worse. Hurts, I reckon. Had my share. Colin Farrell caught me good once on set. Was all pretend, but I missed my mark. Boom. Saw me dead nan waving me to the light."

When Margot and Robyn returned from the farmer's market earlier, things got weird. Aaron stormed off into the house. Robyn went after him. Caleb gave Billy a pained look, like he was torn, but then he followed after his mom and stepdad. Margot and Nikki Kixx stood on opposite sides of the driveway staring at each other. Finally, Nikki said, "Hey, rock star." And then, "Your hair looks really great."

Billy wanted to help Margot—to protect her—but how do you protect someone from something that so dramatically predates you? He felt irrelevant—still woozy, too, from the basketball to the face. Which was when Lawson suggested they take a walk. "Grab a pint, mate? You and me?"

"So, who was the guy with the ponytail?" Billy asks.

"Oy, that cunt?" says Lawson. "Axl Albee. Big muckety-muck at Mar and Nikki's label. Not a nice fella."

"You didn't know he was coming? That *they* were coming? Him and Nikki?"

Lawson looks surprised at the accusation. "You think that was my doing? No, sir. Woulda been clever, though, yeah? Whole thing's bloody perfect, you ask me."

"What?"

"I came here to get Mar back," he says. "Entice her to leave your quaint little town here. What's better than getting half her band back together in your bloody driveway?"

Lawson's bluntness is jarring but informative, like the villain revealing his plan to the audience.

"And as long as we're talking about who knew what when," says Lawson, "I take it you didn't know about Robyn having trouble with the bloke with the hair?"

"No," says Billy. "His name's Aaron, by the way. I guess I just wasn't paying attention."

"That's perfect, too."

"What? Why?"

"Pieces are falling right into place. Mar comes with me. We go about our lives, fame and what have you. Aaron exits stage left, takes his hair with him. You move into the big house like a proper adult. Bob's your uncle. You and Robyn make a go again. Why not? Fit bird, mate, if you don't mind me saying. You've already got an enormous child together. Symmetrical. Ready-made family. Cheers."

Billy understood most of that. "Did you say 'Bob's your uncle'?"

"It's an expression." Lawson clears his throat, rolls his shoulders, then begins speaking in a perfect American accent. "Would it be easier if I talked like this?"

"I don't like that," says Billy. "That's creepy."

"Good, right?" he says, still as an American. "The trick: slower and lower. Tough at first not to sound like you're trying to be a cowboy. Got it down pat, though. It's like the Queen's English, but with all the sophistication and grace stripped away. We can all do it, we British film stars. Our goal is to make American actors obsolete by decade's end. Well on our way." Lawson winks at Billy, then orders two cold Budweisers, briefly confusing the bartender.

"Well, you're wrong," Billy says.

"'Bout what? I said a lot of things there."

"I don't want symmetry. I love Margot." Billy removes the baggie again, pokes at his swollen cheekbone.

The beers arrive, and Lawson groans up at the ceiling. "You do, eh?"

Billy tosses the baggie onto the bar, giving up, because it doesn't matter. Let it swell; he doesn't care. "Yeah, I do."

"You know you're making this difficult for me, mate, right?" says Lawson. "Truth is, I rather like you."

Despite the obvious conflicts here, Billy finds that he rather likes Lawson, too.

"When I saw you at first," says Lawson, "on my phone—you know, the Internet—I was like, 'Well then, this'll be easy enough. Look at this tosser.' No offense."

"Oh, no, really, why would that be offensive?"

"Point being, I underestimated you. Now that I've gotten a look at you—seen you get your bell rung and pop right back up—I understand why she fancies you. You're a likable bloke. Shit, I understand why the *world* fancies you. You should think about getting a publicist, by the way. You could really leverage yourself. You have any idea how hard it is for a *man* to trend online right now, for something *good*? Virtually impossible. It's usually you've punched a valet or accidentally had a wank on Zoom. Well done there."

"Um, thanks?"

Lawson pushes his empty pint glass away, starts on his bottle of

Budweiser. As Lawson checks his teeth in the bar mirror, Billy wonders what's happening back at the house. He keeps thinking about the look on Margot's face when she saw Nikki. It was like when Caleb's plan fell apart at Charm City Rocks weeks ago, and Margot stood silently, lost looking, like a fighter trying to stay upright. He knows that he loves her, because he's begun absorbing her emotions. He feels joy when she smiles—and especially on the rare occasions when she laughs. Now he feels pain at the thought of her pain, a literal ache in his dumb guts.

"I'm gonna be honest with you about something," says Lawson.

"Okay. Have you *not* been being honest?"

Lawson laughs. "Not entirely. Remember, I'm quite good at pretend. You see, up until now, I was intent on essentially ruining your life, because you were my sworn enemy."

"Oh."

"I laid it out for Mar last night," Lawson says. "Was pretty clear about it. Told her I wanted her back. Told her I could help make her famous again. I mean proper famous—not all this Internet rubbish. I kissed her."

"You kissed her?"

"Settle, mate. On the hand. Cheek as well. Cheek or not, it was a good one. And I offered to give her one on the lips as well. And it woulda been ace. A proper knicker-dropper."

"I'm . . . I'm waiting for the 'but' part," says Billy.

"*However*," says Lawson. The actor sips then, smooths the top of his hair in the mirror. "I told you this morning that she said she needed to have a think, you know, me and her—me versus you— all that."

"Yeah?"

"Well, that's not *precisely* what she said. She actually told me to fuck off."

"She did?"

Lawson drinks some more. "In a matter of speaking, yes. I was surprised as well. Kissing. Getting back together. Instant worldwide fame and fortune. Might as well've told me to shove it all straight up my own arse."

Billy catches his reflection again. His face is puffy, but he's smiling. "Wow."

"She fancies you, apparently." Lawson claps Billy's back, which becomes a surprisingly warm squeeze. "Again, well done."

"Thanks."

Lawson points at the bartender. Somehow his Budweiser is gone already. "Oy, enough of this. Back to the Boddingtons. Two of 'em."

"You know it's like not even eleven o'clock, right?" asks Billy.

"Get fucked, mate. I'm drowning my sorrows. Believe it or not, I'm not accustomed to being told no by women."

"Yeah, that makes sense. I've read the articles."

"I've often not been a very good person, Billy," says Lawson. "That was particularly the case with Mar, back then. But I want to do right by her for a change, so I'm gonna step aside."

"You are?" says Billy. "Just like that?"

"Probably for the best. Also, only slightly related, I was informed this morning that if I'm not back in L.A. by tomorrow I'll be sued for thirty-four million U.S. dollars."

"That . . . that's a lot of money."

"It is. I should probably start reading my contracts. But I want you to know two things. First, I'm not just rolling over. If Mar comes to her senses, I'll gladly welcome her home. To whichever home she likes. New York, L.A., London, my little place in the Alps."

"The Alps?"

"French side," says Lawson. "It's lovely there. You should check it out. And second. Mar fancies you. Cheers, you cunt. But I think you need to ask yourself an important question. Is Mar fancying you what's best for *Mar*?"

The mirror again. In it, Billy sees his smile fall.

Lawson waves his hand in a circle over his head. "Baltimore. Charming place. However, doesn't Mar perhaps belong somewhere a little . . . I don't know, bigger? Again, no offense, but perhaps . . . better?"

Billy has wondered this, too, of course. At night, usually, with Margot sleeping beside him. Not just Baltimore. A little apartment above a garage. Trips to a dusty record shop, evenings watching an historically shitty baseball team. A piano teacher with a drawer stuffed full of cardigans. Margot deserves more than all of it, and Billy knows it.

He has two untouched beers to choose from, so he picks the American one. He takes a sip, touches the cold bottle to his face.

"She's a star, mate."

"I know."

"And I'm not psychic, but I have a pretty good idea why Nikki and Axl are here."

"Me too."

The two men drink. People watch, whispering about them.

"The world wants her back," says Lawson.

"I know."

The bartender and two of the waitresses ask Lawson for a photo, which Billy takes for them. He tells everyone to say cheese. A middle-aged couple asks Lawson to sign their menu. When they're alone again, Lawson asks if he can have Billy's Boddingtons, because it's just going to waste there. Then he says, "In a year or two—five years' time, whenever it is—do you want to look at yourself in a mirror like this one here one day and know that you were the bloke who stood in our Margie's way?"

CHAPTER 47

For a few weeks when they were both briefly freshmen in college, Margot wondered if she was in love with Nikki. They'd been staying up late, huddled closely over notebooks and sketch pads as they mapped out their future, chose a band name, doodled potential logos and tattoos, and brainstormed the types of guitarist and bass player they wanted to find.

"Chicks who are cool and badass," said Nikki, "but not as cool and badass as us. Duh."

Nikki was sexy and smart and magnetic. She smelled like vanilla and cigarettes. She made Margot feel cooler than she was. Like a rock star. Margot's sexuality had always felt fluid, too—a tempo that fluctuated with a piece of music. As she looks at Nikki sitting now at Billy's Steinway, she's angry, but she remembers that feeling of maybe-love: a knotted-up stomach, heat at the crooks of her elbows. Nikki is wearing dark, legging-tight jeans and a T-shirt with a strategically shlumpy sweater over it. Her beauty is still vivid, like everyone else in the room has been shot slightly out of focus.

The instant they stepped into the apartment, Nikki went right for the piano. "Hello, gorgeous," she said, tapping out some notes from one of her solo songs. She stops now, like she suddenly remembers why she's here. She looks at the unpacked boxes, the espresso machine, the clutter of two adults living in a space that's too small. "And *you* look great, too," she says.

"What?" asks Margot.

"Sorry. That didn't make sense." Nikki sounds nervous. "I said your hair looks great earlier, in the driveway. It does, but so does the rest of you. *You* look great, Margot."

Her feelings for her old friend have softened, she now realizes, and she knows that this is because of stupid Lawson. He showed up last night and was funny and contrite and not the monster she'd kept casting him as. The bastard went and sucked the oxygen out of her rage, and Margot finds that she wishes Nikki would play one of *their* old songs.

"That girl you sang with in those videos," Nikki says. "She wasn't bad."

"She was all right," says Margot.

"I was jealous of her," says Nikki. "Does that make me a psycho? I was like, shut up, you bitch. That's supposed to be me."

Margot nearly says, *You should've thought of that years ago,* but she doesn't, because it would sound childish—chronologically unreasonable, too.

"Goddamn, girl," Nikki says. "You played the shit out of those songs. I missed that sound. You're like a thunderstorm."

Margot doesn't know how she's supposed to be feeling or what she's supposed to do. Last night, Lawson accused her of disappearing to punish them—him and Nikki. He was wrong, mostly. The two of them feeling shitty was part of it, sure, a bonus. And yes, as Margot told Billy last night, she's doubted herself and her own ability inside and out. She doubted that she was talented enough or hot enough or whatever else enough. Typical artistic neurosis.

But the real reason Margot walked away from it all was so she'd never have to face Nikki again. It took her a few years of being a rock-and-roll recluse to realize that. She was hiding from her former best friend. And now here she is.

"By the way," says Nikki. "Are you and Lawson, like—"

"No," says Margot. "He just showed up, like you did."

"Oh. So, the kinda-cute piano-teacher guy, then, with the swollen face?"

Margot lifts her eyebrows, an expression that says, *Maybe,* but also, *None of your business.*

"I can't tell you how thrilling it is to see you two together," says Axl. "To hear you *talking* again. I've dreamed of this."

If her feelings for Lawson and Nikki have softened, time has only made her hate little Stuart Albee even more. Maybe that's unfair, but whatever. His ridiculous ponytail looks even more asinine now than it did back then. She would be pissed at him for that goddamn thing alone.

"I'd offer you an espresso," says Margot, "but I have no idea how that thing works."

They look at the machine. It takes up a significant portion of the counter space, like a grounded alien spacecraft.

"Sorry to just drop in," Axl says. "But, well, you were being elusive."

"*I'm* not sorry," says Nikki. "I should've dropped in years ago."

"You were, what," says Margot, "seven miles away?"

Nikki smiles, touches the Steinway's middle F key. "You know I hate Chelsea."

"Things have been moving fast, ladies," Axl says. "That's how it is now. Things were glacial before. You needed completed albums, radio stations. Now mountains get moved like that." Axl snaps his fingers.

"What are you saying?" Margot asks.

"Remember how I used to talk about striking while the iron's hot?"

Margot and Nikki look at each other. It was practically the man's mantra.

"Well, that shit's hot again, girls. Red-hot. As Rebecca told you and you for some reason ignored, Margot, Google wants to put 'Power Pink' in a phone commercial. Fucking *Google*. It'll air in every country on the planet. TV, the web. Print. Even an outdoor campaign."

"What's an outdoor campaign?" asks Margot.

"Billboards," says Nikki. "Big pink ones, probably."

Margot laughs. "Billboards," she says. "Jesus."

"And then, boom, we drop an album," says Axl. "We can record in the city—over at Threshold, like before. A single first, for the streamers—maybe a YouTube tie-in. A tour after that. A *reunion* tour. Twenty cities—the big markets—then more. Burnt Flowers is back, baby. Thanks to you, Margot. I simply cannot express to you how big this could be."

"I've got songs," says Nikki. "Enough for an album, easy. You wanna hear some?" She puts her hands on the keys.

"No," says Margot. "Not . . . not right now."

"Okay, yeah," Nikki says. "I'm not warmed up anyway. But they're good. I can feel it. And with you? And with Jenny and Anna? Together? We could make them great."

She doesn't want to look at Nikki being vulnerable, because Nikki is never vulnerable, so Margot looks out the window onto the driveway. Billy's Champagne Supernova sits, dented and unwashed. She wishes he were here, helping her through this with his wholly unearned confidence in her.

"It wouldn't have to be like before," says Axl. "We could come up with a whole new working arrangement. A partnership. A democracy, whatever you wanna call it. The four of you voting on everything. Lockstep."

Margot isn't a kid anymore, signing her name at the bottom of some dizzying contract. She knows that anything that comes out of Axl's mouth is rancid bullshit. She imagines the music, though, the sound the four of them would make together. Because that's what she misses. The push and the pull. The fight. That sound.

"Margot," Nikki says.

She keeps looking outside. The birds have returned to the basketball hoop. The neighborhood has settled. "What?"

"I need you," says Nikki.

If Billy *were* here, he probably would've been quiet, Margot thinks. He'd have made everyone espressos. He'd be sitting now in The Rocker. He'd apologize for the mess, do his best to make everyone feel comfortable and welcome. He'd speak up here, though, because they'd both be aware of Margot's notebook, which rests on the music stand less than a foot from Nikki's face. He wouldn't speak to them, only to her, and it'd just be a whisper in her ear. *But, Margot, you don't need her. You know that, right?*

"I appreciate you coming all this way, Nikki," she says. "I mean that. And you look great, too."

Nikki's face is hopeful, expectant. Axl sets his hand on the Steinway and waits.

"But I think you should both leave."

CHAPTER 48

Robyn really wishes she'd cleaned out her car.

She keeps the outside spotless, thanks mostly to the drive-thru car wash at the Royal Farms she passes on the way home from her office. The inside, though, is a swirl of work papers, marooned to-go coffee cups, and an assortment of backup footwear. She laughs now at the symbolism—the vehicular version of herself.

Looks pretty good on the outside, right? she thinks.

"What's funny, love?" asks Lawson.

"Oh, nothing. Sorry about the mess."

Lawson smiles down at the pair of black flats between his feet. "I'll survive. These are nice, by the way. Classy."

She keeps looking at him out of the corner of her eye as she drives. He probably notices, because how could he not? She keeps veering into other lanes. A guy in a Tesla honked earlier, glaring as he passed. But then he squinted for an unsafe amount of time as he tried to figure out if it was really Lawson Daniels in the passenger seat.

"Appreciate the ride," says Lawson. "I wasn't in the mood to chat with a driver."

"Yeah, happy to," she says.

Half an hour ago, Robyn and Aaron were talking to Caleb in the kitchen, explaining themselves. "I'm still your co-dad," Aaron was saying. "Always. You know that, right, buddy? I'm gonna keep being a part of your life. This is just a living change, not a life change."

"I know," said Caleb. "I just don't understand what happened. Did one of you, like, *do* something?"

Caleb was taking it better than Robyn expected he would—like an adult, not a kid. He was taking it so well, in fact, that it made her realize that all of this—the secrecy, Billy moving in above the garage—was unnecessary, especially since Caleb is now, apparently, going to college three miles away. Maybe the "nontraditional household situation" he'd been born into had prepared him for instability at every turn, as if she and Billy went and built a life for him on a plot of hastily smoothed-over sand.

"No," said Aaron. "Not at all, Cay. It's not like that."

"Sometimes people just . . ." Robyn trailed off. She'd rehearsed the phrasing, but it sounded weak now in her own mind, not big enough to topple their lives over.

Aaron finished for her. "Grow apart. It happens. Not everything is about someone being bad. There isn't always a villain. Sometimes two good people fall out of love."

Then there was a knock at the front door, followed by Lawson's voice. "'Ello?"

He needed a ride to the airport. Not the normal airport, the little one where the private planes go. It seemed strange that he needed their help, as if being famous would somehow make him able to teleport himself across midsize metropolitan areas.

They're just out of the most congested part of the city now. Robyn steers them onto 395, following the nav on her phone. A series of enormous industrial gas tanks sit at the southernmost part of town, one of which is decorated with a mural of blue crabs.

"You love those pinchy buggers here, don't you?" Lawson says.

Robyn admits that they do. "You weren't here for very long, were you?" she asks. "Less than a day."

His arm rests on the console between them. His left hand is just inches from Robyn's thigh, which, despite everything, she's distinctly aware of. "Bit of a legal issue back home. Contract dispute. I'm sorry to leave, though. I like this little place. Maybe next time you can show me how people eat crabs. I can't imagine the logistics of it."

He's just being polite, but it's a fun fantasy. A restaurant on the water. Everyone looking at them. It must be how Billy has felt these last few weeks: special by proximity.

Traffic is thick but steady. The adrenaline from the morning's events has left her body. That, combined with her car's gentle vibration against the road, has a lulling effect, and they drive mostly in silence for several miles. Lawson fiddles with the radio, settling on news. The nav directs her off the highway.

"Can I ask you something, love?" says Lawson.

"Okay."

"You know you're quite lovely, right?"

Robyn hears herself laugh. It doesn't sound like her normal laugh. "Thanks."

"Just a statement of fact, that," he says. "You're beautiful. I reckon you're about my age. Quite fit, still. Well done. I assume you were a sight when you were younger as well, don't mind me saying."

Robyn doesn't know what he's getting at, but she's smiling so hard that her face muscles are on the verge of seizing. "Can I maybe record you saying that?"

Lawson laughs, touches, finally, Robyn's thigh. "Well, we'll see. But back to my point. You're beautiful. And Margie—you know,

Margot? She's lovely, too. Bit shorter than you, sure. Less conventional looking. However, she's got the distinction of being a proper rock-and-roll star. Bit off the map lately, but she's known around the world. Presumably she could have any number of blokes, no?"

"Ohhhkay?" Robyn says.

Lawson twists the volume knob, silencing the radio. "My question is, am I missing something about this Billy Perkins, then?"

"Billy? What do you mean?"

"Yeah. In two decades' time, he managed to shag both of you. Is this what women are settling for? Him? Are things really quite that bleak out there?"

Robyn laughs. And she keeps laughing as she moves left along a bending road. Then, for no reason that she could ever explain, she thinks of sharing a pretzel with Billy a month ago beside the Charm City Rocks van in the parking lot of Caleb's school. She didn't ask him to bring her a pretzel. He just did, because he knows she likes them, and now her eyes are filling rapidly with tears.

"Oh no," says Lawson. "I'm sorry. What've I done?"

"I never cry," she says, crying. "Honestly. It's something I'm proud of."

"You're doing it now, though. I can see it."

"My second time today, goddammit."

"Well, it's been a tough one. Personally speaking, I cry all the time. Mostly because I'm paid to, and I can do it on command. But still, I'm quite an emotional bloke. People don't know that about me."

"Yeah, I've seen you cry," she says. "You're good at it. That scene in the one where you're trapped on that boat. That was fantastic."

"Thank you, love," he says. "Proud of that one. Watch out for the curb, now. I think the airport is right up here, then. Just a bit more to go. Let's not have a smash-up when we're this close."

She turns right, apologizes, crying still. There are signs ahead for the private airport. Through the windshield, a tiny silver plane zooms toward the horizon.

"Tell us what's wrong," says Lawson. "Why are you crying?"

"I get it, okay?" she says. "The cardigans? They're a bit much."

"Insufferable!" says Lawson.

"And the aw-shucks-I'm-just-happy-being-me attitude?" says Robyn. "Maybe a little forced."

"Nail on the head, love," says Lawson.

"But he's very sweet."

"Oh, for fuck's sake. Sweet. I'm tired of hearing that. I can be sweet. I recently voiced a cartoon wombat for Pixar. A bloody wombat! Comes out next year. Wait 'til you see it. I'm bloody adorable."

"No," she says. "No offense, but I don't think you understand how rare nice men are. Especially now. It's like an epidemic of not-niceness. And Billy, God, he was even nicer when we were young. And if I'd . . . I don't know, been more patient, he could've grown up with me. I could've waited him out."

"Well now, that's just unreasonable," says Lawson. "What were you supposed to be, psychic? Entrance is up ahead there. See the little picture of the airplane?"

Robyn has never driven while crying. She's having trouble gauging her speed. Is she going too fast, or too slow?

"What about the other bloke?" Lawson asks. "Aaron? He's quite a bit better looking than Billy. Brilliant head of hair. Aside from him smashing Billy's face with the basketball, he seems like a nice chap, no? What went wrong there?"

"Yes!" She slaps the steering wheel. "He's nice, too. *Really* nice. I had two nice men. What are the odds? And I fucked it up with both of them. One I gave up on too soon. The other I . . . I let fall out of love with me. I let myself fall out of love with *him*. I took us for granted. I put my career ahead of our relationship. I stopped trying."

"I'm sure it's not as bad as all that."

"No, it is. Marriage is work, and I stopped working. And now I'm gonna be alone. This age and alone. In *Baltimore*."

As all that comes out, Robyn somehow manages to pull up below the drop-off sign. It's not like a normal airport—no cops in yellow vests, no harried travelers. Robyn cough-laughs through a sob. "Well, we're here!"

Lawson reaches for Robyn's right hand. He removes it gently from the steering wheel, gives it a squeeze, then guides it slowly to the gear shifter between them. It's perhaps as innocently as she's been touched by a man in her adult life, but for Robyn it makes for a heart-thrumming three seconds.

"How about we put it in park, love? We've made it this far without killing anyone, right?"

"You must think I'm crazy."

"Not at all. I suspect you feel a little better now, don't you? Feels good to get all that out. I could go for a good cry myself, honestly. Maybe I'll give it a go. Do you mind?"

Robyn laughs. "You're the second famous person I've emotionally vomited in front of today."

"Mmm. You cried in front of Margie, did you? Didn't know what to do, I bet. Not a crier, that one. Prefers to knock the piss out of things with wooden sticks. Bit barbaric, you ask me."

Robyn laughs more, wipes her eyes. "She hugged me. Kind of. Like a half hug."

"Oy. Mar hugged you? No way. I think she hugged me four times when we were married. One of those was when my dad accidentally ran over my mum's cat."

It hardly matters whether any of that is true; Robyn suspects much of it isn't. Either way, he's making her feel better.

He unbuckles his seatbelt, faces her, touches her thigh again. "Can I make an observation?"

"Okay."

"Again, you're lovely," he says. "We've been over that."

"We can go over it again if you want."

Lawson laughs. "Right. Your driving skills are questionable. Not sure you should be let behind the wheel again. Before I get on the plane, I'll probably notify the authorities. Aside from that, you're clearly quite capable. Smart. Accomplished."

Robyn decides to go with his assessment. Her face has gone hot, like her body is fighting off something lethal. "I'm the only female senior vice president at my company," she says.

"See?" He touches her thigh again—more of a slap this time. "I know absolutely nothing about business or having a real job, but that certainly sounds like something. So, you're beautiful and smart, and you're a senior vice president. You smell quite lovely as well, which is unrelated, but we might as well add it to the list."

The spaces at the corners of Robyn's vision are blurring, and she knows that she'd faint if she were standing, like a woman in a Victorian novel. She's beginning to understand the phenomenon of celebrity—the mesmerizing power of this kind of charisma.

"So, what in the actual fuck, love," says Lawson, "are you doing worrying about a couple of stupid blokes? Aaron? Billy Perkins? Put them in the bin. Wheel them out with the day's rubbish, and never think about them again. Because you're a beautiful, powerful woman, and you can do whatever the bloody hell you want."

Robyn's seatbelt catches her mid-lunge. Somehow, though, she has the presence of mind to click the release, then she lunges at him again, lips first. Lawson catches her before they collide.

"Easy now," he says.

"Oh my God." Robyn is horrified with herself. "I'm sorry, I don't know what—"

"No, no," he says. "It was my fault. It's happened before. I have a sort of chemistry with women. I've become quite famous because of it, but it's also turned me into a complete bastard. Believe me, normally I'd welcome a bit of that, but I'm trying to put all of it behind me. You know, be a better man. Not take advantage of . . . well, all this."

Robyn longs for an ejection seat—a button next to the climate controls, perhaps, that would launch her skyward. She apologizes again, fearing another wave of tears.

Lawson looks out the windshield, then the driver- and passenger-side windows. He turns around, checks behind them. "All right, fuck it, then. Close your eyes, love."

"What?" says Robyn.

"Go on. Close 'em."

Robyn does as she's told, and Lawson Daniels kisses her. His lips are soft. Sensationally so. She'd have thought the smatterings of beard around his chin and mouth would be bristly, but they, too, are soft. She opens her mouth, and so does he, and the tips of their tongues touch. His fingers graze her collarbone and then gently touch a spot on her throat where her pulse beats, and all she can think is *Holy shit*.

He tells her goodbye, gives her cheek a little caress, touches his forehead to hers. Then she watches as he walks into the private airport.

CHAPTER 49

And now it's Sunday, early afternoon.

After Lawson's arrival on Friday evening, which was followed the next morning by a star-studded pickup basketball game slash Burnt Flowers reunion in the driveway, the house in Roland Park and the one-bedroom apartment above its detached garage felt like a gateless compound. People kept walking by, stopping to look, shielding their eyes with their hands, taking crappy iPhone pictures.

"I think this is the place," they'd say. "Right?"

They'd note the basketball abandoned in the shrubs and the old Mercedes station wagon in the driveway and comment on how normal it all looked, not at all like somewhere musicians and Oscar nominees would hang out.

"It's just, like, a house, though."

As Lawson predicted, pictures of him arriving at BWI airport and then hanging out downtown started showing up across social media immediately on Friday night. Along with the shot of Lawson and Beth and a Natty Boh, the most liked and shared of those images was of Lawson at the Horse You Came In On, pointing at a sticker over the bar that read, I GOT CRABS IN BALTIMORE.

People put two and two together and assumed he was there to see Margot, because why else would he be in Baltimore? Nikki was spotted, too—at the train station, then later in the car on the way to Robyn and Aaron's. Some tourists spotted her in the backseat as two teenagers cleaned the SUV's windshield at an intersection. The weekend team at *HypeReport* posted a story called "Drama in Charm City?" Other sites reported that, according to anonymous friends and representatives, the actress Willa Knight was "devastated." She was also rumored to be in the running for a part in Marvel's upcoming franchise *Impossible Man*. The Internet agreed that she was perfect for it.

This morning, Aaron pulled two roller bags out to his new Audi. The cordial charade of being married, which was all for Caleb's benefit, is over now, so there's no reason for him to stay. He'll crash with a divorced friend for a week or so until his new apartment is ready. He put a deposit down on the place last month, so it has basically just been waiting for him. Aaron said goodbye to his wife, gave her a hug, then high-fived Caleb before giving him a hug, too. "I'm not saying goodbye to you, Cay," he said, "because I'll see you, right? Maybe we can join one of those pickup basketball leagues down in Patterson Park. You and me." He stopped his car on the way out to tell a few randoms who were loitering near the mailbox that there was nothing left to see. "The famous people are gone."

That wasn't entirely true. Margot was up in the apartment with Billy, and she still is. They're on the couch together; the Orioles pregame show is on TV. Margot is looking at pictures from the Internet that Poppy keeps sending her.

Mum, you went to a farmer's market?

Margot is wearing her Target pajamas, and her bare feet are tucked under Billy's thigh. Billy is watching the television but not really seeing it. He feels sick to his stomach, because, unbelievably, he's about to tell Margot that she has to go.

Last night was another one for his pretend time-stopping machine. She told him the story of how she sent Nikki and Axl Albee away. How she stood in the driveway and watched them climb into the big black SUV and drive off. How Nikki looked back over her shoulder, like people do in movies when they're being arrested.

"What are you gonna do now?" Billy asked.

Margot had her head on his shoulder at the time. They were sitting on the same couch they're sitting on now. "Maybe just be with you," she replied, and the joy of being chosen was so powerful that Billy allowed himself to go with it for the remainder of the night, despite knowing that "just being with him" was far less than Margot deserved.

Billy clears his throat. "Margot," he says.

She looks up from her phone. Her hair falls across her eyes, which is unfair.

"You're my dream girl," he says. "I haven't used that term until now, because it's ridiculous, and it makes us sound like kids. And we're not. But that's what you are. You're my dream girl."

She removes her feet from beneath his legs and sits up.

"But I'm not *your* dream," he says.

"What? How do you know what my dream is?"

"Because I've read about it. Because it's common knowledge, and because I've known you for twenty years. Your dream is to make music. To be in a band. It has been since you were a kid."

"I *was* in a band," she says. "I *made* music."

"And you're not done," he says. "Not even close. If the last couple of weeks haven't shown you that, you're out of your mind. Maybe it's with Burnt Flowers again. Axl sucks, but he's not wrong about how big that could be for you. For everyone. Or maybe it's a new band. I don't know. You've got the songs for it, the ability. Either way, none of that's gonna happen here. Not in Baltimore. I love this place, but it's not big enough. Not for you. You can't just hide here, Margot. I won't let you."

She looks around the apartment. Billy does, too, and takes in the embarrassing mess of it all, cluttered and temporary.

"You want me to leave?" she asks.

"No," he says. "Not at all. But I'll never forgive myself if you don't."

Her face loses its expression briefly, and then her eyes begin to well with tears. "But I like it here," she says. "I like you."

It should be such a fantastic thing to hear, but for Billy it's heartbreaking, because he knows that she's only known him for a month. He hasn't had time to disappoint her yet. She hasn't had time to figure out that he'll do nothing but hold her back, the way Robyn figured it out when she walked out of La Scala and wisely chose a path that didn't include him.

"You won't be happy unless you're playing," he says. "Go online. Look at yourself at the Horse and tell me I'm wrong. Shit, not even the Horse. Go watch the video of you playing with Daquan."

"But what if I like you more than I like playing?"

"Then you're lying to yourself." He says this too sharply, and Margot recoils. He's surprised that she's even protesting. By this point in the conversation, Billy imaged her grabbing her bag, switching out her pajamas for jeans, and taking off in her boots, because it's so obvious that she doesn't belong here with him.

"If I'd met you under different circumstances," he says, "it might've been different. Maybe we could've looked at all this and thought it was enough. But that's not what happened. When I found you, the rest of the world did, too. And I can't compete with that."

The sound of baseball on the TV recedes into nothing; the birds, too, along with the gentle hum of suburban Baltimore.

"What if you come, too?" she says. "Back to New York."

"I can't do that."

"Why?"

"My life is here. I can't just up and go."

"Your *life*? The one above your ex-girlfriend's garage?"

The tears are gathering still, but her voice is all sharp edges now. "My students, Margot," he says. "My son."

"Your students can find a new teacher. There are other piano teachers. And I know you love Caleb, but he's an adult."

"That's not tr—" He stops himself, because, of course, it *is* true, but it's somehow wrong at the same time. "My students *do* need me. Some of them have been with me for years. And if I leave Caleb, I'm leaving my family. Don't you understand that?"

Her eyes finally spill over. He reaches for her, but she pulls away. "That's bullshit. Who's hiding now?"

"Hiding?" he says. "I'm not hiding. This is my home. And I'm . . . I'm happy."

Margot stands. The tears are gone because she's wiped them away. Now she just looks mad. "Well, good for you," she says. "I guess you don't need me, then."

Part 4

LESSONS IN ART AND MANHOOD

CHAPTER 50

Beth tells everyone at the Horse to shut their mouths. "Seriously, people, come on! Jesus! Quiet!" With a remote that's held together by duct tape, she turns the volume up on the main TV above the bar. On the screen, about a dozen attractive young people of various ethnicities freeze on a crowded city street. They all have pink phones aimed at themselves, as if about to take selfies. It's unclear where they are, exactly, but that's probably the point, because Google sells things to people everywhere. "Power Pink" starts— the iconic drum intro—and everyone begins dancing in unison.

Nikki Kixx's voice fades in over the action, close to the mic, like a stage whisper.

Drum fills, backed by bass—four big, perfect thuds, like heartbeats—and the dancing intensifies. An electric guitar: one long chord, stretched. Words in white type appear.

Introducing Google Hype
The first phone built exclusively for creators

When the chorus drops, the people on the screen go wild, and there's a flashing montage of sleek product shots, pink earbuds, and beautiful bodies flung into the air. Even on mediocre speakers mounted in the ceiling, the song sounds fantastic. Beth bobs her head behind the bar and shimmies. Gustavo plays air bass. The video cuts to white and Nikki's voice fades out, but Margot's drums play on over more words.

> *It's pink*
> *It's loud*
> *And it gives you the power*

"Oh wow," says Grady. "That's clever."

"Damn, no wonder I'm selling so many of those pretzels," says Gustavo. The Margot Hammer, which Gustavo launched last month, is a soft pretzel dipped in pink strawberry-flavored icing, and it's currently the most popular item on his menu.

Beth kills the sound on the TV, which is now showing a commercial for a local personal injury lawyer, and switches back to music. Billy takes a sip of his beer and tries to ignore the fact that his friends are staring at him. "Guys," he says. "Stop. I'm fine."

Gustavo is next to him, Grady is one stool down, Beth faces them with her arms folded. None of them believe him.

"You don't *seem* fine," says Gustavo.

"And you're drinking in the daytime," says Beth.

"Yeah, you don't normally do that," says Grady.

"G, you invited me here," says Billy. "Beth, you poured this for me."

"Right," says Grady. "Still, though, it's worrying behavior."

Billy has seen a few of the billboards around town. A huge one looms by the Amtrak station. This is the first time he's seen the actual commercial, though, and he's surprised how much it makes him miss her. Margot wasn't on-screen, obviously, because it's a commercial for pink phones. That song, though, is as much her as anything he could ever see with his eyes. Last week, *Rolling Stone* posted a picture of the band on Twitter. They were in a studio together. Margot was in the background behind her kit, and he was offended on her behalf, because Margot should be front and center, always.

After, um, a little time off, Burnt Flowers is recording a new album, the post read. It included a flower and a fire emoji.

"Have you talked to her?" asks Beth.

"No," he says.

His friends exchange solemn glances over his head. He wonders how long they'll keep doing this: treating him like the survivor of something. Forever? Henceforth, will he be the guy who was briefly Margot Hammer's manfriend?

"You could maybe give her a call," Grady says. "You know, just say hi."

"She's busy," Billy says. "They're recording. I'm giving her space. Plus, I doubt she wants to hear from me right now anyway."

Grady and Gustavo nod into their beers, accepting this. Beth, though, leans her elbows on the bar. "Well, that's pretty fucking stupid, Billy."

"Jeez, Beth," says Gustavo.

She shakes her head, unfolds and refolds her arms. "Sometimes women don't need as much space as you morons think we do."

He isn't sure if she's calling *him* a moron or all three of them—or mankind in general.

"I don't know, Beth," says Grady. "Patty asks me to go away a lot, and it usually sounds like she means it."

"Maybe just a phone call, hon," says Beth. "That's all I'm saying." Then she walks away and settles herself at the other end of the bar with an old paperback book. The three men sit in silence watching commercials and drinking, and then Gustavo bumps Billy's shoulder. "I know, man," he says. "Must be tough, seeing that cool commercial and all. But I brought you something I think might cheer you up."

Billy watches as Gustavo digs around in his pocket. He wonders what he has for him. A gift, maybe? More pot gummies? That doesn't sound so bad right now, actually.

"It's in here somewhere," says Gustavo. "Oh, here it is."

It takes Billy two seconds to realize that Gustavo is giving him the finger. He's fallen for this old joke again, and the look of genuine sincerity on Gustavo's face is surprisingly moving. Maybe Beth is right and they're all morons. But for men, sometimes a middle finger from a friend is as good as a hug.

"Too soon?" asks Gustavo.

"Nah," says Billy. "I appreciate it."

"That's really sweet," says Grady. "This beer's making me feel pretty bloated, though. You guys wanna get some coffee?"

Spring has transitioned to early summer, and it's brought humidity with it. It's Saturday afternoon, and Fells Point is crowded, like always. Billy moved into a new place a few weeks ago. It's about five blocks from here, tucked away on a side street. It's not an apartment this time but a tall, skinny row house. It's fine enough, and the Steinway fits in the front room nicely, but it's all too quiet to be excited about, too far from the action.

The three friends walk down Thames Street. They pass Hot Twist, with its BACK IN 15 MINS sign that Gustavo hung up half an hour ago. Billy can hear Charm City Rocks as they approach, the low rumble of it.

"There's still some painting to do up there," says Grady. "You know, crown molding, some touch-up work. I got a guy coming tomorrow. And I need to hang some art that Patty got for us. But we're just about done."

Billy looks inside the record shop, because he can't not look in. Patty is working the register; she waves when she sees him. The Charm City Grinds sign is up and brand new, along with a fluttering banner that reads GRAND OPENING MONDAY!

"You think it's big enough to read from the street?" asks Grady.

"I think it's big enough to read from space," says Gustavo.

They head up the steps. Grady upgraded the glorified fire escape that Billy climbed up and down when he lived here. It's a full brick staircase now, professional looking, with a smooth metal railing. "Here we go," says Grady. "Be nice, okay, you guys?"

Billy can't speak for Gustavo, but he has no intention of being anything other than nice, especially because he can see how excited his friend is to show them. Grady twists the key. The new tinted-glass door opens, and Billy can't believe it. Newly finished wood floors, grayish-blue walls, handsome countertops with a section of matching two-top tables, a few lounge chairs, a love seat by the window. An espresso machine awaits, gleaming. It's brand new, but not that much different from his grandma's old beast.

"Look at this dump," says Gustavo, and Grady smiles.

Billy crosses what was once his TV room and pokes his head into Caleb's old bedroom. There's a conference table there now, with four chairs, a bank of USB ports, and electrical outlets. A framed photograph of the Domino Sugars sign hangs from the wall.

"We figured this could be, like, a little conference room," says Grady. "People can reserve it. Meetings. Stuff like that. You know, telecommuters."

Billy goes to the main window next, leans on the sill. A store that sells expensive baby clothes is moving in next to the 7-Eleven down the street. He sits on the new love seat, which is about where his old couch used to be. He pictures different versions of Caleb sprawled here—from napping toddler to gangly boy to slightly less gangly high school graduate.

"So, what do you think, Billy?" asks Grady.

Billy stands up and rests his palm against the wall. He holds his breath, feels the place vibrating along with the music from downstairs. His old apartment is still humming on. "I love it, man," he says. "You did great."

Grady puts his hands on his hips and smiles again, pleased. "Thanks," he says. "Now, can you show me how this espresso machine works? It's really confusing."

CHAPTER 51

Some 195 miles north of Baltimore again, Margot is at Threshold Recording Studios on West Forty-first Street with the band. It's Saturday, but that hardly registers. She knows it's lunchtime, because Nikki is in the control room drinking a seaweed-colored smoothie.

Jenny naps on one of the couches with a Strand Book Store pillow over her face. Anna is facing Margot, playing, her big red bass crooked on her hip. The low, wobbly sound is being piped into Margot's headphones. She's matching Anna's notes, hitting her kick drum on Anna's F6 chord over and over. Anna has headphones on, too, so it's like they're in their own little world. A deep line of concentration runs across Anna's forehead as they jam over a guitar riff that Jenny laid down a few hours ago. Recording an album is like putting a big, noisy puzzle together while highly caffeinated.

Their eyes meet, Margot's and Anna's, just as Anna changes to E7. Anna smiles and winks, because they've found their groove— the effortlessness from before. It was slow going at first, but they've melded again: one musician, four arms.

———

The first day of work on the new album a few weeks ago, Margot was the first to arrive at Threshold. It was 9 A.M. on a Monday, which is way too early for rock and roll, but a schedule is a schedule. She was nervous to see Anna and Jenny, but mostly Anna, her rhythm-section comrade. Neither Anna nor Jenny could be blamed for what happened. They apologized years ago for not telling her what they knew or thought they might have known about what was happening between Nikki and Lawson. It was a dilemma for them, because it wasn't just some affair within their social circle. Anna's and Jenny's livelihoods were on the line, their careers. Margot told them that she forgave them, but she shut them out anyway, and she hadn't spoken to either of them in years.

As chance would have it, the guitar player and bassist arrived at the same time. They each stopped dead in the doorway when they saw Margot sitting on an old studio couch holding her drumsticks. She must've looked like a junior high kid on her first day at a new school—all nerves and dread.

"As I live and breathe," said Jenny.

"Aren't you that drummer chick from the Internet?" asked Anna. She'd let her curly hair go almost completely gray. She wore a jean jacket and vintage sneakers. She looked every bit as cool as her old bass.

"So, are we really doing this?" asked Jenny. She wore a loose peasant dress under a leather jacket. It was warm out, but recording studios are always freezing.

"Why not, right?" said Margot. "I wasn't doing much else."

"Is it true you told Axl to go fuck himself?" asked Anna.

Margot nodded. She hadn't used those words, but the sentiment was right on. Margot had agreed to all of this—the album, the tour—on one condition: no Axl fucking Albee. She and the band would deal with Rebecca Yang only; Axl wasn't to come within a city block of Threshold.

"Sweet," said Jenny.

"Agreed," said Anna. "Fuck that guy."

The three women—old friends, bandmates once and again—stood in a loosely drawn triangle staring at one another. Finally, Anna slid her jean jacket off and tossed it on the floor. "Well, if we're gonna do it, let's do it, then," she said, then she turned her bare right arm over so they could see the four bass strings tattooed there. Jenny's leather jacket fell next. She'd been marked with the neck and head of an electric guitar from the crook of her elbow to just before the veiny intersection at her wrist. Margot pulled her sweater over her head, revealing her drumstick tattoos, and they put their arms together. They got their tattoos the week before their first tour. They linked arms like this before significant moments as a band. Nikki has a microphone tattooed on the inside of her wrist, its black cord snaking down her forearm and up her bicep. She didn't arrive until nearly noon that first day, though, so she missed out on this.

"You gotta get that shit touched up, girl," said Jenny, poking Margot's arm.

"I know," she said. "I missed you two, by the way." And Margot meant it.

Jenny and Anna smiled, because they'd missed her, too, then Anna asked, "You think we can manage to do this without murdering Nikki?"

"That's hot!" says Wave in Margot's headphones. He's the producer, Marcus Wiley, but he goes by Wave. He's produced Nikki's last three solo albums, and he's wearing leather pants and yellow-tinted sunglasses.

Nikki comes out of the control room with her smoothie. "Yeah, definitely hot," she says. "But, like, is it hot enough?"

Margot and Anna slide their headphones off. Anna looks at Margot. "What does that even mean?" she whispers.

From the couch, Jenny takes the pillow off her face. She isn't asleep after all. "Sounded the right amount of hot to me, Nik."

"So, right now it's very boom boom boom boom, you know," says Nikki. "What if it's more like, boom-biti-boom, boom-biti-boom?" She plays air drums with her non-smoothie hand. "I think that's where the hook's at. Like a hip-hop beat."

"A hip-hop beat?" says Anna.

"These aren't hooky songs," says Jenny. "They're *rock* songs."

"Jenny, have you even seen our Google commercial?" says Nikki. "'Power Pink,' you know, that song that's currently playing every ten minutes in every major market on Earth right now, is hooky as fuck. All our best stuff is. It's how we got on the radio in the first place. We can wear bracelets and put purple streaks in our hair and call ourselves rockers, but we're pop just like everyone else."

The three nonlead singers look at one another.

This has been the dynamic so far: them and her. It always had been, to a degree, Margot knows, because she understands that every band has that one member who's the face—the one who's just enough of a megalomaniac to want to stand up in front of everyone else with no instruments to hide behind.

Nikki sets her smoothie on a guitar case, puts her hands together like she's about to say grace. "Sorry, I'm being . . ." she says. To her credit, Margot thinks, she's doing her best at rock-and-roll democracy. "Maybe we just . . . try it?"

A click from the speaker above them, then Wave's voice from the control room. "Yeah, I'm with Nik on this one, ladies. Hooky's where it's at! What-what!"

Anna puts her headphones back on. "Well, there's a shocker."

———

The driver asks Margot if the temperature is good. He asks her if she wants a Vitaminwater, or a mint, or a Red Bull, or anything, and Margot remembers taking the subway to and from Threshold when they were recording their first album. She'd walk the streets at whatever stupid hour it was and just assume she was about to be murdered.

It's only a little after 9 P.M. now, though. They broke early tonight, each of them leaving by themselves in large black SUVs. She should be tired, but she's not. She looks down at her phone and thinks of Billy. She does this less and less now, but she still does it. You could hardly call it a breakup, because were they even together in the first place? She'd just shown up there; he'd never technically asked her to stay. The label they'd given him was a joke—"manfriend"—like whatever they were didn't quite warrant seriousness. Their nonbreakup breakup happened so quickly, like a car accident. Margot can forgive him for telling her to leave, but she can't forgive him for so adamantly refusing to come with her. His kid. A midsize city. A record shop. A couple of buddies. An occasional free pretzel. He chose these things over her, and it hurt. Still does. Worse, he had the nerve to tell her that he was happy. That *really* hurt.

"I can just get out here, if that's cool," Margot tells the driver.

He looks up at the mirror, hesitant, because he's undoubtedly been told to take her directly to her building.

"What's the worst that could happen, man?" she says.

Margot waves from the curb as the SUV asserts itself back into traffic. She's only a few blocks from home, but she's not in a hurry, because it's an empty home. That's the thing that pisses her off most about having met Billy. Aside from a few plants here and there and an occasional mouse in winter, Margot has been the only living resident of her apartment for years, but she's never thought of it as empty until now.

A few people smile, nod in recognition. There are more celebrities per capita here than in Baltimore, so she's less of a sighting.

A block up, she sees an enormous pink phone on the side of a building. It's the same building from which Lawson's stupid beautiful face once hung, and she shakes her head at the absurdity of it all. Her phone rings. Poppy usually FaceTimes around now—six in the evening California time—as she walks home from work.

"You're never gonna guess what I'm looking at," Poppy says, smiling. It's still light on the West Coast.

"Bet it's the same thing I'm looking at," says Margot.

Both women aim their phones over their shoulders to capture the power of outdoor advertising.

"You're so famous," Poppy says.

"Eh," says Margot.

"How's the album coming?"

"We have a few songs in decent shape, and a few that aren't."

"How's Nikki?" Poppy makes a face. Margot loves her for the fierceness of her loyalty.

"Nikki is Nikki. She's trying."

"Mm-hm."

Margot asks if Poppy has talked to Lawson.

"Willa moved out," Poppy says. "You probably know that, though. The entire western hemisphere knows that. Apparently, she's getting back with that TV actor she dated before Dad."

Margot *does* know these things. Once she lifted her *Us Weekly* ban the floodgates opened, and now she flips through it every week when she gets groceries. Photos of a moving truck outside of Lawson and Willa's house in L.A. and Willa with a pretty twentysomething blond boy from a vampire show.

"You aren't writing, are you?" Poppy asks. "I can tell."

"I don't need to write. I'm here to drum."

They walk together in silence, thousands of miles apart, linked by technology.

"You can call him, you know?" Poppy says. "It's weird that I have to tell you that, because you're an adult and famous and accomplished and you're my role model, et cetera. But apparently you need to be told basic things about how to be a human being."

"I'm your role model?"

"Most of the time."

"That's sweet."

"Regarding the other part of what I said, though?" says Poppy.

"I know I can," says Margot. "But that doesn't mean I should."

Her daughter rolls her eyes, like she did when she was five, twelve, seventeen, twenty-two. "That's dumb. Good line, though. If you were writing, like you should be, I'd tell you to jot that one down."

"I'll remember it for my memoir," she says.

"Oh, I was gonna ask you. Caleb—you know, Billy's kid. Is he really picking Baltimore over Palo freaking Alto?"

Margot mentioned this to Poppy back in the spring, before Margot came back to New York. Still, it's a jarring turn in the conversation. Margot diverts around a sniffing dog on a long leash. "Yeah," she says. "Apparently Baltimore's got quite a hold over its men."

CHAPTER 52

Jackson Barber is the best student Billy has ever had. He's the best student Billy *will* ever have, Billy knows, because that's how talent works, like a once-a-century rogue wave on a beach that nobody sees coming. If they're lucky, music teachers have a Jackson Barber somewhere in their past, present, or future: the kid who sits down one day, takes a deep breath, and stuns them.

That's what happened three days after Margot left. Billy had forgotten all about their first scheduled lesson until there was a knock at the door. *Oh shit! Jackson!* He was still living in the apartment over Robyn's garage. When Billy answered the door, Jackson stood on the steps, shy and tiny next to LaVar Barber, because who wouldn't be shy and tiny next to a man who knocks people to the ground for a living?

"Piano Man! You ready to get this party started?"

Billy wasn't. He was depressed, he hadn't been eating well, and he was slightly hungover. He's self-employed, though, so he knows how to fake it. "Heck yeah, I am."

LaVar asked if he could hang out and watch. Billy doesn't usually go for that, but he didn't have the energy to deliver his spiel about parent-induced anxiety. Plus, Jackson seemed cool with it.

The kid sat at Billy's bench, eyes wide. "Your piano's awesome," he said. "Dad, look at it."

"I know, bud," said LaVar. "Shiny, right?"

Billy settled into The Rocker. "First lessons are just an intro," he said. "You get to meet me and hear about my philosophy. My philosophy is that music should be fun. I want this to be fun for you, Jackson. And I get to meet you and get a sense for where you're at musically. Sound like a plan?"

Jackson didn't look up from the Steinway, but he nodded.

"Well, when you're ready. I'm all ears."

Billy teared up ten seconds into "Für Elise," and it had nothing to do with missing Margot. It was so perfect and so fluid and performed with such reverence that Billy was transported to a place where only the notes and Jackson's skinny fingers mattered. When he was done with the song, Jackson set his hands in his lap and looked up at Billy, awaiting instruction.

LaVar was smiling. It was clear that he'd wanted to stay for the lesson so he could see the look on Billy's face. "What'd I tell you, Piano Man?"

Billy took a deep breath and wiped his eyes. "Not bad, Jackson."

Today's lesson with Jackson is almost over now. LaVar is on Billy's couch, enjoying the show. He won't be here *every* time, he promised Billy earlier, what with offseason workouts starting soon for the Ravens and then the preseason ramping up. It's fine, though, because Billy likes having him around. Caleb is here, too, hanging out in the kitchen with Lincoln, the Barber family's pit bull.

Jackson is working through the Moonlight Sonata, and he's killing it. By the time his lessons wind down, Billy, like LaVar, is pretty much just an observer. "Straighten that back," he says. "Posture."

Normally Billy doesn't say things like that to his students, but he's had to adjust for Jackson's ability, so he basically spends an hour a week parroting the things his grandma used to call out to him when he was learning. *Sit up tall. Round those fingers. Keep your hands steady. You should be able to balance a quarter on those things. Steady rhythm, now.*

When he finishes the song, LaVar and Caleb clap, and Jackson smiles.

"Yeah, okay," says LaVar. "You're good on that one. Now show Mr. Perk what you were working on at home."

"You mean Stevie?" Jackson asks.

"Yeah, I mean Stevie!"

Jackson starts playing "Superstition," smiling the way Stevie Wonder himself would, and Billy remembers stumbling through the song with Margot after their first date while LaVar listened from the sidewalk.

He read somewhere once that sadness is the only inspiration that a musician needs. His electric guitar is right there on the floor, propped up against The Rocker, left over from Alice's lesson earlier. He grabs it now, flips the amp back on, and sets his fingers on the five chord. "Let's try it from the top," he says.

Jackson starts over, and Billy goes five to seven, playing one of the funkiest guitar licks ever written, and he's stunned by how fantastic it sounds.

"What?" shouts LaVar. "Piano Man? You're a guitar man, too?" He gets up and dances, which upsets Lincoln. The dog tries to tackle him, but Billy and Jackson keep playing. "Get off me, you idiot!" LaVar yells at his dog. "I'm dancing here!"

Caleb doesn't dance, because he's far too tall and embarrassed, but he waves his arms in the air. Billy thinks of his grandma up in the cosmos somewhere watching him transition from Beethoven to Stevie Wonder. She'd scowl, probably. She'd shake her head and tsk. That would all be for show, though, because Billy knows that she'd love it.

"So, how much these pianos go for anyway?" asks LaVar. "These fancy Steinway things?"

Billy tells him a ballpark figure and LaVar whistles. "Damn, really? Shoot. Jackson, forget it. I'll just buy you a Caddy instead, we'll call it even."

Jackson gathers his books and papers off the music stand. His homework assignments for the week are aggressive, but he keeps asking for more to do. New songs, theory work, listening exercises.

"You aren't interested in selling this one, are you?" LaVar asks, touching the Steinway. "We already know it works, and the kid loves it."

"Good luck," says Caleb from the kitchen. "He'd sell me before he'd sell that thing."

Billy smiles.

"Yeah, all right," says LaVar. "Figured there's no harm in asking."

"What's this, Mr. Perk?"

Billy is hanging his guitar back up on the wall. When he turns around, Jackson is holding Margot's song, the untitled thing about being lost or maybe being found. Billy wrote the song out from memory after Margot left, setting her words on sheet music, complete with the notes he wrote with her on the fly the night Lawson showed up. He couldn't bring himself to toss it when he packed up to move here from Robyn's place. "Just a song a friend of mine was working on."

"Cool," says Jackson. "Like, an original?"

The kid sets the sheet music up on the stand and starts playing, and it sounds pretty damn good. Jackson plays it again, a little faster this time, and it sounds even better. Billy's new place isn't as noisy as the one above Charm City Rocks, but when Jackson stops, Billy can hear the unmistakable sounds of wooden sticks on plastic coming from a few blocks over.

"Cay, is that Daquan out there?"

Everyone goes quiet; Lincoln tilts his head.

"Um, pretty sure Daquan's always out there, Dad," says Caleb.

Billy's fingers still buzz and sting from the Fender strings as he goes to his music closet. Packed in with his *Rolling Stone*s and stacks of sheet music, he finds his old Kawai electric keyboard. He's held on to it over the years, because it's perfect for traveling or for when his students need him to come to them.

At the sight of a new instrument, Jackson's eyes light up. "What's that?"

Billy blows a bit of dust off the keys. "Jackson, you feel like jamming a little?"

CHAPTER 53

Caleb watches most everything on his laptop now—basketball, shows, movies, whatever—because the resolution is straight-up ridiculous. He taps the full-screen icon on YouTube and the video box spreads wide, practically theatrical. The Wonderboom speaker he keeps on his desk connects as he bumps the volume up.

The video he's about to watch is titled "Car Chase: Official Teaser Trailer." It just came out today—a whole YouTube takeover—and everyone's talking about it online. The caption reads: "A Man. A Car. A Race Against Time." Which sounds pretty badass. He taps the play arrow.

It opens on a low-angle shot of long grass blowing in the breeze beside a highway. "Thunderstruck" by AC/DC starts. There's a shot of a cow chewing, and Caleb snickers. Engine sounds approach, louder and louder until they're a roar, then a silver Porsche bursts across the screen. Cut to a cool head-on shot of Lawson Daniels. He's looking over the steering wheel, but it's like he's staring right at Caleb.

"Holy shit," Caleb says, because Lawson is wearing the same leather jacket that he wore when he showed up in the driveway outside.

Lawson checks the rearview mirror and sees three matching black BMWs chasing him. The dudes in one of the BMWs look like they might be Russian, but bad guys in movies always look like they might be Russian, so who knows?

"Thunderstruck" intensifies. *Nah-Nah-Nanananah.*

One of the maybe-Russians puts his arm out the driver's side window and starts shooting. Lawson jerks the wheel, and bullets whiz by. "Nice try, mate," he says.

There's a shot of the Porsche from the front. The camera lifts, revealing an approaching helicopter closing in from a distance. The pilot is wearing a helmet and a black visor, but he somehow looks Russian, too.

"Oh, is that how it's gonna be, then?" says Lawson.

AC/DC is slowly chanting "Thunder" under drums. The guitar riff skitters along. Words flash on the screen.

From the producers of **Iron Fist** *and* **Throttle Junkies**
Starring Academy Award nominee Lawson Daniels

The road is deserted. There's a tunnel up ahead. Lawson jams the gas pedal down and grips the wheel. The speedometer reads 145 miles per hour as the song's opening lyrics start. The BMWs and the helicopter speed up, too. Apparently, they're all racing to this random tunnel in what looks like maybe England. Close-ups of hands and tires and exhaust pipes and Lawson's furrowed eyebrows.

AC/DC sings, "You've been . . ." Then Lawson says, "Good luck, you stupid motherfu—" but before he can finish swearing, the lead singer screams, "Thunderstruck!" and there's a dazzling montage of shit exploding: two of the BMWs, the helicopter, a speedboat, a black Humvee, the side of a skyscraper. The trailer cuts to black.

Car Chase
Next summer
Only in theaters

Caleb minimizes the video box, revealing the chat app he has open with Justin and Shin-Soo.

Justin: *DAT SHIT IS DOOOOOOPE!*

Shin-Soo: *I like the exploding parts.*

Justin: *Yeah there was a lot of exploding. I'd say more than most movies.*

Shin-Soo: *Which begs the question—will more things explode? I'm betting yes.*

Justin: *Cay you think Lawson would remember you if he saw you on the street? Like you 2 are bros?*

It's hard to imagine that he wouldn't. They hung out. They played basketball. His mom gave Lawson a ride to the airport. It shouldn't be so exciting that Lawson Daniels might know who Caleb is, but . . . it totally is. He imagines a friendship morphing into a pseudo father-son thing. Caleb could have a dad, a co-dad, and a movie star dad.

Caleb: *Prob*

Shin-Soo: *That is so cool!*

Justin: *Totes!*

Shin-Soo: *IMDB says Car Chase 2 is already in development. More ssssploding!*

Justin: *I think I just exploded . . . in my pants.*

Caleb's phone rings, and his laptop rings, too, because it's linked to his phone. A number appears: FaceTime from San Francisco. He freezes. The last time he answered a call from a major American city outside of Baltimore, he pretended to be the father of a tween girl and jacked up a bunch of people's lives. The safe play here would be to ignore it. He's not going to, though, because there is exactly one person in the world Caleb knows in San Francisco.

Caleb: *Gotta go. TTYL*

Justin: *Booooooo*

Shin-Soo: *Lame!*

Caleb opens the call on his computer instead of his phone, and when he does, Poppy appears on his screen in startling HD. Instead of "hi" or "hello" or any of a number of other customary greetings, Caleb says, "Oh. Wow."

"Hey, Caleb," she says.

"Poppy."

Caleb catches sight of his own image below Poppy's and is horrified, because despite being what his doctor once called "shockingly underweight," Caleb appears to have at least three chins. He straightens his neck and pulls his shoulders back.

"You okay?"

"Yeah, yeah," says Caleb. "I'm good. How are you?"

"Fine. Just looked kinda like you got electrocuted for a second."

As Poppy moves a strand of hair off her face, Caleb considers asking, *To what do I owe the honor?* but the odds of getting those words out successfully seem slight. "I just watched your dad's new trailer," he says.

"Oh, yeah, that," says Poppy. "You believe he played Othello? Now he's getting chased in a Porsche."

"We watched *Othello* in English class freshman year," says Caleb. "He was really good."

Poppy half smiles and looks off camera, like she's been struck by a passing thought, and it dawns on Caleb why he's been thinking about her so much since meeting her on FaceTime. She's smart and pretty and cool and confident looking. It's like one of the girls from the Stanford website has come to life on his screen.

"So anyway," says Poppy. "Sorry. I know it's weird I'm calling. I had your number from before. I'm just doing a status check here. How's your dad?"

"My dad? He's good."

"Is he, though, or are you just saying that? Like that meme of the cartoon dog in the burning building who says, 'This is fine'?"

Caleb has a microfantasy about being with someone so smart that he's intellectually depleted at the end of the day, like he's taken a standardized test. Sometimes a crush is just a crush, but sometimes it's aspirational.

"Okay, yeah," he says. "Maybe not *fine* fine."

"Same with my mum." Poppy swears and pushes that same strand of hair off her face. "I'm worried about her. She was happy. Now she's not again, and I don't know what to do."

"I understand," says Caleb. "My dad was pretend-happy. Then he was *happy* happy when your mom was here. But now he's just miserable."

"They miss each other, don't they?"

"Yeah."

"But they're both too stupid to do anything about it."

Caleb leans back in his desk chair. "My dad played one of your mom's songs on the street yesterday."

"Oh my God," says Poppy. "Like, by himself?"

"Yeah," says Caleb. "Well, no. A twelve-year-old boy joined him, and a kid named Daquan who plays Home Depot buckets."

Poppy shakes her head. "That's sweet, but also the most depressing thing ever."

Which was exactly what Caleb thought as he watched the impromptu performance yesterday on Thames Street. Caleb, LaVar, and Lincoln chased after Caleb's dad and Jackson as they speedwalked to where Daquan was set up across from Charm City Rocks. Jackson was hauling the electric piano; Caleb's dad had his

Fender and amp. Daquan was up to jam with them, and Jackson looked thrilled, like he was on a musical adventure. Caleb's dad, though, after running inside the Horse You Came In On to borrow an extension cord from Beth, played Margot's song like he was performing at a funeral, like he might start to cry.

"Trust me, it *looked* even more depressing than it sounds," says Caleb. "I shot it on my phone. I'll text it to you. Warning, though, my dad's voice is pretty terrible."

"Sounds delightful," says Poppy. "Oh, by the way. What's this bullshit I hear about you picking Baltimore over Stanford?"

"What?"

"I mean, none of my business and all, but, dude, it's California."

CHAPTER 54

Tonight, Billy and Caleb finally got around to watching the final episode of the Netflix documentary, which covered the twenty-teens up to the current day. There were a few bright spots, but Billy found it hard to care. The music seemed corporate, and the fashion looked downright dumb. Even the deep-voiced announcer seemed to be straining for enthusiasm as he shoehorned words like "iconic" and "irreverent" into his narration. Not enough time has passed, apparently, for any of it to be interesting.

Toward the end, Caleb said what Billy was thinking. "Margot's way cooler than any of these posers, huh?"

Billy agreed that she was and is.

And now, in a nice reversal of their roles, even though it's not even nine o'clock yet, Caleb is asleep on the couch with his laptop on his chest, and Billy is wide awake. He's committed to finally getting his new kitchen in order. Transition mode has gone on for too long; it's time to make the place feel like an actual home. He found a nice spot for the espresso machine, and he set placemats out on his kitchenette table. As he unpacks a last box of dishware, he looks over at knocked-out Caleb.

With their son in summer limbo until college starts in September, Billy and Robyn have fallen back into their old co-parenting routine in which Caleb volleys back and forth between them. When he's here, he prefers sleeping on Billy's couch next to the Steinway instead of in the little extra bedroom upstairs. He went to his first orientation event at Hopkins the other day: incoming first-year bowling night. When Billy asked if it was fun, Caleb said yeah, "But, you know, I've been to Mustang Alley's a hundred times, so it wasn't exactly special."

Billy gathers takeout cartons and soda cans, a few broken-down moving boxes, and shoves them into the yellow bin under his sink. Tomorrow is recycling day.

There's a quick knock, then the door opens. Robyn says, "Knock, knock," and enters carrying a box of new Tupperware. "Just wanted to drop this off," she says. "I told you it was the world's shittiest housewarming gift."

"Thanks," he says. "I've seen worse, though. Cay got me a Darth Vader spatula that says 'Who's your daddy?' on it."

"We'll call it a tie." She looks down at their son. "Is he asleep already?"

"I think he's faking to get out of helping me unpack."

She looks around at the mess. "Smart move. I'd stay and help, but I don't think it's possible to be parked more illegally than I currently am."

Billy pulls the recycling bin out from under the sink. "Come on," he says. "I'll go out with you."

It's humid outside, so it still feels as hot as it did at high noon. He sets the bin at the curb next to his neighbors' bins. Crushed cereal boxes and empty Natty Boh cans as far as the eye can see. He instinctively looks right, down toward his old apartment. It's brighter in that direction, more signs of life. Robyn's SUV is double parked halfway down the block, near a fire hydrant and two clearly labeled no-parking signs. "You weren't kidding," he says. "That is very illegal."

He walks her down to her car. Robyn reaches for the door handle but stops, and they stand together for a moment. There are so many as-alwayses with Robyn, Billy thinks. She looks great, as always. She smells good, as always. She looks stressed, as always. He points up the street, toward Thames. "You should stop by Gustavo's on your way," he says. "He'd love to see you. Tell him to put a pretzel on my tab."

She leans against her car. "You okay?" she asks.

"Who, me?" he says. "Living the dream over here. You?"

"Being alone is weird," she says. "It was fun at first—uninterrupted me time, you know. Now I just can't believe how quiet everything is, especially when Caleb's with you."

Over the years, Billy's go-to loneliness-fighting trick has been to fend off the quiet by any means necessary. Music, Orioles games on TV, the Steinway.

"I thought about seducing you tonight," she says.

"Oh yeah?"

"I had it all planned out. We'd get back together. Grow old in a state of mild contentment. You'd die before me, because I'm in better shape than you. But first, yeah . . . seduction."

Relationships are like trying to fire rockets into space: if you miss your launch window, sometimes you have to just scrap the whole thing, which is what happened to them back in the day. He spots the Jiffy Lube sticker at the top of her windshield and makes a note to himself to remind her next month to get an oil change. "Why didn't you?" he asks.

She swats a mosquito. "Eh," she says. "You would've rejected me. Or worse, you *wouldn't* have rejected me, but you'd have been thinking about *her* the whole time. Which would've made *me* think about her, and that would've been weird."

"Plus, we would've had to kick Caleb out of the house."

"Ugh," she says. "That kid's such a cockblocker."

Billy laughs. He's known her half his life, and he's never heard her say the word *cock*. "Good kid, though."

"One of the best," she says.

Robyn gets in her car and starts the engine. She opens her window and turns down the blasting NPR.

"I'm sorry I didn't chase after you," Billy says.

"I know," says Robyn. "Sometimes I am, too."

Time goes fluid for an hour or so as Billy slides plates, glasses, and dishes into his new cupboards. Shitty housewarming gift or not, the new Tupperware from Robyn fits perfectly in the pantry and will surely come in handy. He wonders now which option he'd have chosen: rejecting Robyn or accepting and thinking of Margot. He hopes the former, for the sake of being a gentleman, but he'll never know for sure.

Billy has resisted the urge to play Burnt Flowers since Margot left, but he's listening to their second album now on wobbly vinyl, enjoying Margot's drum fills between Nikki's lyrics.

"Hey, Cay, you awake?"

Upon inspection, Billy finds that his son is not. When Caleb was a baby, Billy would check in on him at night and find him sleeping in the craziest imaginable positions, as if he'd been hit with a tranquilizer dart mid-escape. Now, though, he looks peaceful, legs up on the armrest, because he's at least six inches too tall for the couch.

"Cay?"

Billy tosses a blanket over Caleb's legs and takes the laptop off his chest. The movement causes the machine to blink to life, and the screen lights up. Billy doesn't mean to look, because it's probably best not to know what eighteen-year-old males are looking at on their computers. The images he sees, though, are entirely whole-some. A sunset. Some mountains. College-age kids in a lab wear-ing protective goggles. A chef tossing pizza. A pretty girl of East Indian descent in a crimson hoodie. Billy scrolls. Everyone looks so smart and happy, young. The landscapes are beautiful—mountains, sunshine. When he realizes that it's the Stanford Uni-versity website, though, Billy has to sit on the armrest.

"Oh, Cay," he says. "You idiot."

CHAPTER 55

Tonight's 6 P.M./9 P.M. call from Poppy comes in the form of a text message. Margot is alone, taking five, drinking black coffee in a small glass room that's filled with instruments, like a musical graveyard.

you there? Poppy asks.

Am I where? Margot replies. *I could be anywhere.*

She leans back against an upright bass the size of a small bear. When Burnt Flowers first got signed to Stage Dive, she imagined pristine recording studios, dustless and gleaming. Turned out, from the best to the worst of them, they all have rooms like this.

OK smart ass

Why are you texting me? I prefer your voice.

i'm busy

Busy doing what?

none of your biz!

Margot imagines Poppy on the other side of the continental United States going about her young life.

are you happy mum?

The question snaps Margot out of her breaktime daze. She doesn't know if she's happy, but she's busy, and sometimes that's just as good. She's due back in Studio 1 in twenty minutes. She and Anna will work through alt backing tracks for a song called "It's Time Again." They've got five rough songs laid down. They need five or six more, at least, plus a prerelease song to drop on social. The pace is stressful for everyone. Axl is staying away as ordered, but Rebecca brings messages from him every day. Yesterday, his message was: "Axl's not sure he's hearing a single yet."

your silence is deafening . . . and telling

I'm working Poppy, she replies. It's annoying having text conversations with twentysomethings; they type so fast. *Happiness isn't always the point.*

u should write motivational posters for sad people to hang in their cubes. Then she texts: *im sending you a video. caleb sent it to me.*

The upright bass makes a low sound of protest as Margot leans forward. *Billy's Caleb?*

Duh

A video arrives with a swooshing sound.

i know he asked you to leave and that mustve hurt. he thought he was doing the right thing. i dont know. guy logic. whatever. but he misses u.

How do you know?

just watch it mum. Pretty good song btw. wonder who wrote it. gtg ttyl

Poppy?

No typing bubbles. Poppy isn't gone, because people Poppy's age are never "gone" from their phones. Her daughter is done with this conversation, though, and Margot says, "Shit," which, due to the acoustics in the little room, sounds crisp and rich.

When she taps the video, it opens on a street corner in Baltimore, one she recognizes. Daquan is sitting at his buckets, LaVar's son Jackson is cross-legged on the ground with a portable piano in his lap, and Billy is standing between them holding his electric guitar. "Just do whatever you want, guys," Billy tells Daquan and Jackson. "We're just kinda jamming here, okay."

Billy looks tired. He's a little skinny, too, and his face is drawn. He always looked happy, even that first messed-up day at Charm City Rocks. He doesn't look happy now, though. He looks like how Margot feels. He looks like he misses her.

"Are you filming this, Cay?" asks Billy.

Off camera, Caleb's voice says, "Yeah. But what are you doing exactly, Dad?"

"You a lead singer now, too, Piano Man?" says LaVar, also off camera, and Margot thinks about how nice it'd be to be there with them.

Billy counts off and starts playing the same messy chords he played in the apartment over Robyn's garage just before Lawson showed up. Daquan eases into some steady drumming, and Jackson starts playing. When Billy sings Margot's lyrics, it's bad, of course, but it's good, too. Even though he's a piano teacher on a street corner with two kids, it works, because it's rock and roll.

CHAPTER 56

"You're in a good mood," says Billy.

Robyn is smiling. "Who, me?"

They're out to dinner with Caleb, but it's just the two of them, because Caleb excused himself to the restroom a few minutes ago. They're at a table outside of Phillips Seafood in the Inner Harbor, surrounded by tourists. It's sunny and warm, and in a few minutes their waiter will bring them a bushel of steaming crabs to hammer apart with mallets. It was Caleb's choice, and Billy and Robyn are doing pretty much whatever their son wants.

"Why are you smiling so much?" Billy asks. "It's making me nervous."

Robyn looks around, leans in. "So, I had a pretty surreal experience this morning."

He can't remember the last time he saw her like this—practically giddy. She's in a T-shirt and shorts, too, which is weird, because he's so used to seeing her in her various suits of corporate armor.

She takes her phone out, looks around again. "You have to promise you won't tell anyone, though."

"No," he says. "That's like Caleb telling us not to get mad before we know what we're not supposed to get mad about. If you've got, like, state secrets, I'm gonna tell someone."

Robyn groans. "Fine." She taps her screen. "Not state secrets, but definitely an international incident. Here, listen. I don't want to put it on speaker."

Billy holds Robyn's iPhone to his ear. The voice is instantly recognizable. "Robyn. 'Ello, love."

"Is this . . . ?" Billy asks.

She nods.

Lawson Daniels clears his throat on Robyn's voicemail inbox. "Back in your car, after you almost killed the both of us, you asked if you could record me saying what I said. I thought about it, and that was quite cute, as far as requests go. So, listen up, love, I'm gonna do my best. I was riffing before, so forgive me if the details are a bit dodgy."

"Am I about to hear something I shouldn't be—"

"No," she says. "It's not like that. Well, mostly not."

Billy braces himself. "He really does have a good voice, though, doesn't he? It's the accent."

Robyn bends her straw in half. "I know, right?"

Lawson's voice is so deep that the little phone speaker vibrates against Billy's earlobe. "Robyn, you, my dear, are quite lovely," he says. "Beautiful, in fact. Okay, now I'll skip the part where we said mean things about Billy's jumpers, and that bit about Aaron's hair. No sense in rehashing all that, right? You are capable and smart and accomplished, and you, love, need a couple of middle-aged blokes from Baltimore about as much as a fish needs a bloody Jet Ski. Got it? Now, allow me to go off script for a moment. I'm really quite good at improvisational performance. Lotta people don't know that. Anyway, I've been thinking about your lips for the better part of a month now. Hands down the best snog I've had in ages. If I could go back, maybe I wouldn't have jetted off quite as fast as I did. A few more minutes with you . . . well, anyway, maybe another time. All right, love. Best to you and yours. Tell Billy and your freakishly tall child hello for me. Cheers now."

Billy looks at the screen; the message is over. "Did you make out with Lawson?"

Her hands are on her cheeks, *Home Alone*–style. "Yeah."

"When? Where?"

"I gave him a ride to the airport, remember? He kissed me in my car."

Billy laughs—stunned, but also overjoyed by the harmless scandal of it. "Wait, what did you say about my sweaters?"

"Um, don't you think maybe they're a bit much?"

Billy looks at their beers and waters, sweating between them. "Well, shit. That hurts my feelings."

"Don't take it personally," says Robyn. "It's summer now anyway."

"How'd he even get your number?"

"No idea," she whispers. "Famous-person powers."

"The Illuminati?"

They laugh so much that the table next to them looks over. "She kissed Lawson Daniels," Billy tells them, and Robyn slaps his arm.

"Sorry," she says. "My friend is drunk."

"She lies," Billy tells them. "Chronically. It's sad."

Billy and Robyn laugh together some more. Billy scans for Caleb, because he's been gone longer than a trip to the restroom at a seafood restaurant should take. "Where the hell is he? Our food's gonna be out soon."

"So, yeah," says Robyn. "We've both kissed celebrities. Score for us, right?"

Billy tries to keep smiling, but the reference to Margot is a dash of cold water.

"Sorry," Robyn says. "I'm dumb. I just—"

"No, come on. You made out with an Oscar nominee. You're allowed to be happy."

Their waiter drops off rolls.

"You're allowed to be happy, too, you know," Robyn says.

Billy has been enjoying the newfound ease between them since Aaron moved out and Margot went back to New York. They feel like actual friends now instead of people who are just trying to make something work. He holds out his hands, palms up. "What?" he asks. "Who's happier than me, right?"

She takes a roll, tears it in half. "If you say so."

Robyn asks him why they're here, exactly—the three of them. Billy called Robyn last night to see if they could all have dinner.

"I wanna talk," he says. "Need to talk, actually. To Caleb mostly, but you should be part of this, too. We're a team, right?"

She bites into some bread. "Should I be worried?"

"Not at all," he says. "You should be happy. Because you were right about something. And I finally realized it. Oh good, here he comes."

CHAPTER 57

Caleb is eighteen years old, which, mathematically speaking, means he's got a long way to go. He's never had a girlfriend, technically, but he knows that someday he will. That's just how it works, and besides, girls seem to like tall guys, right? That's what he's heard, anyway—hashtags and such.

He'll probably have *several* girlfriends, in fact. Again, mathematically speaking. They'll come and go, and each will affect his life differently. Some dramatically, some hardly at all. Some may hurt him, but he may just as easily hurt a few of them. He hopes not too badly, though. But then someday he'll meet someone who will start out as just another girlfriend, but then she'll become way, way more than that. He'll love that girl—that woman—more than he's ever loved anyone.

For the time being, though, the two people Caleb loves most in the world are sitting at a table together in the sunshine at Phillips Seafood, and they're laughing. Like, *really* laughing. They're laughing in a way he's never seen them laugh together before. He has no idea what they're talking about—probably whatever boring shit people in their forties talk about—but seeing them now, like this, warms his heart, because good for them.

Caleb is finished going to the bathroom. He washed his hands a few minutes ago, checked himself in the mirror. Now he's leaning against a sign for the National Aquarium next door and spying on his parents from about a hundred feet away. His dad keeps turning around and looking for him. Caleb isn't entirely sure why he took this detour on the way back from the restroom, but here he is. Maybe he just needed a minute to himself.

From where Caleb stands, Baltimore looks genuinely cool. A pirate ship full of smiling kids drifts out in the harbor among more smiling people peddling dragon boats. The Orioles and Yankees are on one of the outdoor TVs above the bar. Dogs are on leashes—a freaking ton of them, like, every dog in town is here. A bus lumbers by on Lombard Street. There's an ad for pink Google phones stuck to its side. Caleb laughs, because someone's already tagged it with graffiti.

Caleb has gone back and forth about whether he's happy with his decision to stay here. Right now, he is. Because it's the right thing to do. A little safe? Yeah, maybe. But it makes sense. Not going to Stanford isn't the end of the world. Poppy was right on FaceTime. California *is* incredible. But it's not going anywhere, right? Maybe he'll make it there someday.

His mom is single now, and Caleb likes that he'll be here to hang out with her. Maybe he'll go on mom dates with her—arty movies at the Charles Theatre, so she doesn't have to go alone. His dad is sad about Margot leaving, obviously. It's complicated, because he told her to go, even though he didn't want her to go. His dad keeps saying he's fine, but Caleb knows he isn't, so he's glad he'll be here for him, too.

The breadbasket has arrived at their table. Caleb can see it from where he's standing, and his stomach reacts, because he's so hungry he could pass out. Their salads should be arriving soon, then their bibs and crabs and little bowls of butter sauce. Caleb will eat all his food, then he'll eat whatever food his mom and dad can't eat.

Enough lurking. He should really get back. The two people he loves most in the world are waiting for him. They both need him. And Caleb is happy that he's here to help.

CHAPTER 58

The four members of Burnt Flowers are playing together. They're seven minutes into a jam session, trying to get a potential new song to take flight. Jenny and Anna are at the foot of Margot's kit, the three of them huddled tight, willing artistry through proximity. Nikki is on the other side of the room at her mic. The song is going nowhere.

"Step off!" she sing-shouts. "Go away! It's you! Not me!"

Wave has come out of the control room, and he's dancing. He pumps his fists with each line—Nikki's personal in-studio hype man. The tape is rolling, because it's always rolling, but this is just a band searching, the musical equivalent of casting a giant net into a dark, swirling ocean.

"It's you! Not me! It's you! Not me!"

Chuck, one of the engineers, sits in the control room, head bobbing, staring down at their levels. Over Chuck's shoulder, Margot notices a baseball game on a monitor. It's the Yankees, because they're in New York, but she catches stray bits of orange and black.

She hits the high-hat, but her angle is bad, and the wobbly clamor in the middle of her drum loop causes everyone to look up.

Bands play through all kinds of imperfections when they're jamming, but they've been here all day and into the evening, so the misfire is enough to bring them to a slow-moving car crash of a stop.

"Ladies and gentlemen, the one and only Margot Hammer," says Anna, laughing.

"Sorry. Yeah, that was me."

"It's cool, rock star," says Nikki. "I was feeling that, though. We're close with that one, right?"

"Fuck yeah we are!" says Wave. "Hot!"

Jenny, Anna, and Margot look at one another. That song, if you can even call it a song, is far from close, and as much as Margot would like to give Axl the middle finger, he's not wrong about the distinct lack of a single so far.

"That's the chorus, right?" says Nikki. "It's you, not me. You, not me. A breakup anthem. Breakup anthems are huge right now. Women'll turn that shit up."

Wave punches himself gently in the chest. "I'm feeling it."

Margot rubs her calluses together. "Hey, Chuck," she says.

The studio mics are hooked into the control room. Chuck looks startled. He's not used to the band talking to him directly. He touches a button. "What's up, Margot?"

"Who's playing?"

"Um, pardon?"

"The game. Behind you. Who's playing?"

Chuck turns to the monitor. "Oh, right. Yeah. Yankees-Orioles."

Margot wonders if Billy is watching the game, too. She misses the gentle murmuring of baseball, like the comforting hum of an oscillating fan. "Who's winning?" she asks.

Jenny hugs her guitar. "What the hell, Margot? You're, like, into sports balls now?"

"Just wondering."

"Well, the Yankees, obviously," says Chuck. "I mean, Baltimore sucks, right?"

Margot knows he's talking about the baseball team, but the sentiment hurts, because . . . no it doesn't. Margot actually likes it.

The door from the lobby opens and Rebecca Yang enters. She's carrying a few bags of Chinese takeout in one hand and some rolled-up poster board in the other. "Hey, ladies," she says. "Got a sec? Are we breaking?"

The smell of food does them all in. Jenny and Anna set their instruments on their stands and head for the table at the back of the room.

"What time is it anyway?" says Jenny.

"Something in the p.m., I'm guessing," says Anna.

"Good," says Jenny. "I'm more talented at night. Rebecca, if I open my mouth like a baby bird, can you pour caffeine into it?"

"Stop harassing Becca," says Anna, who has taken to calling Rebecca "Becca."

The guitarist and bassist eat, both wielding chopsticks. Nikki picks up a fortune cookie, and Margot watches an Oriole at bat through the control room window. He smacks the ball between two Yankees and trots to first base.

"All right, so, I've got some layouts for you all to look at," says Rebecca. "Cool?"

Anna's mouth is full of noodles. "Layouts of what?" she asks.

"Album covers, for starters. Tour posters, too, if you're interested."

"We don't even have an album *title* yet," says Jenny.

"It's *Burn It Back*," says Nikki. "Didn't we all agree on that?"

"So, like, we're all in on burn puns, then?" asks Anna.

"Yeah, isn't that a little on the nose?" asks Jenny. "Why not *Burn Baby Burn*?"

"*Flower Inferno?*" says Anna, pointing with a chopstick.

"Fuck yes," says Jenny. "Rebecca, write that down on the brainstorming board. And I wasn't kidding about the baby bird thing. Can you get me a Red Bull?"

Nikki starts pacing. "*Burn It Back* is perfect, though. We talked about this for an hour and a half the other night. It's not a pun, it's a statement. It's the whole point of this. We're back."

"In fairness," says Anna, "*you* did most of the talking. The rest of us just kinda made disapproving sounds the whole time."

Nikki crosses her arms.

"Let's just look," says Margot. "Maybe it'll sound better if we see it laid out, or something else will come to us. Rebecca, go ahead."

Rebecca shuffles in her Chuck Taylors, and Margot knows the girl well enough by now to know that she's nervous to show them whatever's on those boards. "I mean, they're just mockups, okay?" Rebecca says. "Like, ideas. Jumping-off points. Axl just thought, like, directionally speaking, this is where we should be right n—"

"Becca," says Anna. "Enough. We know the deal, babes. Let's see 'em."

Rebecca fiddles, unrolls, stalls for time. She looks for a clear space to display the artwork. All the while, Margot absorbs the dread in the room, like inhaling steadily rising smoke. When the boards are up and on display, no one says anything for several seconds. Wave puts his hands together, nods vigorously. "Yeah, shit, that's right," he says.

"Is this some kind of joke?" asks Jenny.

"What the fuck?" says Anna. "Becca, I'm gonna choke to death on a shrimp right now if you tell me you're being serious."

Margot wants to defend Rebecca—the messenger here—but she's briefly unable to speak. The layouts before them represent the worst possible outcome. There's no other way to categorize them.

They look as if Anna, Jenny, and Margot had been asked to describe the exact opposite of what they wanted and then Axl's team of designers got to work making it happen. The proposed album cover is an image of a giant Nikki Kixx in a crop top, her stomach photoshopped, holding a microphone in the air. The rest of them, Jenny, Anna, and Margot, are behind her, blurred to the point of indecipherability. As terrible as the graphics are, the worst part is that Margot isn't at all surprised. The same, however, cannot be said for Jenny and Anna.

"Reunion my. Fucking. Ass," says Jenny.

"This is just another goddamn solo album for you, isn't it?" says Anna. "We're just your new hired backing band."

"What?" asks Nikki. "No. We can mess with the scaling—shuffle stuff—but, like, look at the flames. They're cool."

"They're hot!" says Wave.

"Yeah, they *are* hot," says Nikki.

"And your body's bumpin' right here," says Wave, pointing at Nikki's navel in the photo. "For real. Dat tummy. This'll jump offa iTunes like a motherfucker. You kidding me?"

"Oh, shut up and pull your head out of Nikki's ass, you fucking dork!" Jenny says.

Wave holds his hands up. "Hey now, girl."

"I can't believe this," says Anna. "I flew all the way to New York to live in a hotel room to be a blurry ant-size blip on an album cover behind your stupid ass?"

"Oh right," says Nikki. "Like you had sooooo much else going on. Axl told me you answered on the first ring."

"Bullshit. I've got my own—"

"What? Bluegrass album in the works? Nobody gives a shit, Anna. I don't even know what bluegrass is."

"Fuck you."

Jenny is standing now. "Guess what, Nikki. Your solo albums

suck. Everybody knows it. Shit sounds like you're diddling yourself next to a drum machine. This was our chance to do something g—"

"*Our* chance?" says Nikki. "Ours? Get off it, Jenny. You and Anna can go to hell. You bitches hid behind me for years. Margot's the only one of you who has any actual fucking talent. And she's the dullest woman in the history of rock music." Nikki turns around and points at her own rear. "You think this ass is stupid? You . . . need . . . this . . . ass! You need *me*! And all three of you know it!"

In the control room, Chuck watches with his mouth open. Rebecca and Wave have been steadily backing up as if an alligator has been released into the studio. Poor Rebecca is covering her ears. Nikki, Jenny, and Anna continue shouting. Their insults turn more and more jagged—the sorts of things none of them will ever be able to come back from. Jenny throws her chopsticks across the table. Anna spills a carton of kung pao shrimp.

The first time Burnt Flowers broke up was like a business meeting. Four women signed documents separately in a conference room at Stage Dive Records. This time their breakup is a screaming match.

No one notices when Margot walks across the room. They continue not to notice as she passes her own drum kit and picks up Jenny's Gibson electric guitar and puts the strap over her shoulder. They do, however, notice when Margot unleashes a power chord. She strums the same chord again, hitting the strings so hard that the tips of her fingers burn. Wave winces. Jenny, Anna, and Nikki finally shut up. And then Margot shouts the lyrics to the song she started writing in a hotel room in Baltimore.

CHAPTER 59

"You're not, like, dying, are you?"

"No," says Billy. "I don't think so."

"Okay, good," says Caleb. "I get the Champagne Supernova if you do, though. Cool?"

Billy watches his son consume bread the way a dinosaur might, and he longs once again to stop time. His son, dressed in baggy shorts and a *Game of Thrones* T-shirt, ravaging his food, forever and ever.

"Billy?" says Robyn. "What's up?"

"We haven't had a lesson in a while," Billy says. "Figured it was time."

"Really? With Mom here? She's a lady, though, Dad. No ladies allowed."

"She's making a guest appearance."

"What are you guys talking about?" asks Robyn.

"Dad's Lessons in Art and Manhood," says Caleb. "It's this whole thing. He explains stuff to me, like how I shouldn't lick doorknobs or judge women based on their crop tops."

"Oh," says Robyn. "Well, this should be interesting."

Billy's goal here is simple and straightforward. Now, though, he finds that he doesn't know how to start. He glances over at the TV above the bar, sees that the Orioles are getting shelled by the Yankees. Finally, he takes a breath and just says it. "Caleb, you need to go."

His son stops midchew, mouth bulging. "But our crabs aren't even here yet."

That probably wasn't the most artful opening line. In Billy's defense, though, for the second time in recent months he's about to tell someone he loves that they need to leave. Billy looks at Robyn, though, and he sees that she isn't confused at all. She sets her bread down; a reflective sheen appears over her eyes.

"You need to go to Stanford," Billy says. "Actually, no. You . . . you *are* going to Stanford."

Caleb swallows. "But . . ."

"And, Robyn," he says, "I know we talked about tuition. All in, Stanford is more than Hopkins. Your financial situation is different now, without Aaron. So, I'm gonna contribute more than we originally discussed."

Robyn blinks, focuses. "Billy, we're talking about a lot of money. How are you—"

"I sold the Steinway to LaVar Barber," he says.

"Dad, no, what?"

"Who's LaVar Barber?"

"He's a Raven," says Caleb. "But, Dad, that's bullshit. You love that thing. You gotta get it back."

LaVar and Jackson came to the house this morning to pick up the piano. Billy had never seen someone look as happy as Jackson did. "You can come visit it any time you want, Piano Man," LaVar told him. LaVar hired the same crew to haul it away that Billy did to take it from the apartment above Charm City Rocks to the apartment above Robyn and Aaron's garage and then back again to Billy's new place in Fells Point. The foreman politely asked how many more times he'd have to move the damn thing, and Jackson said, "Never again!"

As perfect an instrument as the Steinway is, it's more than Billy needs. For the fair price LaVar paid, Billy can buy a perfectly nice new piano and have plenty left over to make a huge dent in Caleb's tuition and living expenses at Stanford.

The people at the table next to them dig into their crabs now. The lady at the head of the table screams with delight when a claw breaks and squirts her husband in the face with crab juice.

"You're right, Cay," Billy says. "I did love it. But I love you more. Also, don't swear."

"He committed to Hopkins," says Robyn. "Wouldn't Stanford have filled his spot by now?"

"I thought of that," says Billy. "Aaron said he can help. Alumni relations stuff. Apparently, they leave wiggle room for situations like this. As far as co-dads go, Aaron's a pretty good one. You're a lucky guy, Cay."

Billy can deal with Robyn tearing up. He hopes, though, that Caleb won't, because if he does, Billy knows that he'll fall apart before their dinners even arrive. Fortunately, though, the kid holds tough. "But I like Baltimore," he says. "I want to be here, with *you*. Both of you. You're my family. My mom and dad."

Robyn puts her hand on Caleb's hand.

Billy decided that he wasn't going to mention the grid of Stanford photos on Caleb's computer. His son is old enough to have his own secrets. "It's not about Baltimore, buddy," he says. "And don't worry about your mom and me. We'll be fine. Especially your mom. Look at her; she's a killer."

Robyn laughs. "Gee, thanks."

"This is about you," says Billy. "Cay, you deserve this. And I know it's scary—*change* is scary. Sometimes it's terrifying. I get it. You've been here your whole life, right? You're safe here. You love this place. And you should, because Baltimore is great. But maybe there's something even better for you out there—something you'll love even more. But you won't know unless you go. Because sometimes . . . sometimes you've gotta take a chance on something."

Across the outdoor dining patio, the doors from the kitchen swing open, and their waiter emerges with a tray of food hoisted over his shoulder. Billy notes this just as he notes that Caleb and Robyn are looking at him. His son is smiling, and Robyn is shaking her head.

"What?" Billy asks. He already knows, though.

"Dad, thanks . . . but, like, are you even listening to yourself right now?"

As their waiter weaves toward them, Billy thinks about Margot. It's an easy thing to do, because he's been thinking about her virtually every moment since she left. And then Robyn takes her hand off their son's hand and puts it onto his.

"Thank you, Billy," she says. "Now, really, get out of here."

CHAPTER 60

Margot doesn't know how long she's been walking, but her feet are killing her.

Her driver inched along slowly behind her for at least two miles after she left the studio. He got stuck behind a few buses and was marooned at several intersections, but he kept catching back up to her.

"I'm not supposed to leave you alone, Miss Hammer!" he shouted out the window. "Mr. Albee will kill me!"

"I'm fine!" Margot told him. "And tell Axl to go fuck himself!"

As a pedestrian it's hard to be inconspicuous when you're being slowly trailed by a giant black Cadillac, so people on the street kept waving at her and calling her awesome. Then, finally, she heard the big engine rev behind her. When Margot looked back, her escort was finally gone for good, and she was free.

Back at Threshold, Margot had played the first verse of her song and the chorus three times in front of Rebecca Yang, Wave, and her stunned bandmates. "But I'm here now! And you're here, too! And that's good enough for me! If it's good enough for you!"

In the control room, Chuck had put his headphones back on,

which means there must be a recording of her playing. She doesn't need to hear it, though, to know that she sounded incredible.

"Margot?" said Anna when Margot finally stopped.

"Holy shit," said Nikki.

Margot took the guitar off her shoulder and gave it back to Jenny. She squeezed the guitarist's hand then hugged Anna. "I have to go."

Four words, unspecific, but they knew what she was saying. This was it. The Burnt Flowers reunion was over. *They,* officially, were over.

"Can we come?" asked Anna.

"Yeah," said Jenny. "Can we?"

Margot winked at Rebecca, and then she looked at Nikki. Neither woman said anything. This entire thing was a gimmick. Nikki didn't need Margot. She didn't need Jenny and Anna either. Nikki didn't *think* she did, anyway. Nikki would rerecord the material they'd already laid down with a new backing band. She'd come up with a few more songs. She'd have the three of them cut out of that terrible album cover, and she'd be fine. Love her or hate her, Nikki Kixx is a rock-and-roll survivor.

Margot kissed Anna's cheek, then Jenny's. She told them, "Not now, okay? But soon." Then she left the studio and stepped out into the evening. She wore jeans and her boots and a pilly sweater. Not exactly a rock outfit, but Margot is a rock star nonetheless. Stupid Lawson was right: she was born to be.

She's walking now in the general direction of home, but there's no way she'll make it in these boots.

For years now, Margot has operated on a day-to-day basis, rarely thinking ahead, her thoughts tangled up in the past— Lawson and Nikki, Burnt Flowers, the MTV Video Music Awards, a mental collage of *Us Weekly* headlines. Now, though, as the crossing light before her blinks on, her future rolls out ahead of her like a red carpet. Tomorrow she's going to clean her apartment. After that, she's going to write a song. And then, by God, she'll write another one. Soon after that, she'll call Anna and Jenny, and she'll ask them if they want to start a new band with her. They'll say yes, she knows, and one of them, probably Jenny, will mention that they need a singer. Margot will tell them that they can all be singers, but that she knows a singer-slash–guitar player in Baltimore named Emma who can really bring it. And if they want to get crazy, there's a kid named Daquan who hits drums like a beast. And if they want to get *really* crazy, there's another kid, even younger than Daquan, his name is Jackson, and he's killer on the piano. They'll make songs together, the first of which will be the song Margot just belted out at Threshold, and they'll release an album. If her bandmates have a better idea, great; but right now, Margot is thinking *We're Fine* would be a perfect title.

But before she does any of that, she needs to call Billy.

Just eyeballing it, there don't seem to be as many benches to sit on in Manhattan as there are in Baltimore, so Margot diverts into a decent-enough-looking bar. It's mostly empty. The few people inside are gathered in small groups. Some solo folks stare at their phones. Margot heads straight for the bartender. "You don't have a beer called Natty Boh, do you?"

The bartender—a guy, fortysomething, with tattoos—knows who she is, but he's being cool about it, like Beth was. "Never heard of it. And I thought I'd heard of everything."

"It's from Baltimore," she says. "It's crappy but good."

"Oh, well, if it's crappy you want." He pours her a beer, yellow and fizzy. She takes a sip and it's perfect, then she touches Billy's name in the contacts list on her phone. There isn't enough time to plan what she's going to say, because he picks up instantly.

"Hello?" he says. "Margot?"

"Hi."

"It's you," he says.

She likes how he sounds, like he's happy to hear from her. "So, here's the thing," she says. "You don't get to tell me what my dream is."

"Okay," he says.

"Because maybe *you're* my dream."

"Really? Me?"

She looks around the bar, which is ordinary and stuffy. A few people have figured out who she is, and those people know her life story, and that's fine. Others are oblivious, or simply don't care, and that's fine, too. Either way, it's nice to be out in the world again. The man she's talking to on the phone right now loves her for who she was, but he loves her for who she is now, too. "Yeah," she says. "You're my dream guy, Billy Perkins."

"You don't think my cardigans are too much?"

"What? I love your cardigans."

"Okay, good," he says.

TVs hang everywhere; one is playing the baseball game. "The Orioles are getting their asses kicked, huh?" she says.

Billy laughs. "I saw that earlier. But I'm not watching it anymore."

"Yeah?" she asks. "Where are you?"

"You won't believe it if I tell you."

"Try me."

"I'm in the Champagne Supernova," he says.

"Where are you going?"

"Well, right now I'm just sitting here in front of my house," he says. "I have a duffel bag. I was gonna come see you."

Margot smiles and touches the weightless foam at the rim of her crappy beer.

"I wanted to surprise you," he says. "The way you surprised me."

"That would've been nice."

"You think?"

"I do," she says.

"But then I realized I have no idea where the hell you actually live."

Margot laughs.

"I pulled up 'New York City' on Google Maps, but that seems vague."

"Just start driving north," she says. "And drive fast. I'll text you my address in a minute."

She imagines Billy in her apartment. She can see him running his hands over the cymbals of her drum kit, taking her guitar off the wall and frowning at how out of tune it is. It's a little presumptuous, because yeah, okay, she hasn't known him long, but she can picture the photograph of them framed and hung up on the wall. Billy about to give her a high five, and Margot smiling as big as she's ever smiled.

"Margot?" he says.

"Hmm."

"The day you left," he says. "I don't know why I told you I was happy. I'm sorry about that."

"Yeah?"

"I wasn't," he says. "And I'm not. I used to be. At least I thought I was. Then I met you. And then you went away. Twice, actually. And that made me realize that I don't think it's possible for me to be happy again without you."

Margot wonders if the bartender can tell that she's about to cry. "It's a good thing I called, then," she says.

There's a grinding sound on the other end of the line, followed by a clunk, then silence. "Shit," Billy says.

"What was that?"

"My car. It won't start."

"You're kidding."

"Hold on a sec. Lemme try again."

Margot listens to Billy talk to the Champagne Supernova. His voice is gentle, like he's comforting a small, frightened animal. "Come on, baby. You can do this. You're a classic. Just one more time. You and me against the world." And then he sighs. "Please?"

She's never heard a car start over the phone before, but it sounds about like she would've thought.

"There we go! That's my girl!"

She can hear the smile in his voice, like joy. "We're good?"

"Never better," Billy says. "I'm on my way."

From her barstool, Margot can see out onto the street. It's getting dark out there. She's turned around—maybe a little lost. But that's okay. She'll be home soon.

ACKNOWLEDGMENTS

As much as I love music, I know very little about how it's made. So I'd like to thank my wife, Kate, to whom this book is dedicated, for helping me with some of the finer points. I'd also like to thank the burly gentlemen who delivered Kate's piano to our house nearly ten years ago. The reverence they showed for that big, beautiful thing was an early inspiration for this book. And as long as I'm talking about inspiration, the joy I've felt over the years listening to my daughters, Caroline and Hazel, tap out classic rock songs in the living room surely found its way into these pages. So, I suppose I should thank them, too.

My friend Catherine McKenzie read an early draft of this a long time ago and had valuable advice for how I could make it better. Another friend, Dave Dundas, let me fictionally borrow his pit bull, Lincoln, for some key scenes. He really does look like a gargoyle (Lincoln, not Dave).

My agent, Jesseca Salky, is simply the best, and I don't know where I'd be without her. Thanks also to the rest of the team at Salky Literary Management, especially Rachel Altemose, Claire Roberts, and Sarah Mroue.

I'm incredibly lucky to be part of the Penguin Random House

family, and I'm so grateful to everyone there for continuing to allow me to tell these stories. My editor, Anne Speyer, helped shape this book from a one-page synopsis into the finished novel before you, and I owe her so much. Thanks to Jesse Shuman and Luke Epplin for their excellent work at guiding this book through the publishing process. Thanks to Emma Thomsach and Melissa Folds for artfully spreading the word. Jessie Bright designed the wonderful cover, and Diane Hobbing made the interior pages sing. Thanks to both of them. And thanks to Mimi Lipson for copyediting this book and me so diligently and compassionately. Kara Welsh, Kim Hovey, and Jennifer Hershey have supported me for three books now, and bless them for that. And, finally, thanks to Kara Cesare for inviting me to join Dell. I'm thrilled to be here.

Rock on, everybody.

CHARM CITY ROCKS

Matthew Norman

A BOOK CLUB GUIDE

Dear Reader:

I can't tell you how much it means to me that you've picked *Charm City Rocks* for your group. It brings me great joy to imagine you and your friends gathered together discussing Billy, Margot, Caleb, Robyn, Aaron, and Lawson. I sincerely hope you like them all as much as I do. As far as imaginary people go, they're a good group.

Over the years I've had the chance to join in on some book club discussions of my work—in person and via computer—and one of the most common questions I'm asked is, "How'd you get the idea?" So I thought it might be useful to address that here.

Sometimes novel ideas show up fully formed. That was the case with my third novel, *Last Couple Standing*. Far more often, though, they arrive sneakily, usually in the form of a seemingly innocuous passing thought that for some reason just builds and builds. A few years ago, that passing thought for me was, "What does a random Tuesday afternoon look like for a rock star?" Because that's the funny thing about rock stars: We typically only see them when they're actually *being* rock stars, like at concerts or in music videos or all glammed up for TV appearances. But, yeah, what about on a Tuesday . . . between albums . . . when they're not on tour . . . and maybe after they've fallen out of the limelight a bit?

From there I started obsessing, because that's what novels require: obsessive behavior. I created a fictional band. I broke that band up in spectacular fashion. I came up with a romance—a couple of failed romances, too. I invented people and I gave them backstories. And then I put those people in Baltimore, Maryland, because that's where I live, and I've always enjoyed writing about places that are right down the street from my house.

But enough about the book. Let's talk drinks. Of course, wine is a popular choice for book clubs. Fair enough. But if you feel like rocking out a little, I recommend getting your hands on some National Bohemian beer, otherwise known as Natty Boh, which is the official beer of Baltimore. If you like it, well, I'm impressed. If you don't like it, keep trying, it's an acquired taste. And I promise that the burning sensation in your mouth is only temporary.

Thanks again for picking *Charm City Rocks;* you've made my day. Have fun talking about it, and say hey to Billy and Margot for me.

Best,

MN

QUESTIONS AND TOPICS FOR DISCUSSION

1. What's a "Lesson in Art and Manhood" that you wish you could teach or learn?

2. Margot seems to be haunted by the word "recluse." Is she one?

3. Margot says, "First loves brand you." Do you agree or disagree?

4. Do you think Margot would have returned to Burnt Flowers if not for Billy?

5. Should Billy have chased after Robyn when she ran away after his proposal? Why or why not?

6. Robyn has been romantically involved with Billy, Aaron, and (briefly) Lawson. What do each of these men bring to a relationship? Whom would you choose?

7. How does the novel depict the relationships between the children and their parents? Did you relate to these depictions?

8. What sacrifices do the characters make for love? Is sacrifice always necessary to find love?

9. Where do you picture these characters five years in the future? Do you think Margot and Billy stay together?

10. If you were Caleb, would you have picked Johns Hopkins over Stanford?

11. How would you have reacted if you were Margot discovering that Lawson was having an affair with Nikki?

MATTHEW NORMAN lives in Baltimore, Maryland, with his wife and two children, and holds an MFA from George Mason University. His previous novels include *All Together Now, Last Couple Standing, We're All Damaged,* and *Domestic Violets.*

thenormannation.com
Twitter: @TheNormanNation
Instagram: @thenormannation
Find Matthew Norman on Facebook

ABOUT THE TYPE

This book was set in Caslon, a typeface first designed in 1722 by William Caslon (1692–1766). Its widespread use by most English printers in the early eighteenth century soon supplanted the Dutch typefaces that had formerly prevailed. The roman is considered a "workhorse" typeface due to its pleasant, open appearance, while the italic is exceedingly decorative.

RANDOM HOUSE BOOK CLUB

Because Stories Are Better Shared

Discover

Exciting new books that spark conversation every week.

Connect

With authors on tour—or in your living room. (Request an Author Chat for your book club!)

Discuss

Stories that move you with fellow book lovers on Facebook, on Goodreads, or at in-person meet-ups.

Enhance

Your reading experience with discussion prompts, digital book club kits, and more, available on our website.

Join our online book club community!

f **g** randomhousebookclub.com

Random House Book Club ™

Because Stories Are Better Shared

 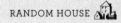